HONOURBOUND

More tales of the Astra Militarum from Black Library

STEEL DAEMON
A novella by Ian St. Martin

CADIA STANDS
A novel by Justin D Hill

CADIAN HONOUR
A novel by Justin D Hill

SHADOWSWORD
A novel by Guy Haley

BANEBLADE
A novel by Guy Haley

THE MACHARIAN CRUSADE
An omnibus edition of the novels *Angels of Fire*, *Fist of Demetrius* and *Fall of Macharius* by William King

• **GAUNT'S GHOSTS** •
By Dan Abnett

THE FOUNDING
An omnibus edition containing books 1–3:
First and Only, *Ghostmaker* and *Necropolis*

THE SAINT
An omnibus edition containing books 4–7:
Honour Guard, *The Guns of Tanith*, *Straight Silver* and *Sabbat Martyr*

THE LOST
An omnibus edition containing books 8–11:
Traitor General, *His Last Command*, *The Armour of Contempt* and *Only in Death*

THE VICTORY PART ONE
An omnibus edition containing books 12–13:
Blood Pact and *Salvation's Reach*

BOOK 14: THE WARMASTER
BOOK 15: ANARCH

• **THE ELYSIANS** •
Audio dramas by Chris Dows
PART 1: SCIONS OF ELYSIA
PART 2: RENEGADES OF ELYSIA
PART 3: MARTYRS OF ELYSIA

WARHAMMER 40,000

A SEVERINA RAINE NOVEL
HONOURBOUND
RACHEL HARRISON

BLACK LIBRARY

A BLACK LIBRARY PUBLICATION

First published in 2019.
This edition published in Great Britain in 2020 by
Black Library,
Games Workshop Ltd.,
Willow Road,
Nottingham, NG7 2WS, UK.

10 9 8 7 6 5 4 3 2

Produced by Games Workshop in Nottingham.
Cover illustration by Marc Lee.

Honourbound © Copyright Games Workshop Limited 2020.
Honourbound, GW, Games Workshop, Black Library, The
Horus Heresy, The Horus Heresy Eye logo, Space Marine, 40K,
Warhammer, Warhammer 40,000, the 'Aquila' Double-headed Eagle
logo, and all associated logos, illustrations, images, names, creatures,
races, vehicles, locations, weapons, characters, and the distinctive
likenesses thereof, are either ® or TM, and/or © Games Workshop
Limited, variably registered around the world.
All Rights Reserved.

A CIP record for this book is available from the British Library.

ISBN 13: 978-1-78193-984-0

No part of this publication may be reproduced, stored in a retrieval
system, or transmitted in any form or by any means, electronic,
mechanical, photocopying, recording or otherwise, without the
prior permission of the publishers.

This is a work of fiction. All the characters and events portrayed
in this book are fictional, and any resemblance to real people or
incidents is purely coincidental.

See Black Library on the internet at

blacklibrary.com

Find out more about Games Workshop
and the world of Warhammer 40,000 at

games-workshop.com

Printed and bound by CPI Group (UK) Ltd, Croydon, CR0 4YY

---

*To Mum and Dad, for every museum trip, every library visit
and all of those plastic dinosaurs.*

It is the 41st millennium. For more than a hundred centuries the Emperor has sat immobile on the Golden Throne of Earth. He is the Master of Mankind by the will of the gods, and master of a million worlds by the might of His inexhaustible armies. He is a rotting carcass writhing invisibly with power from the Dark Age of Technology. He is the Carrion Lord of the Imperium for whom a thousand souls are sacrificed every day, so that He may never truly die.

Yet even in His deathless state, the Emperor continues His eternal vigilance. Mighty battlefleets cross the daemon-infested miasma of the warp, the only route between distant stars, their way lit by the Astronomican, the psychic manifestation of the Emperor's will. Vast armies give battle in His name on uncounted worlds.
Greatest amongst His soldiers are the Adeptus Astartes, the Space Marines, bioengineered super-warriors. Their comrades in arms are legion: the Astra Militarum and countless planetary defence forces, the ever-vigilant Inquisition and the tech-priests of the Adeptus Mechanicus to name only a few. But for all their multitudes, they are barely enough to hold off the ever-present threat from aliens, heretics, mutants – and worse.

To be a man in such times is to be one amongst untold billions. It is to live in the cruellest and most bloody regime imaginable. These are the tales of those times. Forget the power of technology and science, for so much has been forgotten, never to be re-learned. Forget the promise of progress and understanding, for in the grim dark future there is only war. There is no peace amongst the stars, only an eternity of carnage and slaughter, and the laughter of thirsting gods.

'Loyalty, before the threat of death.'

– old Antari saying

The Bale Stars Crusade

HIGH COMMAND

Lord-General Militant Alar Serek

Lord-Marshal Veris Drake

Fleet Commander Gulieta Vallah

High-King Araxis of House Stormfall

Lord-Castellan Caradris

General-Primary Hu-Sul

COMMISSARIAT

Lord-Commissar Mardan Tula

Cadet-Commissar Pollivar Curtz

Commissar Lukas Vander, assigned to the Kavrone Dragoons

Commissar Severina Raine, assigned to the Eleventh Antari Rifles

ELEVENTH ANTARI RIFLES

Command Echelon
General Juna Keene

Grey Company

Command Squad
Captain Yuri Hale
Nuria Lye, medic
Makar Kayd, vox-operator
Ari Rath, standard bearer

Lydia Zane, Primaris psyker

'Wyldfolk' Infantry Squad

Sergeant Daven Wyck

Yulia Crys

Gereth Awd

Karo Efri

Dal

Vyne

Tian

Kane

Jey

Haro

'Duskhounds' Storm Trooper Squad

Captain Andren Fel

Cassia Tyl

Oran Jeth

Afi Myre

Caiden Rol

Blue Company

Captain Sale Devri

Gold Company

Captain Karin Sun

Pharo, primaris psyker

Fyregiants armoured detachment

Lieutenant Frayn, tank commander, Demolisher tank *Stoneking*

Ely Kolat, gunner, Demolisher tank *Stoneking*

Curi, loader, Demolisher tank *Stoneking*
Vurn, driver, Demolisher tank *Stoneking*

Support
Requisitions Adept Lori Ghael, of the Departmento Munitorum

KAVRONE DRAGOONS

Command Echelon
General Kaspar Sylar

THE SIGHTED

Calvar Larat, traitor witch
Cretia Ommatid, Sixth of Nine, *'She Who Watches'*
Ahxon-Pho, Fifth of Nine, *'That Which Creates'*

PROLOGUE

Jona Veer is a dead man, covered in blood.

He runs as fast as his legs will carry him. They are burning nearly as bad as his lungs are from the smoke. The forge complex is thick with it, like fog blown in off the water. It wreathes massive machines that line the aisles, and curls up towards a vaulted ceiling. His boots ring off rust-stained decking as he lurches over thick loops of cabling and splashes through the filthy water sluicing from vast industrial laser cutters and plasma burners that make up the tank assembly line. Panel beaters stutter on repeat, and lifters whine and gasp as they raise and lower sheets of steel. All of that machinery sends ash into the air. It blizzards around Veer, getting in his eyes and making them itch and sting. Everything smells like burning and death. Tastes like it too.

Or maybe that's just from when Chiya's blood got in his mouth.

He retches so hard it makes him stagger, but nothing will

come up except thick ropes of bile. Her face had opened up like a wyldblossom, red and blooming as she shouted at him.

Shoot, you damned fool! Shoot!

Veer hears them behind him. The Sighted. They are laughing and clattering their weapons off the hulls of tanks. Those wicked knives that he saw gut Soli and Fren. They had opened them up slow, laughing all the while, then they'd used the blood to paint things on their skin. Things that made him sick while he hid, still not able to shoot.

Clatter. Clatter.

Clatter.

It comes from everywhere, and it sounds so close. Throne, how he doesn't want that death. That slow spill of his guts or a bullet to the head. But then, Veer doesn't want any death at all. Not an honourable one either, like the others. He wants to live. Veer starts running again and he tastes something else now too, mixing with the ashes and with Chiya's blood.

It's salt, from the tears tracking through the dirt on his face.

'Come back, soldier,' the Sighted shout from behind him. 'We are not finished with you yet.'

Their voices come in the gaps between the thrumming machine noise as the manufactorum keeps working, oblivious to the war at its heart. Servitors trundle back and forth on heavy tracks, paying no heed to Veer as he runs. Half-finished chassis of tanks judder along the line to have their armour machined in place. God-killers, built to fell Titans. Veer isn't a god-killer. He's not a killer of any kind. He couldn't even *shoot*. Not to save Chiya, or even Soli and his damned awful singing.

He's nearly at the end of the line. The chassis of the last Stormlord to roll off the ash-clogged assembly-way waits like a great dark creature in the smoke, terrifying and immobile, complete save for the lighting of its reactor heart. He could hide under it, if he could just get to it.

But Veer doesn't get close. With his eyes full of smoke and sweat and blood that isn't his, he runs right into a shadowy figure that sends him crashing to the ground. The impact of it doesn't hurt him really, but it gets him crying all the worse.

The Sighted he ran into squats on his heels in front of him and cocks his head. His eyes are without irises, just black from centre to edge, and cruel, though the smile beneath them is much crueller. Small silver mirrors and multicoloured tattered feathers hang on a loop of cord around the Sighted's neck. His fatigues are blue and grey under the bloodstains, and his combat vest hangs open to show all of the carvings in his pale skin. This close, Veer realises they are dates. Times. All scored in spirals. There are new ones painted over the top in blood.

'There we are, little soldier,' the Sighted says, in his strange accent.

The Sighted pulls his knife as the others come up behind Veer. He can hear them all laughing, his lasgun cold in his hands. He could shoot. He should shoot. His fingers twitch by the trigger.

'Oh,' the Sighted says, with a black-toothed smile. 'Will you shoot me, Antari? It seems so late to try. Too late for all of your comrades.'

Chiya's voice echoes in Veer's head.

Shoot, you damned fool! Shoot!

But Veer doesn't shoot this time either. His lungs ache and his limbs burn. When he blinks, his eyelids stick from the blood on his face. Veer lets out a shaking, slow breath.

And drops his rifle on the ground.

'I yield,' he rasps. 'Just spare me, please.'

The Sighted laughs so loud that it carries even over the machine noise. His brothers and sisters join in, like a flock of crows cawing.

'And what use would you be to me? A soldier who will not even shoot.' The Sighted pauses, then sighs. 'But your blood. That is another matter.'

He raises the knife, and Veer squeezes his eyes shut. Holds his breath.

But the strike never lands; instead there's a series of loud, flat bangs and the whip-crack of las-fire. Blood hits his face for the second time, only this time it's cold and it smells as though it were spilt a week ago. Veer collapses forwards, retching again. A figure moves to stand above him. He sees the toes of black, mud-spattered boots, and Veer's blood goes cold too. He knows who it is before he looks up. Severina Raine.

The commissar.

'On your feet, Jona Veer.'

He finds that he can't say her name, her rank. He can't say much of anything. When he stands, his legs nearly go from under him. Commissar Raine is a shadow in a shadowed place, all dressed in black with the gilt edges of her uniform dulled by ashes and dirt. Her black greatcoat snaps as it catches in the hot air of the forge. Her silver chest-plate is scored and dented from impacts and knife edges, because the commissar never runs.

Not like he did.

Veer finally looks her in the face. Raine's tawny skin is scarred, and her dark eyes are as cold and still as deep water. Behind Raine there are others wearing Veer's colours. Splintered green and grey. He sees Sergeant Wyck with his squad behind him, and Captain Hale too. There's no movement in

Hale's scarred face, not even a blink. Wyck says something that he can't hear and shakes his head, just a little.

Veer thinks he's saying *stupid*.

Raine's eyes flicker down to where Veer's rifle lies in the ashes and dust.

'Your powercell is full,' she says. 'You haven't fired a shot.'

Veer can't lie now, just as he couldn't shoot before. It's an impossibility.

'No,' he says.

'You ran,' she says. 'In the face of the enemy, you failed to fire your rifle, and then you ran.'

Veer thinks about it. About Chiya's face and all that blood and the way that Fren tried to grab hold of him and snap him out of it.

About how he pushed Fren to the ground so that the Sighted would get him first.

'Yes,' he says, his voice a rasp.

Raine's eyes don't change. There's no malice in them, just that same deep cold. She raises the ornate black and crimson pistol she carries and points it at his face.

'Jona Veer,' she says. 'I find you in dereliction of your duty to the Eleventh Antari Rifles, to the Bale Stars Crusade, and to our Holy Lord on Terra. The punishment is death.'

A tear slides down Veer's face again, and he wishes it wouldn't. Not in front of his own.

'Do you have anything to say in your defence?' Raine asks.

Veer listens to the thunder of the machines around him. Motes of ash drift past his face. He is shaking from head to toe, like being caught out in the cold.

'I just wanted to live,' he says, his voice cracking.

Raine lets out a slow breath. Veer hears the creak of her gloves as she moves her fingers.

'Then you should have stayed to fight,' she says.
And the maw of the pistol lights up.

ONE

Fire and thunder

Commissar Severina Raine slides a fresh magazine into her bolt pistol with a hard click. She has replaced the eight-round magazine four times. Thirty-two shots fired.

Six of them to execute her own troops.

Raine has fought many wars on many fronts across the Bale Stars, and almost all of them have been against the Sighted, or their splinter cults. She has seen the way they turn worlds with whispers and false promises. The way they set workers against their masters, and guards against those that they are meant to protect. It's what makes them dangerous. When you battle the Sighted, you battle the people of the Bale Stars too. Scribes and soldiers. Priests and peacekeepers. The poor, the downtrodden, the ambitious and the reckless. For some of those that serve with her, that knowledge is too much. For some it is just fear that means they find the trigger impossible to pull. No matter the reason, they will find themselves looking down the barrel of her pistol, Penance, in turn. Just like Penance, Raine is made for the act of judgement. For the instant before the strike of the hammer and the burst of flame. She understands what it means to pull the trigger, and what it makes her. She is not driven by anger, or malice. That would undermine her purpose, which is the same no matter the crime.

To eliminate weakness.

Raine crouches down and takes Jona Veer's ident-tags from around his neck. They will not be sent back to Antar as with the honoured dead. They will be disposed of at the end of the fight on Laxus Secundus. His name will go with them, to be forgotten in time by everyone but her, because Raine never forgets the dead, honoured or not.

'Commissar.'

The voice belongs to Captain Yuri Hale. It's rough-edged, like he is. The captain of Grey Company is tall, like most Antari. Three deep, severe scars run down the left side of his face from hairline to chin. The Antari call him lucky because he managed to keep his eye. They say he must have been graced with that luck by a white witch, or by fate itself. Raine doesn't believe in luck. She believes that Yuri Hale survives the same way the rest of them do.

By fighting for every breath.

'More power spikes from the inner forge,' he says.

Raine puts Veer's tags in her pocket, where they clatter against the others, then she gets to her feet and looks to the dust-caked screen on the auspex kit Hale is holding. When the regiment first entered the forges, more than six hours ago, it was registering soft spikes. Now the peaks are jagged, with the regularity of a great, slow heartbeat.

'Whatever the Sighted are doing in there, it's burning hot,' Hale says, and he frowns. 'Kayd's been picking up enemy vox too.'

'On an open channel?'

'Aye, it's as if they don't care if we hear it.'

'Anything of use?' Raine asks.

Hale's frown deepens, and it pulls at the scars on his face. 'The words were Laxian. Kayd reckons they said something like "it draws near".'

Despite the arid heat of the forge, Raine feels a distinct chill at those words. The tactical briefing two days prior had been clear. The primary forge on Laxus Secundus is an invaluable asset, both tactically and logistically, and not just because of the super-heavy tanks built there, but because of what waits in the inner forges. High Command did not disclose the purpose of the machines that Raine and the Antari would find there, only that they must not fall into Sighted hands. That for the enemy to use them successfully would be catastrophic, not just for the battle inside the forges, but for the war effort across Laxus Secundus and the crusade front.

'We are running out of time,' Raine says.

Hale nods. 'And support too. Blue Company are pinned down on approach to the Beta Gate, and Gold have yet to reach the inner forges. I'm calling the push now, before the Sighted can send whatever *draws near* against us, or we lose everything we've bled for.'

'Understood, captain,' Raine says. 'We will not fail.'

Hale glances to where Jona Veer lies dead. Raine knows him well enough to see what he is feeling by the set of his shoulders, and the way his eyes narrow. Hale is disappointed. Ashamed, on the boy's behalf. Raine also knows that, despite all of Veer's failings, it is hard for Hale to accept judgement against one of his own.

'Is there anything else?' Raine says.

Hale looks back to her. 'No, commissar,' he says. 'Not a thing.'

Then Hale gets to rounding up the Antari, voxing orders to the rest of his company pushing up through the machine halls. They have orders to fulfil, traitors to silence, and those machines to retake.

And her judgements are something that Yuri Hale knows better than to question.

Lydia Zane can feel the touch of death on every inch of her body. It makes her ache, skin to bones. The Sighted are doing something in the forges that casts a long shadow. Something that echoes in the immaterium like a scream. It has been the same for Zane since the moment she set foot on Laxus Secundus, death's long shadow clinging to her.

Like that damned hateful bird.

It is sitting there now, talons crooked around the rim of a girder. It is so very still, that bird. She has not yet seen it blink. It never cries, or ruffles its feathers. It just sits still and stares.

On the pillar below the bird's perch is a symbol, daubed in blood. The smell carries to Zane even over the heavy stink of smoke. The symbol is a spiral surrounding a slit-pupilled eye. The mark of the Sighted. The rings of the spiral are just a hair off perfectly spaced, and it makes the breath in Zane's lungs thinner, looking at it. The Sighted who painted the symbol lies broken at the foot of the pillar. So very broken. He is clad in fatigues and feathers, his skin inked with iridescent, metallic tattoos. The Sighted was one of the flock hunting Jona Veer through the machine halls. Zane caught sight of him slipping into the shadows between the half-built tanks during the gunfight. He thought himself hidden, but he was wrong. There is no hiding from Zane, because she does not need footprints or line of sight or even sound in order to hunt. She followed him into the darkness by the stink of his traitor-thoughts and came upon him painting the spiral and the slitted eye.

And then she broke him.

Zane winds her fingers tighter around her darkwood staff. The psionic crystal atop it hums. One at a time, bolts pop out of the pillar and join the objects floating in the air around Zane. Tools. Rivets and screws. Empty shell casings. Splinters of bone. They drift around her absently. The floor tremors under her feet as the panels start to bend upwards. Zane tastes blood, running thick over her lips. Blood on the pillar. Blood that makes up the painted eye at the centre of the spiral, unblinking.

Just like the bird.

'Zane.'

She turns away from the bird and its black eyes and the way it never blinks them. Commissar Raine is standing there with her pistol drawn, but not raised. A threat in waiting. Zane finds she cannot speak. It is as if her lips have been sealed by all of that blood. The objects circle her like a storm, with lightning arcing between them. Raine does not flinch.

'Control,' Raine says, the word carrying clear.

The pistol does not move. The barrel is round and dark, like the eye painted in blood. Like the eyes of the bird. Like Raine's eyes, unblinking.

'Control,' Zane slurs.

More blood finds its way into her mouth.

'Tell me about the tree,' Raine says.

'About the tree,' Zane says, her voice a rasp. 'The singing tree.'

'And why is it called the singing tree?' Raine asks.

Zane blinks. Against the back of her eyelids she sees it. The singing tree standing on the cliff's edge, the roots curling over it like the bird's talons around the girder. The bone-white branches reaching up to meet Antar's thunderhead sky.

'Because that is where we would go to sing to Him on Earth,' she says. 'Because it was as close as you could get to the heavens.'

'And He spoke to you there,' Raine says.

'In the rustle of the leaves,' Zane says.

'What did He say?' Raine asks.

Zane feels the ache in her bones lessen. The objects orbiting her begin their fall to earth.

'That I will be tested,' she says. 'And that I must never break.'

Metal objects clatter off the metal floor, and it sounds like a storm.

'Lydia Zane,' Zane says, finishing the ritual words. 'Primaris psyker. Graded Epsilon. Eleventh Antari Rifles.'

The cables connecting to her scalp click as they cool. Zane wipes her hand through the blood on her face, painting a red streak up the back of it.

'Apologies, commissar,' she says, bowing low. 'It is this place. The darkness in it.'

'The Sighted?' Raine asks.

'I know the shape of their darkness,' Zane says. 'This is different. Things are changing.'

'If you see anything, tell me,' Raine says.

Zane knows that she means *foresee*, not just see, but it still feels like a cruel joke given the bird. The bird that she has been seeing for months now, since she walked the crystal tunnels on Gholl. The bird that she will speak of to no one, especially not to Raine, because to do so would be to invite death.

Because Zane knows that, like every instant of her life so far, the bird is just another test, and that she will not break.

Sergeant Daven Wyck waits until the commissar has gone after the witch before he fetches Jona Veer's rifle. He knows better than to do something like that in front of her. That it's better not to draw her eyes at all if he can help it. Around him, the rest of his Wyldfolk are securing the area at the end of the assembly line, watching for Sighted movement in the smoke. They tend their rifles and replace spent powercells and share out grenades and charges. Clean their bloodied combat blades on their fatigues. Wyck slings Veer's rifle over his shoulder by the strap, then takes his knife and his grenades too. Veer hadn't used even one of them. So stupid, not to shoot, or act at all.

Even more so to get found out.

'Really, Dav?' Awd says.

Wyck gives his second a look. The sort that says *shut up*.

'He isn't going to use them, is he?' he says.

Awd looks as though he's smiling, but it's just the way the burn scars tug at the skin of his face. His eyes aren't smiling at all.

'You'd truly leave him with nothing for where he's going?' Awd asks.

Wyck looks down at Veer's body and remembers the way he spoke, with that lilt of the Vales. It's the same place that Wyck grew up before he was tithed to the Rifles, all deep black lakes and tangled forests. It's a big place, with the people spread thin. Wyck didn't know Veer then. He didn't know him now either, not really, but he was kin all the same. Even if he was a coward, and a stupid one at that. Wyck stoops and puts back the knife. Awd's right. He can't leave Veer with nothing for when judgement comes.

'There,' he says. 'Now it's up to him to answer for his deeds.'

Awd nods. 'As we all will, in death.'

Wyck shakes his head. 'Death will have to catch me first,' he says.

That makes Awd laugh so hard he starts to cough, a wet hacking sound from deep in his chest. It's the flamer he carries that makes his lungs rattle that way. All the ashes from the fuel and the things he burns.

'Death will have to be lucky,' Awd says. 'Sharp soul like you.'

Wyck smiles, but it doesn't go deeper than his teeth. He curls his hands into fists. They ache from fighting. From every trigger pull, every swipe of the knife. From throwing punches and breaking bones. That ache doesn't stop him wanting to fight, though. To cut and shoot and kill. If anything, it makes him want it more.

'Wyck.'

He turns to see Hale standing there. The captain definitely notices the extra lasrifle and the grenades, but he says nothing about either. Wyck has known Hale a long time. Longer than he's had to call him captain.

'We are pushing the Gate,' Hale says. 'I need your Wyldfolk up front.'

The order is no surprise. Wyck runs his twelve-strong infantry squad fast and sharp, so Hale always puts them in the teeth of it.

'Aye, sir,' Wyck says. 'I wouldn't be anywhere else.'

Hale claps him on the shoulder and for the sparest instant Wyck's instinct is to react as if he's been hit. He has to consciously stop himself from throwing a punch at his captain and force himself into stillness. It's the adrenaline, mostly.

'Fire and thunder,' Hale says.

Wyck thinks about the way his blood burns and his

heartbeat rolls like a drum and the old words seem almost funny. He has to stop himself laughing, just like he had to stop himself throwing that punch.

'Fire and thunder,' he says, instead.

It takes Raine and the Antari another hour to fight their way from the assembly lines into the casting halls. The colossal, vaulted chambers are the midpoint of the forge complex, and the most direct path to the forge halls and the Delta Gate beyond. Like the rest of the Forge Primary, the casting halls are still working unabated despite the conflict taking place across the complex. All around Raine, vast machines judder and roar. Overhead, great buckets of molten steel are raised by lifters and poured, spitting, into the moulds beneath. Censers swing over the moulds, and slaved cherubim drop ritual ashes, still running on subroutines that were set long before the war began. The panels move down the line to be beaten, quenched and cooled by blasts of dirty water, filling the halls with smoke, steam and the smell of industry.

To Raine, it feels like running through hell. It makes her long for the icy, ocean-spray winters of Gloam, where she was trained. For clothes stiff with frost, and for the misting of breath in the air.

The casting halls are occupied by dug-in squads of Sighted infantry. Most of them are sworn rebels and traitors that wear blue and grey flak plate and the trappings of heretics. Mirrored glass on bits of cord. Feathers that pierce their skin. The spiral-eye symbol, daubed in red. The rest are faith-breakers, a mixture of manufactorum workers, tech-savants and defected Laxian soldiery that have torn away their icons and excised their loyalty tattoos. Raine cannot say which disgusts her more, but no matter the nature of their betrayal, they will all be granted the same fate.

Death.

'Leave none standing!' she cries, as she charges into combat alongside the Antari.

One of the Sighted looms from the steam and smoke. His eyes are solid black, and his teeth are filed to sharp points. Heretic sigils run and bleed on the Sighted's flak armour, and the heavy, two-handed sword he carries seems to swallow what little light there is. Raine dodges him as he swings for her with that heavy blade. It could take her head clean off if it were to hit her, but the Sighted plants it in the riveted metal of the floor instead, where it sticks for an instant.

An instant is all Raine needs.

She opens the Sighted up from belt to throat with an upward swing of her own powered blade. As he falls, she fires her pistol past him, knocking another of the heretics to the ground in a burst of blood. Behind him, there are more. Dozens more. Hale is right beside her, his laspistol drawn. It's a heavy variant with warding words carved into the grip in Antari script. One sleeve of his fatigues is torn and smoking where las-fire has caught him, and his flak armour has been scored by a dozen blades.

'They are different,' Hale says, between breaths. 'They have always had numbers, and ferocity, but this is more than that. They are well-armed. Organised.'

Raine fires her pistol as the Sighted fall back towards their own lines and the cover of the forge machinery. They are doing it in good order, under smoke. Some carry slab shields, protecting those beside and behind them, making a mobile defensive line. On Drast, they fought her as if their minds were lost, until they had no limbs left to do it with.

They dropped their rifles in favour of knives, because they placed more value on blood than survival. They were dangerous, but they were feral, and fractious. Zane's words echo in Raine's ears.

Things are changing.

'You are right,' she says to Hale. 'But we will kill them all the same.'

Hale nods, and speaks his next words into the company vox-channel.

'All squads advance,' he says. 'We break them as they run!'

Raine raises her sword. Misted water from the machinery hisses on Evenfall's powered blade. 'Give them death,' she shouts. 'In the Emperor's name!'

The Antari of Grey Company cheer. The Hartkin. The Mistvypers. The Pyrehawks. The ones to cheer the loudest are those right beside her in the teeth of it. Wyck's Wyldfolk. They are leading the push, like always. Hale uses Wyck as a blade's edge, because it is what he is good for.

'Yulia!' Wyck shouts. 'Deal with those shields!'

Yulia Crys grins and unslings her grenade launcher. Raine takes cover in the shadow of a casting machine for the moment it fires. The noise of it is like thunder, a series of rapid, automatic thumps that puts half a dozen grenades in the Sighted's lines, in and around those slab shields. They detonate almost immediately. Raine can't see the damage for all the smoke and the fire, but she hears it. The crack of armour and bone. Screams. The scattering of debris landing around her.

'What shields, sarge?' Crys shouts.

Wyck laughs. It is an unpleasant sound.

'Keep pushing forward!' Raine shouts.

The breath she takes tastes of ash and smoke, and blood too.

The Sighted that Crys' grenades didn't kill are running now, much less ordered. Raine fires Penance twice, putting two of them down with quick kill shots. The Wyldfolk light the casting halls with bright flashes of las-fire all around her. The tide has turned. The Sighted are faltering. Dying. But then Raine is hit by a heavy calibre round that impacts against her silver chest-plate and puts a fist-sized dent in it. It knocks the air from her lungs and cracks something in her chest, knocking her aim out. Raine's vision swims, but she catches sight of the Sighted who shot her. He is a tall, whipcord-thin man wearing blue-grey carapace with a cut stone replacing one of his eyes. It is a mark of rank on them, a stone like that. He raises his snub-nosed shotgun to fire again and smiles. Raine raises her pistol, but before she can pull the trigger Wyck slams into the Sighted and knocks him onto his back. Raine hears the shotgun go off. Hears Wyck laugh. She makes an effort to breathe until it isn't agony to do it. The Wyldfolk have the other Sighted dead or running. She makes her way to where Wyck is kneeling. The Sighted underneath him is a mess. His throat is open and pumping blood all over the floor.

'Too slow,' Wyck says, softly. 'Much too slow.'

'Enough,' Raine says to him. 'On your feet.'

He looks up at her. For an instant, there's no recognition in those grey eyes of his. Barely any grey either. It's all swallowed up by the black of his pupils. But then he blinks and takes a ragged breath.

'Enough,' he says, getting to his feet. 'Yes, commissar.'

His voice is deliberate and careful. His use of her rank even more so. Wyck often cloaks himself in obedience and piety when he is being watched.

'He said something,' Wyck says. 'That we can't kill the life they will make here.'

The words, and the implication of them, turn Raine's stomach. She knows what the Sighted are capable of. She has seen it first hand, on Gholl and Drast, and all of the worlds before them. Devastation, and desecration. Whole populations sacrificed in rites and rituals. Blood spilt on a massive scale, all in the name of their false prophets.

And now the Sighted intend to *make life*.

Whether it is soldiers or slaves, or something worse, Raine cannot allow it.

'Whatever it is that they intend, we will stop them,' she says. 'At any cost.'

Raine thinks then of the machines that the Antari have been charged with capturing. Those that would cause catastrophe if the enemy were to use them.

Here, and across the crusade front.

Wyck flinches and turns to look up the avenue, towards the Sighted's lines, where the traitor infantry disappear into the smoke and steam.

'There's something coming,' he says. 'Something heavy.'

Raine strains her ears over the sounds of the casting machines and then she hears it too. Heavy, clanking footsteps.

'Make ready!' she shouts.

The rest of Grey Company have caught up to them now. They take what cover they can behind the casting machines and reload their rifles and pistols. Water spray from the machines runs off the brim of Raine's hat, mingling with the sweat in her eyes. Steam rolls across the avenue like ocean fog.

Through it stride three armoured shapes, half as tall again as the tallest of the Antari. They have domed heads and heavy fists that end in blaster weapons. Carapace-mounted flamethrowers track back and forth on their shoulders. The kastelan automata are stripped back to bare steel, save for the great red spirals painted on their domed heads. At the centre of each is a slit-pupiled eye. With them moves a figure that is human only in shape, dribbling oil onto the forge floor from beneath its black robes. Mechadendrites thrash at its back. The tech-priest turns its face to the Antari, to Raine, and it blares machine noise from the grille of its mouth.

'Pyrehawks!' Captain Hale shouts.

All of the Rifles' infantry squads are named for Antari folk stories, and Raine has come to know most of them since joining the regiment. Andren Fel told Raine that the pyrehawk was said to be the one to light Antar's night sky with stars, setting hundreds of fires in the void with every beat of its wings.

Raine cannot think of a more appropriate name for Kasia Elys and her five-strong special weapons team. They are heavily armoured, with extra plates strapped around their arms and legs, and glare visors in their helmets. The Pyrehawks move up into position and brace their plasma guns, ready to light new stars.

'Set them afire,' Elys snarls.

The Pyrehawks fire their plasma guns in the same instant as the kastelans do their phosphor blasters. Bright white light blooms in the casting halls, printing on Raine's eyes. She is half-blind as she fires her pistol at the kastelan automata and the tech-priest controlling them.

One of Odi's Hartkin is hit by phosphor. Raine can't say who, because there is not enough left to know. The figure is silently running towards the rest of its squad in its blind death throes. Raine puts a bolt in the figure to stop it from passing the phosphor along to the rest of them. It falls, still burning.

In return, one of the kastelans goes to a knee, juddering and smoking from plasma fire. The tech-priest is blaring more machine noise that sounds like a scream. The other two kastelans twist and train their phosphor cannons at Elys and her Pyrehawks as they go for cover. The Pyrehawks fire again as they fall back, trading plasma for phosphor. Their shots land true, staggering the kastelans, but not felling them. Most of the Pyrehawks end up burning like stars themselves and Raine doesn't have enough rounds for all of them.

Not if she wants to kill the tech-priest.

'Zane!' she shouts.

There is no way the psyker hears her over all of the noise, not really. But Zane does not need to truly hear.

'The kastelans!' Raine shouts. 'Break them!'

Lydia Zane walks through the storm as dozens of her kin fall back, firing at the kastelans. One of the automata moves to meet her and the flamethrower on its shoulder angles downwards. Zane raises her hand as the kastelan fires a gout of promethium that would melt her like the steel in the forge if it were to touch her skin. Instead, Zane deflects the liquid flame back over the kastelan in an arc. She feels the heat of it against her kine-shield as a fire in her mind. The cables at her skull creak and the floor under her feet trembles and twists. The kastelan, burning now, reaches for her with a huge, powered fist. For an instant, Zane almost pities the machine. This thing that is made to take commands, and never to question. Only to kill. She sees herself reflected in the mirror of its faceplate. Her nose is bleeding thickly, and her skin is as pale as a lakebottom fish. The crown of cables that thread under her scalp are arcing with lightning.

'Die,' Zane says, and throws up her hand.

The kastelan robot explodes into pieces, disassembled in an instant, all bolts sheared, all seals broken. The floor panels around Zane splinter. Dozens of metres away, overhead cables flex and snap. The shockwave knocks some of her kin to the ground, breaking bones. She hears them scream. The world wavers, and time seems to slow. Zane's heart goes arrhythmic and she distinctly hears the snap of folding wings. She wishes that closing her eyes would stop it, but it never does. Especially not since she lost her real eyes, and had them replaced with false silver discs. Now she sees fire and death in every blink.

It is a test, she thinks. *And I will not break.*

With a scream of effort, Zane refocuses, and turns to the last remaining kastelan and its tech-priest overseer. The tech-priest is slowly raising its arm. Its gamma pistol is pointed at Raine. The commissar's own pistol is raised in answer, but even one as quick as Raine will be ashes if fire from the tech-priest's weapon so much as grazes her. Lydia Zane does not care for the commissar. The psyker is not a hound, loyal and loving to her master. She is caged and tethered, watched and judged, all by Raine. But if Lydia Zane is truly honest, she is sometimes thankful for the strength of this particular tether.

So Zane lifts her hand and curls it into a fist as the tech-priest's fingers ratchet around the gamma pistol's trigger. She turns the gun to scrap, along with most of the priest's arm. It shrieks and rears back. The last kastelan stumbles forwards on jarred, broken legs, still slaved to protect its master. Zane squeezes it with invisible force until the joints burst and it collapses, crushed. Exhausted, Zane falls to her knees, with electricity dancing from the cables of her crown and running along her teeth.

* * *

On Gloam, where she was trained, they would make Raine run the upper gantries over the ocean. They were narrow spans of riveted metal, either slick with sea-spray or with ice when it turned to deepwinter. The trick was to run quickly and surely. Second guess yourself, and the ocean would gladly take you. Raine places her feet just as surely, just as swiftly, as she leaps up on the fallen kastelan's shell and snaps off the last three rounds of her bolt pistol's magazine. They all hit the tech-priest. Chest, throat. Head. It falls backwards, thrashing, the bladed mechadendrites seeking her. Her pistol empty, Raine draws her sabre. Evenfall's power field snarls. One of the tech-priest's mechadendrites cuts Raine's face as another tears a great rip in her greatcoat and her arm. Raine feels blood run hot and fast as she swings her sabre, severing the mechanical arms as they reach for her, until she is close enough to plant the powered blade in the tech-priest's chest. Even then, it takes a moment to stop twitching.

Raine draws a breath, all ashes and the smell of spilled oil. The Sighted have all but disappeared into the smoke, taking cover in amongst the vast casting machines standing between the Antari and the forge halls beyond. Raine pushes another magazine into her pistol. She is down to her last two.

'No respite!' she cries. 'No mercy!'

And around her, the Antari roar and push onwards.

Wyck falls back against one of the casting machines. At his feet, the Sighted takes his time to die, bleeding out slowly across the corrugated floor. The smell of it dizzies Wyck as he cleans the blade of his knife on the leg of his fatigues. Everything seems muffled as if by distance. The thrum of the machine at his back. The las-fire echoing up to the roof.

The Sighted at his feet, choking to death.

Wyck blinks his stinging eyes. He looks back down the aisle to make sure he is still alone before putting his hand in the pouch at his belt and taking out a short, stubby vial with an auto-injector mounted on the cap. Wyck breaks the seal with his thumb, and then punches the needle into his arm, straight through his fatigues. The rush comes quickly, like it always does. Setting him alight from the inside out. Sounds go from murmurs to bellows and everything pulls pin sharp.

Wyck drops the auto-injector on the floor and crushes it with his boot.

'The way is clear,' he says, into the vox. 'Move up.'

His Wyldfolk approach up the aisle, resolving as if from the smoke and the darkness, their green and grey flak plate fouled with ashes and blood.

'I don't like this, sarge,' Crys says. 'We're way out in it.'

The combat engineer is twitching her head from side to side, trying to compensate for the fact she's part-deaf in her left ear. Crys is taller than he is, and so broad across the shoulders that standard template flak plate doesn't fit her all that well. She has her grenade launcher slung across her back and her pistol drawn in its place. Crys has modified the grenade launcher, like she does all of her kit. It's something that she should be sanctioned for, but Wyck has seen how that gun works since. What it can do. The box and cabling mounted on the stock of it increase the speed of the rotary magazine, so that it fires on full auto.

By all rights, Yulia Crys should be deaf in both of her ears.

'We're always way out in it,' Wyck says. 'It's what we're good at.'

Crys shrugs her broad shoulders, but she's still frowning. In some ways, she's right. They are deep into the labyrinth of casting machines, probably cut off from the rest of Grey, but Wyck has the Sighted running and he won't stop chasing until he's bled the lot of them.

Wyck takes point, following after a sound he picks up even over the machines and the gunfire. The ring of boots on metal. He rounds a corner and follows a set of bare plated stairs upwards. It brings him out on top of a rig mounted with plasma torches that are cutting shapes from huge sheets of steel. He moves up the central gantry with his squad behind him. It is noisy, with equally spaced alcoves like confessionals arranged on either side for the machine's slaved servitors. A lot of cover, for those who might hide. Sparks rain from the machines, and smoke blows across the gantry like fog.

No good, Wyck thinks. *This is no good.*

The servitors loll at their stations, operating the torches with convulsive movements of their withered limbs. They don't look up as Wyck passes because their routines don't allow it. Because they are made for the moment of the cut and nothing more. Wyck's fingers twitch by the trigger. The stimms are pressing at him and are making him shake, just minutely.

There's a noise. The barest sound that he wouldn't be able to pick up if his brain weren't so electric.

One of the Sighted lurches out of the next alcove on his left. No carapace on this one. No flak armour. The man is clad in coveralls and he has a heavy, long-handled hammer in his hand. He swings for Wyck, but he is much too slow. Wyck ducks the swing and puts his boot in the man's gut, sending him reeling. He snaps three las-rounds into him before he can get back up again.

More of them come, out of the alcoves, or dropping from ledges above. A dozen or so. They are shouting something over the noise in Laxian. Two of them are down and twitching from chest shots before they can pull their weapons. The sound of them gasping for air they can't get carries to him even as Wyck puts his knife in the chest of a third. He pulls it free again, but the Sighted doesn't go down. Instead he coughs blood onto Wyck's face and swings for him, raking a blunt-edged knife across the front of Wyck's flak armour. It digs a gouge, but doesn't go through. Wyck blinks the blood from his eyes. He can't help but laugh.

'You think you can cut me?' he says.

Wyck cuts the Sighted back, across his arms as he tries to block, then across his throat when his arms finally drop. Wyck gets more blood on his face. His heart is so loud now. Louder than the las-fire and the roaring of Awd's flamer as they finish the rest of them.

'I'm Wyldfolk,' Wyck says. 'And cuts from us always kill.'

'Dav.'

For a moment, Wyck could swear it's Raf's voice he hears, after all this time. There's the same kind of dread in it.

'Dav.'

Wyck blinks and shakes his head. Of course it's not Raf. Raf has been dead for more than ten years. Long since taken. Long since judged. He turns to see Awd looking at him. The others are moving swiftly up the gantry, checking for runners or trip mines.

'What?' Wyck asks.

'These folk,' Awd says, slow and careful. Quiet. 'I don't think they're Sighted.'

Wyck snorts. 'What are you talking about?' he says.

He looks at the body at his feet. The pool of blood that has spread around his boots like a black lake. Wyck realises that the man hasn't cut up his face or torn away his icons. He wears no mirrors or feathers, and his coveralls are Munitorum-issue. The only mark on the man is the worker number branded on his neck. It occurs to Wyck that the blunt-bladed knife is the sort you'd use to pry panels off machines.

'They were behind the lines,' Wyck says, absently. 'They jumped us.'

'I found this on one of them,' Awd says.

He throws something that Wyck catches. Something shiny and silver. No, not silver. Tin. Cheaply pressed.

It's a pendant in the shape of the aquila.

The thunder of Wyck's heart skips a beat. In his head, he hears what Raf said to him, all those years ago, his grey eyes wide with horror.

What have you done, Dav?

The answer is the same now as it was then.

Too much to forgive.

Wyck blinks and clears his throat. 'You know how they are,' he says to Awd. 'The Sighted make soldiers of everyone, even if they don't look like it. They did it on Gholl. On Hyxx too. Even the priests, there. You remember?'

'I remember,' Awd says. 'I won't forget that. Not even when I'm dead.'

'Everywhere they go, people turn their coats for them. This is just that.'

Wyck puts the pendant in one of the pouches at his belt. The one next to where he keeps the auto-injectors.

'I know,' Awd says. 'But–'

Wyck gives him that look again, and just like before, Awd falls silent.

'This is just that,' he says again. 'Now forget it and move.'

Awd nods his head. 'Yes, sergeant. As you say.'

Wyck glances down at the body one more time before following Awd. At the blunt-bladed knife and the wide pool of blood. At the aquila pendant glinting around that man's neck too.

And he knows that when death finally catches him, he'll have so very much to be judged for.

TWO

Brightly burning

Raine's first sight of the Delta Gate is through smoke as it looms at the end of the forge hall. The gate is massive, made for super-heavies and god-machines. It is worked with the icon of the Cog Mechanicus, the shining half-skull grinning and catching the balefire light from the casting machines and warning lumens. A wide avenue leads up to the gate, with vast machinery on either side of it, presses and lifters and rolling conveyers, all still working.

Raine drags Makar Kayd into cover behind one of those machines. The vox-operator has one hand clamped over the bullet hole in his belly, the other still white-knuckled around his rifle's grip. Two more solid rounds are buried deep in the chest-plate of his armour, flattened to fat silver coins.

'Field guns, then,' Raine says.

Kayd nods his head. He is shaking, but when he speaks his voice doesn't waver.

'Yes, commissar.' He looks down and moves his hand

for a moment so that he can see the wound. 'High calibre, mounted on their barricades.'

Raine uses a dirt-dulled mirror to look around the edge of the forge machine. Across the avenue in front of the gate the Sighted have built massive fortifications from heaps of riveted, stamped metal plating, stacked up to half the height of the gate itself. The distinct shapes of unfinished super-heavy tanks make up the bulk of it, their Imperial insignia scratched out and bloody, blasphemous words scrawled on their armour plating. The muzzles of guns in amongst the fortifications light up, and las-fire and solid shot rings from the avenue and the machinery all around Raine as she ducks back behind the cover.

Nuria Lye appears out of the smoke, already unpacking her kit. The medic drops to one knee, and takes a look at Kayd and all of that blood.

'What a mess,' she says.

Kayd scowls. 'The witch could have shielded me from the guns,' he says in a low voice, nodding towards Zane. 'If she'd felt like it.'

The psyker is murmuring to herself, sitting on her knees in the machine's shadow. The hot air of the forge mists where it hits her ice-cold skin. Zane's false eyes move beneath their lids, but she doesn't open them.

'For what it is worth, I have not seen you die,' she says. 'Not today.'

Kayd goes a shade paler. He mutters in Antari. Raine knows the words.

Spare me the ways of the witch.

'You do know that those words cannot hurt me,' Zane snaps.

Raine puts her hand up. 'Enough,' she says.

It is all she needs to say to stop them. Zane goes back to her warding words and Kayd goes back to scowling and bleeding all over the floor. Nuria Lye takes out a wicked-looking injector and primes it.

'Move your hand, Mak,' she says. 'This will hurt.'

'Can't be worse than it already is,' Kayd says, his teeth chattering.

Raine looks at the injector and knows from experience that it will be. 'You should hold your breath,' she says.

Kayd's eyes go wide. She sees him take a deep breath, then Lye pushes the injector into the wound and seals it. It makes him thrash around under Raine's hands as she holds him still, but then it's done and Raine catches a different sort of burning to the rest of the forge smells.

'That really was worse,' Kayd says.

'You're welcome,' Lye says, flatly.

Raine pulls Kayd upright. He has to lean against the wall of the press, but he keeps his feet.

'The gate is adamantium,' Raine says. 'Thick as a fortress wall. Only the highest-ranking members of the Adeptus Mechanicus on Laxus Secundus have the override codes.'

'Let me guess, they would not give them to us because we are not blessed by the machine,' Yuri Hale says.

He ducks back into cover as hard rounds ricochet off the edge of the machine. Hale ejects the spent powercell from his laspistol and pushes a fresh one home. On the other side of the main avenue, the rest of the Antari are taking cover too, behind the forge's heavy machinery and the rust-red pillars that support the vaulted roof.

'No,' Raine says. 'We do not have the codes because those who know them are either dead, or defected.'

Hale spits on the floor at the word *defected*.

'The gate won't be an issue,' he says. 'If it's built, we can breach it.'

Raine can believe it. She has seen the Antari do the same on many worlds before this one. Never has she served alongside a regiment with such a capability for demolishing the undemolishable. Sometimes they joke that they were given the wrong appellation at their founding. That there are words much more appropriate than *Rifles*.

'First things first, though,' he says, nodding in the direction of the gate. 'We have to deal with the little wall they've built.'

'It is too far distant for me,' Zane says, before anyone asks it of her.

'I know,' Hale says. 'And I wasn't going to ask.' He takes the vox handset from Kayd and clicks it live. 'Dern,' Hale says. 'Bring up your Woodcutters, would you? Put some holes in those barricades.'

The response over the vox is distorted by interference, but Raine can hear Meri Dern's smile in his words.

'Got it, captain,' he says.

A moment later, five rattling, clanking shadows emerge from the smoke, moving up the central avenue towards the Delta Gate and the Sighted's barricades. Their heavy tread shakes the ashes from the machines around Raine. The heavy support Sentinels are painted in splintered green and grey, just like their regiment. Hard rounds clatter against the extra armour plates heat-fused to their cabs, denting and scorching but not going through. The Sentinels bristle with rocket pods and missile launchers. Dern's lead Sentinel has a lascannon mounted on its cheek, the barrel charred black with use.

'Woodcutters in position,' Dern voxes.

The Sentinels plant their feet, stablights piercing the smoke. There are a series of booms as missiles launch from them, trailing smoke. Dern's lascannon fires a searing beam of bright white light. There's a loud crack of displaced air. Seconds later, light blooms again at the far end of the avenue, against the Sighted barricades.

More Sighted gunfire chatters off the Sentinels' heavy plating, sending sparks raining to the floor.

'That's their answer,' Dern says. 'Sounds like nothing more than a springtime storm.'

Raine can hear the heavy clatter of the Sentinels' missile pods reloading.

'And again,' Dern says. 'Ready to fire.'

'Fire…' whispers Lydia Zane in horror.

The psyker throws up her hands as the air is split with a catastrophic *boom* that cancels all other noise for an instant, even the forge machinery. Raine's ears ring, but she doesn't blink or flinch. That's how she sees the moment the massive shell fired by the Sighted impacts against Lydia Zane's kine-shield. Raine has seen her use them before to shield whole squads from hellfire and deflect falling stones the size of tanks. But not this time.

This time, Zane's shield breaks.

The shell goes through, hits Dern's lead Sentinel and detonates. The second blast is just as loud as the first. The pressure wave knocks Raine to the ground. Knocks the air from her lungs too. All five of the Woodcutters are caught up in it, swallowed by smoke and flame. The vox crackles for an instant, then falls silent. In the wake of it, the forge halls are still. Not a single gun is fired from either end of the avenue.

Raine gets back to her feet, leaning against the machine press to do it. Her ears are still ringing, and the bright flare of the explosion sticks when she blinks. She has heard that sound before and seen those kinds of detonations. The

Sighted haven't just repurposed tank armour. They are using the guns too.

What they just fired was a Baneblade cannon.

Hale drags himself upright beside her, coughing.

'Woodcutters,' he says, into the vox. 'Any of you still alive?'

Raine knows the answer before she has it confirmed to her by the parting smoke. There is nothing left of Meri Dern's five-strong squad but bits of scrap and blackened ashes.

Yuri Hale thumps one blood-caked, blackened fist against the cover and curses in Antari.

Raine takes her timepiece out of the pocket of her greatcoat. The burr of the ticking through her glove steadies her thundering heart. The brass is highly polished and the glass is unmarked, save for the crack by the top of the dial that has been there since the day she first held it, all those years ago.

By her count, the Duskhounds should be almost in place.

'If we cannot break them, then we bury them,' she says. 'Crush them under their own defences.'

Hale laughs. It's a bitter sound.

'Then go in and bleed any left standing,' he says.

'For every betrayal, for every blasphemy,' Raine says.

'For every death,' Hale finishes.

The vox clicks in Andren Fel's ears as he steps out of the shadowed alcove, a pace behind two Sighted scouts. He knocks the first one into the oily muck with a blow to the back of the head from the butt of his hellgun. The second one turns in time for Fel to kick him hard into the tunnel wall, where he staggers, gasping. Fel puts a las-bolt into the first before he can rise. The second one is quicker. He brings his own rifle up and fires.

But he's not quick enough.

Fel knocks the rifle upwards, sending the shot into the tunnel ceiling. A pipe bursts with a blast of steam. His face mask and carapace protect him. The Sighted doesn't have either. The heated mist scalds him badly, and he screams. Fel cuts it short by breaking the scout's neck. The body slumps down against the curve of the tunnel wall.

The vox clicks again, and this time he answers.

'Acknowledged,' Fel says.

'We are going to need those charges you carry.'

Raine's voice is crackling and distorted, but Fel knows her well enough to pick up the cold anger in it.

'They escalated,' he says.

He hears her take a breath.

'That is one way to put it. Target location incoming.'

Fel keeps moving along the tunnel as the targeting data comes through. The supply network runs all the way under the forge complex. Fel's Duskhounds were sent down into the tunnels to outflank the Sighted, and strike at their backs. Fel knew there was trouble when the roof of the supply tunnel shook like that. He knew it would be so before the battle even started. The leaves don't lie, and there were many dark shapes in those he read in the hours before they deployed. The new target location blinks live on Fel's display. He checks his mission chrono and thinks back to the forge schematics. Fel remembers every detail, because that's how he was trained at the scholam on Antar. Forgetting meant the lash, or the submersion tanks. Recall became second nature as much as firing his rifle.

'Keep holding their stare,' he says. 'We will have the charges set in five minutes and be up top to bleed them with you.'

He saw dark shapes in the leaves, true enough, but that wasn't all he saw. There was the noon sun too. That's light.

Fire. There is more than one way to read it, but Fel chooses to see it as a good omen.

'They will know fire,' he says to Raine.

She used to laugh, back at the beginning, when he told her about the leaves. It's different now. It's not that she has come to believe it, but more that she understands why he does. When Raine answers this time there's something else in her voice. Something close to a smile.

'And thunder,' she says. *'Good hunting, captain.'*

'Hold their stare,' Hale says, bitterly. 'I want to *blind them*. Burn them, like they burned us.'

He spits again. This time, there's some blood in it. 'Do you hear that?' he says.

Raine listens, and she does. It is the Sighted, chanting. Some words are lost to the machine noise and the distance, but a handful stand out clear.

Make dust of the Emperor's bones.

Their blasphemy hits Raine like a physical blow. Anger burns from her heart outwards, a heat that even the forge fires cannot match. She clicks the vox-set live, on the regiment-wide open channel. Kayd sits beside her, keeping the broadcast clear, murmuring soft benedictions as he does so.

'Sons and daughters of Antar,' she says. 'The Sighted want to make us fear. To make us doubt.'

She looks at the faces of the men and women around her. Yuri Hale, his face twisted by those deep scars. Makar Kayd, plastered with blood.

'But fear is for the weak of heart. Doubt is for the weak of mind.'

Nuria Lye puts her fingertips to the aquila pendant she wears around her neck. Ari Rath nods his head, his filthy, bloody fingers gripping the pole of the Antari battle-standard. The icon of the crossed rifles against the wreath of thorns is a spare, bright flash of green in all that grey. It is riddled with bullet holes, but it has never looked prouder.

'We are strong of heart. Strong of mind. We are children of the Emperor, the liberators of the Bale Stars, and we are not afraid. We do not doubt.'

Zane watches too, her hands white-knuckled around her darkwood staff. Beyond her, hidden by the smoke and spread across the massive forge complex, the rest of the regiment will be listening. Nearly two thousand souls, heeding Raine's words.

'We are fire, and we are thunder!'

Raine's fury feels pure now. Her body aches with the want to run and fight. She draws her pistol.

'Now,' she says, into the live channel. 'Let us show them just how loud thunder can be.'

In the moment between the gasp and bellow of smelting metal, Raine distinctly hears the Antari start to sing, their voices made rough by war.

Andren Fel is setting his last demolition charge on the ceiling of the supply tunnel when he hears the words coming tinny through his vox-link.

Through the wylds of winter, through the evenfall.
Brightly burning is He.

There's no mistaking *Soul of Antar*. He has no memories longer held than the words of that song.

Fel switches to his squad's encrypted internal channel.

'Do you hear that, Duskhounds?' he says.

Four *aye, captains* answer him. The rest of his squad are setting their own charges in other tunnels along the line, right under the Sighted barricades. Cassia Tyl is a moment before the others, because she always is. Tyl is fierce and quick in all regards, including words.

'*Would that we were up there singing it with them,*' she says.

Fel smiles. He can't argue with that.

'Set chronos,' he says, instead. 'Three minutes.'

Fel sets his chrono as four acknowledgement clicks come through, again with Tyl slightly ahead of the others. He sends three bursts of vox static to Hale up top to let him know the job is done.

Fel can't listen to his kinfolk sing, but he still lets the words play out in his head as he goes for the ladder that will take him back to the surface. His tread is light and swift, almost silent on the tunnel floor.

Through times of strife.

Fel ducks underneath a pipe that's hot to the touch. The ceiling of the supply tunnel is low, and the temperature is stifling. Machine noise shakes the walls. If it wasn't for his helmet, Fel knows he'd be deafened by it.

Through blood we spend.

He steps over the body of one of the Sighted scouts he killed on the way up.

Brightly burning are we.

That's when Fel notices something. He slows his pace. His hellgun is already up, because there's no place in a warzone that you carry at ease. He blinks the sweat from his eyes and stares into the patch of shadows that he could swear just shifted. Dark shapes. Just like he saw in the leaves.

'Be wary,' he voxes to his squad.

'*What do you see, captain?*' Tyl says.

And then it happens again, just a flicker.

'Shadows,' Fel says, then fires.

The bolt from the hellgun is a whisper, but it punches the shadow onto its back. As it falls, its shape crazes and flickers, then resolves. The shadow is Sighted, and it's not alone. The tunnel fills with las-fire as two more cloaked in the same way fire back at Fel. He catches a las-bolt in the shoulder as he twists to minimise the damage. His carapace armour takes the worst of it.

'Three targets on me,' he voxes. 'Camo gear.'

The shadows grow closer, their footsteps silent. He can only tell where they are by the flickering and the way the puddles of oil in the tunnel move. Even thermal doesn't pick them up. Fel fires and misses. He takes a grazing hit to the leg in return.

'*I have two,*' says Tyl.

Fel fires again and wings one of them. Blood sprays up the tunnel wall, but there's no sound.

'*And here, captain,*' yells Myre.

'*Bastards,*' says Jeth.

There's no answer from Rol, and his signal has disappeared from Fel's display. Fel doesn't get the chance to try the vox again because one of the shadows comes out of the dark and knocks him back against the tunnel wall. Tries to bury a hooked, black knife in his gut. Fel snaps the shadow's arm at the wrist before the blow lands, then drives his elbow into its throat. The shadow staggers back, its camouflage flickering wildly. Fel fires once, dropping it with a neat headshot. Two dead shadows.

The oily puddle at his feet ripples.

Fel turns just in time to block the third shadow's knife with his arm. It clashes off the vambrace and cuts into the soft joint at his elbow. The pain blinds him for an instant, and he loses his grip on his gun. It swings loose by the strap. Fel takes a blunt strike to the throat, and another to the ribs. The shadow is hitting him where it'll hurt, and it does, but Fel is trained to take the hits and stay standing. He grabs the shadow by its flickering edges and the camouflage dazzles and disengages. He sees it for what it is. A man baring pointed, black teeth. The Sighted has blue-grey carapace armour and feathers tied into his lank brown hair. He is kitted with thermal goggles and auditory dampers. He is trying to get past Fel, to run for where he set his charges, but the Sighted isn't a shadow anymore and Fel sees him well enough to return the cut with his own knife. The combat blade goes in to the hilt, and the last shadow falls to his knees, dribbling blood through those pointed teeth. Fel pulls the blade free, and the Sighted gasps air from his throat, and the hole in his chest.

'Tick tock,' he says, before falling over dead.

Fel looks to the datafeed built into his left vambrace. It reads thirty-six seconds.

'Hells,' Andren Fel says. He snatches that auditory damper off the Sighted's body and starts to run.

The last few bars of *Soul of Antar* echo in his head as the timer ticks down.

Walk with Him, know His face.

Fel's injured leg tries to buckle under him. He sees the ladder, but it's far. Too far.

Give your soul, await His grace. Then come home, my dear.

The counter hits zero. Fel drops to the ground, hands over his head. As the tunnel grows light, that last line repeats in his mind.

Brightly burning.

Four detonations blow up through the floor of the main machine hall, spread along the Sighted's defensive lines.

Four fireballs that reach for the ceiling of the manufactorum in white-hot columns. The floor tremors under Raine's feet.

Five, she thinks. *There should have been five.*

There's a part of her, just for an instant, that wonders if the missing charge belonged to Fel. If he's dead. She pushes the thought aside. There is no time for it. Before she can call the charge there's a fifth massive explosion from the centre of the Sighted lines that shakes her eyes in her head and makes her stagger. It can only have been the Baneblade cannon. Scrap is hurled so far by it that it clatters off the machines and the floor around her.

'That's our cue,' Hale says, on the company-wide channel. 'Let's go, Rifles!'

'Fire and thunder,' Raine shouts, with her ears still ringing.

And hundreds of Antari voices answer her.

Fire.

She runs, her heart hammering, up the central avenue.

And.

Everywhere there is steam and smoke. Ash and motes of fire.

Thunder!

Raine's legs burn, but her heart is singing. It feels like the tide turning. She reaches the smoking mess that's left of the barricades alongside Yuri Hale's command squad and the Hartkin, under Rom Odi. The dead are everywhere, some just painted as shadows by the force of the explosion. The metal flooring has been torn up. But the Sighted are many, and they are not quite beaten yet.

Two dozen figures marshal in the smoke, their armour glinting in the forge light. It was Laxian Home Guard armour, once, but the yellow and blue heraldry markings have been scorched off or overpainted. Every single one has marked their face. Raine fires Penance three times. Blood joins the smoke in the air, misted by the explosive rounds. Where it scatters on Raine's silver chest-plate, it looks black. The Antari light the forge with las-fire, moving up to what's left of the barricades and firing over and around them. Two more of the dug-in Laxians fall heavily, their guns going quiet. One of the Hartkin falls in return. He screams before going quiet just as the guns did.

A stun grenade bounces off the barricades and lands among the Antari. Raine sees Yuri Hale throw it back, and follow with one of his own, only he doesn't carry stun grenades. What Hale throws is a frag grenade. When they both go off in short succession, the Sighted are blinded. Then they are burned, just as Hale promised.

'Push forwards!' Hale shouts.

The Antari obey, taking the moment afforded to them by the explosions, but then a whirring sound cuts the air. Raine recognises it.

A heavy stubber.

'Down!' Raine shouts, dropping into a slide as the large calibre rounds put dents and holes in the wreckage of the barricades around her. She hears screams from her side. Hears Hale cursing.

Raine chances a look around the cover. The stubber isn't mounted. One of the Sighted is *holding* it. She is walking braced, letting the barrel run hot as she tracks the Antari going to ground. The roar of the gun is absolutely deafening, which makes the absence of it all the more apparent when it stops suddenly.

Raine looks up over the cover in time to see Lydia Zane raise her hand to the heavy gunner. The stubber crumples and deforms from the barrel down until it detonates in the

Sighted's hands. The Sighted screams, but that stops abruptly too as she is also crumpled and deformed under the telekinetic pressure.

'Mother of spring,' Yuri Hale says, horrified.

The Sighted fall back ragged, evidently just as horrified as Hale. All of them are firing at Zane now. The air around her is a storm of las-fire. Some shots graze her, and she staggers. Others are turned aside by reactionary flickers of psychic shielding. Raine gives chase, Hale and his command squad beside her.

But the Sighted don't get far, because they run right into four matt-black shadows with the howling faces of spectral hounds painted on their masks. Fully automatic las-fire strobes in the smoke. When the firing stops, and the Sighted are dead and smoking at their feet, the lead figure bows his head in greeting. His carapace armour is peeled back to the grey, and he is masking a limp.

'Not dead yet, then,' Raine says to Andren Fel.

The storm trooper captain lifts his closed fist over his heart.

'Not yet, commissar,' he says.

Wyck's heart hammers in his ears. He took another dose in the moments before the explosion, just to be sure. To tunnel his vision for the fight. The stimms make everything sharp. Every sound is crystal clear and loud. Every colour bright and vibrant. Everything else pushes out of his head, to somewhere it can't haunt him.

Wyck vaults the barricades without slowing. He can't, and he won't. Not because of that aquila pendant in the pouch at his belt, or any of what came before. Guilt does no favours for the dead.

He lands amongst the Sighted on the other side. They are

still reeling from the explosions. There is blood up the barricades from where some were caught in it, and a yawning hole in the floor, toothed and dark. Wyck kneecaps one of the Sighted with las-fire and kicks him into that darkness. He distinctly hears the landing. The snap and the scream. Wyck is already moving to the next of them and firing a las-bolt to blow out the Sighted's throat. Wyck takes a round to the shoulder from a third. The pain doesn't filter through, just the impact. It knocks his next shot wide. The Sighted who shot him gets within his reach. She is fast too. Fast and mad, with a deep red spiral cut into the skin of her cheek. She slams the butt of her rifle into Wyck's face, rebreaking his broken nose. He sees stars and loses his grip on his rifle, so he answers her with his knife instead, punching it between her ribs. Something bursts under the blade, and blood runs down his arm.

'Blind,' she is saying. 'You are blind.'

'Better blind than dead,' Wyck says.

He twists the blade and her eyes roll back. Wyck pulls the knife out and drops her.

The rest of the Wyldfolk are over the barricades now. Wyck knows because he hears Crys' modified grenade launcher go off. *Thumpthumpthumpthump.* He turns to shout for her. To ask if she's lost her damned mind, using that thing with the squad so close, but then he sees what she is shooting at and his heart goes cold with fear.

It's a damned witch.

A column of violet light spears up from the Wyldfolk's position, cutting clean through the smoke. A second later, Raine feels an incredible pressure in her head. She stumbles into cover behind the barricades, her eyesight blurring.

The Antari stop firing over the cover and start holding their heads and moaning. Yuri Hale slumps against the piled sandbags and scrap metal, blood running from his nose. Despite the heat in the forge, they all mist the air when they breathe. They would be dead on their feet, if it weren't for the fact that the Sighted are hurting the same way.

The vox crackles in Raine's ear. It is Wyck's voice, and he sounds terrified. Through the distorted wail of the connection, she hears him say the word she knows is coming.

Witch.

The pressure lifts, but the cold grip of fear remains. It's an animal response. A primal clawing at the soul. Raine recognises it and pushes it aside, just as she does with all distractions. She sees Hale regain his feet too. It looks like an effort.

But not all among the Antari are quite so capable.

Dala of the Hartkin breaks formation. Her grey eyes are wide, and she's muttering those same old words.

Spare me the ways of the witch.

'Dala,' Odi says. 'Stay in line, damn you.'

'It'll curse us, sarge,' she says, her voice hoarse. 'You know it, a thing like that!'

'Stand your ground!' Raine shouts. 'Turn away from this, and you forsake everything we have fought for!'

Raine knows that if they break here they will lose the Delta Gate and the forges too. She cannot allow that to happen.

'Turn away from this, and you forsake the God-Emperor's will!'

It's enough to freeze most of them to the spot, but not Dala. For her, the fear has already grown too large to be pushed aside. She drops her rifle and starts to run, and there is only one response to that dangerous kind of cowardice.

Raine levels Penance and fires.

The shot kills Dala outright. She falls heavy and sprawling. The Antari look to Raine now with a new kind of fear. Only this time, it's of her. It's a kind she can use.

'We fight,' she says, loud and clear. 'No matter the foe. No matter the weapons they use, or the armour they bear. Because we fight for the Bale Stars and all of the worlds within. For every soul from here to the sector's edge!'

They know she means Antar too. Raine has served alongside them long enough to know which words will pull at them and which won't.

'For every soul!' she shouts again. 'For the Bale Stars! For the Emperor!'

This time, she gets an echo as dozens of voices answer in kind. She knows that they hate her in these moments. It's another animal response that, while it cannot be prevented, can be controlled, which is exactly what Yuri Hale does when he turns to his troops and gives his next order.

'They may have a witch,' he says. 'But so do we.' He looks to Zane. 'We get you there, and you kill it.'

If Zane feels anything at being spoken of in the same breath as the traitor psyker, she doesn't say so. Instead she bows her head and smiles thinly.

'With pleasure, captain,' she says.

Daven Wyck fires his lasgun at the witch until the powercell blinks red and empty, but not a single shot goes through. When the smoke clears, the thing is still hanging there, about a metre off the ground. It is dressed like a noble, in finely made clothes the colour of the sky at lowlight. Rings set with jewels glitter on its thin fingers and its feet are bare and bloody. The witch turns its head then and Wyck gets a good look at its pale face, carved with numbers and letters and wicked sigils. A red crystal sits where its left eye should be, and a too-wide grin stretches its face.

The witch claps its hands together and to Wyck's right, Karo Efri ceases to be. He doesn't even get time to scream. Just gets swallowed up by blue light until there's nothing but ashes. Just like Dal, and Vyne. Gone quicker than a heartbeat passes. Nothing left to judge. Wyck feels the numb shock of it, even through the way the stimms are spiking. Then the witch turns, still grinning.

Only now it's grinning at him.

Wyck's world centres until all he can see is that grin. Until all he can hear is his heart pounding in his chest like it wants to get out. He is truly afraid, for the first time in a long time, but he can't look away because that makes witches stronger. He remembers the stories. Don't look away, don't turn your back. He murmurs the words they are all taught as children.

Spare me the ways of the witch.

He ejects the spent cell and reloads his gun. He won't turn. Won't run. *Throne*, he wants to do both. The witch floats towards him, trailing smoke and shadow, still grinning.

+A splintered soul, aren't you?+

The voice in Wyck's head sounds like wind across water. His vision goes blurry.

+It is the cutting,+ the voice says. +All the blood you have spilt.+

'Dav!' Awd is shouting for him. 'Dav, move!'

The shape of the witch wavers through the sights of his gun, and then the gun starts to discorporate, turning to ashes in his hands. Wyck still can't move. He's frozen, like an animal caught under floodlights.

+It is your peace,+ it says. +The cut and the spill. You should embrace it.+

The witch hangs in place, right in front of him, still grinning with those needle teeth.

'I already have,' Wyck says, through his teeth.

And he unslings Jona Veer's rifle and fires. This time, the las-bolt punches into the witch's shoulder. Through and through. The scream the creature makes echoes in Wyck's head as well as the forges. It puts him on his knees, with blood running from his nose.

'Stupid fool,' says the witch, in its real voice this time. 'No more words. No more games.'

The witch raises its hand, only to have its arm snapped like a piece of dry kindling. First the wrist, then the elbow. The bones breaking sound like gunshots. Wyck knows what's done that, and it makes him feel no better.

'Oh, now,' says Lydia Zane, as she steps into Wyck's peripheral vision. 'This hardly seems a fair fight.'

One witch, traded for another.

+Little. Pet.+

The Sighted psyker turns to face Zane and looks at her with his one human eye and with the gemstone eye too, though she cannot say how that is possible.

+Gifts,+ pulses the psyker, as if she had asked. +Not that you would know anything of gifts.+

The psyker snorts with effort and the bones in his broken arm reset. His name was Calvar Larat, once. Zane knows this because the unsanctioned blare their thoughts like warhorns. He is not one of the Nine. Not one chosen by the Sighted to lead, though his heart longs for it. He thinks himself a star ascendant. His raw ambition makes Zane want to spit.

+Look at you,+ Larat pulses. +With your collar and your cables. With your watchdog at your back. Such a shame.+

He sends a wave of force at Zane that she turns aside with a flicker of her kine-shield.

+No,+ she answers. +A shame is you resetting that arm, just so that I can break it again.+

Zane claps her hands together, sending a pulse of telekinetic force at Larat. It puts him into the barricades with enough impact to bend the metal. Dust bursts up around her, and false wind stirs her robes. Zane does not wait, but attacks again as she walks forwards, slamming the psyker against the barricades over and over and over. For a moment, she is lost in it. In the fury of using her power. She does not feel the way her bones sing with aching, or how her skin opens in wounds from pushing her limits. She does not pay heed to the snap of wings. She will prove to the thing once known as Calvar Larat that she is more than a pet. To the Antari that she is a good soul who uses her power in the right. To herself that she can take all the tests and pass them, because she is strong and she will not break.

Zane stops in front of Larat's broken form, looking down at him. He is a mess of tattered finery and blood and splintered bone. Every spare inch of his skin is scarred with words and numbers, some overwriting others.

+You see my marks,+ Larat pulses. +They are fates, little pet. A hundred twists in time's rope. Knots and loops and nooses all. Every one of them a new truth.+

Zane raises her hands to put him out of his misery, but finds herself frozen in place. Pinned, like an insect on a board by Larat's wicked power. He laughs, dribbling blood through his pointed teeth, then rears up, limp and broken and bleeding. His gemstone eye glitters.

+And I have a truth for you too. Would you like to see it?+

And he takes hold of her face with his clawed, bloody hand.

Lydia Zane's eyes open to a wide blue sky. She is falling. The wind whips at her robes and rattles her crown of cables. She is not afraid, though she should be. It is a long fall. Her staff is nothing but a splintered shard in her hand. Her fingernails are broken and bloody. There are three great dark stains across the front of her robes where she has been shot. All of this Zane sees, and all of it she understands.

But still, none of it makes her afraid.

When the ground finally embraces her, she lands in soft loam, between the boles of white-barked trees. From that terrible height, the impact still breaks every bone in her body. It is an instant of incredible pain, then a peace like one that she has never known as her nerve endings fail her. With her lungs punctured, Zane can't breathe. With her organs pulped, she cannot live. So Lydia Zane lies on her back in the loam as blood soaks into it, dying slowly and in absolute quiet. The last thing to go is her bionic eyes, because they are made of metal and wire and they feel no shock at the fall. Before they fail, Zane sees four birds pass across that wide blue sky.

Ghosts, in silent feathers.

Daven Wyck can't move. He is pinned in place when the temperature drops and more blood bursts from his nose. It hits his skin and freezes. The blood is the last thing he sees before he blacks out.

Wyck watches blood drip from the point of his combat knife. Regular, like a slow heartbeat.

Drip. Drip. Drip.

He breathes in and catches that iron smell. Realises that his hands are slick with it. The sleeves of his fatigues are soaked through. They stick to his skin.

Drip. Drip.

Wyck's mouth is dry and there's an itching behind his eyes. A pressure against them. More blood. His, this time, firing in his veins. Pushed by the stimms. Making him shake. Making more blood drip off that knife.

Drip.

The body at his feet is in dark armour. Hard plate. Carapace. But it's still a body. Still dead. Stabbed through the soft joints. Elbows. Under the ribs. Throat. Armour can't protect everything. There's always a weakness. Always a place that can be cut. If you're fast and vicious.

And Daven Wyck knows he is both.

There are markings on that armour, underneath the bloody handprints and smears. And on the other bodies he sees when he turns. All dead. Cut through the soft parts. The markings are silver.

Laurels.

Skulls.

The knife drips again.

Drip. Drip. Drip.

Twin-headed eagles.

Raine sees the darkness roll out from Zane and the traitor witch like smoke. Like fog rolling in off the ocean.

'Hold!' she shouts to the Antari, in the moment before it hits her.

Severina Raine is six years old and standing on a rain-lashed landing pad far above Gloam's furious ocean. Her clothes are soaked and sticking to her. They don't fit quite right, those new clothes. The dark tunic marked with the icon of the Adeptus Ministorum. The rough weave trousers and soft-soled shoes. The belt with a loop for a blunt training blade. The people that brought her here said that she'll grow into the clothes in time. That eventually everything will fit that doesn't, but Severina misses her books, and her maps. She took nothing from her home on Darpex, because she hadn't really believed she'd never see it again until setting foot on this platform and listening to that angry ocean. It sounds like it wants to swallow her up. Severina looks up at the hive spire. At the way it reaches up into the dark and the clouds, lights glittering on the side of it from torches and lumens. Kilometres high, and the same again deep. It looks as though it would swallow her up, too, and then she'd just be another one of those tiny lights.

'It is always dark here.'

Lucia's voice is raised, so that Severina can hear her over the wind. Her sister is standing beside her, rain gathering in the neat, dark braids of her hair. She is taller already, though she is barely two years older. The two of them stand close together, but they don't hold hands or link arms because that will make the group of people approaching across the landing pad think that they are afraid, when they are not. They are cold and sad and a little angry too, but not afraid. Never that.

Lucia did take something from home. Something that belonged to their mother. She has her fingers locked tight around the timepiece as she watches those people approaching across the landing pad. The brass case of the timepiece is the only bit of warm colour in the world right now except for those tiny lights.

'It stays dark because the people who made this place poisoned the sky,' Lucia says. 'A long time ago.'

'Why?'

Lucia looks at her and smiles. It is a sad sort of smile.

'Because they wanted to build a new world,' she says. 'And poison seemed a small price to pay.'

Andren Fel does his best to stay on his feet as his Duskhounds fall beside him, one after another. Fel doesn't want to lose them like he lost Rol, so he tries to reach for them, but then the world turns around him and he falls too.

Andren Fel sits cross-legged on the floor of the house. The wind pulls at the timbers, and whistles through the eaves. There is frost on the inside of the thick windowpanes. He hasn't eaten in a long time, but he can't go and hunt for something, or fetch it from the trader down the way, because he has to stay and watch.

Because otherwise the duskhounds will come for his mother. It's what they do. Come for those that fate forgot to take.

His mother is lying where she has been for days, pale as that frost on the windows. Andren turns the heavy blade he is holding in his hands. There are fanged faces carved into the hilt. It's too big for him to use yet, really. It was hers when she went off-world to the crusade. Before she was hurt so bad she couldn't fight. So bad it should have killed her, they said.

Only now it is killing her. The old doctor from down the way said so. That they didn't do a clean job when they tried to heal her in the first place. They didn't get all of the pieces out. So now she is dying the death she should have had before. Andren knows that's how it works. He's been taught so since he was old enough to understand the stories. Fate comes for you, no matter where you go.

But just this once, he thinks maybe he can stop it, if he's quick and ready when the duskhounds come.

His mother shifts, just a bit.

'My boy,' she says. 'My son.'

Andren gets up from the floor on numb legs and walks over, still carrying that blade.

'I told you to go,' she says. 'Why didn't you go?'

He tells her all the reasons why and she smiles, just a little. It's something she doesn't often do, because it hurts her to do it. Not on the outside. On the inside.

'We all have our fates,' she says. 'This is mine. You have yours. You will do something great. A righteous thing. I know it.'

That's something else he's been taught. Something else she has always said. She read it in the leaves.

'What, though?' he asks her. 'What will I do?'

'Your heart will know it,' she says. 'When the time comes.'

And then there's a noise from outside the house. Andren moves to the door as it opens wide and fast. He raises his mother's knife and he goes for the shadowed shapes that enter the house. The duskhounds, come to finish fate's job. He knocks into the first one and nicks at the shadow. It cries out, and he thinks he can do it. He can stop them and make them wait a bit longer. But then a second one grabs him and locks his arms so he can't fight them. Andren kicks instead until they stop him doing that too.

'Boy cut me,' says one of the shadows. 'Look.'

Another of them laughs, and Andren realises they aren't hounds. They are men and women, though their armour makes them look like monsters. It's the same sort of armour his mother wore when she went off-world. He stops kicking.

'Let me go,' he says. 'I need to watch her. To keep the duskhounds away.'

The man he cut bobs down and shakes his head.

'No,' he says, sounding a little sorry. 'No, you don't.'

Andren Fel looks back and sees that he doesn't. That they have already taken his mother, but that even so she is still smiling, just a little. He couldn't keep the hounds away, no matter how quick or how ready he was. How much he watched.

'Fate still found her,' he says.

The man he cut nods. 'And now it has come for you too.'

Aching, bleeding and her mind alight, Lydia Zane finally puts Calvar Larat on his back, not to rise again. He just lies there, his throat clicking with blood and his arms turned to ragged, splintered stumps. Zane can see the unlight of his soul twisting away to be judged. It's the same as the unlight that makes the Antari dream.

'Little pet,' Larat says, and now he uses his mortal voice too. 'Little monster let out of her cage. Off her tether while her watchdog sleeps and her kinfolk dream.'

He grins still, even now.

'Freedom, just for a moment,' he says. 'That is my last truth. My last gift, to you.'

Zane twists her hand, and silences Larat for good by breaking his neck. The light in his human eye dims. Even the gemstone appears to go dull. The psychic storm Larat created begins to clear, and the Antari around her stir. Zane does not move. Instead, she stands and stares at Larat's one remaining fate-mark that is clear to see, cut into his chest just above the collarbones. It is a date and a time, just like the others. The date is today's. The time is marked down to the second. To the exact second that Calvar Larat's soul finally twisted away.

His death, writ in his skin. Foretold to the moment.

Just as her fall was foretold in the vision he showed her.

The bird has returned, the way it always does. It perches on what is left of Larat's face, still watching her with those black eyes, but this time it opens its beak and speaks.

Fall, croaks the bird.

And Zane feels the rush of wind on her face. Her stomach turns over. She cannot get a breath.

'Mists alive.'

The bird and the feeling vanishes and Zane snaps around to see Daven Wyck leaning against the barricades, holding the rifle he took from Jona Veer. For once, there is not a trace of a smile gracing his even features. Just fear, which like so much else turns to anger inside Daven Wyck. Zane knows that she is the source of that fear and that Wyck hates her for it. He has never made a secret of it.

Not like all of those other secrets he carries. Ugly secrets.

'Is it dead?' he asks her.

Zane glances back at the mess she has made of Calvar Larat.

'He is dead,' she says.

Wyck lowers his rifle, but not completely. Always armed, that one. Always ready to fight. His hands are shaking, and his mind is like white noise, or a storm against glass. Loud and roaring.

'It put lies in my head,' he says. 'Made me see things.'

Zane thinks about what she saw. About falling into that loam, and the breaking of all of her bones. The pain and the silence. The birds, passing in front of the blue sky.

And she knows that it was not a lie.

'A truth,' she says. 'That is what Larat said. Yet to come, or been and gone.'

Wyck laughs, and it is a cruel sound.

'A truth,' he says, flatly. 'From a witch, and a traitor one at that. I don't think so.'

For a moment, Zane wants to break his bones the way she broke Larat's. She cannot tell if the feelings are hers, or Wyck's. Violence bleeds from him like ink into water. A tremor rolls from her, rattling the plasteel of the floor. Wyck's eyes go wide and he raises the rifle that he took from his dead kin, but then something eclipses Zane's anger altogether and she reins in her power.

It is the shadow at the heart of the forge. She had thought it to be Larat, but now she feels it anew. Stronger.

Zane looks past Wyck, towards the Delta Gate. 'Look,' she says. 'Something comes.'

He turns and looks. Sees what she sees.

The Delta Gate is opening.

Raine is one of the first to gain her feet. All around her, the Antari are shaking and struggling to get up. They murmur superstitious words in their own tongue. Some are still and lifeless, killed by the shock of the dreams they were given. Despite herself, Raine finds that the dream clings to her too. The cold. The thousands of tiny lights. Lucia's voice too.

It is always dark here.

She shouldn't call it a dream, because that's not what it was. It was a memory, and one that she hasn't thought of in a very long time. Raine shakes her head to clear it. She pushes it aside, just like before.

Far aside.

'Fate.'

The voice is Andren Fel's. To anyone else, he would sound perfectly calm, but not to her. She knows him better than that. Fel is kneeling in the dust and ashes, turning his combat blade in his hand. Light catches on the carvings on the hilt. Raine asked him once if he made those markings, and he told her no.

'It was fate,' he says, absently.

'Are you with me?' Raine asks.

Fel stirs as if waking, and looks up from the blade.

'With you,' he says. 'Of course.'

'Get the others on their feet,' Raine says. 'Now.'

'Aye, commissar,' Fel says.

There is a change in his bearing, as if he has found his balance. He gets up and goes to rouse the Duskhounds, and Raine goes for the others. She pulls Hale upright first. His skin is as grey as his eyes, and he is shaking with the after-effects of the psyker's dream. He struggles to keep his balance, and Raine realises that it isn't just Hale who is shaking. It is the floor under their feet too. She looks up and over the last remaining barricades to see the two halves of the Delta Gate sliding slowly apart beyond the smoke.

'Why in Terra's name would they open the bloody thing?' Yulia Crys says, leaning on the barricades. 'After all they've done to keep us from it?'

Zane comes up through the smoke. The psyker is in such a state that Raine is surprised she can stand. Her grey robes are tattered, and her furs are matted with blood and filth. There are deep shadows around Zane's false eyes. Her veins show dark through her paper-thin skin. Wyck is a pace behind Zane, watching her warily. He is shaking too, but it is nothing to do with either psyker's work. That kind of shake is the sign of a stimm-user. Wyck thinks that Raine doesn't know, that he can escape her judgement. He doesn't realise that he is only running ahead of it, like the tide. That when he becomes more of an issue than an asset, he will be overtaken by it and made to answer for his weaknesses.

'Something comes,' Zane says. Her teeth are pink with blood.

'Another witch?' Hale asks her.

Zane sniffs wetly. 'Something comes,' she slurs again.

'What's wrong with her?' Hale says to Wyck.

Wyck spits on the ground, still watching the psyker. 'Damned if I know,' he says. 'She started saying it when the gate began to open, and now she won't stop.'

Crys' eyes have gone wide. She starts pulling at the pouches on the bandolier across her chest to reload her grenade launcher. 'Zane's right,' she says. 'Something is coming. Something with a bloody great engine.'

Raine can't understand how the Antari can pick it out from the sound of the gate grinding open and the forge machinery, especially half-deaf, but if there's one thing Crys knows, it's things built to kill.

'What is it?' she shouts up to Fel. 'What do you see?'

'Something bad,' Fel shouts back. He drops down off the high portion of the remaining barricades. 'Something they have *made*.'

Raine looks over the barricades. She sees it now too. Not a tank. Not a war machine or a Cybernetica robot. It is an abomination. The Sighted have fused parts of a super-heavy tank onto a set of jointed mechanical legs. Exhaust stacks stick up from the back of it like spears in a sea monster's back, spewing thick dark smoke. It is metal and crystal and thick clots of oil where the two materials meet. Its hooked limbs punch holes in the plasteel of the floor as it approaches them.

She wonders if this is what the Sighted with the gemstone eye meant. If this *thing* is the life they have made here.

'Throne of Terra. What have they done?' Crys looks distraught. 'Those guns mounted on it. Those are Vulcan mega-bolters.'

'On your *feet!*' Raine shouts, moving among her soldiers. 'Now!'

Hale is beside her, shouting for grenades and for the missile teams. For the Antari to fall back firing. He orders them to aim for the vision slits and the joints of the limbs and to try to halt it. But then Raine loses the sound of Hale's voice. She loses every other noise in the forge, because the Vulcan mega-bolters begin to fire. Raine sees Crys, firing her grenade launcher. She can't hear it over the racket of the mega-bolters. She just sees the barrel of it lighting.

Flash. Flash. Flash.

The grenades land in front of the abomination and against it, but when the smoke clears, there's barely a dent in the armour.

'Keep firing!' Raine shouts over the vox, and she can hardly hear her own voice. 'Collapse the floor! Make a grave for it!'

They are losing their ground. Losing their lives. Next to her, Jole of the Hartkin is hit. He vanishes, and blood-spray mists across Raine's face. The guns track. More of the Hartkin are torn away. Craters are punched into the barricades. Fel is throwing demo charges for the abomination to find as it chases them. Rounds tear up the floor. Missiles trace overhead from the Antari heavy weapons teams. There's an arc of plasma fire from Elys, last of the Pyrehawks. Then there are no Pyrehawks at all because she's gone too. Vaporised. Raine knows the likelihood of breaking anything on that thing with a bolt pistol from this range, but she fires anyway, because she won't die without fighting it. And in that moment, a part of her is certain that is what is about to happen. That she'll die here. Turned to a mist of blood like Jole and Elys and all of the others that are simply gone now. The abomination puts one of its metal claws over the barricades and onto Fel's charges. They go off, splintering the limb and unsteadying it, but the abomination doesn't stop. It makes a sound that is all too much like a scream and pushes through. It is right on top of them.

Then Lydia Zane steps up beside Raine and throws out her hand.

For a handful of heartbeats, the abomination's guns spin down. Its legs freeze and twitch. Zane is locking them. Holding it still. In the ear-ringing absence of the sound of it firing, Raine can hear Zane screaming. Her back arches and lightning runs up and down her thin limbs. In the moment of respite, while the abomination is without its teeth, the Antari fire on it. Their last missiles. Last grenades and demo-charges. Las-rounds and flamer fuel and solid shot from snipers. Raine fires her pistol, too, until it clicks empty. The abomination is engulfed in flame and Raine's heart leaps. She hears Wyck laughing, though she can't see him for the smoke. But then Zane collapses and the smoke clears and the abomination's guns begin to whine and spin again. The barrels are red-hot spirals, like the markings cut into the faces of the Sighted. Raine takes a breath. Blinks. Light fills the forges. Blinding and white. She thinks this must be it. Death.

But the light doesn't come for her. It spears into the abomination instead. A beam fired from behind the Antari. A second shot follows it, cutting deep into the thing's armour and rocking it on its clawed legs. The abomination staggers backwards and ratchets its guns upwards in answer, only to be struck again. Raine chances a look back, and her heart sings.

Behind them, through the smoke and the ashes and misted blood, stride two Imperial Knights. The massive, bipedal war machines are halved in violet and white, armed with glowing thermal cannons and hung with pennants that ripple in the hot air of the forge. They blare the sound of victory horns from their vox-emitters. Between them rolls a command tank, trimmed in red and gold, a roaring lion sculpted on the forward-facing armour. It bristles with guns and trails devotionals. Hundreds of foot soldiers follow behind, silhouetted by the smoke. The Lions of Bale. Raine knows them as she knows the man she can see in the cupola on top of the command tank, lit in gold by the forge light, his fist raised in the air in defiance. The hero of the Bale Stars Crusade. Living avatar of the Emperor's will.

'Serek,' she shouts, into the vox. 'The Lord-General Militant!'

And every one of the Antari answers by shouting his name as more furious spears of light arc towards the Sighted's ailing machine creation.

Serek!

The machine reels. Staggers backwards.

Serek!

The ammo hoppers for the Vulcan mega-bolters rupture, then so does the abomination's reactor.

Serek!

There is a scream and a flare of white light as the abomination collapses. Raine is knocked to the ground, winded and bruised and momentarily made blind and deaf by the explosion.

But she is smiling too.

THREE

The Lord-General Militant

Daven Wyck ejects the last powercell from the rifle he took from Jona Veer, and uses the gun like a club instead to put the Sighted down with a blow to the face. Killing him takes three strikes, and it is noisy, and messy.

'They are running,' Awd says, from beside him. 'Routed.'

Awd has been out of flamer fuel ever since the machine that tried to kill the lot of them succumbed to the barrage from the Knights. He's using a knife and his fists now because they are the only weapons left to him as they push up through the halls behind the Lions' tide, sweeping up what remains of the Sighted.

'Damn right they are routed,' Wyck says.

He goes to take a drink from his canteen and finds it empty. It's the stimms that do that. Dehydrate him. Make his brain feel as though it's pulling away from the insides of his skull. Especially on the comedown, which is hitting him like that rifle stock hit the Sighted's face. It's been worse lately, and he knows it's because he's been upping the dose.

He also knows he hasn't got a choice. Less will do nothing, and what's a bit of extra pain on top of the rest?

'Why do you think they do that?' Crys asks.

The combat engineer nudges at one of the bodies with the toe of her boot. The Sighted has cut up his face, like they always do, but Wyck knows that it's not that she means. It's the eye. Or more precisely, the jagged red stone in its place. He thinks about that witch. The one who put a nightmare in his head.

'Because they are mad,' Wyck says. 'Corrupted. Faithless. Pick a reason. They're all true.'

Crys nods her head, but she drops into a crouch to look closer.

'If you're not careful, you'll go the same way,' Wyck says. 'Looking too far into that stone.'

'He's right,' Awd says with a soft laugh, though Wyck didn't mean it as a joke. 'You know the stories.'

'It's not that,' Crys says. 'It's this.'

She pulls the Sighted's lasrifle free, snapping the strap at the fastening. She turns the rifle in her hands.

'A rifle,' Wyck says, flatly. 'There are plenty like it.'

'Look at the mark on it,' she says, and throws it for him to catch.

Wyck does as she says. It is stamped with a Departmento marking, like all standard issue lasrifles. The serial code reads STE12550021. It just looks like a normal serial code. He frowns, and it makes the headache growing behind his eyes even worse.

'Like I said, there are plenty like it. Well over twelve million of them. What's your point?'

Crys puffs out her cheeks and takes the rifle back from him.

'This rifle was manufactured on Steadfast,' she says. 'And it isn't standard issue.' She ejects the powercell and weighs it in her hand. 'It has a larger capacity cell, and they counterbalance the rifle, so you don't feel the difference. They are good guns.'

Wyck holds out his hand, and Crys puts the cell back in and passes the rifle to him. He tests the weight of it and realises she's right. It is a good gun.

'Thing is,' Crys says, 'they've only been manufacturing that type of rifle on Steadfast for the past two years.'

Wyck's headache is rooting properly now. The light is dim in the forge, but it still hurts his eyes. 'So?' he says, impatient.

'So how did the Sighted get them?' Crys says. 'Steadfast has been under Imperial control for over ten years. It's the best protected world in the sector.'

Wyck looks at the rifle in his hands. There's a silver aquila on the stock that the Sighted has tried to remove with the point of a knife. He can't help thinking of what the witch showed him. The thing Zane called a truth. The five dead, marked with their silver eagles. The blood dripping from the point of his knife.

He shakes his head to clear it. 'I don't know,' he says. 'Killed for them, I'd bet. Took them off the dead.'

Crys frowns, her tattooed arms folded across her broad chest. 'You're probably right, sarge,' she says. 'But I'm taking it to the commissar.'

Wyck shrugs. 'If there's one thing I know,' he says, 'it's killing, and the why of it.'

'Don't we all?' Awd says, laughing again, loud this time.

Crys joins in as she takes the rifle back and slings it across her shoulders. Wyck doesn't laugh, though.

He didn't mean that as a joke, either.

* * *

Andren Fel approaches Lydia Zane slowly. It reminds him of his training on Antar. When they sent him out against the wyldwolves with nothing but the blade that his mother had left to him. They dropped him in the middle of the black forest, where the roots are a tangle and the canopy is so thick it is dark always, only here and now the tangle of roots is a tangle of the dead. The canopy is the vaulted ceiling, and the smoke makes the darkness.

The wyldwolf, sitting perfectly still, is Lydia Zane.

She is on her knees at the foot of the Sighted's abominate machine. It has fallen onto its back, punched with holes by the Imperial Knights, then finished by one of their roaring chainblades. Fel can see the cut curving up and over the repurposed tank chassis. Inside the thing is dark, and something darker dribbles out onto the plasteel floor. The puddle spreads slowly towards Zane.

'The spiral,' she is saying, softly.

Fel keeps his gun raised. She is so still, and covered in wide open wounds that wrap around her arms and criss-cross her scalp. They are psycho-stigmatic. Witch-marks. Zane has one hand pressed against the metal hull of the dead thing, where the Sighted have painted their own mark onto it.

'The spiral,' she says again, and she turns her head slowly to look at him. 'The spiral is broken.'

Fel doesn't lower his gun, even when she looks at him. Zane's false eyes are without pupils or irises. They are just silver, from edge to edge, like old ice, and surrounded by cruel old scars. She peels her hand away from the machine's hull, and Fel sees where the spiral has broken. One of the blasts from the thermal cannon has gone right through the armour at the centre of that mark. Right where they paint the eye.

'The spiral is broken,' Zane says. 'But the shadow remains. Can you feel it?'

Fel feels a lot of things in that moment. The searing pain of the las-wound in his leg. The ache in his bones from where the explosion in the tunnel caught him. The other ache that comes from the loss of one of his own, because Rol never came up with the rest of them. Most of all, he feels a cold, deep fear, not of the Sighted or their war machines, but of Lydia Zane. But Andren Fel is made for the moment when fear cuts close, and trained to act against it, so he doesn't freeze, or run. He walks over to Lydia Zane, lets his rifle fall loose and puts out his hand.

'On your feet,' he says. 'You need to move.'

Zane blinks her strange, unnatural eyes. Though they are silver, they will never again be grey. They will never again be Antari eyes.

'You do not feel it,' she says. 'But then, how could you?'

She lets him help her get to her feet. The moment of contact, even through his gloves, is singularly unpleasant. Like ice water and needles under the skin.

'What shadow?' he asks her. 'What do you mean?'

Zane looks over towards the Delta Gate, to where the Knights and the Lions are breaking the Sighted.

'It is impossible to say,' she says. 'Because it has no shape, just depth. Like water, it changes to fill the space.'

She leans heavily against that staff of hers. There are cracks running up the darkwood. They are dark and wide like the cuts that have opened in her skin.

'And just like water,' Zane says, 'it would seek to drown us.'

Severina Raine steps over and around the dead as she walks towards the Delta Gate with Yuri Hale beside her. Raine's boots stick where blood has been spilled. Each step nudges shell casings aside and sends a dull ache through her bones. She is exhausted. Injured. Out of ammunition and hoarse from shouting orders.

But there is still the inner forge. The dread machines still need securing. Their duty isn't finished.

The two Knights from House Stormfall stand sentry now on either side of the Delta Gate, painted in their new heraldry of war. They are scorched and burned, pockmarked by gunfire. Their banners are tattered and trailing loose threads. The barrels of their thermal cannons are blackened, their chainswords reddened. They are so still, you would be forgiven for thinking them statues. Raine walks into the long shadows cast by the war machines. This close, she can feel the thrum of their reactors running along her bones. Still, but not sleeping. The Delta Gate yawns open, the interior lost to smoke and flame. Somewhere inside, the rest of Serek's Lions are fighting. Raine can hear the sound of gunfire carrying on the hot forge air.

One of the Lions of Bale posted at the Gate breaks the line and approaches. She is a tall woman, built like a slabshield wall, with a fur-trimmed cloak that makes her look bigger. She carries a chainsword, and a heavy laspistol at her hip. Her hand rests lightly at the grip of it.

'Commissar,' she says, prompting Raine to introduce herself, before turning to Hale. 'Captain Hale. Still lucky, I see.'

Hale snorts. 'Apparently,' he says. 'Good to see you, Karandi. Or should I say *Captain* Karandi?'

'You should,' Karandi says, with a smile that doesn't quite reach her eyes.

'The Delta Gate–' Hale begins.

Karandi raises her hand to cut him off. 'Is no longer your

concern,' she says. 'The Lions have it, and the machines within.'

'The duty is ours,' Raine says, levelly. 'And it is unfinished.'

'With all due respect,' Karandi says, 'it may not be finished, but you are. You have fought hard, and well, but you are in need of reinforcement and resupply, and we are not.'

Hale shakes his head. 'I can rest when I'm dead,' he says. 'Until then, I'll do what I came here to do with the troops that I have.'

'I am afraid I have to agree with Captain Hale,' Raine says. 'Our orders come from High Command, and nobody else.' She allows herself the sparest smile. 'With all due respect.'

'Then take it up with the Lord-General Militant,' Karandi says. 'Because I have my orders too.'

'Take what up with me, captain?'

Raine knows the voice. The warm rasp, like steel on stone. She snaps to attention, and sees Hale and Karandi do the same.

'At ease,' says Alar Serek.

A kastelan automaton stands at the Lord-General Militant's back, painted in the same red and gold as his Lions of Bale. The robot's arms end in two massive power fists that are oxidised from use. Raine is reminded briefly of the corrupted automata that they fought in the forge. Of their single-minded defence of that which they were ordered to protect. The kastelan robot is not the only one accompanying the lord-general. No more than five paces back, five more of his Lions wait, all clad in carapace plate and armed with hellguns.

Serek has changed little since Raine last saw him, save for the strands of grey in his fair hair, and the new scars on his angular face. He still wears a cloak of fur on one shoulder and carries a sabre at his hip. His blue eyes are still intelligent and keen. And then there is the way that his mere presence is a pressure, like standing in a holy place and knowing you are to be judged. Serek is a tall man, built strong and made even more so by a life spent serving the crusade, but it is not his physicality that sets him apart. It is his sheer force of will.

That has certainly not changed, either.

'Captain Hale and Commissar Raine are concerned about their duties regarding the inner forge, lord.'

Karandi's voice is different now, more measured. She keeps her eyes at a point somewhere around Serek's collar as she speaks, as if she cannot look him in the eyes.

'The duty is ours, lord,' Raine says. 'And we do not leave them unfinished.'

Serek looks at her with those keen eyes, and Raine finds it hard to hold them too. She prides herself on being able to read those she serves with, but with him it is impossible. It always has been, which is why it is such a surprise when he smiles.

'Captain Karandi,' he says. 'You are charged with guarding the Delta Gate. Go back to it.'

His voice is even, with no displeasure in it, but there is no question as to whether or not it is an order, or whether Karandi will obey.

'Yes, lord,' Karandi says.

She does a neat half-bow, and then marches back to her post.

'You will have to forgive my Lions for showing you their teeth,' Serek says. 'They are fierce in every regard.'

Raine thinks about the way they fought in the forge halls, putting the Sighted to sword and flame, and she cannot deny it, nor will she ever forget it.

'Then our orders, lord?' Hale asks.

Raine has never heard that kind of tremor in his voice before. Not in the moment before a charge, or at the news of terrible losses. Not even when speaking of that traitor psyker. That thin smile flickers on Serek's face again.

'You are relieved of them,' he says. 'You fought with honour and conviction, and without your regiment's sacrifices there would have been nothing left of the forges for us to secure.'

Serek puts his hand on Hale's shoulder.

'This victory is yours as much as ours. Gather your troops, leave the forges to the Lions and go forward to win me another.'

Hale bows his head. Another order without question, impossible to refuse.

'Aye, lord,' he says.

'For the Bale Stars,' Serek says. 'For the Emperor.'

Raine makes the sign of the aquila and says the words back in the same moment as Hale, her blood burning with pride.

'Commissar Raine,' Serek says, before she can move from the spot. 'A moment.'

'Yes, lord,' she says.

Hale glances at her once, then bows and walks away to gather what is left of his company. Serek moves too, towards the Delta Gate. Raine keeps step beside him, with the kastelan and the Lions at her back. Both are silent and watching.

'It is three years since last our paths crossed,' Serek says.

Raine doesn't have to think about it. She remembers it with absolute clarity.

'Hyxx,' she says. 'At the collapse of the Temple of Unlight.'

He nods. 'You were serving with the Tolus Fifth Mechanised then.'

It seems a lifetime ago now. The cold Ecclesiarchy moon,

where the Sighted turned the cathedrals into fanes and slaughterhouses. Where so many of the Tolus Fifth were lost that the regiment was dismantled and absorbed into several others. It seems a lifetime ago, but Raine can still recall every name and face, because she never forgets the dead.

'Yes, lord,' she says.

Serek stops, looking up at the Delta Gate. 'Much has changed since Hyxx,' he says. 'The Sighted twist and change shape like a blood sickness. They adapt to our weapons and our tactics, and the only cure is total elimination. Purification.'

'Through blade and bolt, lord,' Raine says. 'Through faith and fury.'

Serek does something else then that surprises Raine. He laughs.

'Three years since I last saw you,' Serek says again. 'In that time you have only grown more like her. Your mother would have had no qualms about looking me in the eye and speaking her mind, either.'

Raine feels unsettled, as if the floor has tilted under her feet. There are few people who speak to her of her mother, and fewer still who she will allow it from. But she can deny him the words no more than she can deny his orders.

'I cannot say I remember her well,' Raine says. 'But I remember a little.'

And they are things she holds tight to. The discerning darkness of her mother's eyes. The clear sound of her voice, like the ringing of the prayer-time bells as she read from treatise and tacticae. The gold of her medals and commendations. Then she remembers the man who came wearing braiding and bearing a letter to explain to two daughters that their mother was dead. His dress boots echoed so loudly on the marble floor.

'She always told me that fury is the flame that tempers faith's edge,' she says. 'That makes it keen and strong.'

'They are good words,' Serek says. 'Thema always was an inspiring speaker. She had a fierce heart.'

His words pull at something in Raine's core and make her miss her mother more keenly than she has in years.

'Words are powerful, lord,' Raine says. 'They can begin wars and end them. People will die in the name of them, or to defy them.'

Serek nods. 'And they can bleed you as soon as shield you,' he says. 'Those are good words, too, Severina Raine.'

Gloam, before

The ceremony chamber is hung with tapestries depicting the Emperor and His nine angels. Censers burn in sconces on the walls, filling the air with a richly spiced smoke. Cherubim flutter to and fro, snapping their part-mechanical wings and playing hymnals through vox-emitters grafted into their throats. Severina stands with those of her age and class, as she has been taught. Back straight. Hands knitted behind. Feet spaced. The smoke stings her eyes, but she does not blink. The stone floor is hard and cold through her soft-soled shoes, but she doesn't shift and shuffle, because to do so is to show weakness, and today of all days is not the time for such a thing.

Lord-General Militant Alar Serek stands at the lectern on the raised dais at the head of the hall. He is dressed in white, with a dark red sash across his chest, pinned with medals and commendations. A sabre is belted at his hip, the hilt worked in gold. He puts his hands flat on the lectern, and speaks without a vox-caster, his voice carrying easily across the vastness of the audience chamber and the heads of hundreds of progena.

'Children of the Emperor,' he says. 'Today is an auspicious day. Today these progena will be granted the honour of service in the Bale Stars Crusade.'

Severina looks to the side of the dais. She can see her sister standing there amongst the graduating cadets. Lucia's hair is tied in a crown braid that Severina made. She had twisted it tight and pinned it in place so that it could not come loose, like their mother taught them to do. Severina's heart is alight with pride, seeing her sister standing there. It is an effort not to smile.

'Today one fight ends, and another begins,' Serek says, looking back over the crowd. 'Because the truth of it is that there is no moment in life in which we do not fight. No easy victories, or respite.'

Severina knows this to be true. She has been fighting since the day she arrived at the scholam, and long before. Fighting those who would seek to discourage her, or test her. Fighting herself when she felt weak. Fighting the doubt that arises from her blood, that she knows Lucia feels too. The doubt that comes from their father's failings, and the cowardice that got him killed. From their mother's successes, and trying to live up to her legacy. Their heritage is a blade that cuts both ways.

'I wear this sash to honour the memory of such a fight,' Serek says. 'On the world we now call Steadfast, I fought and killed the heretic known as Dektar the Ascended.'

Severina moves in the same instant as all the other progena, raising her closed fist over her heart in recognition of the legend. The sound of so many salutes is a reverent murmur. Serek salutes them all the same way in return, before drawing his gold-hilted sabre and placing it on the lectern. It catches the light the way the brass casing of Lucia's timepiece does.

'I fought Dektar the Ascended alone, with this blade. He was strong, and clever, but he was reckless. And I had something that he did not.'

He looks to the progena awaiting their ceremonial rites.

'Tell me what that was,' he says.

Severina's heart sings as her sister steps forwards. Her polished boots click loudly on the stone of the dais.

'Lord,' she says, with a neat bow. 'The answer is faith.'

Serek looks at her for what seems a long time. Severina can't even track it with heartbeats, because it feels as though hers have stopped.

'Your name, cadet.'

It isn't a question. Those of Serek's rank and glories do not ask questions.

'Lucia Raine,' she says, somehow keeping all but the barest tremor from her voice.

'A good answer,' Serek says. 'Return to your place, Lucia Raine.'

Lucia does, and in doing so, Severina catches her eye for the sparest moment and gives her sister the smallest of nods. It is a fractional movement that could earn her a caning or two days without food if it goes noticed, but in that moment, Severina doesn't care. She considers it worth any amount of reprimand to convey how incredibly proud she is of her sister.

'Faith is what makes us all children of the Emperor,' Serek says. 'It is what gave me the strength to keep fighting, even when I was cut by the heretic Dektar, from here, to here.'

He puts his fingertips to his shoulder and follows the shape of the sash to his hip.

'That is why I wear the red,' he says. 'Not to remind me that I won, but to remind me that without faith, I would have been killed there and then. Or I would have died walking back through the ruins of Steadfast. Or on the operating table as those who served me worked to save me.'

He takes the sabre, and puts it back in the scabbard with a soft click.

'I endure because I am a creature of faith,' he says. 'As you must be, in all things, at all times. Unbreakable.'

He looks to the progena arrayed at the side of the dais once more.

'Unbreakable in mind. In spirit. In sheer will.'

Serek raises his fist in the air.

'Unbreakable,' he shouts.

Severina answers him with the other progena, and with Lucia too. Hundreds of voices as one, in a roar to challenge the cry of the ocean.

FOUR

The red line

Raine's first duty on the return to the Antari muster grounds is always the same: to debrief Lydia Zane.

The debrief takes place at the far end of the Antari medical block, in a small room that smells of counterseptic and cold steel. The room's walls are whitewashed flakboard, like the rest of the block, but there are no cots or stretchers, just two chairs and a table with drawers, all heavy-duty steel, and all bolted to the floor. Raine takes her own seat, then unlocks and opens the drawer and takes out Zane's file. It is a thick binder full of loose sheaves, wrapped in cord. Hundreds of battles, captured in ink. The chair that sits opposite Raine is tarnished from oxidisation. It has inbuilt restraints for the wrists, and a locking collar studded with sedative injectors that are slaved to a button under Raine's side of the desk. A cautionary measure. Raine cannot hear the wounded or the dying from this room. There are deliberately empty rooms left between the debriefing suite and the wards, to ensure that anything said during debrief is not overheard. To ensure that there is distance between the psyker and the wounded, in case anything should go wrong.

Another cautionary measure.

This time, it is Andren Fel who escorts Zane into the room, and the psyker practically falls into her seat when he lets go of her. One of the aides has to hold Zane's head up while the other bolts the restraint collar around her neck. The only time Raine has seen her look worse was after Drast. After she lost her eyes, saving those of her kin that she could. The aides move silently around them, connecting cables and activating the psy-reader on the table. It starts to scratch out a pattern with jagged movements of its auto-quill. One of the aides draws a vial of Zane's blood. If it hurts her, she says nothing. She doesn't even flinch. Then the aides bow low and retreat, still without speaking a word. Fel goes too, though he doesn't look happy about it. Raine knows that the process makes him uneasy. That despite all of his training, he is still Antari, and still filled with dread at the thought of a psyker, even one that is bound and monitored like Lydia Zane.

After almost two years of serving alongside them, and seeing all of the things that Zane has done, there's a part of Raine that can understand his dread.

Raine clicks the vox-thief live and opens Zane's file.

'Post-mission debrief,' Raine says, turning to a new page. 'Operation one hundred and seventy-five. The retaking of the Forge Primary on Laxus Secundus.'

She writes it into the file too. It isn't strictly necessary with the vox-thief recording every word, but the file is Raine's choice. It's the act of taking notes. The unequivocal black and white of ink on page. One of the few things in life that are quite so clear-cut.

'Name and rank,' Raine says.

Zane coughs. The breath she takes afterwards is as if she's come up from underwater.

'Lydia Zane,' she says. 'Primaris psyker. Graded Epsilon. Eleventh Antari Rifles.'

'How long have you served the Rifles?' Raine asks.

It's a question she knows the answer to, and that's the point.

'Fourteen years,' Zane says. 'From the moment they would let me, I chose to serve.'

Raine takes her notes. The psy-reader pushes out parchment.

'You always wanted to serve?' Raine asks.

Zane coughs again. The psy-reader's auto-quill trembles.

'There are few other choices, for a witch,' Zane says.

Raine stops writing and looks up at Zane. 'I thought that you loathed that word.'

Zane's pale cheeks colour, and she frowns. 'I do,' she says, bitterly. 'There is no dignity in it.'

'Then why use it?'

Zane draws her broken fingernails along the arms of the chair. 'Today has been a test,' she says, haltingly. 'I misspoke. That is all.'

Raine makes a note of the psyker's words. She can feel Zane's false eyes on her, and on the words she writes into the file.

'And if you were to choose?' Raine asks. 'If there were an option other than service, what would you do?'

It is not one of her usual questions, but that in itself is usual. It is protocol to pressurise Zane. You cannot test the strength of something by pushing gently.

'There is no choice,' Zane says.

'Pretend there is.'

Zane scowls. A fat drop of blood falls from her nose into her lap.

'I am caged,' she says. 'Bound. Tempered, by what they did to me. I do not pretend. I cannot.'

Lightning crackles across Zane's scalp, and the psy-reader spikes.

'They cut deep, and built walls,' she slurs. 'Iron bands to bind me on the inside. Collar to bind me on the outside. It is what you do to an animal that you expect to bite or thrash. Bind it. Watch it, always. Shoot it when you need to.'

The psy-reader is close to the red line. Zane is rattling and twitching as much as the needle. As with every duty Raine has, it is a choice she has to make.

Trigger the collar.

Shoot the psyker.

Keep pushing.

Her pistol is on the table. The emergency trigger for the collar is under the desk. Raine makes the choice, and she reaches for neither.

'I won't shoot you,' Raine says.

Zane smiles, though it is more like a snarl. The psy-reader dips again. 'Not today,' she says.

Raine frowns. She sounds so sure. 'Tell me about the shadow,' she says. 'The one that you sensed at the heart of the forge.'

It takes Zane a moment to muster her answer, as if she has to dredge it up.

'Fel gave you my words,' she says. 'I should have known it.'

'Does that make you angry?' Raine asks.

Zane shrugs. 'He does what he does,' she says. 'He is faithful, that one. Another one bound and tempered by what was done to him.'

Raine stops writing. 'The shadow,' she says, changing the subject. 'I asked you about the shadow.'

Zane closes her eyes, the lids stretching thin over her bionics. The scars in her eye sockets look dark, like crazing in pottery.

'If Fel truly gave you my words, then you know all that there is to know,' she says. 'I cannot take the shape of it, because it keeps none. I cannot tell you what it is, only what it wants.'

Raine watches her carefully.

'Which is what?' she asks.

The psy-reader bottoms out completely. Zane's breathing has slowed. Her breath no longer mists the air.

'Everything,' she says. 'The stars and all of the spaces in between.'

Raine can't help it. The words run a chill along her bones. For a moment, the both of them are quiet. The only noise is the scratching of the psy-reader and the sound of the rain drumming on the roof of the medicae block.

'Will that be all, commissar?' Zane asks.

Raine can see where the psyker's fingernails have dug half-moons into her palms, but even with that, and the misting of the air and all of the pushing, the needle on the psy-reader never crossed the red line.

'Yes,' she says. 'That is more than enough.'

When Raine arrives at her command tent, Yulia Crys is waiting outside it, wrapped in a raincloak. She is holding a lasrifle that she took from the forges. A kind of rifle only made on Steadfast, she says, that the Sighted definitely shouldn't have.

'I didn't know who else to tell, sir,' Crys says. 'Thought you might know what's to be done about it.'

Crys has never had the same qualms about Raine that most of the other Antari do. But then, she doesn't have qualms about anything much. It makes her a good soldier, if a little direct.

Raine takes the rifle from her. It is solidly built. Well made. Unscarred, save for where the Sighted have tried to remove the Imperial insignia.

'Troubling, don't you think, sir?'

Raine glances up at Crys. It is a good word for many things about today.

'Yes,' she says. 'I do. Leave it with me.'

'Aye, commissar,' Crys says.

She ducks into a neat half-bow and then disappears off into the rain to join her kin as they prepare to be redeployed. Raine takes the rifle into her tent. It is dry inside, but no warmer. In one corner, there is a cot with the thin sheet folded as she left it. In the middle of the space is a metal table with a chair either side of it. The tent is bigger than the Antari get for four berths, and it always seems needlessly so to Raine, who slept in a shared dormitory for most of her youth.

She walks around the table and takes her seat. Turns the rifle in her hands.

'How did you end up here?' she says. 'And in the hands of a traitor?'

The rain drums on the tent canvas over her head. It is always raining on Laxus Secundus, because of the filth thrown into the air by the working of the forges. The sound lulls her, reminding her of that cold night she arrived on Gloam. Of Lucia and the warm glimmer of the timepiece in her hand. To be shown that memory again, on today of all days. It seems like fate. Raine blinks the thought away, her eyes heavy. It is an Antari thing, to think of everything as cast by the hand of fate. It is superstitious, and illogical. She is seeing connections where there are none because it is late in the day. Because she has been awake for almost forty-six hours and fighting for most of that time. Her uniform is still filthy with ash and blood from the forges. It is under her fingernails and settled into the grain of her skin. Impossible to scrub out. Just like her own memories, and the feelings tangled up in them. Raine breathes a slow, measured breath.

'Commissar.'

The voice is familiar, and welcome.

'Captain,' Raine says, looking up from the rifle to see Andren Fel standing in the tent's doorway.

'A moment of your time?' he asks.

Fel's matt-black armour is a ruin, stripped back to the base layers and punched through with holes. He goes without his Duskhound mask. His fair skin is bruised and there is still forge ash in his dark hair and his close-cropped beard. It has settled into the deep, old scar that runs down one side of his face from his jawline to his nose.

'Of course,' Raine says.

She pushes out the other chair with her boot and Fel comes and sits down opposite her. He is still carrying a limp, and his throat is discoloured with bruises that blur his dense Antari tattoos.

'It is about the Sighted,' Fel says. 'The way of the fight back there.'

'I thought it might be,' Raine says. 'Tell me what you saw.'

Fel nods. Rainwater drips from where it has collected in his dark hair and paints trails through the ash on his armour.

'We were supposed to be the shadows in those tunnels,' he says. 'But they were hunting us.'

He leans forwards and puts something on the table. It's a metal disc, small enough to be held in the palm of a hand.

'They had camouflage gear. Auditory dampers and mirror-cloaks. It's better kit than we have. Better kit than the Lions, even, if I had to guess.'

Raine frowns and takes the disc. Unlike the rifle, there's no marking to see. She has never seen the like before.

Fel exhales a slow breath. 'They killed Rol,' he says. 'Came near close to killing me too. It wasn't just that they had the kit, it was that they knew how to use it. They were prepared. Trained, even.'

'Crys took this rifle off one of the dead,' Raine says. 'More kit that is better than what they should have. Then there were the field guns too. They were properly maintained, fully functioning. This isn't just scavenging and scrap.'

It's Fel's turn to frown. 'This is different,' he says. 'They have always been fierce, but not like this.'

'Yuri Hale said the same thing to me,' Raine says, sitting back in her chair. 'And he is right. It's not just the weapons, or the equipment. It's the way they were fighting today.'

'Like an army,' Fel says.

Raine nods, drumming her fingers on the table. 'Then there is the matter of the machines, and whatever they were hiding in the inner forge.'

'Evil things, surely,' Fel says.

'Indeed,' Raine says. 'If it must be left to the Lions to deal with them.'

She thinks back to the abominable machine they did see – the one that nearly made the Antari no more than a name to be remembered – and wonders what could be worse than that. What it would take to stop something that bad. She thinks about Lydia Zane, and the shadow she felt.

The one that wanted the stars and all the spaces in between.

'You asked me if they escalated earlier,' Raine says. 'I think that is exactly what they are doing.'

Fel narrows his eyes. 'So what is to be done about it?' he asks.

Raine stops drumming her fingers. 'What we always do,' she says. 'We escalate too.'

Fel smiles. 'Sounds about right.'

'But first we have to know the threat to match it,' Raine says. 'Speak to the troops. Find out what they have seen and heard. Anything and everything. They will tell you things that they would never bring to me.'

Fel nods. 'Consider it done,' he says.

He has to put his hand on the table to get to his feet.

'Andren,' Raine says.

There's an easing in him at the sound of his given name. It's only slight, but it's clear for Raine to see.

'Tread carefully,' she says. 'There are still stories that I owe you.'

He nods, and raises his closed fist over his heart for a moment.

'Consider that done, too,' he says.

Daven Wyck picks his way through the medicae block, past the injured and the dying, looking for Nuria Lye. He spots her in the corridor, leaning against the lightweight boarding of the wall and holding a tin cup of water in her bloody fingers.

'Nur,' he says.

She looks at him sidelong and scowls. 'You had better be hurting, Dav,' she says. 'Or you had better get out.'

Wyck laughs, and it makes him dizzy. His head is aching

like he's split it open, and it burns behind his eyes. Every noise is like needles against his eardrums.

'You know I am,' he says. 'I used it all. Every dose. I need more, Nur.'

Lye's scowl grows deeper, and she grabs him by his fatigues and pulls him into a room at the far end of the corridor. One where the shelves are lined with sterile wraps and bottles and jars of murky liquid. One where they won't be overheard.

'You damned fool,' she hisses. 'You will get us both strung up, mouthing off like that.'

Wyck shakes his head. His heart is slow and arrhythmic. Uncomfortable.

'So give me what I'm after.'

She looks at him again with that same scowl, then comes closer and takes hold of his face with her rough, bloody hands.

'What are you–' he starts.

'Shut up,' she hisses, then she lets go. 'God-Emperor, Dav,' she says. 'When did you last dose?'

He tries to remember doing it, but when he thinks of the injector and pressing it he just thinks of the hiss and the rush and the blindness that comes with it. The fast rush of his heart.

'I don't know,' he says. 'Too long ago.'

She shakes her head. 'Your pupils are fixed, and if you didn't know, your nose is bleeding.'

Wyck puts his hand to his face. It comes away with a red stripe painted on the back of it.

'Huh,' he says. 'So it is.'

'Those doses are killing you,' she says.

Wyck's temper spikes. That has been getting worse lately too, as if some of the fury that the stimms bring gets left behind when they wear off.

'Not taking them will kill me,' he says, deliberately. 'It'll make me slow. Slow enough for death to catch up. At least this way, I get to choose my fate.'

He presses his fingertips against the bridge of his nose. The burning is so bad now.

'Give me the stimms,' he says.

She folds her arms. 'No. I won't do it. Not anymore.'

He blinks. 'You owe me,' he says. 'For deeds, and secrets kept. You don't forsake that kind of owing.'

She looks at him with those eyes of hers. The eyes that used to look at him differently, before all of this. Before Gholl and Hyxx. Before she got a good look at his soul.

'No,' she says again.

Wyck's temper snaps like a frayed cord. He doesn't realise he's hit her until she's hit him back. Until he sees stars and spits blood. Then he hears something smash and feels a sharp pain in his hand.

And finds himself holding a shard of glass from a broken bottle pressed against Nuria Lye's throat.

'You bastard,' she hisses through her teeth. 'You unforgivable bastard. Do it. You'll only prove them all right.'

She's wearing an aquila on a silver chain. Like the man in the forge. The wings catch the light like the icons on the dead in the witch-dream.

Too much to forgive.

Wyck blinks. He lets up on the pressure, and the shard of glass comes clear of Lye's throat. The next thing he knows, he sees stars again as Lye punches him in the face. He falls back against the shelves. More glass breaks. Lye hits him twice more. Hard enough to burst his lip and send him blind for an instant, but then someone grabs her and pulls her clear. Wyck sees who it is through half-lidded eyes, and honestly wishes she had just kept hitting him.

It's Fel. The commissar's damned dog.

'Are you done?' Fel asks, holding her still.

Lye doesn't answer. She is breathing hard, her hands curled into fists. Wyck waits for her to say what he did. What he's been doing all of this time. To throw him into the jaws of death.

'I asked you a question, chief medicae,' Fel says, his voice firm and cold.

Lye doesn't look at Fel when she answers. She looks right at Wyck with nothing but hate in those grey eyes. Deep grey, like those stones he used to pitch into the lake.

'Yes,' Lye says. 'We're done.'

Fel lets her go, but he keeps himself between them. 'Whatever the hells that was, it never happens again. Is that clear?'

'As a springtime sky, captain,' Lye says. 'It was a moment of weakness, and nothing more.'

Wyck knows she isn't talking about herself.

Fel narrows his eyes, but he doesn't question it. 'Get to your duty,' he says.

Lye turns and walks out, glass crunching under her boots. Wyck knows that she meant what she said. That no matter what has gone before, Nuria Lye is done with him. That by sparing him like that, she has paid any debt he might claim of her.

She owes him nothing.

'You had better find somewhere else to be,' Fel says.

Wyck pushes himself away from the shelves, and the room spins lazily. Lye really did hit him hard. Fel's armour is burned and battered, ruined from the forge, but the icons survived. They catch his eye with their silver edges.

Twin-headed eagles.

Something from one of the broken jars drips off the shelf at his back.

Drip. Drip. Drip.
Wyck shakes his head to clear it.
'Gladly,' he says.

'The lord-commissar requires your presence.'

That's what the runner that brings Raine her summons says when he turns up at her command tent. He is a young commissariat cadet who introduces himself as Curtz. The cadet can be no older than twenty, but he has already earned a deep scar that carves a line into his dark hair, front to back. He is carrying an umbrella instead of wearing a raincloak, which Raine finds faintly ridiculous.

'Then we should not keep him waiting,' she says.

It is best never to do so, with an officer like Mardan Tula.

Raine follows Curtz to a Taurox transport that is sitting on the edge of the Antari encampment with its engine idling. The constant Laxian storm thunders overhead, churning up the mud and putting runnels through the gravel.

'What is this about?' Raine asks.

Curtz collapses the umbrella and climbs up the step into the Taurox.

'The lord-commissar requires your presence,' he says, again.

Raine is sure that Curtz isn't being deliberately obstructive. It's just that he hasn't been told the answer. She climbs into the Taurox and takes a seat in the troop bay opposite the cadet. Curtz thumps on the separating wall between the troop bay and the cab, and the Taurox starts to churn away on its tracks. The transport smells of cold iron and petrochem, and the deck of the troop bay is caked in muddy bootprints. Curtz sits there with his hands folded in his lap. The cadet is impeccably dressed, his uniform crisp and pressed, and his boots polished to a high shine. Raine is still wearing her bloodied tunic and trousers. Her dirt-caked boots and gloves. It's all uniform, as far as she is concerned.

'What happened to Aeryn?' Raine asks. 'I hadn't heard that he made officer.'

Curtz shakes his head. 'He was shot, sir,' he says. 'On Gholl, during the siege for the second city. He took a bullet for the lord-commissar.'

Raine closes her hand into a fist and holds it up over her heart.

'Emperor keep his soul,' she says.

Curtz looks surprised for a moment. It's the first time she has seen a natural expression on the boy's face.

'Did you know him, sir?'

'Yes,' Raine says. She had met Tula's previous cadet several times. He had been unsettlingly clever. Looked at you the way a bird of prey might. He would have made a good commissar. 'But that is not why I said the words.'

'If I may, sir,' Curtz says, 'then why?'

'I serve with the Eleventh Antari Rifles,' Raine says. 'Do you know them?'

She knows that he does. All cadets are required to learn of every regiment they may serve with. It is the responsibility of all within the commissariat to know their friends as well as their foes, for when the moment comes that you cannot tell them apart.

'They are tithed from the wild world of Antar,' he says. 'Their heraldry is a pair of crossed rifles against a loop of thorns.'

'That is true,' Raine says. 'But an adept could tell me that. What else?'

Curtz almost smiles. She can tell he revels in being tested, which is fortunate for him. He will find no shortage of that, being Tula's cadet.

'The Rifles are superstitious,' he says. 'Steeped in tradition. They name their infantry squads for myth and folklore.'

'There we are,' Raine says. 'Now that is an answer.'

This time Curtz does smile, just barely. The Taurox squeaks and rattles around them as it churns the rough ground under its tracks. The engine is a thunderous, bad-tempered roar.

'In the Rifles, those left behind always do two things for the honoured dead,' Raine says. 'First, they make a fire, and use the ashes to paint the name of the lost. Then they speak their words. The same words that have been spoken by generations of Antari, that speak of passing on to be measured and judged, and the peace that comes after.'

'But you did not use their words,' Curtz says.

'No, because I haven't earned them,' Raine says. 'I am not Antari.'

She sits back in her seat, letting the roar of the Taurox's engines tremble her bones.

'But the tradition is a good one,' she says. 'It costs nothing to bid a good soul farewell.'

Andren Fel meets his Duskhounds at the edge of the muster ground, where rows of Chimera transports sit under plastek covers and camouflage netting, just big dark shapes in the rain. There are no trees on Laxus Secundus, so they will have to use one of the collapsed buildings. It isn't as good a place as a forest for a send-off, but it's better than no place at all. All of the squads have their own ways, but the Duskhounds by their nature are separate from their kin in many things, mourning included.

'It's strange,' Tyl says. 'To think this whole place was habs, just a month ago.'

She is right behind him, like always. Fel steps over the

puddles that have collected in the collapsed block, by habit more than intent. It's hard not to tread quietly when you have spent your whole life doing it.

'Is it strange?' Myre says. 'It is the same everywhere. Stay somewhere long enough, and it will go to rubble. War finds all of us in the end.'

Myre has always been melancholy that way. Fel waits for Rol to balance it out, but of course he doesn't, because Rol is why they are here.

'Here,' Fel says, when they reach an open chamber high enough to stand up in. There's enough roof left that it isn't full of water, but enough missing so the starlight hits the puddles. It's as close to a tree canopy as they'll get.

Tyl opens one of the pouches at her belt and takes out a roll of parchment paper made from Antari trees. She sets it down amidst the rubble and ruin.

'You should light it,' Fel says.

Tyl looks up at him. She isn't wearing her carapace, just her black fatigues and her rank pins. Her red hair is shaved clean on the sides and braided long on top. She has washed the forge ashes and blood from her face, as they all have.

'Aye, sir,' she says, softly.

He hands her the tinderbox, then sits on the cracked rockcrete floor. Jeth and Myre do the same, so they are sitting like the points of a star around the roll of parchment paper. Tyl strikes the flint and steel and the paper catches quick. Fel thinks for a moment about the rush of the fire down in those tunnels. About how it was so bright that his mask's visor dipped to compensate. He shut his eyes but still saw it through the lids.

He wonders if Rol did the same. If he saw it too.

The paper curls, rolls and collapses in on itself. It takes

a few minutes for the embers to die, and for the ashes to go dark and quiet. In that time, not one of them says a word, because you don't while the fire is burning. Once it's done, Tyl sits forwards and puts her fingertips into the ashes, because those who light the fire always write the name too, and it couldn't have been anyone else but Tyl. Not for Rol. The two of them trained together at the scholam. They were family in all but blood. Kith, but as good as kin.

She paints the letters of his name carefully on the rockcrete. Tyl has steady hands from all of her years of training. From being the one who inks tattoos into any of the Antari who ask it of her.

But now, she shakes, just barely.

Tyl draws to the end of the 'L' and stops. She puts her hand flat on the painted letters of Caiden Rol's name.

'Blood and bone dies,' she says. 'But the soul goes on.'

Jeth leans forwards next and puts his hand beside hers. 'To be weighed and measured,' he says.

Myre puts her hand beside Jeth's. 'To be known and counted,' she says.

Fel is last of all. He puts his hand down too, feeling how the rockcrete is cold but the ash is just barely warm.

'And taken up into His light,' he says. 'Evermore.'

Then they all say the last word again, together.

The command camp has been established in what remains of Laxus Secundus' secondary city. The locals used to call the city Overspill, because it is built on top of a network of massive storm drains that take Defiance's fouled water and empty it into the distant sea. The crusade forces renamed it upon capture, as they often do, calling it Resolve instead. As Raine steps down from the Taurox into the mud and the storm and catches the foul, stillwater smell of the place, she thinks that perhaps the old name was better suited.

The commissariat hub sits at the heart of the command camp, a prefabricated building made of dark flakboard panels and rigid iron framework. Raine follows Curtz inside, past a pair of Tempestus Scions guarding either side of the door, rain-slick and absolutely still in their carapace plate. They are not sworn to any regiment here, just to Tula and the commissariat. Like Curtz, their armour is gleaming and in perfect condition. Glossy black, like ocean stones.

Curtz stops in the corridor and bows low. 'The lord-commissar awaits you in the meeting chamber,' he says.

Raine nods and thanks him, and Curtz marches away, his polished boots clicking on the flakboard floor. Raine wastes no time. She pushes open the door to the meeting chamber.

The room is a large space, mostly occupied by a large wooden table. Projected above it is a slowly turning hololith depicting Laxus Secundus. Six figures in black stand around the hololith and the table, and they all look up as Raine enters the room.

'Ah,' says Lord-Commissar Mardan Tula, from the head of the table. 'Severina Raine.'

Like his cadet, Tula is absolutely immaculate. His uniform could be tailored from dark steel, all sharp edges and crisp folds. His weapons gleam with the dull warmth of polished chrome and bone. The only untidy detail about Mardan Tula is his face. It's a patchwork of burns on burns that crease around a smile of silver teeth. It's a face that shows the fights it's been in. A face Raine feels she can trust.

'Lord-commissar,' she says. 'I apologise for my late arrival.'

Tula waves her apology aside, though she knows he

appreciates it. He places a great deal of value on correct decorum for someone who need not use it at all.

'Come,' he says. 'Let us begin.'

Raine takes her place at the table between two figures she recognises. Commissar Arienne Mourne she knows by reputation alone. Mourne serves with the Lions of Bale, and wears a fur cloak over one shoulder as a mark of it. She is dark-skinned with golden-yellow eyes that seem too bright to be anything other than bionics. The other figure is one she knows from past meetings, and past battles. Commissar Lukas Vander is assigned to the Kavrone Dragoons, a regiment that has served alongside the Antari and Raine many times. He is tall and lean, pale as marble, with neatly cut hair that has gone to silver despite the fact he is not much older than she is. As always, Vander is wearing his antique longrifle across his back. It is the sort of thing that could be taken as an affectation if Raine hadn't seen him use it. Vander glances at Raine as she takes her place. He is brutally honest in all things, including his complete and utter disdain for her. Raine nods her head at him in greeting. Vander scowls, and his eyes go back to the map.

That disdain and the scowl on his face are the reason that she chose to stand beside him at the table.

Raine hears reports from her comrades fighting all across Laxus Secundus. Twelve regimental commissars, spread across the world's face. From the ports. From the oil fields. No matter the location, or the officer delivering the report, there are elements that remain the same. A noticeable change in the Sighted's strength and disposition. A weakening of morale. And of course, many deaths.

'Now,' says Tula, looking to Vander. 'Your report, if you please. How fares Defiance?'

Vander nods. 'Progress through the city is slow,' he says. 'And rates of dissent are high, even among the command ranks. I have served with the Kavrone for six years, and have never had to execute so many. Company Captain Farain was commended at Steadfast for his actions. He wore the Lion's Honour. Today he threw down his rifle rather than fulfil the order to clear the hospital sector of traitors, and those too weak to stand against them.'

Raine sees Mourne scowl at the mention of the Lion's Honour. It is a mark that is only earned by exceptional sacrifice in the name of the crusade. To show cowardice while wearing it is unthinkable.

'I shot him, of course,' Vander says. 'But three of his platoon command turned on me for it. Said that Farain was right to put a stop to it. That they wouldn't stain their honour by killing those they swore to protect. That they wouldn't kill any more healers, wounded or sick, even if they have taken up arms.'

Vander leans on the table, and frowns as if the movement pains him. Raine notices for the first time the bandages wound around his arms under his coat.

'They must have thought three against one good odds,' he says. 'They should have known better.'

Arienne Mourne smiles thinly at that.

'I have seen the same problem,' Raine says. 'Here, and on Gholl and Hyxx before it. The Sighted subvert and arm everyone. Priests. Workers. Adepts. They send civilians to spend their blood in the hope that it will make us falter or pause.'

She exhales a slow breath.

'It has always served them well,' she says. 'And with every new warzone it seems to serve them better. Our troops grow weary of killing the people of the Bale Stars, while the

Sighted revel in it. That is why even those wearing the Lion's Honour are throwing down their guns.'

Vander scowls. 'Their weariness does not matter,' he says. 'Nor their opinion on what is right. They will do as they are ordered, or they will die.'

Raine looks at him. 'I am not suggesting differently,' she says. 'Merely making an observation as to why. We are executioners, but we are also judge and jury. The moral hearts of our regiments. If you do not understand the why of the trigger pull, then you are no more than a butcher.'

Vander's green eyes are furious. 'Then call me a butcher, but at least I can say that my blood is clean. I was not born of a coward.' His face contorts in disgust. 'And as for your sister–'

He doesn't get to finish his sentence, because Raine drives her fist into his face. The sound of Vander's nose breaking is loud in her ears. Vander touches his hand to his face and then looks at it. At the blood on his fingertips.

'You *dare*,' Vander says. He goes for his sword.

And Mardan Tula's voice cuts the air.

'Enough,' he says, without raising his voice even a fraction.

It is enough to make Raine uncurl her fists, though her heart is still hammering in her chest.

'Your words lower you, Vander,' Tula says. 'They lower all of us.'

Vander at least has the good grace to colour at the lord-commissar's words. 'It is the truth,' he says.

Everyone around the table is looking at Raine now, even those present by flickering hololith. She sees in them the same thing she has seen many times from her peers and her betters. The narrowing of the eyes. The judgement. It only makes her even more determined to prove every one of them wrong.

'And do you think that I do not know it?' Tula asks. 'Do you think that I would allow Commissar Raine to stand beside us if I thought her unworthy?'

'No, lord,' Vander says, carefully.

Tula turns to Raine now. She finds that she can't meet his eyes.

'And you,' he says. 'I expect better.'

The ache in Raine's hand from striking Vander is drowned out by the ache of shame in her core.

'I apologise for my misconduct, lord.'

Vander shakes his head. Tula waves her words away for the second time.

'We here have all earned our place,' Tula says. 'Our pistols and badges. Our scars. That is the way of the commissariat. Our value is in our deeds.' Tula looks at Raine. 'You will receive your new orders officially before long. You and your regiment are being reassigned to Defiance, to assist Vander and his Dragoons in the taking of the primary city. The Lord-General Militant demands the western sector to be cleared. He will wait no longer.'

Raine sees Vander's jaw set, but he's clever enough not to challenge Tula.

'Aye, lord,' she says.

'I said that our value is in our deeds. Work together to secure that city, keep your regiments fierce and fighting.' Tula pauses and looks at them both in turn. 'Prove your worth,' he says. 'Prove you have earned your scars, and your place at this table.'

'May I speak with you in private, lord?' Raine asks Tula, once the conclave is over.

He pulls the datakey that maintains the hololith, and the

image of Laxus Secundus disappears. Tula puts the datakey into the pocket of his greatcoat and nods.

'I can spare you a moment,' he says. 'Follow me, if you please.'

Tula leads Raine to a smaller room at the end of the corridor. It is Tula's quarters, without question. Raine can tell by the way the paperwork stacked on the desk is perfectly square to the table's edge and by how spare and clean it is.

'Take a seat,' he says, as he takes his own behind the desk.

Raine does. The seats are cushioned, which makes her more uncomfortable than if they weren't.

'I hope that you are not going to request a different deployment,' Tula says, taking the first sheet of paper from the stack and inspecting it.

Raine blinks. She would never have considered such a thing.

'No, lord,' she says. 'Absolutely not.'

Tula picks up a stamp from his desk and presses it into black ink, then against the paper. Raine knows they are chastisement orders. Punishments and executions awaiting. Tula places the stamped form on the other side of the table. Again, it is aligned carefully to the edge.

'Good,' he says. 'Vander might be discourteous, but he is a good commissar.'

Raine can think of words other than *discourteous* to describe Lukas Vander, but she doesn't say so.

'He is not alone in his prejudice,' Tula says. 'There are many who would see you stripped of your rank because of your blood alone.'

'I know,' Raine says. 'But they are wrong, lord.'

Tula glances up from his sheets of paper.

'They are,' he says. 'I know this. You know this. But you

will always have to answer for your blood, deservedly or not. You cannot do so by fighting everyone who speaks ill of it.'

Raine feels shame colour her cheeks.

'My actions were unacceptable,' she says. 'Whatever penance you deem necessary, I will undertake.'

Tula stamps the sheet of paper and stacks it on top of the others, then he rests his hands on his desk, his fingers laced neatly.

'Defiance is penance enough,' he says. 'I meant what I said. I want you to prove your worth. I want you to make Vander see it too. We have few enough allies without fighting amongst ourselves.' Tula frowns. 'Deeds, Severina,' he says. 'They are what made your mother, and your father. Your sister too. In time, you will have to answer for yours, so make sure that you choose them carefully.'

'I will,' Raine says.

'I know that too,' he says. 'Now, what was it that you wished to speak about?'

Raine puts her hand into the pocket of her greatcoat and takes out the auditory damper disc given to her by Andren Fel. She takes the rifle, strapped at her back, and puts both on the desk in front of Tula. If the rain-slick rifle in close proximity to his paperwork angers him, he doesn't show it.

'What do you see, lord?' she asks.

Tula picks up each item in turn. He looks at them the same way he looks at everything. With a careful, discerning gaze.

'These were taken during the battle at the forge,' he says. 'From the Sighted.'

Raine nods. 'The rifle–' she begins.

'Is Steadfast marked, which is troublesome.' Tula picks up the small, silver disc. 'But this is more so. I have seen the like before.'

'Where?' Raine asks.

He narrows his dark eyes. 'I cannot tell you,' he says. 'Needless to say, those who were using them would not have given them up, or been easily killed.'

A chill rolls up Raine's spine at his words. She can't help thinking of Zane's long shadow again. That perhaps it is longer and deeper than she thought.

'It was not just traitors we fought today,' she says. 'They had machines. Automata, and things they had created.'

Tula's face twists at the word *created*.

'Heresy,' he snarls.

'It is not just the machines, either,' Raine says. 'Or the rifles, or the equipment. It is the Sighted themselves. They are changing. Growing stronger. We fight them as fiercely as we ever have, but we are being held to a standstill all over Laxus Secundus, and I would not be surprised were it the same across the crusade front.'

Tula sits back in his chair, turning the silver disc in his fingers.

'If they are gaining strength then we need to stop it,' Raine says. 'Cut off their supply lines and disrupt their hierarchy. If we don't, the Bale Stars will be bled white and there will be nothing left to fight for.'

Tula stops turning the disc and puts it back down on the desk with a soft click. There is an expression on his face that she has never seen before. It takes Raine a moment to realise that what she's looking at is Lord-Commissar Mardan Tula unsettled.

'Leave it with me,' he says. 'I will take your words to High Command.'

Gloam, before

Severina is running the ice-rimed iron walkways when she sees a familiar figure leaning on the balustrade by the scholam's heavy outer doors. A figure dressed in black and gold, wearing a peaked hat. A figure with a beautiful, snub-nosed bolt pistol holstered at her hip, and a gold chain from a timepiece reaching into the pocket of her greatcoat.

'Lucia,' Severina says, in disbelief. Her words mist the air.

Lucia turns away from the angry ocean and looks at her. She has changed much in the months since Severina saw her last. Lucia has earned a handful of scars that sit pale against her skin. She has become lean and corded, like an animal made to run.

'Sister,' Lucia says, with the slightest of smiles.

Her voice is still the same, though. Severina returns the smile. They don't embrace because they stopped doing so long ago, but they clasp hands for a moment, Severina's cold, numb fingers lacing with Lucia's gloved ones. Then they let go and Lucia goes back to leaning on the balustrade. Severina joins her.

'I truly thought I would never see you again,' Severina says. *'Certainly not here.'*

Lucia nods. 'I did not think that I would return either,' she says. 'But my master has business to attend to with the drill-abbots.'

Severina thinks to the letter that Lucia sent. The one that was spare on detail, and marked with dirty fingerprints at the edges.

'Commissar Morbin,' she says. 'What is he like? And the Kavrone Dragoons. I want to know everything that you can tell me.'

Lucia laughs. 'Some things do not change,' she says. 'Still asking so many questions.'

Severina nods. 'It is important to know everything that you can,' she says. 'The truth is often found among the details.'

'You know, those words sound familiar,' Lucia says. 'I think they must belong to someone terribly wise.'

This time, Severina laughs. 'Tell me about your master,' she says. 'About the crusade.'

Lucia nods. 'Commissar Morbin is a good master,' she says. 'He is uncompromising and cold, of course, but he is fair. He does not treat me like a child.'

'And the Dragoons?' Severina asks.

'They do not treat me like a child either,' she says, with a half-smile. 'They hate me, as you might expect.'

Severina nods. She has been taught that very lesson many times since she arrived at the scholam. That she cannot expect hatred from her enemies alone, but from every quarter.

'They are fierce, though,' Lucia says. 'Strong of faith, with many victories to their name. It is an honour to serve with them.'

She flexes her fingers absently as if they ache.

'Would that you could have seen them on Paxar, sister,' Lucia says. 'The armoured companies catching the sun's light. Dozens and dozens of tanks. They rolled over the Sighted like the ocean rolls over stones.'

'Paxar,' Severina says. 'Then the Lord-General Militant was present?'

Lucia nods. 'Making legends,' she says, with a flicker of a smile. 'As always.'

'I heard the abbots say that he killed one of the Nine there, as on Steadfast,' Severina says.

'Not just one of the Nine,' Lucia says. 'A whole coven of their traitor psykers too. He faced them with only a handful of his Lions and emerged victorious nonetheless.'

Severina feels that same rush of awe that she felt on the day of Lucia's graduation. The Lord-General Militant has a score of stories to his name, and each one only makes her admire him more fiercely.

'Unbreakable,' Severina says. 'Just as he said.'

'Yes,' Lucia says. 'He is. As we all must be.'

She looks down to the ocean for a moment, lost in thought. To Severina, it looks as though Lucia is dreaming awake.

'What is it?' Severina asks.

Lucia shakes her head. 'Nothing, sister,' she says, and the moment passes like a cloud passes before the sun. 'And what of you? Those bruises tell me that you have either been training, or fighting.'

Severina puts her hand to her face. She had forgotten about the black eye.

'Training,' she says.

Lucia frowns. 'Don't lie,' she says. 'I can always tell. Who were you fighting? Illariya?'

Severina shakes her head.

'Cozelt,' she says. 'And Pallard.'

'Severina.' The way Lucia says her name, it is like a sigh. 'You know what can come of fighting like that, without authorisation. I am not talking about the lash, or even the undervaults. They could hang you for it, if the mood takes them.'

'They kept talking about father,' Severina says, interrupting her.

Lucia lets out a slow breath. 'What did they say?' she asks.

Severina looks out over the ocean now, because she can't look at Lucia as she says the words.

'That he deserted his post,' she says. 'That his whole unit were killed because of it.'

'That is the truth,' Lucia says. 'You know it as well as I do. He paid for it with his life, as is right.'

'I know that,' Severina says. 'That is not why I fought them.'

'Why, then?' Lucia asks.

'They said that I have coward's blood,' Severina says, gripping the freezing railing with her hands. The cold metal stings her skin, but she pays it no mind. 'They said that I am weak. That one day I will break like he did and I should be put to death before it can happen. They told me that my soul will go nowhere when I die because the Emperor has no place for cowards.'

Severina turns away from the ocean and looks at her sister.

'But that is not why I fought them either,' she says. 'I fought them because they said the same of you, and I will not have it.'

Lucia puts out her hand and grips Severina's shoulder. It is a strong grip.

'My fierce sister,' she says, softly. 'You are not weak, nor a coward. You will never break, and neither will I. That is how you prove yourself. Not by fighting those who doubt you, but by proving yourself beyond all doubt. Honour, duty and faith. That is all that matters.'

Lucia's dark eyes are unflinching. Proud. She has never looked so much like their mother.

'And that is how we will earn our place at the Emperor's side,' she says.

FIVE

Fighting for every breath

The mess hall is busy and noisy by the time Fel arrives. His kinfolk have cleared the long hall, dragging the benches and tables out of the middle, before making a circle in chalk in the space that's left. The mess hall is built of the same flak-board and corrugated plasteel as the other large buildings at the muster, so it does a little better than a tent at keeping out the wind and the ever-present Laxian rain. It is warm from the strip-heaters placed at the edges and from the many people present. Smoke coils in the air from leaf tobacco and the lanterns on the tables. Tonight, there are not just Antari in the mess. Fel spots a handful of logisticians and Munitorum support crew in jumpsuits and work boots. He knows some of them from transit. Some from resupply. There are a couple of Navy pilots too. They aren't wearing their pins or their dress jackets either, but Fel knows they must be from the 4470th Naval Wing, because there are no others of their kind fighting in the major city or the forges. All of the outsiders sit together around one table, their uniforms a blot of colour in a sea of Antari green and grey.

Yulia Crys stands in the middle of the chalk circle under the flickering lumens, talking to another of her squad called Kane, who is helping Crys wrap her hands for fighting. The combat engineer is dressed in her fatigues and a vest, but she's barefoot and without her flak armour or her patches or pins. It's the way of it, and it always has been. On the nights before a new deployment, the Antari fight for the joy of it. The fights only have two rules. No weapons, and the only way to stop it is to yield or go out cold. There is one more rule, which applies to everyone under the roof, fighting or not. There is no rank, no class. Everyone here is at ease, finding peace in something, for a few hours at least.

Fel walks past lines of benches and takes a seat opposite Yuri Hale. The others at his table are Sale Devri, Captain of Blue Company, and Gereth Awd of the Wyldfolk. Lara Koy of the Mistvypers is there too, sitting with a short-necked lute across her, playing soft notes that Fel can just about catch. Three of Koy's fingers are augmetics, but the song is no worse for it. There are tin cups at their elbows. Hale's, Devri's and Koy's are half-full. Awd's is empty, but he has a second in his hand.

'Now look who it is,' Awd says. His voice is a lazy slur. 'Andren bloody Fel.'

'It is,' Fel says. 'Good eyes on you.'

Awd laughs so hard that he coughs and almost loses what's left of his drink.

'Don't see you often on these nights,' Koy says, without looking up. 'Not you, or yours.'

She's right. It's not often that the Duskhounds join on nights like this one. It's not for a lack of wanting to, but more that they are separate in this too, just as they are in mourning. They don't fit here, because they don't fight unless they are training, or killing. They don't drink or bet. Those things are bred out at the scholam as surely as others are bred in, like how to tread quietly and which bones are the best to break. Those reasons stand for Fel, too, but for him there is another. Fel has taken to spending the hours before they deploy speaking with Raine instead. That is where he is at ease. Where he finds his peace. He knows for a fact that not one of them would understand it, because all they see of her is the peaked cap. The greatcoat. The gun. That's how it needs to be, for her and for them. So Fel keeps their meetings a secret, hidden even from his Duskhounds. Secrets don't sit well with him, nor lies, but when it comes to Raine, he doesn't have a choice.

Because he cannot be without her.

'He is likely just tired of seeing Crys win,' Devri says, with a snort.

Koy laughs.

Awd drains his drink and slams his cup on the table. 'Aren't we all?' he says. 'Speaking of which…' Awd turns in his seat as Crys shouts for their attention. She is alone in the circle now.

'Third fight,' Crys says, as it goes all but quiet. 'Who will it be?'

There's murmuring. Laughter. The soft twang of the strings of Koy's lute. The Antari start to clap in time.

'You're here now,' Devri says, grinning at Fel. 'Seems a waste not to try.'

Fel shakes his head. 'You know better than to ask me that.'

Awd sighs. 'Such a waste,' he says. 'Might win something if I bet on you.'

'Come on now,' Crys shouts. 'Or are we all tired and soft?'

There's a cheer from the next table along and Fel sees one of the Munitorum logistics crew stand up. He is a good deal shorter than Yulia Crys, but he is built strong. His right arm is augmetic from the elbow down. It'll hit hard.

'Try me,' Crys says. 'If you can remember how it is to fight after spending so long moving crates.'

She makes a show of cracking her knuckles. He laughs and takes a bow.

'My name is Leonar Krall,' he says, stepping up to the circle's edge. 'And after watching you, I do not think it is me who needs reminding.'

Awd laughs. He pushes a couple of crumpled ration slips into the centre of the table to join the ones already sitting there.

'All in for Krall,' he says. 'Perhaps he can win me something.'

'Perhaps,' says Devri, before looking over at Fel. 'If you're not going to fight, then tell me you're going to bet.'

'Let him be,' Hale says. 'You know he won't.'

Devri shrugs, and bets on Crys. Hale does the same. Koy shakes her head and keeps playing her lute. All around them, the Antari watching bang their hands on the tabletops as Crys and Krall bow for the fight. Crys does it with theatre and a grin on her face. Fel can see what she's going to do before it happens.

'You're winning nothing,' he says to Awd, as Crys snaps up from the bow and knocks Krall reeling. A welter of blood hits the flakboard floor and the Antari cheer.

'Hounds' *teeth*,' Awd says.

He gets to his feet unsteadily and starts shouting at Krall to keep his hands up. To dodge her when she swings for him. None of Awd's advice sticks, but a lot of Crys' punches do. She takes a couple in return. Gets her lip burst and has to take a step backwards. Krall is leaning into the weight of that augmetic, trying to knock her clean out. It leaves him open on his off side. Fel can see it clear as day, and from the way Crys moves around him, he can tell she sees it too. Krall's next swing glances off her shoulder, and then Crys gets inside his guard, puts her arms under his and lifts him clean off his feet before slamming him onto the ground, flat on his back.

Devri pulls a face. 'You know,' he says, to Fel, 'perhaps you do right, not fighting.'

Crys has her knee on Krall's chest now. He throws his hands up, gasping the word 'yield' through bloody teeth. The Antari whoop and cheer and Fel has never felt so apart among his kin. Not because of the fight, but because of the noise and the way they use it to drown out the day and what they have lost. Fel finds himself longing for quiet, but that will come later. He has questions to ask and answers to find.

He swore it to Raine.

'That's that,' Hale says, with a smile.

Awd shakes his head. 'Looks like it,' he says, mournfully. 'I need a drink.'

He walks off to find one, a little unsteadily. Hale picks up all of the ration slips. He hands Devri's back and puts the others in his pocket.

'I'll give his back tomorrow,' Hale says, nodding in Awd's direction. 'He will only lose them to someone else otherwise.'

Hale pauses and picks up his tin cup. His fingertips are still black with ash from speaking the names.

'And I think we have all lost quite enough today.'

Fel thinks about the way Tyl's hands shook as she painted Rol's name on the rockcrete.

'Now that is the truth,' he says.

* * *

Lydia Zane stands outside the mess hall, listening to her kinfolk cheer and shout and laugh. She takes a step forwards into the shadow cast by the building and lets it swallow her up. Zane knows that Crys is fighting, and winning, not because she has seen it, or even foreseen it, but because she knows that is always the way.

Zane puts her hand flat against the flakboard. It is cold under her fingertips and slick with rain, but Zane feels something else too. The warmth of lumen light. The coursing fire of spirits drunk from tin cups. She tastes the iron tang of blood and smells leaf tobacco. She hears the gentle thrum of the lute.

'A bright thing,' she mutters. 'Such a bright thing.'

Zane pulls her hand away and shrinks against the wall as two figures emerge from the mess hall. It is Pav, the pretty one, and Dol, from the Fenwalkers. They are drunk. Laughing. Kissing. Zane does not hear their thoughts so much as catch the edge of their feelings. It is like turning the pages of a book. The first pages are the surface feelings. The ones shown on their faces. Want and need. Go further and you find the truth of it. They are afraid. Angry. Hurting. Desperate not to be alone.

They disappear off into the camp, and their feelings recede like the tide going out until Zane is left with nothing but her own. They are no different, really. She is afraid. She is angry. She hurts.

But *she* is different. She cannot choose to simply be the feelings she shows on her face, nor can she drink and fight and forget. She cannot kiss someone pretty. It does not matter what she wants, or needs, because Zane will always be alone in all the ways that matter. More so than ever, her only company will be that of shadows.

Especially now that there are two birds, instead of one.

They sit there on the lumen string that rattles in the wind and rain. Their curved talons hold them steady. The black one is unchanged. Unruffled by the weather. The rain cannot touch it, because it is nothing but a shadow. A ghost, born of the wildness of her mind.

The other is white, with feathers missing in places. The hook of its beak is chipped like the edge of well-used pottery.

Fall, says the first bird.

Free, says the second.

They repeat their mocking, croaking words until Zane cannot tell the order of them. Until they blur together at their edges and become one word.

Freefall.

The painkillers that Wyck picked up off the floor of the medicae block are wearing off. He feels every step he takes as a jolt behind his eyes. Every raindrop stings like it has cut him as he walks down the rough dirt track out of the encampment, towards the tankers' lot. Wyck passes by grey, weatherproof tents and temporary buildings painted in Antari splinter pattern. He passes piles of rubble made from the city that was here before. He passes the latrines and the pits. The smell of that turns his stomach and makes his headache even worse. He is cold too, and shaking, and still covered in filth from the forges. One eye is lidded from where Lye kept hitting him.

We're done.

That's what she said. Just thinking of the words makes him angry all over again, but there's something else along with it too. It takes him a long time of walking through that stinging rain to recognise it.

Regret.

He would have cut her, back there, if he hadn't caught himself. If it hadn't been for the pendant catching the light that way. They were friends, once. Trusted each other. She owed him, sure enough, but he owed her too. She was the one who helped him cheat death the first time, and has been helping him outrun it ever since. Now that link is severed. Snapped like a worn thread. Wyck goes in the pouch at his belt and takes out the necklace with the tin aquila on it. He can see the tool marks on it. It was made crudely, by hand, from an offcut of something bigger.

He would have cut Lye just like he cut the owner of the necklace. She'd be dead, and so would he. Fel would have shot him, or dragged him in front of the commissar for her to do it. The hounds would have finally had their due, for all of the deaths he's owed.

For all of the ones he's caused.

Wyck shakes his head. If Lye had just given him the stimms like always, none of it would have happened. He wants to throw the necklace away. To pitch it up high into the rubble that surrounds the camp so that he doesn't have to look at it. Instead he puts it over his head and tucks it inside the collar of his fatigues, then he keeps going through the rain down to the tankers' lot. To where he'll find Kolat, because Kolat doesn't care about what's right or whether the doses Wyck takes really are killing him. He won't argue over anything but the cost of it, and that, along with death, is another thing that Wyck has become skilled at avoiding.

'What did you see?' Fel asks.

Devri is slouching, holding his tin cup in his hand. He washes the liquor up the edges while he talks.

'A lot of death, I'll tell you that,' he says. 'Too much.

Thought it'd be the lot of us before the Lions turned up like that.'

'Not to forget the Lord-General Militant,' Koy says. She is still plucking out songs on the lute. 'I have never seen him in person before. The man who killed Dektar the Ascended. They say he walked back alone afterwards, miles through enemy territory, bleeding all the while. That he should have been dead a dozen times over.'

'But the Emperor spared him,' Devri says. 'Because he yet had legends to make. The stories I know. Hyxx and Virtue and the rest. But I don't think that I truly believed it. Not until today.'

Fel thinks about what he saw. About the brightness of Serek's presence, even at a distance, like the story of the pyrehawk's feathers. So fierce that it hurts to look for long. He can believe it too. All of it.

'I'll tell you something,' Yuri Hale says. 'I have never felt a fear like the one I felt standing before him and hearing him speak.'

Hale has been quiet until now. Distant.

'Not a fear like in a bad fight, or when there's a blade coming for you,' he says. 'More like the fear of something much greater than you. Something that could break you soon as look at you. It was like being judged before my time.'

'What did he say to you?' Koy asks.

She isn't strumming the lute anymore. They are all watching Hale and listening.

'That we fought with honour. That the victory was ours as much as theirs,' Hale says. 'And that we must go forward and win him another.' He shakes his head as if to clear it. 'And I don't plan on failing him in that, no matter what the Sighted send against us.'

Devri nods. 'It was like they knew exactly who they were facing today,' he says, looking into his tin cup. 'They had mined the entire way to the Alpha Gate. Longshots took out my mortar teams. My demo teams. They took our teeth, one by one.'

'They did the same to us,' Hale says. 'Took Dern and his Sentinels. Elys and her Pyrehawks.'

'They came after mine with camouflage gear,' Fel says. 'Kit like I have never seen. Crys took a rifle off one of their dead too. Steadfast-made.'

'That's bad,' Devri says, and takes a slug of his drink. 'I knew it would be, from the first day on this world. There's something in the air. Feels like a curse on the land.'

'Like a long shadow,' Fel says, thinking about Zane after the machine fell and how she kept murmuring.

Devri gestures at him with the hand holding the cup. His knuckles are split along the lines of old scars. 'That's right,' he says. 'Like a shadow. That's exactly right.'

Devri leans in then, elbows on the table. Like Fel, Devri is heavily tattooed, though his aren't made up of myths or stories. Sale Devri has warding sigils inked into his skin, surrounded by densely-packed words from prayers. The purpose of their tattoos is the same, though. Commemoration, and protection.

'I'll tell you what,' Devri says. 'I didn't see it, but I heard about it. You know Gold Company's witch?'

Fel nods. Everyone knows Pharo. If Zane is frightening because of what she can do, Pharo is frightening because of what he can hear, which is everything.

'I heard the Sighted took him,' Devri says. 'That he wandered clean off when they got close to the Beta Gate. It was as if something had taken his mind.'

Fel can't help thinking about Zane again, and what she might have done had she the strength to stand.

'They tracked Pharo by his locator, but all they found was his collar,' Devri says. 'And quite a slick of blood.'

Fel shakes his head. He doesn't like Pharo. Nobody does. But he still doesn't like to think about what the Sighted might do to him. Raine told him what happened on Gholl, about them taking the eyes of their captives. It's no fate.

'I hope Pharo is dead,' Fel says, and he means it to be kind.

Devri nods. He picks up his cup again, but it's empty.

'Should probably be my last anyway,' he says. 'Tomorrow will hurt enough as it is.' He gets up from the bench with the awkward limp that comes from his augmetic leg, but then he raps on the table. 'Steadfast-made,' he says. 'That's what you said about the guns.'

'That's what I said.'

For a moment, Devri's eyes are clear. Not clouded by the day or the drink or all that death, but they are troubled.

'You should speak to Ghael,' he says.

The tankers' lot is noisy with the sounds of repairs being made. The mechanised support company took a beating getting the rest of the Rifles to the forges in the first place, and almost every machine on the lot is wounded. The sound of the tech-priests singing their soft, atonal songs carries to Wyck on the wind.

He walks down the line through the spots of floodlights. Each circle of light dazzles him like looking into the sun. Kolat's machine, *Stoneking*, is at the end of the line, rain running off the lip of the armour plating and tracing around the wide mouth of the cannon. Kolat himself is sat up on the edge of the Demolisher's turret. He's a dim outline in the starlit dark, save for the light of his lho-stick. That's how Wyck knows it's him, even in the dark. Most Antari don't smoke lho. But then, most Antari don't deal in illegal combat drugs either.

'Ely.'

Wyck speaks up over the thrum of tools and engines. He hears Kolat cough and sees the light of the lho go out. Kolat's dim shape moves from the turret down the hull of the tank to a place where he can drop to the ground. He makes a dull sound when he hits the mud.

'Thought I knew the voice,' Kolat says, stepping into the circle of light.

Ely Kolat is of a height with Wyck, though he's stooped and strong across the shoulders from years spent inside the tin can of the tank. His teeth are mostly steel, and often smiling, though it's always mocking on Kolat's face. He's smiling that way now. Wyck's fists curl. They ache from hitting Lye.

'Not seen you for a time,' Kolat says, in his lilting southlands voice. It sounds mocking, just like his smile. 'Thought you must have died.'

Wyck shakes his head. A hollow cold roots in his bones. He realises that by now he will have missed saying the words for those they lost today. For Efri and Dal and Vyne and the others. He should have been there with his Wyldfolk to do it, but instead he was fighting with Lye, and now he's here. That's something else that he'll pay for, in time.

'Lots of us have,' he says. 'But not me.'

'Then you're lucky,' Kolat says, absently, glancing at his machine.

There are grooves and dents pushed into the thick armour plates like fingerprints pushed into wet clay. The tank's tracks are black and clotted with forge ash. Wyck knows that Kolat's unit don't knock out dents like that unless they compromise the tank's armour. They wear their scars with pride, just like the infantry do.

'Not lucky,' Wyck says. 'Just quick and vicious.'

Kolat snorts and looks back at him. He has dirt painting his face, save for around his eyes where his goggles have been sitting. The mocking smile is back in place.

'Isn't that the truth,' he says. 'What happened to you, anyway? Those bruises look too keen to be from the forges.'

'One of Crys' fights,' Wyck says, because he gives no more than he needs to.

Kolat doesn't drop that damned smile. He leans against the Demolisher's mud-caked tracks and takes out another lho-stick. He takes the heavy satchel slung over one shoulder and puts it on the ground at his feet.

'I don't think so,' Kolat says. 'You don't fight in those chalk circles. Everyone knows that.'

He lights the stick and breathes out blue-grey smoke.

'If I had to guess,' he says, 'I'd say it's got to do with why you're here, talking to me. There is only ever one reason for that.'

He nudges at the satchel with his boot. Kolat has the sleeves of his coveralls rolled back, showing the tattoos that patchwork the skin of his arms. All of the tankers Wyck knows have the same mark. The fyregiant, burning as he breaks down a mountain with his fists. They think of themselves that way. Mountain-breakers. Demolishers, just like their machines. Especially gunners like Kolat. Wyck knows of another story that they tell in the Vales. The one that says that the riverfolk fooled a fyregiant into following them onto a cliff's edge before collapsing it and sending it to drown in the river below. It's easy to trick the arrogant, and even more so to collapse the ground from under them. You just have to know the moment to do it.

'It's not standard, what you need, and I would bet that you need a lot of it by now, too, for it to work at all.' Kolat grins. 'It's going to cost you.'

'Cost me what?' Wyck asks.

'Triple,' Kolat says. 'Or a debt. Your choice.'

Wyck shakes his head. He doesn't have triple, and there is not a chance that he's giving Kolat a debt to call on.

'Come on, Ely,' Wyck says. 'That's no way to treat a friend.'

Kolat laughs. 'We aren't friends.'

'We should be,' Wyck says. 'Otherwise there's no need for me to keep quiet.'

Kolat's smile falters, just for a moment. He blows smoke through his nose.

'About what?' he says. 'You say a word about what you get from me, and you're dead too.'

Wyck shakes his head. 'I don't mean about that,' he says. 'I mean about Edra.'

Kolat drops his lho-stick at his feet, though there's still a drag or two left in it. He glances up the line, but there's nobody around to hear them.

'You don't know a thing about it,' he says.

It's painful to smile, but Wyck can't help it. It pays to know things. More so when you can collect on them.

'Let me count the things I know,' he says, holding up his hand. 'Edra was your loader. A good soul too. He led the hymnals when your lot sang.'

Wyck watches Kolat's weight shift as he stops leaning on the tank.

'Edra used to come to Crys' fight circles, though yours aren't usually the kind to do so,' Wyck says. 'He'd come to patch up the wounded and drink with the rest of us. A good soul, like I said.'

'None of that means a thing,' Kolat says.

'Oh, it does,' Wyck says. 'Because a good soul like that doesn't sit well with a bad one like yours. Too principled. Too concerned with right and wrong. When a good soul like that notices wrongs he feels ill about them. Talks about them. Might even report them, given enough time.'

Wyck watches Kolat carefully.

'Which I suppose is why Edra ended up under a black sheet,' he says.

'Shut your mouth,' Kolat snarls.

Wyck shakes his head. 'I came down here looking for you, you know. Saw you when you'd done it.' He smiles. 'From the state of you, it must have been a really ugly kill.'

That does it. Kolat's calm collapses, just like the mountainside under the fyregiant's feet. He pulls his service pistol, but his movements are angry and obvious. Wyck strikes Kolat's outstretched arm with one hand, and grabs the pistol with the other, disarming him. Then he snaps a kick into Kolat's knee, putting him in the dirt and making him cry out. The tankers' lot keeps singing around them, because nobody is close enough to hear it.

'Like I said,' Wyck says, ejecting the pistol's powercell. 'Quick and vicious.'

He throws the powercell up and over the Demolisher. It lands somewhere in the darkness with a clatter. Wyck walks past Kolat and picks up the satchel. He goes through it until he finds what he needs. Two silver tins. Ten auto-injectors each. He takes them both, then throws the satchel at Kolat's feet.

'We'll call my silence the cost,' Wyck says. 'That seems fair to me.'

Kolat gets upright by leaning on the chassis of his Demolisher.

'You should go and find that cell,' Wyck says, handing the empty pistol back. 'You wouldn't want to be caught out of hand, now.'

Kolat scowls at him and spits on the ground. He snatches the pistol back.

'You have secrets too,' he says. 'In the end you will be found out as surely as I will. You will answer for what you've done.'

Wyck thinks about that. About the deaths and the oaths broken. The betrayal and the blood. Heavy and cold, like the pendant around his neck. There's another weight now, though. The weight of those two tins and their contents in the pouches at his belt.

'In the end, sure,' Wyck says. 'But I am not there yet.'

Lori Ghael is sitting on one of the mess hall benches, telling Antari stories to those who don't belong to the regiment. She works in requisitions, a Munitorum adept by rights, but she dresses and acts like a soldier. Most from Antar do. Today she wears the same boots and fatigues as the rest of them. Her hair is shaved on one side, and she has dog tags around her neck. The difference with Ghael is that where those of the fighting companies are marked with blood and with ash from the forges and the funerals, she is marked with ink stains. Her only augmetic adjustment is the bionic lens that replaces her right eye and her skin is pale and unscarred from a life spent away from the front. Out of the sun and the field of fire. That means that Fel doesn't know her much at all other than by sight. When she spots him, she stops her story and holds up her hand before he can speak.

'Let's see,' she says. 'Black fatigues. That's a storm trooper unit. Red bars mean a captain. I saw you sitting alongside

Hale, and Awd and Koy too. That's a safe bet for Grey Company. Those taken together means a Duskhound.'

She looks at him and narrows her eyes. Something in that look reminds him of a hunting bird. It's the keen sense of being observed.

'Captain Andren Fel,' she says. 'Am I right?'

'You are,' he says. 'On all counts.'

Ghael grins widely and applauds herself.

'I told you,' she says to those sitting around her. 'I know everyone, name and rank, if not by sight or sound.'

Fel suspects she knows a good deal more than that, with keen eyes like hers.

'I have a question,' he says. 'And I think you may have the answer, or a part of it.'

Ghael's remaining Antari eye brightens, amused. 'Questions I like,' she says. 'But first, you have to tell everyone here why your unit is named the way they are.'

The outsiders all look at him, curious. To Fel, it feels like an intrusion of a kind. He doesn't speak their stories to just anyone, so he tells them the simple version.

'Because the story goes that the duskhounds come to take those who fate passed over,' he says. 'Where they go death walks in step beside them. Given what we do, it seemed a good name.'

Some of the Munitorum workers laugh in a way that suggests unease.

'Throne,' says one of the Navy pilots. 'Your world must be dark, to give rise to those kinds of stories.'

Ghael shrugs. She is still smiling. 'Sometimes,' she says, before sliding off the edge of the bench and getting to her feet. 'Now, what was it you needed to ask me?'

Fel pulls her aside and the outsiders go back to their own murmured conversation.

'What do you know about Steadfast pattern lasrifles?' he asks.

She frowns for a moment. The expression is mismatched where her bionic pulls the skin taut.

'That you get twice as many shots for one pack out of them,' she says. 'That they are thirty per cent less likely to overheat because the venting is better. That no amount of requisition will get any for our troops.'

'Because they are rare,' Fel says.

Ghael snorts. 'Not that rare,' she says. 'If that were true, the Kavrone wouldn't have them.'

'You're sure about that?' he asks.

She nods. Taps the shaved side of her head with her forefingers. Fel notices the long scar that runs front to back there for the first time.

'This bionic isn't all they gave me,' she says. 'I don't forget. Not names. Not ranks. Especially not guns.'

Fel frowns. Two thoughts drift ashore in his head. The first is the easiest. That the Sighted really did take the rifles off the dead. There are certainly plenty of Kavrone dead on Laxus Secundus to account for a few stolen guns. But then it isn't just guns. It's the camo gear. The field artillery. The machines.

Zane's long shadow.

Then there's the feeling he's getting. Instinctual. Like when you're clearing a series of blind corners and switchbacks and you know that there's a blade waiting for you around one of them.

'Honestly,' Ghael is saying, 'you would think the Kavrone were the Lions of bloody Bale, the way they are treated.'

'What do you mean?' Fel asks.

She nods over at the outsiders in their Munitorum coveralls and workers' boots. They are back to their laughing and their drinking, a spread of faded playing cards out on the table between them.

'Ask them,' she says.

'It's like I said to Ghael,' Krall says. 'They had us reassigned. Made us redirect the landers and move everything so that they could use the largest of the bays for their own.'

He puts his cards out in front of him, and one of the Navy pilots laughs.

'Looks like you can't win at this, either,' the pilot says, with a grin on her face.

Krall scowls. The expression is disrupted by the bruising from where Crys hit him.

'On the orders of the Kavrone general, you said,' Fel says.

Krall nods.

'He was down there himself,' one of the others says. His name is Brannt, and he's in the same coloured jumpsuit as Krall. 'General Sylar, I mean. Didn't speak to any one of us directly, of course. Not someone of his rank.'

The way Brannt says 'rank' makes it sound as though he has given the word a second meaning. The others in Munitorum gear smirk or snort laughter. Fel lets it pass. From what he's heard muttered about the Kavrone general, Sylar has earned the bad blood.

'If the general was there, then they could be using the bay for reinforcements,' Fel says. 'I can't think my kin are the only ones to get cut badly today.'

Krall shakes his head. He collects up the playing cards and shuffles them together.

'That's the thing,' he says. 'They aren't bringing anything in. They are sending it out.'

The other Navy pilot snorts as he picks up his new hand

of cards. 'Typical,' he says. 'We have over half of our birds on the ground, wounded or dead, and we are sending supplies off-world. And they wonder why the crusade has been going for over forty years.'

Fel gets that feeling again. That same unease.

'There will be a reason,' the other pilot says. 'There always is. Someone needs it more.'

'Who could need it more?' Fel says. 'If it's as bad as you say.'

Krall looks at his hand of cards and puffs out his cheeks. He is incapable of hiding the truth in his face.

'The Strixian Ninety-Ninth,' he says. 'Apparently.'

Brannt hisses and punches his arm. 'You could get the lash for repeating that,' he says. 'Idiot. Shut your mouth and play cards.'

'He won't get the lash,' says Ghael. 'Because he's wrong.'

She has been quiet until now, watching the others play.

'Are you calling me a liar?' Krall says. 'I saw the orders with my own eyes.'

Ghael snorts. 'Such eyes they are too,' she says. 'But mine is better, and I'm telling you, you're wrong. The Strixian Ninety-Ninth won't be getting those guns, because you don't give guns to the dead, which is precisely what that regiment is. They caught fire on Hyxx to a soul, if I remember right.'

The Navy pilot rolls his eyes. 'And now we are sending guns to the dead,' he says, his tone caustic. 'Glory be to the holy Munitorum, and all of their mistakes.'

Fel knows that it happens, now and then. The Bale Stars is a big place. There are many deaths. Reports from the field can be conflicting and confused and lead to mistakes. They are rare, but they do happen.

But he cannot help feeling that is not the case this time.

'We are not sending guns to the dead,' Ghael says. 'And mind your bloody words too.'

The pilot holds up his hand in apology, knowing when he has overstepped his mark.

'Krall is just wrong about the Strixians, that's all,' Ghael says, nodding at Krall. 'Just like he was wrong about winning against Crys.'

Krall's face colours. Another feeling that he's incapable of hiding.

'I suppose I'm wrong then,' Krall says, then throws down his cards. 'And I'm out too. The odds are stacked badly in this game.'

Fel watches the cards hit the table and thinks that Krall's words might apply to more than just the game. He gets to his feet and Ghael pulls a face at him.

'You're leaving?' she asks.

Fel nods. 'There is a lot to do before dawn,' he says.

SIX

Bad blood

It is well into the early hours when Raine arrives back at her tent, but she cannot sleep. Not yet. It is always difficult, on the nights before a deployment. Usually she has her routines and rituals to pass the hours. She speaks with Fel, or she trains, or she takes to her prayers.

But not tonight.

Tonight is different.

Raine tends to her weapons first. She cleans and hones the blade of her sabre. She takes apart her pistol and uses a fine brush to scrub and knock the blood and ash from the component parts. She mends the tears in her greatcoat. Other commissars would give this duty to their cadets, or rely on an aide. Raine does not. When her weapons and uniform are restored, she takes a shower herself. The water is colder than the Laxian storm outside, and it only lasts a minute, but it cleanses her of the worst of the dirt. She realises now how badly she was cut in the forges, so she cleans, binds and stitches what she can with the field kit she has. The bruising across her chest from the impact of the shotgun round she cannot do much about but suffer. She only ever goes to Lye if she needs to. If her injuries compromise her ability to perform her duties. Anything else is just another scar. Then Raine puts on a clean uniform and binds her long hair into a tight crown braid. Restored, just like her weapons, there is nothing else to be done but the last thing.

Raine goes to her greatcoat and takes out her timepiece. The hands tick softly, like a heartbeat. The brass warms in her palm. Raine turns the timepiece over to look at the back of the case, and the word scratched there.

Lucia.

She remembers pushing the point of her training blade into the soft brass to make each mark. The letters are jagged and angular. Angry. Broken up. Just like she was, the day she received the timepiece in that box. Just like she has been in some ways every day since.

'Ten years,' Raine says, to herself, and to the timepiece.

Ten years to the day since Lucia was executed by firing squad.

Ten years since Lucia betrayed her. Dishonoured her.

Absolutely and irrevocably broke her heart.

Raine closes her hand around the timepiece and her knuckles go pale. Every year, it's the same. She tries to think of the moment it happened. The moment that Lucia fell. Raine thinks that if she can find it, that moment of weakness, that she will be able to prevent herself from falling the same way and from giving in to the weakness of her blood, as Lucia did. She remembers every word. Every frown, every smile. The way her sister would teach her about the Bale Stars and every one of its worlds. How they would read by candlelight long after they should have been sleeping. She thinks of braiding Lucia's hair for her graduation ceremony. Of the way she changed, every time she saw her. Leaner and more haunted. Last of all she thinks of Lucia standing there on that stage in front of everyone and saying those words that she was so proud to hear but that mean nothing now.

The answer is faith.

The remembered words snap something inside of Raine. She drops the timepiece to the floor of her tent and drives her boot down onto it again and again and again until she hears something break. The anger blows away like parchment torn free in a gale, and she realises what she has done. Raine goes to her knees and picks up the timepiece. The glass face is shattered. The chain is snapped. The brass is dented.

Somehow, though, the hands are still ticking.

'Fool,' Raine says to herself. Her jaw aches with the want to scream or shout or cry. 'You fool.'

She runs her thumb around the outside of the casing and it comes away, hinged open by the force with which she crushed it. She can see the workings of the timepiece glitter. Wheels and cogs and tiny needles.

Then she sees something else. Not a wheel. Not a cog.

A datacrystal.

Raine goes cold and her heart feels as good as stopped. She pulls the case away a fraction and tips it so that the datacrystal comes loose and lands in the palm of her other hand. Raine looks at it for a long time, listening to the second hand of the timepiece tick around and around.

It could have been in there all along, Raine realises. From the day her father gave the timepiece to her mother, all those years ago. Before his weakness earned him his death. Or it could have been hidden there by her mother, a message for her daughters.

Or it could have been put there by Lucia.

She should get rid of it, but Raine cannot find it in herself to tip the crystal onto the floor and crush it. Instead, she finds herself carrying it over to the table where her datareader sits and clicking it into place. The machine whirs and spools and ticks over, just like the timepiece. Raine closes her eyes.

When she opens them again, she is faced with a hololith projection.

For my sister, it says, in flickering text. *The truth is contained within.*

Raine has to put one hand on the table's edge to keep her feet. She feels hollow. Shattered. Just like the timepiece. She should definitely get rid of the datacrystal now. Lucia's words are the words of a traitor, no matter their intent. But Raine's eyes keep going back to that word.

Truth.

Underneath Lucia's words is an input field for a passcode. Raine types in her commissariat authorisation slowly, deliberately, telling herself that she doesn't do it because of the pain or the anger. The guilt. That she does it because it is her duty to seek the truth in all things.

Raine hits the input key and the hololith flickers. She closes her eyes again.

When she opens them, she finds no truth waiting for her. Just the same hololith screen, only now it is overlaid with new words that make Raine's heart sink.

Access denied.

Gloam, before

Severina kneels on the hard flagstone floor of the scholam's chapel. Outside and inside, deepwinter howls. The altar sparkles with frost, save for where the candles flicker and the tallow drips. The wind twists through the rafters, bringing flurries of snow to land around her as she prays. The snow stings her skin and the floor makes her knees ache. Severina can't feel her fingers or her toes, but she remains unmoving.

'Service is my duty,' she says.

The candles flicker in the wind.

'Duty is an honour.'

The shutters on the windows clatter together.

'The greatest honour is to know true faith.'

It is the last of her prayers, and the simplest. That is why it is her favourite. The most calming. There is serenity in simplicity. In the plainness of words that mean just what they say.

Severina gets to her feet slowly. They prickle with the rush of blood coming back. She puts her hand to her heart and bows her head one last time to the golden figure of the Emperor that stands at the head of the chapel. Severina knows that there is someone else in the chapel who has been there for several minutes. The flow of the winter air changed when they opened the door and entered, bringing with them the smell of gunsmoke and cold metal. But that is not all the person brought. There is a sound too.

A soft ticking.

'Sister,' *Severina says.*

This time Lucia comes to stand beside her, playing opposites to that day on the gantries all those months ago. She bows her own head to the Emperor and makes the same gesture as Severina. One hand, over her heart.

'Courage in His sight,' *she says.*

The words are strange to Severina. She wonders if they belong to the Kavrone. Lucia looks as though she belongs to them now. The heavy coat she wears is lined with a blue fabric that Severina catches sight of when she moves. There is something else too. A pin wrought in iron and gold that Lucia wears on the collar of her tunic.

Severina smiles, broadly and without thought for the chapel's solemnity.

'That is a mark of office,' *Severina says.* 'You are no longer a cadet.'

Lucia smiles in return, though it is thinner and gone as quickly as the snow in the candlelight.

'Yes,' *she says.* 'For almost a month now.'

'Tell me of it,' *Severina asks.* 'Please.'

'Still the same. Still asking questions.'

That thin smile flickers on Lucia's face again. It reminds Severina of the painted faces of saints. It is the sort of smile that has a weight.

'The world was Virtue,' *she says.* 'What can you tell me about Virtue?'

It is a game they used to play as children. Lucia would teach Severina the names of planets. Their exports. Tithed regiments. Their saints and their stories. Then the two of them would sit by candlelight, late into the night, and Severina would repeat back to Lucia all of the things she already knew. Those memories are still some of Severina's fondest.

'Virtue,' Severina says. 'Virtue is a cold world in the western arm of the sector. Ice and rock. No regiments are raised there because all they do is mine promethium.'

'We gave it the name Virtue,' Lucia says. 'Though there is nothing of virtue on that world. It is fuel, to be taken and used for the crusade's ends. Something to be hollowed out and left behind.'

Severina frowns. It is not just Lucia's thin smile that is weight for her to carry. For the first time, she notices the deep scars that craze their way up her sister's throat. They are healed, but not pale yet.

'You are troubled,' Severina says.

Lucia doesn't acknowledge the words. She keeps her dark eyes trained on the Emperor.

'The Sighted had taken all but one of the mines,' Lucia says. 'They slaughtered some of the workers, but a good portion of them simply turned. Cast off their allegiances and threw their lot in with traitors and fools.'

Severina's stomach turns at the idea of it.

'They will find no peace,' she says. 'Not even in death.'

Lucia nods. 'And we did grant them their deaths. Every one of them.'

'Good.'

'We fought for days inside those mines,' Lucia says. 'But we could not root them out. They collapsed tunnels on us. Buried whole squads and platoons in ice.'

'How did you answer that?' Severina asks.

'We buried them in return,' Lucia says. 'We turned the mines into mass graves.'

She shifts, rubbing at her left arm absently as if it pains her.

'It wasn't just the enemy that we buried,' she says. 'It was our own too. The ones who were cut off or trapped or just too deep into the mines. It was necessary, but it caused outcry and disorder. Disobedience. I was with Commissar Morbin when they turned on him.'

Severina looks at her sister. The cold air seems unwilling to fill her lungs.

'The Kavrone defied orders,' Severina says, softly. 'They attacked him.'

'And me,' Lucia says.

'What did you do?'

Lucia looks sidelong at her.

'What should be done, in such a case?' she asks.

Severina doesn't have to think this time.

'Every dissident must be shot. Every weakness ended.'

Lucia nods. 'That is what I did. Morbin and I shot every one of them, though we both got cut badly for it. When it was over, I thought Morbin dead, but he kept breathing long enough for us to get back to High Command. Long enough to graduate me to full officer.'

'Then what?'

Lucia blinks. 'Then he died,' she says, simply. 'It is to be expected, from so many cuts.'

Severina doesn't say that she is sorry, because you do not apologise for death. Instead, she bows her head.

'Emperor keep him,' she says.

It feels a long time before Lucia finishes the words.

'Once and always,' she says, eventually.

Even with the story told, that heaviness remains in Lucia's face *and her posture. She doesn't turn to leave. She just stands there, looking up at the Emperor's golden eyes.*

'It is more than Morbin's death that troubles you,' Severina says.

Lucia is still for several ticks of the timepiece. Then she nods. Mouths the word 'yes' in silence.

'Tell me,' Severina says. 'Please.'

Lucia looks at her then, properly, then grabs her and draws her into an embrace. The last time they held each other in such a way was the day their mother died.

'Change,' she whispers in Severina's ear. 'That is what troubles me. The crusade is not as it was, nor are the Bale Stars. It is no longer about duty, or honour. It is about ambition and greed. It is broken, sister. Faith has been broken.'

Severina breaks free of her sister's grasp. Her mind rings like the muster alarms, and her heart is beating loudly in her ears.

'Don't say that,' Severina says. She is shaking. Shaken. 'Don't say those vile things. Not you. Not ever again.'

Lucia covers her mouth with her hand. She blinks once. Twice. Then her dark eyes clear and her hand falls away. She bows her head.

'Forgive me,' Lucia says. 'It is Virtue. Morbin. The Kavrone. I allowed it to unsettle me.'

'Then they were just empty words,' Severina says.

It would read like a question, but she doesn't mean it as one, and Lucia knows that too. She nods.

'Just empty words,' she says. 'And nothing more.'

SEVEN

A matter of loyalty

While the rest of the forward operating camp sleeps, or trains, or heals wounds, the landing fields are awake and active, moving materiel and souls. Bulk landers lift off and touch down, their engines burning like new stars. Heavy lifters move to and fro. Soldiers shout and gesture. The place is floodlit to ward off the night, but there are still shadows to step into if you know how.

And there's nothing Andren Fel knows like shadows.

He watches through a set of magnoculars from the top of a rise as the Kavrone soldiers patrol the largest of the landing bays. The one that Krall and Brannt spoke about. It is a massive open square that's been panelled flat and surrounded by temporary storage hangars that can be collapsed with ease when the crusade front moves on. In the middle of the square sits a bulk lander with its ramp down. Figures move up and down that ramp, loading materiel, just like Krall said. Fel can't tell exactly what, from this distance, but he can see the size of some of those containers. It looks like more than just guns, but he won't know without getting closer, which is exactly what he is working out how to do.

Around the edge of the landing field there is a high, double-thick wall that looks to be easily twice his height. It's definitely scaleable, especially given that he's without his heavy carapace and his gun. He is unmarked in all ways, wearing plain fatigues, gloves and a cloth mask that hides everything but his eyes. Just in case. There are two direct entry routes, both large gates, wide enough to take a tank. One to bring supplies in at the front, one at the back to send them out again. The one at the front, closest to Fel, is guarded by two Kavrone sentries. It would follow that the other gate is the same. Then there are the roving patrols. The Kavrone move from floodlight to floodlight in pairs, with overlapping routes. They are armed with rifles and wear their raincloak hoods up against the weather. That's one thing that helps him. The noise of the storm is loud anyway and inside a hood like that it will be like vox distortion in the ears. Added to the rest of the racket of the place, it will more than cover any kind of noise he might make.

Fel watches for another couple of minutes, memorising the routes the Kavrone take. The overlap of their patrols means that any disruption in the pattern would be noticed within two minutes. It's not long, but it could be worse. Fel takes note of the Kavrone themselves too. He picks out the tired ones from their pace, and the way they shift from foot to foot when they stop. His best option is to wait for those Kavrone who are the most tired and distracted, and to let them pass before going over the wall in the darkest space between the floodlights. He'd come down on the other side behind one of those storage hangars. Minimal risk of contact. If he has to drop anyone to get away unnoticed, he'd rather do it on egress.

Fel's best option comes back around. It's the two Kavrone who are slouching. One of them is smoking a lho-stick as he walks. Fel stows the magnoculars and moves down the rise as they walk their route, marked by that coil of blue smoke. He sticks to the shadows as he moves towards the landing field and everything goes out of view but the fence and the floodlights and the distant dark shape of the bulk lander over the top of them. The ground between the landing field and the rest of the camp is open, but it isn't flat. They only collapsed the parts they needed, so there's enough rubble and broken stone to keep him hidden until he's close enough to make the wall. It's just about knowing when to go still.

When he gets close enough, Fel can hear the Kavrone talking as they come to a stop under one of the floodlights.

'I wish I were being shipped out with those boxes,' the one with the lho-stick says. 'Another day in that city will kill me.'

The other one shakes his head. 'If you don't stop with that griping, I'll kill you myself.'

Lho-stick laughs. 'Go ahead,' he says. 'It'd be a damned mercy. Spare me from walking around here for the rest of the night.'

He looks up at the fence and blows smoke.

'I don't see the need,' he says. 'For the sake of some munitions and whatever else it is they are moving. The supplies aren't even ours.'

The other Kavrone growls. 'Thought I told you to stop griping,' he says. 'We guard it, like the general ordered us. You know how it goes if you question Sylar. You heard what happened to Halliver and the others.'

Lho-stick's shoulders slump. 'Yeah, I heard,' he says, with some cold in his voice.

The two of them get to walking again. Fel waits for the distance to make the stablights on their lasguns go dim, and their voices a murmur, then makes for the spot at the wall where the shadows are deepest. He crosses the open ground at a run, putting his momentum into a jump right at the wall to propel himself up it. It hurts, with the stitches in his arm and the weakness in his leg where he was shot, but both of his hands hit the top and he pulls himself up and over, then drops to the ground on the other side. He crosses straight to the back of one of the storage buildings. Straight into the shadows. He goes still and waits a moment, listening for noise from the other side of the wall. Fel hears nothing but the rain. The wind. The sound of the landing field activity. No vox chatter. No shouting.

No contact.

Lydia Zane sits cross-legged on the floor of her tent and tries to meditate. To calm the storm of her mind and send the bird away.

No. The *birds*.

She opens her eyes slowly and lets out the breath she has been holding. It steams in the cold. Around her, objects turn lazily in the air. A handful of glass beads. A straw doll. A tattered old pict. Several shining rounds of ammunition. Beyond them, the birds sit and watch. One black. One white. Both utterly still.

She ignores them.

Zane hums as she sends the objects spinning. The temperature drops another couple of degrees. Frost begins to form around her feet. The song is one that Zane's mother would sing to her when she was just a child. When her gifts were still hidden, and her hands were unbloodied. Zane usually finds calm in the song when all else fails, but not today. She cannot rid herself of Calvar Larat's mocking words.

Freedom, just for a moment. That is my last truth. My last gift, to you.

Freedom. It is a violent gift, and she had revelled in it as she killed him. A moment unwatched. Unjudged. But then she thinks that perhaps that was not the freedom he meant after all. That he was speaking of the death he showed her. Her death. Painful. Agonising. But oh, so quiet. Those four birds against a bright blue sky.

Four, not two, so there is still time yet.

The glass beads clatter together and one cracks. Flakes of old straw splinter from the doll's arms and legs. The wounds on Zane's own arms ache and sting in sympathy. She hums her song louder, but the pain grows worse and not better and Zane realises that it is not just because of Calvar Larat, nor is it because of the birds. That there is another reason that her mind cannot grow calm, despite the song.

It is the long shadow. The one from the forges.

She can still feel it, here on Laxus Secundus.

Shapeless. Deep. Dark.

Without name.

No.

Is it?

There is a noise outside Zane's tent that disrupts her thoughts, and then her mind does calm. The objects drop out of the air around her, hitting the floor of the tent in sequence. Zane gets to her feet and steps out of the circle of scattered earth that she made for herself. She ducks out of her tent, her staff in hand, and finds herself looking at four figures. Three of them are soldiers, wearing black and silver carapace plate. Their helms are enclosed, with round green eye lenses. The fourth figure is unmasked. He wears a dark uniform with no marks on it that she recognises. He is not Antari. He has not the height or the lean weight and his eyes are blue, like winter ice.

He should not be here. Not unescorted.

'You are Lydia Zane,' the uniformed man says instead. 'Primaris psyker. Antari Rifles.'

Something about him makes her want to scream. Her skin crawls. Not one of the soldiers moves. They just stand there, rain slick and still, their faces hidden behind their masks and their glowing eyes locked on her.

'Aye,' she says. 'Who is asking?'

'Requisitions Officer Andol Toller,' he says, with a bow. 'On behalf of High Command.'

Zane cannot tell if he lies, and that frightens her. Her mind is not just calm now. It is silent. Blind. That sickness and panic grows worse by the moment.

'You are soulblind,' she says. 'A blank.'

Toller's face stays careful. Neutral. He does not acknowledge her words.

'We have come here to collect you,' Toller says. 'You are being reassigned.'

Zane takes a step backwards. It does not feel like a reassignment. It feels like a snare. Blind the animal. Trap it. Use it. She is suddenly very aware of the distance between her tent and those of the rest of her regiment. The witch circle that makes them feel safe, that now serves against her. She is aware of her fragility, without her gifts. Of the ache in her bones and the guns carried by those silent soldiers.

'Reassigned to what?' she asks. 'To where?'

Toller shakes his head. 'Classified, I'm afraid.'

'If you cannot tell me, then I cannot go,' Zane says.

Toller narrows his ice blue eyes. 'It is not optional,' he says. 'It is an order.'

'Not unless it comes directly from my superiors,' she says, keeping her voice level.

'High Command *are* your superiors, which makes me your superior also,' Toller says. 'But if you insist.'

He produces a data-slate from the pocket of his dress coat. On it is Lydia Zane's name, and her assigned code, given to her at the Scholastica Psykana, along with many other things. The bindings, inside and out. She blinks rain from her eyes and stares at the screen. At the words that glow red like a harmful thing. Like something that can poison.

Approved for reassignment.

Nowhere does she see a signature, facsimile or otherwise, from any of her regimental commanders. And then there is the matter of Toller himself. They would not send a blank after her unless they were expecting conflict, or to have to take her by force. Toller's presence is a threat.

And Lydia Zane does not like to be threatened.

'Your slate changes nothing,' she says. 'Return here with Captain Hale or General Keene and have them explain it themselves. Until I have word from my own, I go nowhere.'

The smile that flickers across Toller's face is ugly.

'Your *own*,' he says. 'It is strange that you think of them that way, when they don't extend you the same courtesy. They fear you. Hate you. You owe them nothing.'

Zane knows that her kin fear her. Hate her. But she knows them, and the way of their hate. This man she does not know, and she cannot know, because he is soulblind. Because he has been sent to disarm her, with three soldiers at his back.

'Word from my own,' she says, again. 'Until then, I have nothing more to say to you.'

Toller scowls. 'You are an asset, like a gun or a tank. Nothing more. Neither of those things question their reassignment or use, and neither will you.'

He snaps his fingers, and the three soldiers in carapace step forwards with their guns raised.

'And like any other asset,' he says, with that ugly smile still in place, 'if we have to dismantle you to move you, then so be it.'

Daven Wyck is halfway back from the tankers' lot when he hears raised voices carrying on the wind. That's not strange to hear around the encampment, especially for the night before a deployment. It's hard for any one among them to wait until morning to fight. What's strange is the fact that he's not *in* the encampment yet. He is in the empty, rubble-strewn land between the tankers' lot and the tent fields, not far from the edge of the witch's circle that separates Lydia Zane's tent from everybody else's. Another cry carries to him, and this time Wyck is certain that the voice belongs to Zane. He frowns. The witch is always murmuring. Whispering. Speaking in her damned riddles. But she doesn't shout, not like that. That means something is wrong, and the idea of all of the things that could be wrong when it comes to her sends his bones cold.

Wyck wants to keep walking back to camp. To pretend he's not heard it and leave the witch for someone else to deal with. Preferably the commissar, with a bolt-round. Maybe they could kill each other into the bargain and then he'd be free of both of them and the way they look at him like they know what he is. But he doesn't keep walking. Can't take another step.

'No good,' he says, to himself. 'That's no good.'

If something is wrong then Zane could kill the lot of them the way she killed that traitor witch. Turned it into meat and blood and nothing more. It's no fate at all, to die that way. He can't let it happen. Not to his kin. So he turns on his heel and chases the noise. Pulls his knife, and one of those injectors he took from Kolat.

It's just in case, he thinks to himself as he punches the needle clean through his fatigues into the meat of his arm.

Just in case I have to kill her.

Fel moves down the side of the storage hangar, keeping to the shadows cast by the buildings and the equipment stacked between them. Through the space between this hangar and the next, he can see clear out into the landing field, where the materiel is being moved. Fel can only see Kavrone troops moving to and from the lander. No Munitorum in their coveralls. No logisticians, or adepts, just soldiers. It's another strange thing in a series of strange things. The crusade runs on routines. Repetition. There's an order to all things, top to bottom, from Crys' fight club to the reassignment of regiments. All things have their rules and their reasons, but this is in breach of most of the ones he knows.

And then there is the matter of Kaspar Sylar.

The Kavrone general is standing by the bulk lander, cast in half-shadow by the hard light from inside. He is watching his soldiers load up the crates and containers. His continued presence means he sanctioned what they are doing. That they are sending guns, and whatever else is in those containers, to a dead regiment on his orders. If all of that is true and Sylar knows it, then that makes him complicit in the misuse of assets, and of providing misinformation to High Command. The idea of that sits very poorly with Andren Fel.

He has to get back to Raine, to tell her what he has seen, but he won't do that without one last thing. He needs to look at the crates themselves to know for sure whether they are really being sent to the Strixian 99th. As much as he'd like to trust Lori Ghael's eyes, he trusts his own more.

The storage hangars are all built to template with sliding steel doors at the front, like an aircraft hangar, but there are also smaller, single access doors on the sides. The one Fel comes to is locked, but it doesn't take much to break the mechanism. It's just a case of knowing where to apply pressure.

Inside, the hangar is lit by unstable strip lumens that make the shadows dance. He can hear the Kavrone moving around at the top of the hangar, but they won't see him behind the stacks of containers. Whatever they are moving is big. Each container is at least five metres deep and twice as long, like caskets for giants. They are also disruptor-fielded. Fel can feel the hum of it in the air. It makes his teeth ache in his head.

He drops to a crouch to get a better look at one of the containers. They are plasteel, and unmarked in all ways save for one. There's no insignia. No wear and tear. The only markings on the containers are the serial codes stamped on them and the silver inlays glimmering in the metal. The patterns of it remind Fel of Devri's tattoos. That unease he feels grows worse. Dizzying. For the first time in a long time, Fel feels the urge to turn and run. He has to shake his head to clear it and choose to slow his breathing. He has to put his hand down to stop himself from falling against the containers.

And then he hears footsteps at his back and the whine of a lasgun power pack on the charge.

Hells, Fel thinks.

'Stand up slow, or I drop you.'

The voice is male. The accent Kavrone. There's a waver in the voice that suggests that the speaker is wary. Nervous, even. Fel gets to his feet and raises his hands so that the Kavrone can see he isn't armed.

Not with a gun, anyway.

'This area is off limits,' the Kavrone says. 'But then you broke a lock to get in here, so I think you know that.'

Fel says nothing. He won't give the Kavrone his voice. Instead he looks at how the stablight mounted on the Kavrone's gun is casting against the containers and works out how far away he is. Arm's reach, surely. From the level of it, Fel would guess he's got height on the Kavrone too.

And he would also guess that he's quicker, at a push.

'Now, turn around,' the Kavrone says. 'Go for that knife you carry and I'll shoot out your throat.'

Fel does as he's told. He turns around, and he doesn't go for his knife. Instead he lunges for the Kavrone and grabs the rifle before it can go off, twisting it clear of the Kavrone's hands. He hears one of the soldier's wrists go with the force of it. He drives the butt of the rifle into the Kavrone's face and sends him reeling. Before he can recover, Fel gets him in a choke-hold until he goes still. Unconscious and bloody, but not dead.

Just like with the door, it's a case of knowing where to apply pressure.

Fel drags the Kavrone into the shadows between two of the containers, leaving him sat upright so he won't suffocate before he comes to. As well as the rifle, the Kavrone has a knife. Fel throws both of them among the containers at the back of the hangar so that he'll have to look for them. Last of all, he takes the order script the Kavrone is carrying. It's a neat roll of parchment with a list of serial codes stamped on it. One of them matches the container he checked earlier.

Right at the bottom, there's the despatch order and an icon that Fel doesn't recognise. A hunting bird in white, wings spread against a circle of flame.

For immediate and secure redeployment to the Strixian 99th regiment, the order says.

Underneath it, there are words printed that make him go cold.

Handle with care, it says. *Cargo is live.*

Lydia Zane sees the rain-soaked ground through half-lidded, bleary eyes as one of the unmarked soldiers pulls her to her feet, holding her arms so that she cannot fight him. They took her darkwood staff when she tried to crack their heads open with it, and they have disabled and removed her locator collar. The soldier lifts her with such ease, as if her bones are hollow, just like those of her birds. She cannot see them, because Toller has taken them from her along with her gifts. For the first time, Zane longs to see those birds and their watchful black eyes.

She longs to break Toller and his toy soldiers like she did Calvar Larat.

'You will see,' Toller says. 'You are wasted amongst your so-called kin. We will put your gifts to use for the crusade. For the Emperor.'

With considerable effort, Zane lifts her head and spits at him. Toller raises his fist and strikes her, and the world turns again. Dazzling.

'Let's go,' Toller says.

'And where are you going, exactly?'

The voice startles Zane. She manages to lift her head again to see Daven Wyck standing there. He must have been far from the encampment to hear the trouble and come running, given the witch-circle of open space between Zane's own tent and the others. Wyck is rain-soaked and smiling, holding his combat knife in a loose grip. Of all her kinfolk, he is the last she would have asked for. The one who has thought often about whether he would be able to kill her, given the chance. She would not put it past him to try it, either, if he thought he could do it.

She knows that he has done worse, over less.

Toller looks at Wyck's fatigues and his mark of rank.

'Above your clearance, I'm afraid, sergeant.'

The two soldiers either side of the one holding Zane in place raise their rifles and point them at Wyck. It doesn't seem to bother him. He nods, still smiling. It should be handsome on a face like his, but it just looks jagged, like the edge of something broken.

'Oh, you have me wrong,' Wyck says. 'You'll have no trouble from me.'

His eyes are dark as the night around them, the black of his pupils flooding over the grey. Zane can see how he breathes rapid and shallow and realises that even now, after the day's fighting is done, he is still poisoning himself with those stimms he takes. One of his ugly secrets.

'You can kill her, for all I care,' Wyck says, with that smile still in place.

'Bastard,' Zane hisses.

'See, now,' he says. 'And you wonder why I'll be glad to see the back of you.'

He looks at her, and there is something more than just cruelty in those flooded eyes of his. Wyck takes another step forward, closing the distance between them.

'Even if you are my kin,' Wyck says.

Zane flinches.

Kin.

He said *kin*.

'Whether or not trouble was your intent, you have already caused it,' Toller says. 'For yourself, at any rate.'

He raises his hand and around Zane the toy soldiers move.

'Kill him,' Toller says.

With Kolat's stimms boiling Wyck's blood, the armoured soldiers seem to move slowly, as if through water. Big, obvious movements. Glints from their guns as rain hits the metal. The rain is slow too. Much slower than his heart as he lunges forwards to close the distance before either of those unmarked soldiers can shoot him. The one in the dress uniform hasn't even drawn his pistol yet.

Stupid.

Slow.

Wyck jumps into the first soldier and puts him on his back. His knife goes into the soft joint at the soldier's neck. Straight through. He feels something go inside and the soldier thrashes and shakes and spasms. Wyck puts the knife in him twice more before he dies. Through the soft joints. Then he blinks the blood from his eyes and moves for the other one. The soldier doesn't flinch or step backward. Brave, or just stupid too. The soldier fires his rifle and Wyck drops into a slide so that the shot grazes his shoulder instead of dropping him. His knife hand goes numb from it, but he doesn't let go. The soldier twists to follow him and fire again and Wyck cuts through the backs of both of his knees where there's no armour. The soldier cries out and goes down heavy, losing his gun. A kick to the second soldier's head while they are both on the ground makes him go as still as the first. Wyck gets to his feet.

'Enough!'

The uniformed man's voice is slow just like the rain and the way everyone moves. He is pointing a pistol at Zane. The psyker is dribbling blood because she fought them. For a second, it's almost enough to make Wyck want to like her.

'I will kill her,' he says, in his slow voice.

Wyck laughs so hard it hurts his throat. 'Do it, then,' he says.

He doesn't do it. Of course he doesn't. You don't kill what you came for. Instead he hesitates, frowns and then falls over backwards with Wyck's thrown knife buried in the middle of his chest. A good throw. Heart level. In to the hilt. The minute the uniformed man hits the earth, something in the air changes. The temperature drops like a stone and Wyck finds he can't move because of the pressure that's coming from Lydia Zane.

The pressure that breaks every one of the last soldier's bones before he can even scream. He folds like parchment paper and finally lets go of Zane. It's the only thing that seems to happen faster than Wyck's heart can beat. Then Zane falls forwards and the pressure lets up and the night falls silent, save for the rain and the way his heart thunders like a storm of its own. Wyck looks down at his hands. At the body of the soldier at his feet.

Black armour, trimmed with silver.

Twin-headed eagles.

Rain and blood all falling and running and dripping.

Drip, drip, drip.

He starts to laugh again without meaning to. It bubbles up like blood out of a deep cut. The dream the witch gave him was true. Just not the way he thought. It's not his own he killed.

Not this time.

'Why did you do that?' Zane asks him, snapping him out of his thoughts. 'Come here to help me?'

Her voice is a rasp that's hard to pick up over the storm. Wyck crosses over to her, stopping out of her arm's reach. He won't get closer than that to a witch. Zane looks like a drowned thing. All pale and bruised with those false, flat eyes.

'I didn't,' he says. 'I came here because I figured you had lost it. That I would have to kill you.'

Zane looks up at him, her face blue-pale and streaked with rain.

'You could try,' she says.

Then she starts laughing. It's like a cough, or something wounded trying to die. It unsettles Wyck so badly that he takes a step backwards without intending to. She gets to her feet and puts out her arm, pulling her splintered staff through the air towards her. It lands in her palm with a snap.

Wyck walks over to where the uniformed man is lying with his open eyes fixed on the night sky. 'What was he?' he asks. 'What did they do to you to catch you like that?'

'His name was Andol Toller,' Zane says. 'And he was soul-blind. A blank.'

Wyck doesn't know whether that distresses him more or less than the idea of a witch. Cursed is one thing, but to be without a soul is something else entirely.

'They must have wanted you badly,' he says. 'To kill for it.'

'They wanted my gifts, whether I would give them or not.' Zane frowns. 'That last one to die. His mind was full of empty spaces, as if he had been made to forget.'

Wyck can feel his headache coming back before time.

'Did you find anything else in his head?' he asks her.

'Shapes,' Zane says. 'Sounds and sights and smells. Cold, like mid-winter. The song of machines. Needles being pushed into skin.' Her frown grows deeper. 'The smell of fire, and the touch of silent wings.'

Her cable crown is humming loud as she remembers. Wyck can hear it over the rain.

'So, nothing useful,' he says, with a shake of his head.

'Toller said that he was sent on behalf of High Command,' Zane says. 'And now they are dead.'

Wyck puts his foot on Toller's chest to get purchase enough to pull his knife out, then wipes the blade clean on his fatigues. There's not a patch on them that isn't dark with mud or blood. Camouflage for camouflage.

'They shot first,' he says. 'Or they tried to, anyway.'

'That might be true, but we cannot report it,' Zane says. 'The commissar would have us for dead.'

Wyck nods. His heart is still hammering but the want to laugh is wearing off. He can feel the cold of the rain and the wind. The burn of the las-wound in his shoulder. The old, familiar dread that comes with the idea of being found out.

'What do we do now?' Zane asks.

Wyck looks around at the four dead men, who are rain-slick and still. He looks at the collapsed habs and manufactoria and the deep darknesses exposed by shelling.

'We hide them,' he says. 'And we make a secret of it.'

Raine meets with Andren Fel with two hours to go until dawn. The storm has turned soft, the rain to mist, like fret blown from an angry ocean.

They meet in what was once the palace of the forgefathers. It would have been grand, once. Great iron and brass cogwheels line the atrium on either side of Raine, supporting the domed ceiling far above. The ceiling had been leaded crystal, before, stained with angular depictions of the god-killers built in Laxus Secundus' forges. Now Raine crunches a world's legends under her boots as she walks to where Fel waits for her, at the foot of the stairs to the palace proper.

'You have been gone a long time,' she says. 'I take it you turned up more than just idle talk.'

Fel nods. He sits down on the stairs, and Raine sits beside him. The stairs are marble, inlaid with hexagrammic patterns that have been splintered and shattered. It is not the first time that they have met here, on these steps, under a night sky. They did the same on the night before the primary forge too. Just to talk, like they always do. To share stories. Those meetings are a habit that Raine knows that she should not have, just as much as she knows she cannot give them up.

'It is as you said,' Fel says. 'Things are changing.'

Fel is turning a parchment screed in his gloved hands. His restlessness makes Raine uneasy, because he is not the type to act like that. Not unless something is really troubling him.

'And I don't think it is just the Sighted,' Fel says.

He holds out the parchment and she takes it. It is speckled by rain, but otherwise undamaged. She unrolls the parchment and looks at it as he explains to her what he learned and what he saw. First from the Antari and the logisticians, then from the landing fields.

'The Strixian Ninety-Ninth,' Raine says, when he stops talking. 'They are dead.'

Fel nods. 'On Hyxx, I know.'

Raine frowns and shakes her head. The name means something to her, because she doesn't forget the dead.

'No, not Hyxx. It was the Coris Belt, I'm sure of it. A whole flotilla, shot to scrap.'

Fel goes still when she says those words.

'Regiments have been rebuilt in the past,' he says. 'Forged together from broken parts to die again.'

'That is true,' she says. 'But I don't think that is the case here, do you?'

'No,' he says. 'I don't.'

Raine looks at the parchment in her hand. At the words, printed in red.

'Cargo is live,' she says.

'Live or not, whatever the Kavrone were moving cannot be good,' Fel says. 'It felt like submersion, just standing beside those containers. Like being held under with no light to see the surface.'

He is flexing his fingers as if they hurt him. As if what he is trying to say hurts him too.

'One of them got the drop on me,' he says. 'I didn't hear a thing until he was close. I should have, but there was something about that place, and those containers.'

'Did he see anything to know you by?' Raine asks.

Fel shakes his head. 'He won't forget it in a hurry, though. I had to hurt him pretty badly.'

'That sits poorly with you,' Raine says.

He nods. 'Until I know what they have done. If they have broken faith.'

'We will find out,' Raine says. 'And then we will drag it all out into the light so that it is plain to see. If faith has been broken, then those guilty of it will be broken in turn.'

'Including Sylar?' Fel asks.

Raine nods. 'Including Sylar.'

'What could be worth it?' Fel says. 'Worth breaking faith over.'

Raine thinks about what she had heard about Kaspar Sylar. About how his cruelty is only outstripped by his ambition.

'Power,' she says. 'Glory. The stars, and everything in between them.'

'Said that way, it sounds like something from the old stories,' Fel says. 'Like the King of Winter.'

Raine rolls the parchment neatly and starts to turn it in her own hands.

'Our next posting is to fight alongside the Kavrone,' she says. 'High Command are sending us to the primary city.'

'Seems like fate's work,' Fel says.

'Or something like it,' Raine says.

She puts the roll of parchment into her inside pocket and gets to her feet, suddenly unable to sit still. It is because of Sylar. Because of the Kavrone. Because they were Lucia's regiment, before.

And that really does feel like fate's work.

She thinks of Lucia's words in the chapel that day, so long ago, and the fear in her sister's eyes as she spoke about change and ambition. For a moment, Raine wonders if Lucia could have seen this corruption taking root, and earned her death by trying to stop it. That thought stirs a dangerous hope inside her, long extinguished. One that she should ignore, or smother. One that she should know better than to heed.

Raine puts her hand in her pocket, and her fingertips brush against the timepiece. She has put the datacrystal back inside and bent back the casing to hide it again until she finds a way to unlock it. It feels heavier now than it ever has, that timepiece. Heavy and cold.

It is a lot to carry, alone.

She looks at Fel, sitting there on the step under the mist of rain that comes in through the shattered ceiling.

'Do you trust me?' she asks.

'With my life,' he says, without even a pause.

'Despite what I am?' Raine asks.

Fel gets to his feet now too. 'Because of what you are,' he says.

'And what is that, to you?' Raine asks him.

He stands there unarmed and unarmoured, without his pins or his colours. For a moment, they are both just souls.

'Strong,' he says. 'In all of the ways that it matters.'

Raine thinks that she should know what to say to him then, but she cannot find the words. It is a strange feeling, to not know. Ill-fitting, like clothes made too large.

'Something is troubling you,' Fel says. 'Something more than the Kavrone or the guns or the Sighted.'

She wants to take the timepiece out of her pocket and explain it to him. All of it. Her father, and his coward's blood. Her mother, a dead hero.

Her sister, the traitor.

But Raine cannot make her hand close around the timepiece, and she cannot find those words either. It takes her a moment to recognise the feeling.

Fear.

She is afraid of seeing that look on Fel's face that she saw on the faces of those at the commissariat conclave, and the scholam before it. She is afraid that once he knows about the failings of her blood he will not trust her anymore. He said that she was strong in all the ways that matter, but in this Raine finds that she cannot be.

Not yet.

'We need to return to camp,' she says, instead. 'It is a story for another time.'

He smiles, just barely, and nods.

'Another time, then,' he says.

* * *

Daven Wyck stands halfway down the steps of a ruined habitation block looking into the deep, dark water that has flooded the hab's lower levels. It looks black, like the lakes of the Vales. The hab block is a part of the collapsed cityscape, out in nowhere between the Antari encampment and the tankers' lot. It's a place that nobody would care to go until the crusade front moves on, which makes it good for hiding things.

Like bodies.

All of that black water swallows up the dead blank and his soldiers with ease, and as Wyck watches them go he thinks about the water wraiths, and wonders if they take those who are dead already, or if they just like to drown the living.

He wonders if Raf found one all that time ago, down there in the dark.

'Someone will know,' Zane says. 'The blank and his men will be expected or missed by those that sent them, and then they will come for us.'

The witch is sitting next to him on the step, watching the water lap against the stone.

'Not for me,' Wyck says, with a shrug. 'For you, maybe.'

'What was done was both of ours,' Zane snaps. 'Your hands are as bloody as mine.'

Bloodier. The word surfaces in his head like a bloated thing breaching the skin of a lake.

'So that is it,' she says, bitterly. 'We make a secret of it.'

'Unless you want to die,' he says, then turns to go up to the surface and back to the forward camp.

Zane doesn't move from the spot. She just keeps watching the water. Wyck is careful to keep half an eye on her as he goes, because of what she is.

'You have so many secrets,' she says. 'It is a wonder there is room inside you for another.'

Wyck stops on the steps. His knife is in his hand, though he can't remember drawing it.

'Get out of my head,' he says. 'Or I'll put you in that water too.'

Zane gets to her feet, leaning on her staff to do it. She finally turns away from the black water.

'I am not in your head,' she says. 'I do not need to be. Your mind sings loudly, especially when that poison you take is burning your blood.'

Zane has known about the stimms since Gholl. Since they went into the mountains and the Maw, and he made the mistake of trying to drag her to her feet to stop them all from dying. It was touching her that did it. You should never touch a witch.

'If you say a word about it–' he starts to say.

'I will not,' Zane says, interrupting him. 'Because I owe you a debt.'

Wyck scowls. He knows the value of an owing, but he doesn't want that from her kind. It seems more a curse than anything else. Zane tilts her head. It reminds him of a bird, the way she does it.

'And because we are kin,' she says. 'That is what you said, back there.'

'They were just words,' Wyck says. 'And they didn't mean a damn thing.'

'It is the truth, though,' she says. 'That we are kin, in more ways than you think.'

'You're a witch,' he says. 'Save for where we call home, I am nothing like you.'

'Death,' she says. 'That is what makes us the same.'

Wyck snorts a laugh. 'We all make death. We all know it.'

Zane smiles, and it kills the laughter in his chest. Her smile is a cold thing, as if she has only ever watched one happen and never tried it herself.

'You are followed by it,' she says. 'And by what happened on Cawter.'

Wyck finds himself frozen there on the steps. Not by her witch's power, but by her words and the things that come back to him as she speaks them.

Jungle heat. Sweat on the walls of the transport and everyone inside. Keller, humming.

'Shut up,' he says.

'You were the only one to walk away, when that transport was torn to pieces,' she says. 'Death took a look at you, and it passed you over.'

'Shut. Up.'

He says the words through his teeth as he remembers what came after. The bloom of light. The noise, that he thought had made him deaf until the ringing came back. Blood in his eyes and his nose and his mouth. The heat of the fire as it burned everyone else but him. Keller and Heyn and Duni and all of the others. He had to write their names in the ash that was made of them because he was alone and lost and the tinderbox and the paper had been with Duni. He never speaks of Cawter, not with Awd, or even Lye. Not with anyone. But now he finds he can't stop himself, because she won't *shut up* and he can't make her because if he touches her she'll take even more from him than she already has.

'You talk as though you know of it, but you don't. You couldn't.'

'How can you be so sure?' she says, with that tilt of her head again.

Mists and moors, he wants to hit her.

'I wrote my *name*, back there,' he snarls. 'I wrote it in ashes in the list of the dead because I thought that soon I would be too, but when the Sighted came I kept killing them until my gun went dry and my knife went dull.'

'You were afraid,' Zane says.

'I was angry,' he says, though there are times when the two are hard to tell apart. 'I wanted to bleed them for what they had done to us, and I did. They cut me back for my trouble. Badly.'

The scars are such pale lines now, all those years later. Shoulder, collarbone. Chest. Stomach. That one had been the worst. All of the bloodstains had spread so much they joined up and painted him red.

'But you did not die as you had thought,' Zane says. 'Death passed you over again.'

Lye had been the one to find him. Wyck hadn't recognised her at first. He'd taken her for Sighted too and tried to cut her before she'd knocked him down.

Enough, she'd said. *That's enough.*

Then Lye had stuck him with a needle and put him under so he'd stop fighting her. Her lakestone eyes had been the last thing to go when the darkness rolled over.

'I kept trying to tell Lye, but she didn't listen,' he says, half to himself.

'Tell her what?' Zane asks.

Wyck can see it then, written in ashes under the jungle canopy.

'That I hadn't scrubbed out my name,' he says. 'I left it for death, and now it knows me.'

Zane nods. 'That is what I meant,' she says. 'When I said that we are more kin than you think.'

'What?' Wyck asks.

Zane laughs, and it echoes in the hollow space. She goes

to leave, turning into no more than a shadow as she goes up the stairs.

'Death,' she says. 'It knows me too.'

Ely Kolat watches Grey Company's witch come up and out of the collapsed hab through a set of grubby magnoculars that paint her in shades of green and make hollows of her eyes. Kolat can't help the face he pulls. He can't abide witches. He waits, though looking at her is turning his stomach. He knows it'd be worse were he closer. She might be able to hear his thoughts, and he can't have that.

Can't have her spoil his fun. His payback.

Kolat sits and waits a bit longer for Wyck to follow her out of the darkness. Just like he thought, they were using the place to hide those bodies they were moving. The ones in carapace plate and officer's colours. That's bad. At least for Wyck, anyway. Kolat has no quarrel with the witch. Not that he'd have the heart to do anything about it, even if he did. Wyck's the one who damn near broke his leg. Stole from him. Laughed at him. Wyck is the one who thinks himself free of consequence, but he'll learn the hard way once word gets out about those bodies.

Kolat can't help but grin now either. He slides off the collapsed wall he's sitting on and stows the magnoculars. Then he limps back towards the tanker's lot, whistling softly. A song from home.

One called *The Hangman's Wish*.

When she returns to the Antari encampment and her command tent, Raine makes a request for information from the office of Lord-Commissar Mardan Tula for all deployment and materiel requisition in relation to the eastward arm of the Bale Stars Crusade.

'This will take time,' Tula says, over the secure hololith link. His image flickers, but his gaze is no less discerning for it. 'It is a substantial request.'

Raine nods. She asked for everything, because it is the easiest way to hide that you are looking for something in particular. Dragnets always catch more than just their intended quarry.

'I understand,' she says. 'But it is necessary.'

Tula's eyes narrow. 'I doubt you would ask otherwise,' he says. 'I will get what you need, and send it with Curtz. The boy is diligent, and trustworthy.'

There is something in the way Tula says *trustworthy* that gives Raine pause.

'It is a valuable thing, lord,' she says, carefully. 'Trust.'

'And rare,' he says.

Tula's image flickers as thunder rumbles overhead. Raine hears it through the hololith too, a moment later.

'There is a storm coming,' he says. 'It will make the next days more difficult. Be watchful in the primary city.'

At the scholam, Raine spent long hours learning to read others. To find their weaknesses and their fears. To catch a lie when it is being hidden, or a truth, in equal measure.

'Always,' she says. 'Emperor go with you, lord.'

Tula makes the sign of the aquila as the hololith crazes and flickers.

'And with you, Commissar Raine,' he says.

And then the connection fails and Tula disappears. Raine sits back in her seat.

'He sounded wary,' Fel says.

He was quiet while she spoke with Tula, because protocol dictates he should not have been there at all. Given everything she has come to suspect, Raine finds that particular breach doesn't bother her all that much.

'Yes, he did,' she says. 'And that is troubling in itself.'

'Do you trust him?' Fel asks.

If Fel had asked her a week ago, she would have said yes. Now the word won't come, no matter how badly she wants to say it.

'He will get the records,' she says. 'If nothing else, he is a man of his word.'

'Often that is good enough,' Fel says.

Raine nods. 'Until we know what we face, this must stay between us,' she says.

'I know,' Fel says.

'It might mean lying to your kin,' she says. 'To your Duskhounds.'

He nods. She sees the way he crosses his hand over one of the tattoos on the inside of his left arm. The shadowy shape of the duskhound made in ink there. The mark his kin all bear too.

'I won't speak of it, not to them or anyone. You have my word.'

She knows what these choices mean for him. How hard they are to make. Andren Fel is Antari, his identity rooted in the place he was born and made. She is not. Not Antari. Not a soldier. By rights, he should not choose her at all.

'So, what now?' Fel asks her.

She looks at him. He is mud-spattered and soaked with rain. The sleeves of his fatigues are rolled back to the elbow, so Raine can see blood soaking through the bandage from the cut he took in the forges.

'Let me look at that,' she says.

Fel shrugs. 'It's not so bad,' he says.

'It wasn't a question.'

Fel smiles at that, despite everything. That easy smile of his was strange to her at first. Over time, though, she has come to find it a comfort. Raine fetches her medical kit and moves to sit on the edge of the folding table, close enough to look at the damage properly. She cleans her hands with counterseptic, then takes hold of his arm and unwinds the old bandage. The cut is bleeding badly. Too badly just to bind it.

'That story you spoke of earlier,' Raine says. 'I don't think I know it.'

'The King of Winter?' Fel says. 'I must have told you that one.'

Raine shakes her head. She takes a clean wad of gauze and holds it in place on his arm with enough pressure to stop the bleeding. She can see where he's taken a dozen other cuts on that arm. Old scars under and over the tattoos he has of scripture and of the wicked creatures from his stories.

'I would remember it if you had,' she says, with a smile.

He laughs. That was another thing that surprised her to start with, until she realised that he doesn't share that laugh with everyone.

Just with those he trusts.

'True enough,' he says. 'The story of the King of Winter is one of Morrow too.'

Raine nods. 'The first and most revered of Antar's saints,' she says, as she checks how badly the cut is still bleeding. Too badly to stitch, yet. 'That name, I do know.'

She knows the look of Morrow, too, because she is the subject of one of Fel's tattoos. Morrow looks strong, the way she has been inked into his skin, with fierce dark eyes and her pointed fingers held steepled, in that Antari gesture for oaths.

'The story is old,' Fel says. His voice has softened the way it does when he tells stories. 'Even for Antar. It goes that when the world was first made, the winters were fierce and long, and it was a king who brought them. One with claws and wings, but that wore the face of a man. Because the Emperor, wisest of all, knew that the forests would die if winter did not pass, he made Morrow to balance winter's king. She was a fierce creature, with thorns woven into her hair and a cloak of leaves.'

'That is why you call her Our Lady of Thorns,' Raine says.

Fel nods.

Raine takes away that wad of gauze now, and sets to cleaning the blood away. Fel doesn't flinch, though she knows it must hurt. That is how he is in all things. Unflinching.

'When the time came for winter to pass,' Fel says. 'Morrow would go to fight the king in the heartwood of Antar's oldest forest. As they fought, the sky would grow fierce with fire and thunder, but after three days, Morrow would always emerge triumphant and the King of Winter would retreat to the mountains, where he kept his castle and where winter never passed.'

Raine goes back in her medical tin and takes out her suture kit. She sets about stitching that cut closed while he talks.

'Over time, the king grew jealous. The people of Antar loved Morrow because she brought with her flowers and food. They did not love the King of Winter. They spoke his name in whispers and dreaded his coming.'

'So what did the king do?' Raine asks.

'He knew that he could not beat Morrow fairly, so he made a deal with the vypers of the earth, that they could have his mountain seat if they gave him their poison to kill her with.

'So the vypers gave their poison to the king, and he came down from the mountains and brought winter with him, and then waited for Morrow to come to the heartwood to face him. Like always, they fought for three days, and the sky grew fierce, but on the last day, the king plunged his poisoned claws into Morrow's chest. Into her heart, where the light that made her was. Morrow fell, and her cloak of leaves turned brown in an instant. Her hair turned brittle and her eyes to dull stones, and then she was gone. The King of Winter rejoiced then, because he had beaten Morrow, and all of Antar would be his kingdom. And the King of Winter did rule. All of Antar wore a cloak of snow. The forests died, and there were no more flowers. The people starved, and in their desperation, they beseeched the king, but his new kingdom had made him no less bitter. No less cruel. He allowed them to have the heartwood to grow food, but for a price. Every year, on the day he defeated Morrow, he would take a sacrifice from amongst the folk of Antar.'

'What kind of sacrifice?' Raine asks.

'A good heart,' Fel says. 'And he would eat them, and grow stronger.'

'Now, that cannot be the ending,' Raine says, as she finishes her work. 'That would be a dark story, even for you.'

She sees him smile out of the corner of her eye.

'No,' he says. 'It is not quite the ending. The King of Winter ruled over Antar for ninety-nine years. He took ninety-nine good hearts and grew stronger and stronger ruling from his throne in the heartwood. On the hundreth year, the folk of Antar brought their sacrifice as they always did. It was a young woman, with fierce dark eyes, and when the king looked upon her he knew that taking her heart would make him stronger than any other. Stronger than the Emperor, wisest of all. It would make him strong enough to take the stars from the sky.'

'That sounds terribly arrogant,' Raine says, absently, as she winds a new bandage around Fel's arm. She can't help thinking of Sylar as she says it. Of the long shadow, that wants the stars, and all the spaces in between.

'It was,' Fel says. 'But the king could not see his arrogance. He just saw opportunity. So he got up from his darkwood throne, and he made to take the young woman's heart. He plunged his claws into her chest, but he found that hers was a heart that he could not take, because it burned too fiercely. It scorched his feathers and his fur and lit the forest in gold. The light spread and touched every corner of the world, melting the snow and the ice. The king drew back his claws, but it was too late, because the fire had caught him, and he saw the young woman truly now. Saw that her hair was spun with thorns.'

'Morrow,' Raine says.

Fel nods. 'She took every bit of strength from the king and gave it back to the land, then took his crown of bones and broke it, because there could be no more kings. Only the Emperor. With his crown broken, the king became nothing more than just winter, and he was taken up into the sky for the winds to watch over.'

'And Morrow?' Raine asks.

'Morrow's heart had saved every soul on Antar,' he says. 'But she fell into a deep slumber. The folk of Antar broke down the darkwood throne and built a bower for her in the heartwood. She sleeps there now until she is needed. Until the Emperor wakes her again.'

Raine finishes sealing the bandage and lets go of Fel's arm.

'And do you believe He will?' Raine asks. 'Wake her again?'

'I believe that her heart was fierce,' he says. 'And that fierce hearts are the kind that endure.'

EIGHT

Defiance. Defiant.

From the new staging post, Raine can only see the city of Defiance. It is lit by the last dim rays of daylight as the sun falls somewhere behind the clouds. The spires punch up into the sky on all sides, black iron and slabs of rockcrete. Their edges catch fire, painted bright by those last moments of light. Thunder rumbles in the distance, both from the constant Laxian storm, and from the ongoing battle. The building that the Antari have been billeted to in order to push into the city proper is an old scholam, built in the Laxian way. An odd mixture of functional and decorative, with silvered inlays in the walls, and bare rockcrete for floors.

'It is strange, isn't it?'

Raine turns away from the upturned claw of the city and the arched embrasure that serves as a window and looks at Andren Fel. He isn't looking at her, but at the letters painted on the wall of the corridor, ten feet high. Lumens clasped in gargoyle hands jut out of the wall above it, casting hard light.

'Duty, honour,' Raine begins.

'Faith,' Fel says, finishing the adage. 'I haven't set foot in a scholam since my own,' he says. 'Not one still standing, anyway.'

'Neither have I,' Raine says.

'The way it is written is exactly the same,' he says, absently. 'Down to the colour of the paint.'

Fel puts his hand out, gloved fingers to the word 'faith'. The armourers have repaired his carapace plates well. All of the damage from the forge is hidden now, though Raine notices a difference on the inside of his left vambrace as he holds out his arm. There are twelve deliberate nicks out of the red paint, where before there were only eleven. Raine knows the shape of a mark when it is made by the point of a knife.

'For Rol,' Raine says. 'The new mark.'

Fel glances down at his vambrace and nods. He drops his arm back to his side.

'It feels right,' he says. 'Carrying the lost with you.'

Raine thinks about the timepiece in her pocket and can't help but agree. She has tried three more times to unlock the datacrystal with words or phrases Lucia might have used.

The-Answer-Is-Faith.

Truth-Among-The-Details.

Always-Asking-Questions.

Still, it remains locked. Raine feels as though she is playing one of her sister's word games. The sort that they would play as children. Only in this instance, there is much more at stake than who will be the one to lead prayer or greet their mother from duty.

'The delegation from the Kavrone are barely minutes out,' Fel says.

'Then we should go,' Raine says.

'Hale told me that the general is with them,' Fel says.

The wind coming through the embrasure at Raine's back feels colder.

'Good,' she says. 'Then we will know him.'

She takes another look at those words painted on the wall. There is a worn patch on the word 'faith' where generations of progena have put their fingers to it as they walked past, just as Fel did.

'Being here makes me think of how the scholam masters would put us out into the forests to train us,' Fel says. 'Have us hunt to feed ourselves and take skins to sleep under.'

'Tell me about the hunt,' Raine says. 'About how you would do it.'

'There are many ways,' Fel says. 'You can chase the animal until it tires, but you will yourself end up tired. You can lay snares, but that is a chance, and you might starve before the animal chooses to take from them. You can lure it, with food or scent, but you might lure wyldwolves that way too. It is dangerous.'

'You said there were many ways,' Raine says. 'What else?'

'You watch and you listen. Learn its strengths and its weaknesses,' Fel says. 'Stay nearby and let the animal grow used to you.'

Raine puts her fingers to the word 'faith' too. The stone is cold under her fingertips.

'Then when it is inattentive. Careless. When you know that it will not run,' she says. 'That is when you make your move.'

Fel nods. 'That is when you make your move.'

The briefing is held in what used to be the scholam's audience chamber. Like all things on Laxus Secundus, it has architectural overtones of the mechanical. Squared-off edges.

No windows and a heavy set of doors. To Raine, it feels like a gilded strongbox.

Or a casket.

When she arrives with Fel, the rest of the Antari captains are already gathered around a heavy wooden table that is flaked and bleached with age. It is real wood, though. Raine catches the smell of it. A hololith projection flickers above it, showing the seal of the Bale Stars Crusade. Serek's roaring lion. Around it stand Hale, Devri and Sun. Grey, blue and gold. Three companies for this particular operation in Defiance's western district. Fel takes his place beside Hale. Raine goes to the opposite side of the table, because that is how things are. Her, in opposition, always.

'They are late,' says Karin Sun, checking the chrono on his wrist and scowling.

Gold's captain could as well be made of ferrocrete. He is squarely built and strong, with a face made of blunt angles and scars. There is a visible, dull steel plate set into his scalp from where he took a solid round that should have killed him.

Devri laughs. By contrast to Sun, Blue's captain is lean and tall, even as the Antari go. His dark hair is unruly, and he always looks as though he has forgotten to shave. Devri is almost as heavily tattooed as Fel is, with prayer-words showing easily above his uniform collar.

'It wouldn't surprise me if they are doing it on purpose,' Devri says. 'Proving a point. You know how the Kavrone can be, especially when it comes to us.' He shakes his head. 'They call us wild, as if they know what the word means.'

'As if wildness is a bad thing,' says Hale.

'I fail to see what point they could be trying to prove,' Sun says. 'That they are incapable of keeping time?' He folds his arms across his chest. 'Lateness is laxity,' Sun continues. 'Laxity is–'

'Sin,' Devri interrupts him. 'Spare me the words, Kar. We are not the ones to break them.'

'That is enough,' Raine says, at the sound of footsteps approaching the doors. 'From the lot of you.'

Hale nods. Devri shrugs. Sun keeps scowling, but he doesn't argue. Then the footsteps draw close and the doors to the audience chamber open wide.

'Oh,' Devri mutters, with a smile. 'An honour guard.'

Two Kavrone Dragoons in full regimental dress stand by the doors. Their uniforms are royal blue and crisp white, snow and sky, with not a mark on them. They wear torin caps with their regimental badges in gold. A flaming lance, framed by the sun. The honour guard stand to attention as two Kavrone captains enter the chamber, in flak armour and cloaks that clasp across the chest. They introduce themselves as Ellervin and Jeraine, of the first and third companies, respectively. Raine knows the names of all of the Dragoons' captains. Or she did. Neither one of the soldiers before her held the rank before Laxus Secundus. Vander was not exaggerating when he said they had taken losses.

The Kavrone's commissar is the next to take his place. Vander stands at the table beside Raine, in opposition to the troops, just as she is. Like his regiment, he is immaculate. Ornamented. Save for one thing.

'Vander,' she says.

He glances at her and she gets a proper look at the deep bruise under his left eye from where she hit him.

'Raine,' he says, with arctic civility.

The careful lack of disdain in his voice would surprise Raine more, but she is not giving him her full attention, because the generals are taking their place at the head of the table. One Antari. One Kavrone.

Juna Keene is dressed like her captains, in flak armour painted in greys and greens. The Antari general wears no cloak. No cape. Her rank is only shown by her pins and her medals, and the brutally decorative chainsword she carries at her waist. Her hair is shaved down on the sides, and dark, tight curls on the top. Her ears are pierced a handful of times each.

Kaspar Sylar is as much an opposite to her as it is possible to be. The Kavrone general's armour is glossy enamel. His cloak is crimson and heavy and trimmed with gold thread, the clasp set with stones. His medals and pins glitter in the lumen light. The degree of ceremony seems strange to Raine, after serving with the Antari for so long. She knows, though, that it is not unusual for other regiments. What is unusual is Sylar's face. It bears the strange distortion of juvenat and cosmetic attention that has left him unscarred despite all of those commendations, and all of his wars. The consequences of his years have been erased, made all the more apparent by their absence.

A dishonesty, made of his skin.

Keene puts her hands on the table. Her sleeves are rolled back to show one well-made augmetic arm. Her other is flesh and bone. Her dark skin is heavily tattooed in the Antari way.

'Let us begin,' she says.

She inputs an authorisation code, and the hololith changes.

'The local name for the western district of Defiance is the Healer's Ward,' Keene says, as it appears before them, rendered in miniature. 'As well as their forges and factories, the Laxians made augmetics. Good ones too. That is where the name comes from, though they did a good deal in the Ward besides heal.'

The hololith flickers, displaying different schematic angles. When it draws out to encapsulate the full scale of the Healer's Ward, Devri whistles.

'That is an ugly heap,' he says, with a grin.

The hololith display shows the entire fifteen hundred square kilometre district in miniature, a vast urban sprawl of stacked manufactoria, habs and places of worship joined by wide avenues and bridges. At the centre of the Healer's Ward, a cluster of spires juts upwards.

'Thank you, captain,' Keene says, with some humour in her voice. 'Helpful as ever.'

Devri nods, still smiling.

'Your objective will be the Sanctum of Bones,' Keene says. 'It is the central spire, and the main medicae facility in the Healer's Ward.'

Keene adjusts the hololith again and the rest of the district falls away to isolate the tallest of the Ward's spires.

'The Sanctum of Bones?' The name is a question, the way Hale says it.

'It is a local name.'

The words come from the Kavrone captain called Ellervin. In the light of the hololith, Raine notices just how young he is, and how tired he looks.

'The Sanctum of Bones is the facility where the Laxians built those augmetics mentioned by General Keene, as well as other things. Servitors. Cherubim. It is the place where they mind-scrubbed the weak. Repurposed the broken.'

Ellervin looks back to the hololith.

'That is where they have us at a standstill,' he says. 'The facility is on a war footing.' He scowls. 'The Sighted have it locked down with shielding, on the inside as well as the outside.'

'They locked down a good portion of our second company too,' the other Kavrone captain, Jeraine, says. 'This is the last we heard from them before the shielding fell.'

Jeraine takes a datakey from the pocket of his fatigues and feeds it into the cogitator-system. It starts to play crackling vox-capture. Raine can clearly hear las-fire in the background.

And screaming.

'This is Burdian, of the second,' the recorded voice says, through wavering distortion. *'If you can hear this, we need support. Guns. Souls. Anything you can spare. They are everywhere.'*

There is more screaming and the recording skips and breaks up into fragments with only one more sentence coming through clear. A sentence Raine suspects that Burdian never intended to transmit.

'Throne, no. Please. Not like this–'

Then the recording falls silent.

Jeraine pulls the datakey and holds it tightly in his fist as if he wants to crush it. Beside him, the Antari captains all steeple their fingers. It is a gesture associated with benedictions. Oaths.

And sometimes with the passing of souls.

'The blast shielding on the outside is adamantium-mix, and can be broken,' Ellervin says. 'The inner shield, though, is a different matter.'

The young Kavrone captain points to a highlighted location in the upper third of the Sanctum of Bones, over half a kilometre from the base.

'Whatever powers the inner shield is on this level, but we have been unable to reach it.'

'I take it you have tried a direct strike,' Fel says, pointing at the same location. 'Through those heat exchange vents.'

Raine sees them when he points them out. Jutting pipes, like exhausts.

Ellervin blinks. 'No,' he says, slowly. 'The blast shielding–'

'Won't block those,' Fel says. 'Unless they designed it to suffocate everyone inside the Sanctum. They might be grated, but that's not a trouble to breach.'

'That is high risk,' the other Kavrone captain, Jeraine, says. 'The Sighted notice you, and you are dead without question.'

Fel looks at him. Raine knows that look.

'Then you don't get noticed,' he says, simply.

Jeraine falls quiet, scowling. Raine sees Devri smile in the hololith light.

'Gaining access is not the end of it,' Keene says. 'Intelligence reports tell us that one of the Nine is present in the spire.'

Raine feels the mood around the table shift at the mention of those who control the Sighted. Always nine. Every one they kill replaced with another. Karin Sun snarls through his teeth and Raine knows why. Sun was there with her on Gholl, in the crystal caverns. Like her, he was captured by Arcadius Verastus, who called himself Ninth of Nine. Gold's captain was almost killed by Verastus, just as she was.

'Who, sir?' Raine asks Keene. 'Which of the Nine?'

'Cretia Ommatid,' Keene says. 'From the transmissions intercepted, they are calling her *She Who Watches*.'

'Sounds like another witch,' Sun says, with some venom.

'It is unclear,' Keene says. 'But likely. The Sighted rarely elevate those who are not warp-touched.'

'If that is true,' Sun says. 'If we know one of the Nine to be there and the spire is proving so hard to capture, then why are we trying at all? Why aren't we just bombarding it?'

'Because our second company are still inside it,' Jeraine snarls.

'You know as well as I do that your second company are likely dead by now,' Sun says.

Jeraine looks at Sun like he wants to crush him, now. Sun ignores him. Instead he reaches out and points to several locations around the Sanctum of Bones.

'Hit it in the right place, and you'll collapse the lot. Sighted and all. One of the Nine, made as dust.'

'No.'

Sylar's voice carries easily. It is a snarl that ill-suits that strange softness of his face.

'We are to capture it,' he says. 'To excise the Sighted, no matter their strength, and preserve what is left of the facility.'

Raine thinks about those containers the Kavrone were moving, and wonders if there is something in the Sanctum of Bones that Sylar wants to move too.

'The facility must be of great value,' Raine says. 'To spend as much blood as this, instead of choosing to rebuild.'

Sylar looks at her and Raine is reminded of those debriefs she undertakes with Zane.

Apply pressure.

Observe the results.

The Kavrone general's eyes are dark, and seem set further back than they should be, like deep pools. There is not a flicker in his distorted face.

'Commissar Severina Raine,' he says. 'The Lord-General Militant spoke to me of you. He said that you conducted yourself with honour in the war for the forges.'

Raine can feel the Antari looking at her at the mention of Serek's name. Vander is too, though in an altogether different way.

'The lord's words honour me,' she says, carefully.

'Then honour them in return,' Sylar says. 'And do not question. Capture. Excise. Preserve. Those are your orders, and your only concerns.'

She can see what he is doing. Using Serek's name as a mirrored shield because it means something to everyone around the table. It is a coward's play, and a conceited one at that.

And Raine counts that as two things she has learned about General Kaspar Sylar.

'The Bale Stars will require a good deal more blood to be spent before our work is done,' Sylar says. 'Before it belongs to the righteous and the worthy.'

Raine nods. 'Yes,' she says. 'Of that, there can be no question.'

Sylar's face twitches into a sneer, but he is the first to look away.

And Raine counts that as another thing learned about the Kavrone general.

Lydia Zane has not slept an hour since the blank and his soldiers were taken by the black water. When she closes her eyes, the image of it swallowing them up paints itself on the lids. When she opens her eyes, her two birds sit there and watch her. Their unblinking black eyes seem judgemental, now. So Zane spends her time before the battle to come in her assigned quarters in the old scholam building, keeping her mind occupied with training and meditation. With prayer, and with offerings.

'In my time I have killed many,' she whispers. 'Traitors and monsters and heretics.'

The white one ruffles its untidy feathers.

'But never have I killed like that,' she says. 'Never have I had to make a secret of it.'

The black bird opens its beak as if to speak, but says nothing. A cold wind blows through the gaps between the stones that make up the wall of her quarters. The room is small and spare, with no furniture. Zane can sense from the sorrow soaked into the stone that it was used for punishments. For the type of training that leaves scars. It seems appropriate, given that it now belongs to her, however temporarily.

'There is much that I already bear,' she murmurs. 'But this secret is a heavy thing.'

She shakes her head, thinking of those shapes that she took from the soldier's mind before he died. The needles. The flame. The wings. At first she had taken those for the wings of her white bird, but now she realises she was wrong. There was no snap of feathers, only a soft and near-silent beat, like the heartbeat of something colossal, booming and regular.

'There was a darkness in those men. A malice.' Her voice wavers. 'But still the secret of it is heavy. Still I doubt. If what was done was sin, then I welcome judgement.'

The wind howls and the building around her creaks, but Zane hears no judgement in the song of the storm. Even her birds remain blessedly silent. Then the wind dies down and Zane looks up to the idol. It is a simple thing that she spun from wood, using her gifts. The Emperor, seen as she knows Him, with a halo of leaves and a cloak of sky and arms outstretched like branches. As He must have been when she heard His voice through the rustle of the singing tree's leaves, all those years ago on the cliff over the ocean.

'My soul is a good soul,' she says. 'I swear it. I know it. In all things I am guided. In all I am tested. This weight is but another test.'

The Emperor's eyes are burned dark by the act of making. Unblinking. Zane takes a ragged breath. She looks down at the thing she has made, just as she made the idol all that time ago. It is a dagger, freshly spun from wood. One that she will use should High Command send any more soulblind. She will not be caught without talons or claws. Not again.

'And in this test,' she says, to the Emperor and the blade at her feet, 'as with every other, I will not break.'

When the briefing comes to a close, Raine returns to her assigned quarters. It is high in one of the scholam's dormitory wings, where the wind howls loudly. Pollivar Curtz is waiting for her accompanied by two commissariat-sworn Tempestus Scions, and several double-locked crates stamped with the crusade seal.

'Sir,' says Curtz. 'The lord-commissar sends his regards.'

Raine nods. She unlocks her quarters and picks up one of the crates.

'Bring them inside,' she says.

Curtz nods to the Scions. They say nothing, but they move the crates as ordered until they are all stacked up inside the spare concrete cell. It was a dormitory chamber at one time, and still bears the standard proclamation painted on the wall in that same red paint.

IDLENESS IS SIN.

With the crates moved, the Scions leave the cell and take up position in the hallway without Curtz having to say a word. Curtz hands Raine a hard case last of all. It's the sort that carries datacrystals.

'There is one more thing, sir,' Curtz says. 'Words, from the lord-commissar. He would only have me speak them directly to you.'

Raine takes the case and puts it in her pocket. The same pocket as the timepiece. All data together.

'Then speak them,' she says.

Curtz hesitates and clears his throat.

'He asked me to tell you that escalations have been made,' he says, then he frowns, just a little. 'And to ask you to think on his words. What he said to you about deeds.'

Raine knows the words he means. Tula's rich voice comes back to her immediately.

Deeds, Severina. They are what made your mother, and your father. Your sister too. In time, you will have to answer for yours, so make sure that you choose them carefully.

What she cannot be sure of is whether the words are a warning, or a threat.

'I can return a message,' Curtz says. 'If you have one.'

Raine thinks on that for a moment.

'Give the lord-commissar my thanks,' she says. 'And tell him I will fight fiercely, just as he ordered. No matter how large the storm grows.'

Daven Wyck sits on a supply crate in the Wyldfolk's billet with his rifle across his knee. The room was a mess hall, or something like it once. It is built of cold, old stone, the mortar turned black with age. What kit they have is in boxes, or part-unpacked. Crys has already pitched her cot by the window, because she likes to listen to the rain, and nobody has the heart or the want to argue with her. There is room enough in the billet to sleep twelve, though Wyck doesn't have twelve anymore.

But then that's why the new folk are standing in front of him.

The two of them are just about eighteen, both wearing clean fatigues and armour with not a nick out of them, nor out of those faces, either. Before today they were regimental support. They undertook training in preparation for the day they would join the regiment proper. They cleaned guns and helped put kit on the line. They have never been on the line themselves. Never fought a proper fight. But now they are both standing in the Wyldfolk's assigned quarters, watching him and waiting for him to say something.

'Told you,' Awd says, from beside him. 'They are just new growth.'

Wyck puts his rifle down, and his knife. He'd been scratching loops of thorns into the gun's barrel. Making it his, and not Veer's. The action of it was helping him keep his headache at bay. He can feel it coming back now, rising in his head like the sun over the world's edge.

'Names,' he says, to the two new folk.

'Haro,' says the first one.

She is tall and corded like rope, with rings through her ears.

'Haro, *sir*,' says Wyck. 'Try again.'

Haro colours, and stands up a little straighter. 'Sorry, sir,' she says. 'I meant to say my name is Haro, sir.'

'And you?' Wyck asks the other.

'My name is Jey, sir.'

His voice is low and soft, and he is pale as fog, even to his eyes. They are the grey of young ice. Jey and Haro both look like Antari, but they don't sound like it. Wyck picks up the wrong kind of lilt from both of their voices.

'You are both void-born,' Wyck says. 'Isn't that right?'

They look at each other then, just for a moment. Then Haro nods.

'Yes, sir,' she says. 'Me on the *Wrath Unending*.'

'And me on the *Pyre's Light*,' Jey says.

'Then you've never seen home,' Wyck says. 'You have never known Antar.'

'No, sir,' they answer together.

Wyck looks at Awd. 'This is what they give us,' he says. 'To replace Efri and Dal and Vyne. Void-born.'

'Looks that way, sergeant,' Awd says.

'No. I don't think so,' he says. 'You'll both have to go back.'

'We can't,' Jey says. 'Sir, please.'

Wyck shrugs. 'Not my problem,' he says. 'If you can't go back, then find something else to do, because you're not needed here.'

Wyck picks up his rifle and goes back to etching the thorns into the barrel of it.

'It *is* your problem.'

Haro's voice is a snarl. Wyck glances up at her. She's got her hands rolled up in fists.

'We aren't going anywhere,' Haro says. 'We were sent here to be Rifles. To be Wyldfolk.'

He laughs, and watches her face colour again when he does. This time it's because she's angry.

'To be Wyldfolk,' Wyck says. 'When you haven't seen home but on maps. You're barely Antari, never mind Wyldfolk.'

It's Jey this time who speaks up. He's not soft-spoken now.

'Our eyes are grey just as much as yours are. We might need your say-so to be Wyldfolk, but we need nobody's to be Antari.' He twists his face as if he wants to spit. 'That's something your words can't change, *sir*.'

There's a moment of quiet while the rain lashes against the windows, and then Wyck laughs again.

'I think I could like them,' Awd says, laughing too.

Jey and Haro just stare, still furious.

'Antari, maybe,' Wyck says. 'But you are not Wyldfolk. Not yet.'

He puts the rifle down again and gets himself up off the crate. He keeps hold of his knife in a loose grip.

'Tell me what you know the Wyldfolk to be,' he says.

To their credit, both of them ignore the knife. They keep their eyes on his. Grey, just like they said.

'Wyldfolk are the spirits of the woods,' Haro says. 'They defend the land from those who would hurt it.'

'And how do they do that?' Wyck asks.

'They bleed them,' Jey says. 'Take the shape of briars and cut them.'

'And if you are cut by the Wyldfolk?' Wyck asks.

'Then you die,' Haro starts.

'Because those cuts always kill,' Jey finishes.

'Deep or shallow,' Wyck says. 'Many or few. It doesn't matter. The Wyldfolk cut you, and you die.'

He holds out his hand, so that they can see the flat of his palm, and the scar across it. It's one of his oldest ones. Keller did it with his combat blade all those years ago, back before Cawter and the fire and the ashes.

'The only way to pass safely is to pay up front,' he says. 'That's the way of it.'

Awd shows them his hand too. The scar that runs the same way.

'You take this mark and you're one of us,' Wyck says. 'Until you're dead, so you had better be sure before you pay.'

They don't glance at each other, or hesitate. They both put out their hands. The left, like his. Just like the old stories say. Wyck makes the mark on Haro first, then takes her hand and makes her roll it into a fist so that the blood bubbles over and off it. It hits her boots and the stone floor. Then he does it for Jey too. More blood on the stone. Wyck tries not to think of the blank or the soldiers. Not in this sacred kind of moment. He pushes the thoughts under so they sink, just like the dead.

'That's payment made,' he says, when there's enough blood spilt. 'Now you defend the land, as we do. You cut those who would hurt it. You fight sharp and fast and you never stop when you chase.'

The two of them smile, though the cuts will be hurting them. That's the moment where he truly sees it in them. A wicked spirit.

'That payment grants you the name of Wyldfolk,' Wyck says. 'Now you just have to earn it.'

Severina Raine finishes reading another of Tula's records and flips it closed. She leans forwards, and puts it onto a pile to her right. Raine is surrounded by folders in jagged stacks and loose sheafs of parchment, spattered with ink. She has been sorting and reading the documents for hours, going back through almost a decade's worth of redeployment and requisition. She has found records for guns and for tanks. For fleets of ships. Lives, in the millions, all captured in droplets of black ink. But what she is really looking for still eludes her.

And it feels more than a little deliberate.

Raine opens the next folder on the unread stack. It is one of many detailing troop movements for the battle at the Coris Belt. She scans the pages, her frown growing deeper with each turn of the parchment.

It has been redacted, just like the others. Locations. Troop numbers. Executable orders. Everything but the regiment name.

The Strixian 99th.

Raine closes that folder too and puts it on top of the previous one, on the pile to her right. The pile that contains reams of similar documents pertaining to the Strixian 99th, and the Kavrone Dragoons. Just as Fel suspected, the Strixians have died several times over only to reappear months or even years later, on a different front. They are resupplied, and reinforced, just like any other regiment. Then they die, again. That is where the peculiarity lies.

Because the Strixians always die to a soul. No survivors.

Unfortunately, with the other details redacted, that is the only peculiarity that Raine can prove. It is flimsy at best. Easy to attribute to a Departmento error, or inaccurate reports. Easy to dismiss, for the right people.

Raine sits up straight and pushes her hair from her face. She allows her eyes to close, just for a moment, hiding the room and the documents from view.

So many things, hidden.

Raine lets out a slow breath and opens her eyes. They sting, even in the dim glow of the overhead lumens. For a moment, she is tempted to close them again. To sleep, even just for a few minutes, but those painted words on the wall of her quarters draw her eyes.

IDLENESS IS SIN.

Raine can't help the wry smile at reading the words. It just finds its way onto her face.

She leans over and picks up another folder.

The scholam's abandoned undercroft is a maze of interlinked corridors that Andren Fel treads alone, following the trail left by his targets. Boot prints on the stone. He passes by cells with their heavy doors ajar. Fel knows them to be isolation cells. That there will be no lumens in them, that the walls and floor will be bare, the cell not big enough to lie flat in. He knows how dark it would be if he were to shut himself inside one and pull that heavy door closed. So dark his mind would make shapes of it, whether his eyes were open or closed. He remembers it clearly, from a different time. A different world.

From home.

The first two targets come from the darkness of those cells to try and kill him with a pincer attack. One left, one right. Fel disarms the target on the left and knocks her legs out from under her, putting her wheezing on her back in the water and old dirt. Her laspistol skitters on the floor, and he kicks it further. The target on the right fires his pistol with a flash, but Fel knocks it wide and high before answering with a killshot of his own. One dead, but the first target is back up now and she gets Fel in a chokehold.

'You're dead,' she says, in his ear.

'Not yet,' Fel says.

He slams her back into the wall and her grip goes loose, then he rolls her over his shoulders and puts her on the floor again. This time, he fires his pistol before she can get up. Another kill. In the quiet that follows, Fel can hear water running and hitting the stone floor. The hum of old lumens as they flicker overhead, erratic. He hears something else too. Footsteps. They are soft and measured, but he can hear them all the same, approaching where the corridor bends sharply. Fel puts his back against the wall and slows his breathing as if he's taking line of sight. He moves up to the bend in the corridor but not beyond it.

The footsteps are close. Perhaps fifteen paces. He waits a moment.

Ten paces.

Another moment.

Five.

Then Fel rounds the corner with his laspistol already raised and points it square at Cassia Tyl's face. He pulls the trigger and the gun lights with a mock flash.

'You're dead,' he says.

She lowers her own pistol. It was risky to jump her, because usually she's quick. Quicker than he is, sometimes.

'Myre and Jeth?' she says, trying to look past him.

'Dead too,' says Jeth.

They are already on their feet. Myre stoops to pick up her pistol from where Fel kicked it.

'You made a mess of it,' Myre says to Jeth. 'Fired before you had a killshot.'

'At least I kept hold of my gun,' Jeth says.

'You both made a mess of it,' Fel says. He points back to where they fought. 'Boot prints on the floor, never mind the marks you left in the dirt when you opened those cell doors wider to hide.'

Jeth scowls, but he nods assent. 'Aye, captain,' he says.

'It won't happen again, sir,' Myre says.

'And you I heard,' Fel says to Tyl. 'Just whispersteps, but it was enough.'

Tyl looks more than disappointed. He sees shame in her face. 'Next time you won't,' she says. 'I swear it.'

'I know,' Fel says. 'And I know that our balance has changed. That losing Rol is like losing a limb or an eye.'

The three of them nod.

'But we will be four until we can get a fifth,' he says. 'Until I can choose a fifth.'

He has tried to avoid thinking about it so far. The idea of assessing candidates to take Rol's place still sits poorly with him, even after saying the words and saying goodbye. It's not the way most regiments do it. Usually a replacement would be selected without their say so. But then most regiments don't run their own storm trooper units, either. They certainly don't allow them to hold onto their past or their homeworld as the Antari do. Fel has fought alongside Tempestus Scions before. Those who are mind-scoured and carved out from the inside. All of their stories lost. It is a practice that Antar's scholams stop short of, because it is the Antari way to make a soul strong not by forgetting, but by remembering. That is the way that things have always been done. It is tradition, and one that has never failed them.

'Until then we need to make ourselves balanced,' Fel says. 'This world will try to kill us plenty more times before we are finished, and I don't want cause to light another fire.'

He puts his hand out, palm down. The three of them put their hands on top of his. In that moment of contact with his kin, his family, he feels like a fraud. It might not just be the world that's trying to kill them, or the Sighted – it could very well be their own.

But he can't say a thing. He swore it to Raine.

'Eyes and ears,' he says, instead. 'That's what you trust in the Sanctum. That and your hearts. Is that clear?'

If they think it a strange thing to say, they don't question it. Instead they all nod their heads.

'Aye, sir,' his three Duskhounds say, together.

'Now,' he says to them, dropping his hand away. 'We go again.'

The hour is late when Raine notices something in the report that she is reading. It is not related to the Kavrone, or to the Strixians, but it is still something. She goes through the carefully arranged piles of records, pushing them aside until she finds one to match it. Then another. Then another. Reassignment requests. Redeployment orders. All for sanctioned psykers. All being moved from their parent regiment. Raine didn't notice it at first because it was sparing. Irregular. Now they are being moved in greater numbers, more often, but it is still the same as the earlier records.

Once the psykers are reassigned, they disappear, never to re-join their regiments. They are not reported as KIA, or MIA, warp-lost, or executed.

They are ghosts, just like the Strixians.

And just like the Strixians, the records are untraceable to those making the request. To those who redacted it. It's the absence of information that proves the connection.

Consequences, erased.

Raine thinks about the shadow Lydia Zane sensed at the heart of the forge. The one that wants everything. The stars and the spaces in between. She thinks about what Fel found at the landing grounds.

Cargo is live.

Those thoughts put a cold in her more fierce than a deep-winter gale.

And then her long-range communications set begins to chime.

Raine gets to her feet. They sting and ache with sitting for so long. The hour is late. She picks up the receiver, enters her authorisation and is greeted with an automated message.

Priority signal, the message says, in icy machine tones. *Immediate attendance is required. Central command. Commissariat hub. Priority signal.*

The message repeats itself until Raine shuts down the link. She picks up her coat and her hat. Her pistol and sabre. Then she stands for a spare moment, looking at the records at her feet, before picking those up too. Just a few. The hardest to dismiss. Tula asked her to think on his words. To choose her deeds carefully, for when she is made to answer for them.

But Raine cannot choose carefully now. She cannot ignore the shadow, or the ghosts.

She can only do what is right, and brace herself for the answer.

NINE

Oaths and promises

When Raine arrives at the commissariat hub, there are no Tempestus Scions guarding the entrance, and Curtz is nowhere to be seen. She does see a figure that she knows, though.

Lukas Vander.

He approaches as Raine drops from the Taurox's steps into the churned mud. Vander doesn't look immaculate now. He is soaked from the weather and muddy to the knees. His green eyes are wide.

'Raine,' he says. 'The priority signal.'

'I received it,' she says. 'Why do you think I am here?'

He grabs at her arm to stop her as she passes him.

'Wait,' he says. 'Listen to me.'

Raine shrugs him free. 'I came here to speak with Tula,' she says. 'Whatever you have to say can wait.'

Raine heads for the commissariat hub, the records held

safe in a weatherproof case. The storm is roaring overhead, bringing flecks of ice on the wind that sting her face.

'Raine!' Vander is shouting. 'Wait, damn you!'

She doesn't. Raine ignores him as she goes inside and follows the corridor. That is where she finds Curtz. The cadet is sitting with his back to the flakboard wall, his legs drawn up. He is turning something in his hand and muttering. A badge, marked with a golden eagle. The words are prayers, soft-spoken. He flinches when he notices her.

'Sir,' he mumbles, getting to his feet. 'My apologies.'

'Where is Tula?' Raine asks.

Curtz doesn't answer, but he glances to the door of Tula's office. It is ajar.

'Wait,' Curtz says, just like Vander did.

Raine ignores him too. That cold feeling has taken hold of her again, a vice grip on her heart and her mind. She goes to the door and pushes it open the rest of the way and sees what Vander must have seen, and Curtz before him. That vice grip tightens so that she can't speak or blink or move. She almost drops the record case.

Because lord-commissar Mardan Tula is dead, hanging from the iron support beams of his office by the rope around his neck.

Raine stands in Tula's quarters, looking at the way the paper has spilled from the desk. It is scattered across the floor. Dog-eared. There are wet, muddy boot prints on some of those pages, made by the militarum wardens and the medics that came to remove Tula's body.

It is such a mess. A mess that he would have hated.

Raine drops down and starts to pick up the papers.

'You should not have moved him,' Vander says.

Raine turns to look at him. Vander is standing in the doorway, his green eyes narrowed. Sylar's words from the briefing come back to her.

The Bale Stars will require a good deal more blood to be spent before our work is done.

Raine looks at Lukas Vander and the coat he wears that's lined with Kavrone blue and she feels a rush of heat behind her eyes. He is either complicit, or oblivious. She is not sure which she would hate more, but she knows that she wants to hit him again. Over and over. But she won't. Not here. Not now.

'You should not have cut him down,' Vander says.

It had been hard to do, to cut Tula down. To saw through the thick cord that had twisted itself tight, and to lower his body to the floor amongst those scattered papers.

The weight had been a lot to bear, alone.

Raine straightens up, with Tula's papers held in her hand. They are creased and crumpled, and becoming more so because she's gripping them so tightly.

'You would have had me leave him,' Raine says. 'You would have let him hang, in dishonour.'

Vander scowls at her. 'It is not about dishonour,' he says. 'It is about procedure. About doing things correctly, not that I would expect you to understand that.'

'*Procedure*,' Raine says, in disbelief. 'We are not talking about thievery or laxity or a minor infraction. Tula is *dead*.'

'I know that!'

Vander shouts the words. It is the first time Raine has heard him raise his voice away from the field. There's a break in it, and there's a break in Vander too. In his posture and his bearing. He crosses to her, standing no more than arm's reach away.

'Suicide,' he says. 'It is a crime. Worse than that, it is cowardice.'

Raine stares at him. His green eyes are clouded.

'Tula was no coward,' she says.

Vander isn't like Tula was, or Serek is. He isn't so hard to read. Raine can see the conflict in his face, like two waves colliding before they reach the shore.

'No,' he says. 'I do not believe that he was.'

Raine watches him carefully.

'Then what do you believe?' she asks.

Vander shakes his head. His eyes stop looking quite so clouded.

'That everyone is capable of making poor choices,' he says, his voice cold again. 'Selfish choices.'

He straightens that blue-lined coat. Raine can see where it has been mended up close, the lining replaced and repaired. It is not quite so immaculate, under hard light.

'You wanted to speak with Tula,' Vander says. 'What was it about?'

Raine turns her back on Vander and puts Tula's papers down on his desk, square to the edge. The topmost form is marked and countersigned in red by Departmento adepts and holds the seal of the Bale Stars Crusade. Her breath catches in her throat. It is Tula's copy of the requisition form for the records she had him secure.

'Nothing,' she says, slipping the form off the stack and into her coat. 'Just a matter of paperwork.'

Lydia Zane follows her two birds through a corridor built of stone and black mortar. Ironwork juts from the walls on either side of her, razor-edged, like pharyngeal teeth. All around her, her kinfolk are frozen still in the moment of the fight. Picked out in detail, like a painting in oils. Zane walks between them. She passes by Yulia Crys, locked still in the moment of putting down one of the Sighted with a thrown punch. Zane can see where the impact of it has shattered the Sighted's teeth as well as his jaw. Fragments hang in the darkness. There is a snarl on Crys' face. A show of her own teeth. Her eyes are bright with fury. Zane sees all of this by the light of Gereth Awd's flamer. Caught as it is, the flames remind her of blooming flowers, bright and aching. Zane puts her fingertips close, but she feels no warmth from it. She pulls away like she did from the mess hall. This brightness is not for her. Awd is not looking to what he is burning. He is mid-shout, and he is looking to Wyck.

Wyck is alone, further out than any of his Wyldfolk, like always. Furthest into the darkness. He has drawn his knife through the throat of one of the Sighted, and an arc of blood follows behind it, glittering. Zane moves closer. There is a fury in Wyck's eyes too, though it is a different kind to that she saw in Crys'. Bright and aching, just like the fire. Behind Wyck, another figure looms from the darkness, barely a heartbeat from burying his knife in Wyck's back. The figure is all shadow, no matter how closely Zane looks. No matter how she concentrates, all she can see is the silver of the blade. The serrated edge.

Zane hears a cry from her birds, and turns to look for them. They wait at the very edge of the light, watching her as they always do.

'Free,' says the first bird.

'Fall,' says the second.

And then the birds take wing and flutter further into the darkness. Zane continues to follow them, leaving her frozen kin behind. The floor becomes wet against her bare feet. She cannot feel her toes. Zane stops a moment and crouches on her heels. It is oil, she thinks, slicked on the floor, though it smells so rich and heady, like the smoke does at a speaking of the words. She puts her fingers into it and they come away black.

Zane rubs her hand clean on her robes. They are tattered and torn. Spattered with blood, though she cannot recall the making of the damage nor the stains. She cannot remember where it is that she left her darkwood staff, but she misses the weight of it and the cooling presence of the crystals it carries.

Zane follows her birds until it is so dark that she cannot see the oil-slick floor or the jutting ironwork of the walls. She can only see the birds because they seem to make their own light, soft and indistinct, like candlelight. They perch on something, tapping their clawed toes. It is colder here. Colder the closer she gets. Through her robes and her skin and her muscle and marrow and bones.

'Free,' says the first bird.

'Fall,' says the second.

Zane approaches the birds, and by their flickering light she sees what it is that they perch upon. A casket of dark metal. It is the source of the spreading oil. Of the rich smell like earth and smoke and death. Of the cold. So cold. She blinks frost from her eyelashes.

Zane puts out her hand. It is bony and pale and crooked like the talons of her birds. She places it flat on the casket and it opens with a hiss and a roar and a blast of icy wind. The birds cry and snap their wings and fly free. Zane can only hear the second as it echoes away into the darkness and leaves her with the casket and what is inside.

'Fall,' it says. 'Fall. Fall. Fall. Fall.'

Zane looks down through coiling mist and dancing motes

of ice. She sees then by the light spilling from inside the casket, blue and cold like stars.

'No,' she says.

Inside the casket, she sees herself. She is pale as death, her skin stretched thin over her bones. Wires puncture her arms, her legs, her throat. Her head nestles within a coiling mass of cables that hum and sing and scream. They are draining her. Taking her gifts.

No. Not gifts.

Her power.

Her life.

In the light spilling from the casket, Zane can see the others too. Dozens more caskets that hinge open around her, all cradling the gifted. Other psykers. Some are military, as she is. Some are future-dreamers and gift-sellers. Some are barely old enough to be tithed. The other psykers are all being drained too, turned to nothing but skin and bones by their cable crowns. Figures in black carapace plate stand guard around the caskets. Their eyes are green, glowing discs.

'No,' Zane says, again, taking a step backwards.

And she feels, rather than hears, the soft beat of great wings at her back. Zane turns and looks and sees it then, looming over her. A man. No, a monster. With a king's noble face and hooked claws that reach for her and wings that could curve around every one of those caskets. Its talons grow so close that she cannot focus on them.

'No!'

This time, Zane shouts the word as she snaps awake.

'The King of Winter,' she whispers, as her artificial eyes adjust to where she is.

Zane is not in her quarters. She is not even inside the once-scholam anymore. She finds herself outside in the darkness of the muster yard, with the icy rain lashing her skin. It feels like being cut open.

Like talons, raking her skin.

Zane's robes are filthy and soaking, and her feet are bare and numb from the walk she made whilst dreaming. She clutches not her darkwood staff, but the spun dagger that she made for herself, holding it out in a shaking hand as a threat to the darkness.

Zane thinks of how it felt to stand before that great wicked monster with its mighty wings. The King of Winter is here, on Laxus Secundus. It is seeking the gifted and the cursed alike. The men who came for her did so for the king.

It is not one of the Sighted.

She remembers the look in the monster's eyes. The feelings, boiling from it.

'You are a creature of wanting,' she says, though she knows that the king cannot hear her. 'Of pride and ambition.'

Zane wavers on her feet.

'But that is not all that you are,' she whispers, slowly lowering her knife. 'You are hurting. Angry. Afraid.'

A smile stretches over her teeth.

'Because you too have known the touch of death.'

And then Lydia Zane stands there and laughs, alone in the rain and the cold and the darkness.

'I think they thought you serious, you know,' Awd says. 'Jey and Haro.'

He is sitting opposite Wyck on the cold stone floor of the Wyldfolk's billet, heating two tins of protein mash over a gas stove. They both could have gone down to the mess to fetch something with Tian and the void-born, but Wyck couldn't face the noise, nor their earnest faces. Awd could have gone anyway, but he hasn't, which means he's got something to say. Probably something Wyck's not going to like much. Awd takes one of the tins off the flame with his bare fingers and lets it sit for a moment before sliding it across the floor. Wyck picks it up and pries it open with the edge of his combat blade. The protein mash inside the tin is hot, and the smell of it makes Wyck want to throw up.

'That's because I was serious,' Wyck says.

He knows he has to eat what's in that tin. The headache will only get worse if he doesn't. It'll get blinding, and when it gets that way he gets stupid, and after killing those men High Command sent, he really can't afford to be.

Awd laughs. 'Come on now, Dav,' he says. 'You know we cannot choose what they are, but we can make them into something.'

'You sound like you're after my stripes,' Wyck says. 'Words like those.'

Awd snorts. 'Not likely,' he says. 'That is a headache I do not need.'

Wyck can't help laughing at his choice of words. It sends him dizzy, so he rests his head against the bare stone of the wall for a second. It is comfortingly cold. Wyck starts eating the protein mash. Like always, it smells worse than it tastes.

'You know what I think?' Awd asks.

Wyck shakes his head, pushing his food around with the flimsy tin spoon. 'No, but I would bet you're about to tell me.'

'I think you gave them all that spite because you feel sorry over Efri and Dal and Vyne.'

Wyck stops pushing his food around and puts the tin down.

'What?' he says.

Awd doesn't take heed of the tone he gives that word. He just keeps eating his food and talking in between.

'You weren't there,' he says. 'When we said the words. You should have been. Don't pretend that doesn't put hooks in your soul because I know that it does.'

Wyck stares at him. 'I gave Jey and Haro all that spite because they looked like *prey*,' he says. 'Because they looked at me like I was going to mind them, or keep them safe.' He shakes his head. 'I needed them to understand they won't find that here, or anywhere. That being of a squad doesn't make you safe. It doesn't mean anyone will mind you. It means that your kin will fight with you. Bleed for you. Die for you, even. It means you had better be worth it.'

'Efri was worth it,' Awd says. 'And Dal. And Vyne.'

'I know,' Wyck snaps. Then he sighs. 'I know.'

'You should have been there,' Awd says. 'Crys is stung over it too, though she'll never tell you so.'

He nods over at where Crys lies flat out on her cot underneath the window, snoring. She never has trouble sleeping. Never has trouble with much of anything.

'I should have been there,' Wyck says. 'You're right about that. But what's done is done. Guilt does no favours for the dead.'

Awd frowns at him. 'That's what you say,' he says. 'But you are wearing that chain now all the same.'

Wyck puts his hand to where the silver chain rests. He tucks it back inside his fatigues so that it is hidden. The comedown must be bad. He is bleary-eyed and shivering. An idea pushes up in his head like someone else put it there.

Outside.

He should go outside. The air will help.

Wyck gets himself up off the cold floor by leaning on the wall.

'Where were you, Dav?' Awd asks. 'What were you doing?'

Fighting, Wyck thinks. *Lying. Stealing.*

Killing.

'Never you mind,' he says instead, and goes to leave.

'And now where are you going?' Awd shouts after him.

Wyck blinks, but his eyes stay bleary.

'Never you mind that either,' he says.

Left with little option otherwise, Raine reaches out to one of the last people to still retain her trust.

She sits cross-legged on the floor of her quarters and waits for the hololith link to be established. It is a secured line with theta-level encryption, bounced to the fleet in orbit over Laxus Secundus by the high-gain communications linkup established at the command camp. Even with those powerful transmitters, it still takes time, but Raine cannot trust the vagaries of an astropath, and she cannot go there herself. So, she sits and she waits, turning her timepiece in her hands.

The link clicks live, and the image resolves, jagged and flickering. The woman that looks out at Raine has changed little since last they spoke. Even shaped from hololith light, her face is angular and hard and made more so by her years. Her hair is white and curled, held in place with silver pins. Her eyes are mismatched. One green, one blue. Not augmetic, but a natural asymmetry.

'Hail, Lord-Marshal,' Raine says.

Veris Drake doesn't smile, but her eyes narrow in a way that is the equivalent on her face.

'Severina,' she says, chiding. 'Such formality. One of the scholam's many gifts to you, I am sure, but you know better than to speak so with me.'

Drake has always had little patience for ceremony. Raine

remembers the day of her mother's remembrance service. The honorary banners and rifle salutes and devotionals. The rich, spiced incense smoke. She remembers Drake scowling.

Ridiculous, she had said. *Your mother lives not in the stitching in these flags, or the song of guns. She is her deeds. Her legacy.*

Then Drake had looked to Raine, that honest, untempered scowl still in place.

She lives in you, she had said.

Since then, Raine has considered Veris Drake a soul to trust, and she has proved it several times over.

'Of course,' Raine says. 'Apologies.'

'Now, my dear,' Drake says. 'The hour is late, especially to one of such a dreadful age as me, so tell me what could possibly have unsettled you enough to necessitate a theta-encrypted communication.'

Raine looks down at the requisition form in her hand. The creases that fold across it that have worried at the ink. Faded and cracked it.

'I believe that there is a corruption taking root in the Bale Stars Crusade,' she says. 'I believe that there is a faction within our ranks looking to seize power from the Lord-General Militant and from High Command, and that they are willing to kill to conceal it.'

She glances up. The Lord-Marshal's image destabilises for a moment, and when it resolves again, Drake has her fingers steepled before her face.

'Who?' Drake asks, her voice wintry.

'I suspect that it is orchestrated by General Sylar, of the Kavrone Dragoons,' Raine says.

Drake laces her fingers and rests her chin on them. Her mismatched eyes are adamantium-hard. 'Is that because Sylar is hateful and self-aggrandising, or do you have proof?'

Raine tells her everything she knows. The landing sites. The live cargo. The guns and the psykers. The discrepancies in the records.

Tula's death.

Drake listens throughout, with her scowl unchanging.

'And you want me to take this to Serek, and the rest of High Command,' Drake says.

'Yes,' Raine says. 'I know it is a risk, but I did not know who else to turn to.'

Drake waves her hand. 'Risk does not concern me,' she says. 'As I said, I have lived to be dreadfully old. What concerns me is your lack of evidence.'

'The records–' Raine starts.

'Tell you nothing,' Drake finishes. 'Only that there are excisions. I need whatever was cut out. I need documents and data. Otherwise it is just your word against Sylar's, and whoever else he has managed to convince.'

'And Tula's death?' Raine snaps. 'What of that?'

Drake's face softens then, just for an instant.

'It is regrettable,' she says. 'If he truly has been betrayed, but that too requires proof to persecute for. Anything else is suicide, if you will pardon me the use of the word.'

Raine's heart is thundering, and she has put more creases in that paper in her hand, but she knows that Drake is right.

'And if I get you this proof?' she asks.

'Then I will speak with Serek as you ask,' she says. 'But not before. This is a political matter, Severina. You cannot solve it with your fists or the edge of your blade. You have to play their game, by their rules.'

Raine wants to spit, thinking about it. She has always considered solving problems with a sword's edge much the cleaner option.

'Understood,' she says. 'Though their game feels unbalanced to me.'

'It always is, by its nature,' Drake says. 'The odds are always stacked against the righteous. It is what makes us righteous.'

Drake's eyes narrow again, that approximation of a smile.

'There is a Munitorum complex on Laxus Secundus,' she says. 'A lens through which the crusade's information must travel, as it does on all worlds. That is where I would go, were I looking for errant records. After I had awaited the necessary passcodes to access the most restricted areas, of course.'

Raine nods.

'Thank you,' she says. 'Veris.'

Drake waves her away again. 'Gratitude can lie with ceremony as far as I am concerned,' she says. 'Just keep your eyes open, my dear. I promised your mother I would watch for you, and I would hate for this terrible business to make a liar of me.'

It is late when Fel and his Duskhounds return to the wing of the scholam where the squad are billeted. Late enough to be early. There are only a few hours left before the sun rises. Before the Healer's Ward and the Sanctum of Bones.

'Something is worrying at you, captain.'

Tyl looks exhausted. There's a bruise starting to close her right eye from one of her deaths in their training games. She's not the only one who is hurting. In the end they managed to kill him several times over between them, which had been the point of doing it.

To make sure that if they had to work without him, just as a three, then they could.

'What makes you say that?' he asks her.

Her mouth quirks in a try at a smile.

'Because I know you,' she says. 'Because you have that look about you that you get when you think overlong on something.' She gives up on the smile. 'Because you disappear on the nights we don't fight and you never say to where, or why.'

Fel can't find it in himself to be surprised that she has noticed. No matter how quiet he might be, Tyl has always been watchful. She's the best marksman of the lot of them with a longshot. There's a part of him that's proud of her for noticing, even if he can't explain where he goes.

'It's nothing to speak of,' Fel says.

'That doesn't mean it's nothing at all,' Tyl says. 'It means it's important enough for you not to say.'

He won't lie to Tyl, so he's left with only one choice.

'Which means you should stop asking,' he says.

Tyl holds up her hands, palms out. It's a deference. A show of no weapons. Fel can't feel surprised at that either. The lot of them are made for it. The want to obey is instinctual, like throwing up an arm to block a strike.

'Right you are, captain,' she says.

She turns away to leave.

'Cass,' he says.

She looks back at the sound of her given name.

'There is something that I do need to tell you,' he says.

'What's that, sir?'

'I am making you my second.'

Tyl blinks. He knows she is thinking about the fact that it was Rol's place before.

'Not Myre,' she says. 'Or Jeth.'

'No,' Fel says. 'You.'

Tyl is a good choice because she is quick and fierce in all things. Quicker than him, sometimes. But it wasn't speed or fire that won her the place, it was what she just did and said. Because she was the one to notice when he goes, and because she had the heart to ask him about it, even if he can't give her an answer.

'Thank you,' Tyl says. 'I won't let you down.'

Fel nods. 'Just remember what I told you,' he says.

Tyl salutes the old way, with her hand closed over her heart. 'Eyes and ears,' she says. 'And hearts.'

And then she does go, leaving him in the corridor alone. Fel waits until she rounds the corner and he can't even hear her whispersteps anymore, and then he looks again at the mark left in chalk on the face of the door to his quarters. Three short strikes, and underneath them three words written in a familiar hand.

Duty. Honour. Faith.

Wyck finds his way out into the rain and sleet and keeps walking until he's well out of the muster yard's floodlights. It's pitch dark, save for the city burning in the distance. He hears fighters scream overhead, though he can't see them. The icy weather doesn't really help with the shaking, and now that he's here, he can't remember why he thought it would.

'I was not sure that you would hear it.'

He flinches and turns at the sound of the voice. Lydia Zane looks like a drowned ghost, standing there with the rain ringing off her witch's crown. Droplets hit the surface of her silver eyes without making her blink.

'Commanding others is not my strength,' she says. 'But your mind is open and closed in equal measure.'

Wyck realises what she is saying. That coming outside was a poor idea after all, because it wasn't his in the first place. He starts shaking worse, and pulls his knife.

'You did this,' he says. 'You put witch-words in my head.'

'I needed to speak with you,' Zane says.

Wyck laughs, despite the cold and the shaking and the fear locking his limbs.

'No,' he says to her. 'You think what we did gives you that right? It doesn't. Not now. Not ever.'

Zane tilts her head. 'Listen to me,' she says. 'It is important.'

'*Listen to you,*' he says. 'You are lucky I don't cut you. Crawl back to your cursed circle and stay away from me.'

Zane snarls. She moves fast. He tries to stop her, but finds himself frozen as Zane puts her cold, clammy hands on either side of his face. Images flash in front of his eyes.

Black ironwork.

Flame and fury.

Razor edges, snapped teeth. Oil-slick water.

The blade of a knife, ready to bury itself in his back.

In his back.

The images disappear. Zane's hands fall away and she steps backwards as Wyck falls onto his knees and violently throws up what he'd managed to eat onto the gravel of the muster yard.

'Now will you listen?' Zane says.

Wyck spits on the ground. He is shaking so completely that he can't get to his feet. He looks up at her.

'I truly hate you,' he says, through his chattering teeth. 'Do you know that?'

Zane shakes her head. 'You are welcome,' she says, flatly.

'What?'

She tilts her head. 'Death means to take you tomorrow,' Zane says. 'I thought to let you know that you should take care for knives at your back.'

Knives. At his back.

Wyck shudders and blinks his bleary eyes. When he does,

he sees something else that she showed him, printed in the darkness made by his closed eyes. Machines. Cables. Zane stuck through with wires inside a metal casket.

'Going by the casket, it wants the same for you,' he says.

That makes her laugh bitterly. The sound of it turns his stomach again, but there's nothing left to throw up.

'No,' she says. 'That is not death. That is something much worse.'

Wyck gets to his feet, finally, slowly. The rain feels like a pulse outside his body.

'Worse,' he says. 'Than death.'

'Yes,' Zane says. 'That is why I called to you. Why I brought you out here.'

She puts her hand into her robes and takes something out of them. In the darkness, it takes Wyck a second to realise what he's looking at. He almost laughs.

'You made yourself a blade,' he says.

'Next time they come for me, I will not be found without teeth,' Zane says.

'And what, you want to know the secret of using one?' Wyck asks her.

She nods. That's when he does find it in himself to laugh. It's all ridiculous. Delirious.

'Your spells,' he says. 'How do you use those?'

She frowns. 'It is instinctual,' she says. 'A reaction. And calling them spells is ignorant.'

Wyck shrugs. He doesn't much care to know what they really are. 'A blade's the same,' he says. 'Instinct. You cut them so they can't cut you. Fast and deep. No hesitation.'

Zane looks down at the blade in her hand. It looks as though it is made from wood. Wicked and jagged. He has to hand it to her, it looks as though it'll leave a nasty wound.

'That is all?' she asks.

'That's all,' Wyck says. 'Killing isn't hard to do, no matter how it's done.'

It's the truth. He's never found the act a hard thing to do. It just happens. Instinct, like he said. It's the after that's the problem. The nightmares and the ghosts. The blood all over his hands.

Zane is looking at him with that tilt of her head. He hates that look, like she's looking right through to his core.

'I see,' she says.

And before he can ask her exactly what she sees, she turns and walks away into the darkness.

Raine waits by the red-painted words in the old scholam's upper corridor at the stroke of three. The scholam bell is loud and doleful, still set to ring time, even with no progena to hear it. Wind howls from the end of the corridor, through the open embrasure that serves as a window. It tugs at Raine's coat, and makes the candles lighting the corridor flicker, casting dancing shadows. Raine can't bring herself to put her fingers to the worn spot on the wall where the word 'faith' is painted like she did when she met with Fel before. Not now.

Not after Tula.

He helped her. Listened to her. Escalated, on her behalf, and it earned him not just death, but dishonour.

Dishonour, like Lucia.

Raine looks away from the letters painted on the wall at the sound of footsteps made deliberately louder so she will hear them. It's a courtesy.

'Commissar,' Fel says.

His face is honest, so Raine can see the concern in it, but they can't speak openly so close to the Antari quarters.

'Captain,' she says. 'Follow me.'

Raine walks with Fel in silence to a narrow room in one of the abandoned wings of the scholam that the Antari haven't taken as their own. Before the city fell and the scholam with it, it was a library filled with devotional texts and treatises on tactics. A star map covers the entirety of one wall, showing the full extent of the Bale Stars. Every world and every war. It is embroidered on heavy cloth that has grown damp and started to rot. Their boots disturb the scattered parchments and torn pages that lay strewn across the floor. They have started to blacken and mould too, the way things do when they are left untended. Raine knows that Fel is waiting for her to speak, but it takes her a moment to do it. The smell of the paper and damp cloth is cloying.

'The lord-commissar is dead,' she says.

There's a tremor in Fel that most people wouldn't catch. 'How?' he asks her.

'They made it look like suicide,' Raine says. 'By hanging.'

'Throne,' says Fel.

Raine has never once heard him use that word as a curse. Not in nearly two years.

'Because of the records,' he says. 'Just for requesting them.'

Raine nods.

'They murdered him, and made him seem a coward,' Fel says.

'Yes,' Raine says.

Fel takes a slow breath. 'Whatever Sylar and the Kavrone are doing, they truly don't want it seen.'

Raine nods. 'They are willing to kill for it,' she says. 'Even someone of Tula's standing and reputation.'

Raine looks to the star map. Laxus Secundus is a tiny silver knot of threads. One of hundreds, joined by starlanes and marks of fealty.

'I suspect it is a grasp for power,' she says. 'A coup. It is no secret that Sylar is ambitious.'

'I overheard two of the Kavrone talking at the landing fields. They made it sound as though he is removing any who refuse him, even his own.'

'We cannot trust any one of them,' Raine says.

'What about their commissar?' Fel asks.

She looks at him. 'When I arrived at the commissariat headquarters, Vander was already there,' she says.

'So, he is a part of Sylar's plan,' Fel says.

Raine thinks about that conflict she saw in Vander's face.

'Or he is ignorant to it,' she says. 'Either way, he has failed.'

'And the records?' Fel asks. 'What do they show?'

'That the Strixians have died more times than they should have,' Raine says. 'And that regimental psykers are being reassigned.'

'Psykers,' Fel says. 'Do you think they took Pharo?'

'Perhaps,' Raine allows. 'Or perhaps that truly was the Sighted.'

'I don't know which is worse,' Fel says.

That Raine can agree with, without question.

'Cargo is *live*,' Fel says. 'That is what the script I took said. Are you telling me that those caskets were for moving witches?'

'In all likelihood.'

Fel shakes his head. 'I left them there, to be moved and used like animals. That's not right, witches or not. We need to find them.'

'The records did not say why they were being moved, or to where. The details were either redacted or omitted.'

'Under whose authority?' Fel asks, with a frown. 'Could Sylar do that?'

'Not all of it,' Raine says. 'Not without help. Nor could he have done what he did to Tula without allies.'

Fel is all tension now, of the kind that comes from the implication of threat. 'You were the one to request the records from Tula,' he says. 'Could it be traced back to you?'

Raine reaches into the pocket of her greatcoat and takes out the form she took from Tula's office and unfolds it. 'I found the request form when I cut Tula down, which means that they either missed it, or they left it behind deliberately.' She smiles, bitterly. 'Though I suspect they would have come for me already, had it been the latter.'

Fel shakes his head. He definitely isn't smiling, bitterly or not.

'We need to do something before they do find out. This has to stop.'

'We cannot act without proof,' Raine says. 'We need the original records. All of them. Without redactions or omissions.'

'And how do we go about doing that?' Fel asks.

'I have an ally left to me in High Command,' Raine says. 'I will go to the Munitorum complex in the secondary city and get them myself.'

Fel shakes his head. 'We are about to deploy,' he says. 'The regiment needs you on the line to watch over them, and the Kavrone.'

Raine frowns, because he has a point, and because she knows what he's going to say next.

'I'll go, and bring the records back to you,' he says. 'It's far less risk.'

Raine cannot help thinking of Zane's words, then.

He is faithful, that one.

She thinks about the creak of the ironwork supports in Tula's office and the scattered paper on the floor, and she knows that it is time to say what she came here to say.

'No,' Raine says. 'You have done enough already. From now on, I will deal with this. It is my burden to bear.'

Raine knows how to read Fel's face. His voice. His bearing. She can see how her words wound him as surely as a cut might.

'You are asking me to turn my back on this,' Fel says. 'On you.'

'Yes,' Raine says.

He frowns. 'No,' he says. 'I won't do it.'

Raine can tell that his heart is clashing with his head, and with the conditioning that makes him what he is. She knows it because she feels it too. It is agony.

'Then I won't ask you,' she says. 'I will order you. Leave it. Forget it. Walk out of here, and back to your kin.'

She sees him flex his fingers as if they hurt.

'No,' he says again.

Raine draws her bolt pistol in one movement and points it at his face. She can see the shake in her hands as she looks at him through the iron sights. That isn't right. She never shakes.

Never doubts.

'Think about what you are doing, captain,' she says. 'I am giving you a direct order, on commissariat authority. This is insubordination.'

Fel doesn't move, nor does he look away.

'Then you had better shoot me, Severina,' he says. 'Because I'm going nowhere.'

Raine shakes her head. 'Tula is dead,' she says. 'Murdered because he chose to help me.'

'It was his choice,' Fel says. 'And I have made mine, to stand at your side no matter what fate brings.'

'Truly,' Raine says. 'That is your choice?'

She cannot help but feel they are talking about more than just duty, now.

Fel nods. 'Until the end,' he says.

Raine lets out the breath she has been holding. She lowers her pistol and holsters it. 'Until the end, then.'

She puts out her hand and Fel takes hold of it in his own as a way to seal the promise. Both her hands and his are scarred and rough from lifetimes spent fighting. The moment of contact is brief, and then it is over and Raine knows what she needs to do.

'There is something that you should know, if we are going to do this,' she says. 'A story I owe you.'

She puts her free hand in her pocket and takes out the timepiece. Even with its broken face, the ticking is still a comfort.

Fel nods, with understanding in his grey eyes. He asked her about the timepiece once before, a long time ago now. Raine had only told him that it had once belonged to her sister and that her sister was dead. That was all she could bring herself to say, and he had known better than to ask any further.

'This was a gift to my mother from my father,' she says, tracing the curve of the case with her thumb. 'So the story belongs to them as much as me.'

She keeps looking at the timepiece as she talks.

'My mother was Thema Raine,' she says. 'She was Lord-General Militant before Serek. She was fierce and strong. An Imperial hero.'

Fel must know the name, but he doesn't speak. He lets her continue. Raine is glad of it, because if she stops, she knows she would not be able to begin again.

'My father was not. He was my mother's greatest mistake.

His name was Ewyn Lauder.' Raine pauses, letting the words hang in the air. She has not said her father's name aloud since she lost Lucia. 'He was a line soldier, a captain in the Darpex One Hundred and Seventy-Fifth.'

She rolls her fingers tighter around the timepiece and the case creaks under them.

'Five years after I was born, he was fighting in the first civil war on Paxar. It was an ugly war, like this one. There were many losses. Weakness was rife.'

She finally looks Fel in the eyes.

'His platoon got cut off from the rest of their regiment behind enemy lines, and instead of standing to the last or fighting his way back with his soldiers, my father chose to flee. He abandoned his men and left them to die at the hands of traitors.'

Raine's heart is loud in her ears as if she is running under fire.

'I have seen the records,' she says. 'The transcription of his confession. He said that he ran because of his daughters. Because he could not bear to die, knowing that Lucia and I would be left behind. He made us the cause of his cowardice, and then he died anyway, and left us to bear that. To bear the weakness of his blood. A coward's blood.'

She waits for that change in his face, and the judgement she has seen everywhere else, but it doesn't manifest. There is no change in Andren Fel.

'Severina,' he says. 'You are not your father. His weakness does not make you weak.'

'We spent our lives telling ourselves that,' Raine says. 'My sister and I. That we would do better than our blood. Lucia took this timepiece from my mother's things when she died as a reminder of what made us.'

She turns the timepiece in her hand and looks at Lucia's name etched into the back of it.

'But then I lost her too,' she says.

Gloam, before

Severina spits blood onto the old wooden boards of the training hall floor. She is breathing hard, which hurts from whatever is cracked in her chest. Illariya is trying to get up with fury in her eyes. Cozelt is out cold.

'Cease.'

Drill-abbot Ifyn's voice carries across the hall. He waves two aides over, who pick up Cozelt and carry him clear. Illariya won't accept help to get up. She leans on her training blade to do it instead.

'Raine,' Ifyn says. 'I must speak with you.'

Severina sheathes the training blade in the scabbard at her belt. She tries to think what his words might be as she follows him from the training hall. If she performed poorly, or if there is a lesson in the fight that she did not perceive. Even now, with hardly a month left until her graduation to cadet, there are always more lessons.

Ifyn's office is a spare cell, like a devotional chamber, save for the wooden desk that dominates it. He takes a seat on the far side.

'Sit,' he says to her.

Severina does as she is told. She keeps her back straight and her hands knitted in her lap. She cannot think what it might be. She has undertaken every duty. She won the fight against Cozelt and Illariya fairly, even though they worked together against her.

'Severina,' he says.

Ifyn's face is impassive and cold, as ever, but the use of her given name steals the breath from Severina's lungs. She blinks. In the moment before he speaks again, she feels a long shadow bear down on her. Heavy on her shoulders, like a weighted cloak.

She can see that his words are going to hurt.

'This concerns your sister,' he says.

Severina blinks again, and sees a hundred deaths for Lucia on the backs of her eyelids. They are all violent and cruel and each one of them breaks her heart, just a little.

'She is dead,' Severina says. 'Is that it, master?'

Ifyn shakes his head.

'No,' he says. 'She is not dead.'

For the first time since she was introduced to Ifyn, all those years ago on the landing platform over the ocean, he looks troubled. Severina's mind begins to rush with even uglier possibilities.

'Your sister has been found guilty of acts of treason and dissent,' he says.

The words hit Severina like a physical blow. Her chest aches, worse than before. She clenches her fists, feeling her fingernails press into her palms.

'No,' she says.

But she is thinking about that day in the chapel. The day that has haunted her since. The fear and wildness in Lucia's dark eyes.

'Your sister has chosen to stand against High Command,' Ifyn says. *Severina notices that he will not say Lucia's name.* 'She has been leaking information to the enemy for months in order to *orchestrate the elimination of key members of the command elite. She intended to destabilise and destroy the crusade.'*

'No,' Severina says again. Her jaw aches.

Ifyn shakes his head. 'She broke faith, Severina. Your sister is a traitor.'

Severina wants to scream. To shout. To throw herself at Ifyn and lock her hands around his throat and make him go silent and still. She does none of these things, though. Instead, her injured, shattered heart turns inwards and draws up walls around itself, and she asks the question that she knows and dreads the answer to.

'What will happen to her?' *she says.*

Her voice doesn't sound like her own. It sounds like some other young woman, cold and distant, as if heard through glass.

'She faces summary execution by firing squad,' *Ifyn says.* 'In one week's time.'

Severina thinks of every time she has fired her pistol in training. Of the squeeze of the trigger. The hammer strike. The flame. Then she thinks of Lucia's eyes. Of the fear she saw in them that day in the chapel. But not just that. She thinks of her sister's laugh. Of her cleverness and her wicked temper. Of her hand taking hold of Severina's own on that day on Darpex so long ago. The day they lost their mother. She tries to let the memories go, to push them aside along with her sister and that terrible pain in her chest that cannot just be a broken rib or bruising. It feels like dying.

'That will be all,' *Ifyn says.* 'Return to your duties.'

Severina slowly uncurls her fingers. The nail-marks in her palms are purple and deep.

'Yes, master,' *she says.* 'To my duties.'

TEN

Into shadows

Andren Fel goes to speak with Tyl before dawn. Before the muster. She is sitting in her quarters cleaning her tattoo needles carefully in boiled and salted water. Fel can see where she has used them to ink a set of balance scales on the inside of her forearm. The arms of the scales look like tree branches, and in each weighing pan, there is a heart.

'Balance,' she says, when she sees him looking. 'Thought it made a good reminder.'

'That is why I need to speak to you,' Fel says. 'There is something I need to do. A duty. One that means I won't be going with you into the Sanctum.'

The needles ring against the dish as Tyl drops them and allows them to sink in the salted water.

'A duty,' she says, slowly. 'Captain, what are you talking about?'

Fel wants to tell her. He trusts Tyl with his life, and with his Duskhounds too. He knows she would help them without a second thought. So would Myre and Jeth, if he asked it of them.

But he can't say a word. He swore it to Raine.

'It's need-to-know,' he says. 'I can't tell you.'

That's the moment. The one that cuts like taking hold of a loop of thorns to keep from falling. She looks at him like he has turned his back on them.

And he knows that he has more than earned that look.

'It's important, this thing,' he says. 'If I could let it be, I would, but I can't.'

That's when he sees that instinct kick in for Tyl. The need to obey that weighs heavy. The same instinct he had to fight all the while when he was talking to Raine.

'I won't ask you to, captain,' Tyl says. 'It's not my place.'

Tyl takes the needles out of the salted water and lines them up on a clean linen to dry. The water and the heated steel must burn her hands, but she doesn't flinch from it.

'Watch carefully in that place,' Fel says. 'From every corner. Every angle. Understood?'

Tyl frowns at him. 'I will,' she says. 'Fate guide you, captain.'

On hearing those words, Fel can't help feeling as if it is now, more than it ever has.

Do you still truly believe that your sister betrayed the crusade?

That is what Fel had asked her, after Raine had told him of Lucia's execution and the way she had changed in the lead up to it. The wildness of her eyes.

Raine had been unable to answer the question honestly, so she had not answered it at all, but the question has made a space inside her to call its own, and now she cannot stop thinking of it. Of the hate and anger that she used to repaint every memory of her sister, and what it would mean if that were unjustified.

What it would mean if Lucia were betrayed, and not the betrayer.

Raine looks to her timepiece held tight in her hand, knowing the datacrystal to be inside. The one that is meant to hold the truth, but that she has still not managed to unlock.

It is like being back at the scholam. Being tested without knowing the limits of the test or what it is meant to teach. Those were always the hardest lessons to learn, the ones that hurt the most, but in the end, they were often the greatest lessons too.

The timepiece ticks over to the mark and Raine puts it back into the inside pocket of her greatcoat. She pushes everything aside but what is immediately before her and steps up to stand in front of her regiment. The strength of three companies of the Eleventh Antari Rifles stand ready on the rockcrete beside their troop transports and armour support and Valkyrie wings. There is ice on the wind, bitter and cold. The Laxian dawn is dim and throttled by storm clouds.

To Raine, it's a comfort.

'Today, we stand in the city of Defiance,' Raine shouts the words, her voice carrying easily across the muster yard. 'A city that has been tainted by our enemies, and must be made fit to once more bear its name.'

She draws her sabre, and holds it in the air. Up to the storm.

'Defiance will once against stand defiant. We will make it so, by faith and fury!'

They answer her as one, with her own words.

Faith. And. Fury.

And Raine answers them with their own words.

'By fire and thunder!' she cries.

And this time, their answer is louder even than the storm overhead.

Haro's gear is new. Fresh stamped off the line. Her helmet runs a little large, and she's struggling with the fastening on the strap used to tighten it, though Wyck knows that's got nothing to do with the fit or the size of the helmet. It's because Haro's hands are shaking too badly. He's seen that kind of shake before. The sort that comes from the wait and the fear. From being lined up in the muster yard and listening to the commissar talk that way. From knowing that your place on the line used to belong to someone else and that you're only filling it because they're ashes. It's different to the shake that he's trying to hide. The one that goes right to his marrow that tells him he needs to dose soon.

Mists and moors, how he needs to dose.

'Hey, void-born,' Wyck says.

Her eyes snap over to him and she drops her hands.

'Sir,' she says.

'Take a breath,' he tells her. 'A proper one. Count it out slow.'

He sees her frown, but then she does as she's told, and her hands stop shaking quite so badly. She finally manages to get that clasp closed and then opens her mouth as if to say something. Probably thank you.

'Don't,' Wyck says. 'Just do me a favour and keep breathing.'

He walks away from her to check on the others and Crys stops him. A laugh rolls up from her chest like thunder.

'Inspirational words, sarge,' she says. 'Poetry.'

Crys is kitted up with all of her demolitions gear. It makes her even bigger than she already is. Awd would usually laugh at something like that, but he doesn't today. His eyes are sombre above his burned-on grin.

'You want poetry, then you can go and join Koy's Mistvypers,' Wyck says. 'She can play that lute of hers for you.'

Crys snorts another laugh and thumps him on the shoulder. It sends Wyck's arm a little numb and makes his already aching head ring like a bell.

'They'll do alright,' she says, dropping her voice. 'The void-born.'

Wyck looks back to Haro and Jey. They are with Tian. He's having them paint thumb stripes on their faces with oil paint from a tin. Wyck can't help thinking about what Zane showed him. The black slick water.

Knives at his back.

Something worse than death.

He shakes his head and it makes his vision swim.

'It's you that bothers me, sir,' Crys says. 'You don't look right.'

Wyck frowns at her. 'What?'

'That nosebleed, for one,' Crys says.

Wyck puts his hand to his face and sees she's right. He tastes it then too. Wonders how long he's been bleeding.

'It's nothing,' he says, like he would an order.

Crys purses her lips at him like she wants to ask again, but she doesn't. She never does, when he pulls that tone with her. The rest of the regiment are all moving around them to deploy behind the Fyregiants. Wyck hears the tank squadron's engines all kick in as one.

More thunder.

More headache.

'Let's go,' Wyck shouts to his Wyldfolk.

He catches Nuria Lye looking at him as they move up to

follow the tanks into the city. She scowls and shakes her head at the sight of him, before turning away.

Crys whistles, low. 'What did you do to earn that kind of scowl?' she asks. 'Ask her for a midnight dance?'

'Yeah,' Awd says. 'What did you do?'

Wyck knows he's not just asking about Lye. That Awd suspects something is up. He's always known one of them would figure out about his dosing eventually. He always thought it might be Awd. Wyck has thought some nights about what that would mean, and whether he could kill Awd, if he had to. But it's as he told the witch, it's not about whether he *could* do it. That part he knows for sure. He's quicker than Awd, and much more vicious.

The problem is that Wyck's not sure he could live with it afterwards.

Wyck runs the sleeve of his fatigues under his bleeding nose, leaving a red stripe against the green and grey.

'A midnight dance,' Wyck says. 'No. If I'd have asked Lye for that then I'd be dead.'

Crys laughs loudly at that. Awd doesn't.

'Maybe she would have done us a favour, sarge,' Crys says, oblivious. Her grin is bright and wicked. 'Then we'd finally get a proper speech before a fight.'

For the second time, Wyck realises he's being watched, only this time it's not by Lye. It's much worse than that.

It's the commissar.

Raine materialises from amongst his kin like a rogue shadow.

'We will be first through the breach,' Raine says. 'Your squad will run the edge.'

Wyck becomes very conscious of the way his nose is still bleeding, sluggish. He slings his rifle and makes the sign of the aquila.

'The edge,' he says. 'Aye, commissar. It's what He made us for.'

Raine doesn't blink, but her dark eyes narrow just a fraction. The wind catches her greatcoat. Water beads on the material, and drips from the brim of her peaked hat.

'In His name,' Raine says.

Wyck nods. 'In His name,' he says, carefully. Levelly.

Wyck has occasionally wondered, just like with Awd, if he could kill Raine, should he need to. Looking at her then, at the black depths of her eyes, he more than knows the answer.

Not a damned chance.

Cassia Tyl runs up the Valkyrie gunship's ramp. The thrusters are already firing, loud and hot, cooking the rain right out of the air. Tyl smells burning and fuel and beneath all that, the close press of thunderstorms. Electric. It feels heavy, and in that moment, so does she.

Myre and Jeth are already on board, armed and armoured, ready to go. Their red-lensed faces turn to look at her.

'Where's the captain?' Jeth asks.

'Going solo,' Tyl says. 'Something important.'

Jeth shakes his head. 'No,' he says. 'That's not how this works. We go together.'

'Not today,' Tyl says. 'Today I'm in charge, and we're a three.'

Jeth bows his head, but he has the look of a threatened animal about him. All tension.

'We may be a three, but the captain's a one,' Myre says, in her downturned voice. 'He's alone in whatever he is doing, and you know what they say about lone hounds.'

'Don't say it,' Jeth says. 'You know better than to tempt fate like that.'

Tyl knows that is where the heaviness is really coming

from. It's not so much the fact that they are going without Fel as it is that he's acting alone.

That, and the fact that he wouldn't tell her why.

'He has a duty to do and so do we,' Tyl says. 'And that's all. We stay balanced and watch careful, like he said.'

Jeth and Myre both nod their heads. Tyl thumbs the vox-link on the wall.

'We are a go,' she says.

'Right you are,' says the pilot, Jova, from the cockpit.

Tyl looks out as the ramp closes and her view of the muster ground narrows to a thin line and then nothing at all. She pulls on her mask and everything gets washed in red. In one corner she sees Myre's heart rate and Jeth's. They are both steady and patient, because they are built to be calm, even when they are just a three and not a five. Even when their captain is hiding something from them. Usually Tyl would be able to see Fel's life signs, too, but not today.

Because it only works when they are close.

Andren Fel looks at the schematic of the Munitorum complex that Raine gave him. It is a big place. A warren of corridors and records halls. Circles within circles, to the centre, where the most dangerous data is kept. The most high risk. He puts out his hand and traces the shapes of the chambers and corridors with his fingers. The ventilation systems and the switchbacks. Lefts and rights and dead ends. He makes landmarks out of some of it and patterns out of the rest. The act of memorising the map is calming, in a way. It helps him forget what it is that he is doing, when you look at it in abstract. Abandoning his kin. His duty.

Even though the choice was right, what he is doing is desertion.

Fel lets out a slow breath. The schematic is crumpled in his fist. He folds it into squares and proceeds to tear it into shreds, before closing his eyes for a moment. The Taurox is slowing. He can hear it in the way of the engine and the snarl of the tracks.

'We are close,' comes Curtz's voice from the cab.

Raine told the cadet very little, and Fel has told him nothing else. It's as much about trust as it is the fact that Fel doesn't want to see Curtz die like Tula. Dishonoured.

The Taurox grinds to a stop, and Fel gets up and out, into the shadow of a tall building hung with tattered, rain-soaked pennants. This district of the secondary city has been broken and remade in war's shape. The buildings are pockmarked and strung with razor wire and the roads are cracked and flooded and marked with dirt from tracks and treads.

'That will be all?' Curtz asks.

The cadet looks worn thin. His knuckles are split as if he has been fighting.

'That's all,' Fel says, and he turns to go.

Curtz nods, then he frowns. 'Commissar Raine told me that the Rifles have a tradition,' he says. 'Of speaking words for the honoured dead.'

Fel shouldn't, but he nods.

'And what about the others?' Curtz asks. 'The ones who have had their honour stripped away?'

Fel tries to see deceit in the cadet, but all he can find is rage. That, and grief.

'All go on to be judged,' Fel says. 'And the Emperor alone knows the truth of a heart, honoured or not.'

Curtz nods slowly. 'He does,' he says. 'Of course He does.'

Then he shakes his head as if to clear it, and gets back into the Taurox without another word. Fel watches the transport go, tracks churning, and once it is well out of sight, he moves off into the crooked paths behind the buildings.

The approach to the Sanctum of Bones is a wide avenue, lined on either side by partially collapsed habs and manufactoria. Everything is jagged, grey and ugly, shot through with snapped rebar that reminds Ely Kolat of broken bones. Small arms fire rings off *Stoneking*'s skin from the buildings on either side of the avenue where the Sighted have dug themselves in like wood larvae. Kolat ignores it, watching through the lens of his targeter as the Sanctum of Bones grows closer. The Sighted are manning barricades outside the spire, despite the blast plating locking it down. The heretics have scrawled their bloody, hateful sigils all across the metal as if it'll offer them protection from the Fyregiants. As if anything can. Five other Demolishers roll alongside *Stoneking*. Two on either side, and then *Mountainsong* in front, like always. Quite a way in front this time, because Chori is damned impatient to get to breaking. Behind them, Hale's Grey Company follow in columns on foot, protected by the bulk of the Fyregiants. Kolat can't see them, but he knows they are there. He has spent so long inside the Demolisher that he's come to appreciate the value of a narrowed view. Just seeing the threat. The target. Nothing more.

'Five hundred metres to range,' he says.

'Cannon's up and waiting,' says Curi in his slow, lazy voice.

The loader isn't especially clever, but that suits Kolat just fine. He only needs him to do his job, and nothing else. He doesn't need another soul like Edra.

Edra, who had been clever enough to notice the extra tickets and trade-coins Kolat had managed to hoard and wondered how. Who had then been naïve enough to ask him about it instead of just reporting it, and trusting enough to turn his back when Kolat promised him he'd stop shifting stimms and go straight.

Edra, who had been tougher than he'd expected, and taken quite a bit of killing.

'Hold speed,' Frayn says, from behind Kolat. 'We can't get ahead of the troops. Much as I'd like to.'

The tank commander might be a sight more clever than Curi, but Frayn isn't a threat to Kolat's off-duty habits either. She's so damned pious that every minute she's not in the tank is spent at prayer, or having holy words inked in any space she's got left.

'No, sir,' says Vurn. Kolat can hear the smile in the driver's voice.

Stoneking shrugs aside debris from another of the Kavrone's wrecked Chimeras with her dozerblade. The shell of the transport is still burning. It's been torn up from the middle outwards to open up like a wyldblossom. Big exit wound. More small arms fire rings against *Stoneking*. Kolat sees bodies too, for moments at a time, through the framed focus of the targeter. There was a time long ago when the sound of *Stoneking*'s engines rattled his ears, right down into his throat, but now he finds he misses it when she is quiet.

He loves hearing her sing, in all of the ways that's true.

'Sixty seconds,' he shouts, as the overlay zeroes towards green.

And then an impact shakes *Stoneking*, rattling dust and grit from the tank's frame above Kolat's head.

'Long-range missile fire,' Vurn says. 'From the Sanctum's barricades.'

Curi laughs, loud over the engine's roar. 'That won't come through,' he says. 'They should know better.'

'You're right,' Frayn says, and there's something in her voice. 'They should.'

Kolat keeps his eyes on the Sanctum and the avenue and catches sight of another Chimera afire, another with that same big exit wound. From the inside out.

And he goes cold just the same way.

'Mines,' he shouts. 'They've mined the avenue!'

'Full stop,' Frayn yells.

Kolat hears her shout over the vox to the other Fyregiants and the column behind, but he loses her words to a catastrophic explosion that shakes more than just dirt and dust. Kolat cracks his head off the targeter mount and goes blind for an instant. When his sight comes back it's narrow by nature. Lidded, because he is dizzy and aching and there's blood running into his eyes. *Stoneking*'s engine is still roaring, but differently to before. She's hurting like he is. Over the noise he can hear Vurn cursing over and over.

'We're not dead,' Kolat slurs.

'No,' Vurn shouts. 'But *Mountainsong* is.'

Kolat blinks and tries to focus through the targeter. The view is awash with fire and smoke and smears that might be the glassaic or might be his eyes, but when they pull back enough and he blinks enough he sees it. The shell of their sister machine, torn up from the inside. Like a wyldblossom.

'Lieutenant,' Kolat shouts, twisting in his seat to try and see her. 'We need a plan.'

Frayn's face is a mask of blood, but she's alive. Awake. She pulls down the vox handset and clicks it live.

'To the hells with a plan,' she says. 'What we need are wings.'

Cassia Tyl looks out from behind the door gunner on the Valkyrie, hanging on to the handhold built into the wall of the troop compartment. The wind howls past as the gunship turns sharply, angling her towards the avenue below. Inside her enclosed helm it just sounds like whispers. She sees the wreckage of the lead Demolisher, burning like a fire for the dead.

'It's *Mountainsong*,' Tyl says, over the Duskhounds' internal channel. 'Slain by fire.'

Jeth curses. Myre says nothing. The Valkyrie screams as it dips below the buildings and into the avenue at speed. The airframe shakes and rattles right down Tyl's arm. Grey stone and metal rush by and the gunners on their heavy bolter turrets open fire into the buildings on either side of the avenue, though they can't hope to hit much at such a speed.

And then the rocket pods fire from under the Valkyrie's wings.

Clusters of rockets streak over the top of the rest of Grey Company and the remaining Fyregiants in the avenue, impacting the open ground between the tanks and the Sanctum of Bones in rolling waves and triggering the mines buried under the rockcrete. The explosions happen in quick succession, throwing dirt and chips of stone so high in the air that some of it finds its way into the Valkyrie and clatters off Tyl's carapace plate. She can't help but smile.

'Now *that* is thunder,' Jeth says. He is at the other side door, braced in it with his hellgun up at his shoulder.

'Quite the racket,' Myre replies, flatly.

The Sighted fire back from their gun-nests in the buildings on either side of the avenue, and from the Sanctum itself. Dozens of squads in blue-grey flak are arrayed in front of the spire behind crude fortifications, protecting the shielded face of the spire with missiles and solid rounds and hails of las.

'Hope you're hanging on!' the gunner yells as he answers the enemy fire with his own.

Then the Valkyrie pulls into a steep climb up the face of the Sanctum. Tyl's world tilts, but she has a snap harness attached to her plate and she clings to her handhold as the engines howl and the airframe groans under the stress and then they are up and away and out of range of the Sighted's guns. There are holes in the Valkyrie's hull big enough to see through in places where they took high calibre rounds. The world tilts back and the gunner turns. His face is weather-tanned around his goggles and breather. Tyl can tell he is grinning even with most of his face covered like that.

'Just a detour, sir,' he shouts.

'Coming up on your drop,' Jova, the pilot says. *'Thirty seconds.'*

Tyl nods at Jeth and Myre, and they move their way to the back ramp of the Valkyrie. She feels the way the aircraft cuts speed as a tug on her bones, followed by the vertical thruster jets kicking in as they move into position above their drop.

'Quickly now,' Jova says. *'We have hawks on radar.'*

'Ready,' she says, to her Duskhounds.

Because in that moment, without Fel, that's what they are. Hers. Her responsibility.

'Aye,' the two of them say together.

Tyl hammers the release switch for the Valkyrie's rear ramp. The ramp lowers and opens to the roar of the wind and the gunship's jump-jets. The blast shields are pitted layers of adamantium-mix that cover the whole side of the spire, save for those three heat exchange vents, each tall enough for a soul to stand up in and protected by heavy, industrial grating. A lip of black iron no more than two metres wide runs beneath them. That's it. Their designated drop. Beyond that ledge, the spire drops dizzyingly towards the ground. Almost half a kilometre of freefall.

And not one of the heartrates in Tyl's helmet display flickers at the sight of it.

Tyl fires the grapnel line down onto the ledge where it sticks and then hooks the cable to the rappel anchor in the airframe of the gunship. The cable autowinds in and goes taut, even in the high wind.

'Let's go and make some fates,' Tyl says.

And she takes hold of the cable and swings out into a quick descent. Tyl feels the pull of the wind. The temperature measure in her helmet's display drops sharply. The slide is fast and over in seconds. Tyl's boots hit iron and she moves straight to the heat exchange vents, with Jeth and Myre right behind her.

'Duskhounds free and clear,' she tells Jova, over the vox.

Myre gets to setting the heat-charges. They activate with white-hot flashes of light and start eating their way through the industrial-grade plasteel of the vent covers.

'Acknowledged,' Jova replies. *'Maintaining cover.'*

The Valkyrie turns, holding position over the spire, and then Tyl hears the scream of hawks on the chase.

'You might want to hurry yourselves,' Jova says. *'It's about to get noisy out here.'*

Tyl looks out to see the enemy fighters drop through the cloud cover. Lightnings. Two of them. Jova's Valkyrie moves out at speed to engage.

'Myre!' Tyl says, putting her hellgun to her shoulder.

Her rifle is modified with a longshot scope and an extended barrel, but even that won't allow her to hit the Lightnings, not at that speed.

'Ten seconds!' Myre replies.

It's nothing, ten seconds. Ten heartbeats. But in those ten seconds, Cassia Tyl sees Jova's Valkyrie fire its lascannon. A spear of light. The Lightnings both answer with their hellstrike missiles in the same instant. White smoke and fire flashes. Countermeasure flares burst around the Valkyrie, making a halo for it. Her helmet display dims. Tyl takes a breath. Fires her hellgun anyway.

Despite herself, for the sparest instant, she thinks about that half a kilometre of freefall.

The bolt from the lascannon takes one of the Lightnings, turning it into a fireball. It stops screaming and falls out of the sky. The second fighter peels up and away into the clouds with a roar of afterburners, and in the last of Tyl's ten seconds, both hellstrike missiles hit Jova's Valkyrie. The gunship keens and tilts sideways, smoking. Spinning. Losing altitude and fuel in a stream of liquid fire. The vox-link with Jova clicks live in her ears, but not a word is said. Tyl only hears altitude alarms and feedback.

'We're in,' Myre says.

Cassia Tyl blinks, then turns away from the edge and the city and the Valkyrie falling to earth.

'Let's go,' she says, and walks into the darkness of the vent system.

'Now,' Frayn says. 'We break them.'

Kolat's eyes are still dazzled from the mines going up as Vurn guns *Stoneking*'s engine and she rolls forwards again, into the devastation left by the mines. Her joints and her tracks creak and sigh. Beside them, their sister machines do the same. Behind them, the troops follow.

'Thirty seconds to outside range,' Kolat shouts.

This time the Sighted aren't trying to bait them, they are trying to break them. *Stoneking* shakes and cries around Kolat as the targeter hones towards zero, but he doesn't want to hear that. He wants to hear her *sing*.

The instant they hit outside range, he calls it out and waits for the words.

'Main cannon fire!' Frayn yells.

Kolat thumbs the firing stud and *Stoneking* sings. Her sisters join her a moment later. The detonations from the Demolisher shells shake his bones, even at outside range.

'Load!' Kolat shouts, as smoke blooms and rolls, obscuring his view of the barricades.

'Aye!' Curi shouts, not slow now. Quick when it counts.

Vurn keeps pushing *Stoneking* forwards as Curi reloads the main cannon. Close range is all the better for breaking. The closer they get, the more Kolat can see the damage they've done. The Sighted's barricades are a ruin and their guns are quieted, but the blast shielding on the spire is still up.

It doesn't seem a good trade. Not for *Mountainsong*.

'Up!' Curi shouts. 'Cannon ready!'

'Fire!' Frayn shouts.

Kolat fires again and *Stoneking* sings and screams at the same time as more enemy fire rocks her. He cracks his head again. Curi curses from the loader's run. The massive detonation from the fired shell rattles Kolat's bones and crashes his teeth together. He can't help but shut his eyes, but when he opens them again and the glare has stopped printing on them he can see it. Kolat puts his hand up against the tank's frame, proud and hurting, just as his machine is.

'It's broken,' he shouts, hoarse.

'Move up!' Hale shouts. 'Into the Sanctum!'

Raine keeps pace alongside the Antari of Grey Company as the Fyregiants push their way through the rubble they've made. Enemy fire has all but ceased in the face of the armoured detachment's fury. Raine's ears ring from the sound of it and when she blinks, the fireburst prints on her eyes. Pride burns in her chest.

Beside her, Yulia Crys laughs loud. 'Now that's a sight,' she shouts.

The smoke and the ashes clear to expose the great dark wounds opened in the face of the spire by the Demolisher shells. They are ragged and toothed by snapped supports. As the Fyregiants grind through, they don't look like giants at all. The scale of the Sanctum and of the wounds they have given it make them look like toys. The darkness swallows the tanks whole. As Raine charges after them through the rubble and thick, choking dust, she feels it do the same to her. The darkness is absolute. Heavy. Ahead of her, the Fyregiants make a wall of armour, their engines echoing balefully. The high-powered stablights mounted on their hulls fade to nothing before they find the Sanctum's opposite wall.

Around Raine, the Antari of Grey Company fan out to secure the entryway. The way the dust clings to their uniforms and their skin, they truly are grey. Shadows in the shadows. The depleted first company of the Kavrone Dragoons take up their positions too. Raine sees the way they move, disciplined and ordered, and she hears Lucia's words as clearly as if she were standing beside her.

It is an honour to serve with them.

'Raine!'

The shout comes from Vander. In his clipped accent, her name is made of edges. The Kavrone's commissar is made of edges too, his face locked in a scowl.

'Capture,' he says. 'Excise. Preserve. Those were our orders.'

Raine looks around at the Antari in position. 'This is a capture,' she says, calmly.

'And preservation?' Vander snaps. 'What of that?'

'The Antari know exactly how to break an opening,' Raine says. 'The Sanctum can more than withstand the damage.'

Vander stares at her.

'If you are proven wrong, then you will answer to Sylar as well as Keene,' Vander says.

Raine holds his gaze. 'I am right,' she says, and she means it in an altogether different way.

'Commissar.'

Raine turns to see Hale standing there. Grey Company's captain is plastered with masonry dust.

'The perimeter is established,' Hale says. 'But there is something you need to see. Both of you.'

Raine nods. She follows Hale to the most forward point of their beachhead with Vander at her side. The Demolisher tank *Stoneking* waits there, growling into the dark. Beside it stands Lydia Zane. Picked out in the diffuse glow from the tank's stablight, she looks like an apparition.

'The Sanctum of Bones,' Zane says, in her kindling-dry voice. 'That is the name, is it not?'

'It is,' Raine says to her.

'It seems they made a truth of it,' Zane says, absently, pointing out into the darkness.

Raine cannot see the things that Zane can. Most of the time, she is grateful for that. In this moment, all it does is run chills through her bones.

'Show me,' Raine says.

Hale takes a flare launcher from his belt and fires it, up and high into the Sanctum. The flare bursts red and falls, throwing enough light to see the heavy ironwork arches and support pillars that bear the weight of the Sanctum above. The hanging devotionals and loops of broken cable. The statues of the Emperor in His guise as healer, hands outstretched.

And to see the bodies. Hundreds of bodies. Twisted, contorted and so very still.

'The Sanctum of Bones,' Zane says again, as a whisper.

Raine's eyes aren't printed with the glare of the Fyregiants' work anymore, or the red glow of the flare in the darkness. When she blinks now, it's those bodies that she sees.

'Our orders are clear,' she says to Hale. 'Our obligation to the dead too.'

'Excise?' Hale says.

Raine narrows her eyes.

'Excise,' she says.

ELEVEN

Those who are lost

Cassia Tyl breaks the neck of the Sighted scout with a swift, quiet movement and catches him as he slumps against her, dead weight. The sawn-off shotgun the scout carries swings loose by the strap. Beside her Jeth does the same with the other Sighted unlucky enough to be patrolling the corridor.

Emergency lighting paints everything red as Tyl and Jeth drag the bodies out of the hallway and into an adjoining chamber they have already cleared. The level was once part of the augmetics facility. Chromed surfaces reflect the red light back at Tyl and there are runnels cut into the tiled floor to collect spilled blood and drain it away. There's a good deal of it blackening the central drain. Bare, wicked instruments are arranged on trays.

Something about it prickles at Tyl's memories. Something just beyond recall, long buried. She reaches out and touches one of the cutting knives and it spins on the tray, flashing in the light.

'Ready?'

Jeth's voice makes her flinch. She turns fast.

'Whoa,' he says.

Tyl shakes her head. 'Sorry,' she says. 'It's this place.'

He nods. 'I know,' he says. 'There's a wickedness here.'

Tyl feels a wry smile cross her face at that.

'We wouldn't be here otherwise,' she says.

Jeth laughs at that. Myre doesn't. She never laughs.

Tyl rounds back out into the hallway with them following her as shadows. In the red light, the Duskhounds could for all the world be inside a dead, desiccated thing. The Sanctum's arches are like black iron bones. The cracked plaster like skin.

The Sighted are like vermin, chewing their way into the carcass.

Tyl moves up to the next corner and stops, before holding up her hand for the others to do the same. The temperature gauge in her helmet's display has dropped sharply, just like outside the spire. Like a winter wind. Frost slicks the floor and walls. Tyl picks up noise. Footsteps. Low voices with Laxian accents.

Four targets.

Tyl listens a second longer.

No. Five.

'Rend and blind,' she says. 'Left. Fifty metres.'

Myre and Jeth send bursts of vox back as acknowledgement, then the three of them round the corner.

Five Sighted stand between the Duskhounds and the edge of the shield they have been tasked with dropping. Tyl sees it behind them, catching the light like smeared glass. The Sighted are dressed in heavy boots and helmets. Padded, layered fatigues and flak armour plates hung with feathers and bits of broken glass on dirty cord. None of it does them much good against hellguns on full charge. Two of the scouts go down, punched through with smoking holes before they can react. The other Sighted aren't quite so slow. Two raise their autorifles and begin to fire as the flash charge that Myre slid along the floor goes off and blinds them. Shots go wild around Tyl as she keeps moving, unflinching. Her visor dips to compensate for the flare of light, which is how she catches the third of the Sighted fleeing towards the shield. He's the alarm.

'We've got a runner,' she says, over the internal vox.

Her hellgun whispers and puts one of the shooters on his back. Jeth takes two hard rounds against his carapace plate in order to put the other against the wall. He hits the Sighted so hard that the scout goes limp and leaves a streak of blood down the tiles as he collapses into a heap. Myre drops the runner with a whisper from her own rifle when he's just metres from the shield's edge, sending him sprawling across the floor. Tyl can hear him breathing still. Cursing too. She steps over the other dead. The scout is trying to drag himself for the shield, but his legs won't obey him because of the hole through him and the blood running into the gaps between the floor tiles. Tyl fires another las-bolt and the scout stops scrabbling with a long, ragged gasp and goes still.

This close to the shield, it's even colder. Tyl realises that flakes of snow are dizzying around her. Where they hit her armour, they melt and bead. Where they hit the shield, they evaporate with a snap of blue light. The cold is strange, but not as strange as the feeling she gets standing near it. Like looking at those knives again. Unsettling. It makes her want to turn and run and she can taste grave dirt, despite her breather's filters, which tells her exactly what kind of shield it is.

'This is witch-work,' she says. 'A psychic shield.'

'Well, shit,' Jeth says.

'There has to be a way through,' Myre says. 'Unless they trapped their scouts on the outside.'

Tyl frowns, and it's not just because of the shield, it's because of what she can hear coming from beyond it.

'What is that?' Jeth asks.

Tyl can tell from the way he says it that he knows as well as she does what it is. From the way his heart rate spikes in her helmet view.

'Singing,' she says, absently. 'That's *Soul of Antar*.'

Raine steps over and around the dead as she leads the Antari deeper into the Sanctum of Bones. Mist scuds, knee-high, moving like a tide. Like one hundred thousand exhalations of breath. Above Raine, the ceiling seems impossibly high, lost to darkness and distance. Even with all that space, Raine still feels the pressure of the Sanctum all around her. The weight of it, like water waiting behind a dam as the stone of it begins to crack.

'We have put them to the chase,' Vander says. 'They know the fury they face, and they hide from it. Cowards.'

He doesn't sound disdainful this time. He sounds disgusted. Vander has his longrifle drawn and braced. The gold decoration on the barrel of it glitters where it catches in stablight beams. His eyes glitter too, like green gemstones.

'I don't think this is hiding,' Raine says. 'I think it is waiting.'

Vander scowls. 'Whatever it is, they should know better. Their deaths are assured. They will answer for their sins.'

The smell of death carries to Raine on the air. Overhead the Sanctum creaks, tectonic.

'As all sinners will,' she says to Lukas Vander.

For an instant, Vander's scowl disappears, replaced with a fleeting uncertainty, but it is just an instant, and then it is gone and his control reasserts itself. He turns away from her, to what is left of his company.

'Vengeance does not wait,' he calls out. 'Pick up the pace!'

Then Vander stalks away through the mist. Raine follows him, keeping her pistol raised and her finger close to the trigger. As she pushes through the mist it parts and shifts enough for her to see the bodies. The bloodied vacancies where their eyes should be and the marks made in their skin.

The rictus grins on their faces.

'This is bad,' Yuri Hale says, beside her. 'All of this death. All of this quiet.'

'They've made a curse of it,' Makar Kayd says. The vox-operator is twitchy, sweeping his lasrifle back and forth. 'Trapped the souls of the dead where He can't find them.'

His words are superstitious, but Raine can't disagree with all of it. The Sanctum really does feel cursed.

Tainted.

'Keep your hearts fierce, and your minds strong,' Raine says, loudly enough so it carries. 'This place is meant to make us fear. To make us falter. We will do neither.'

The vox crackles in her ear.

'Not everyone in here is dead.'

The voice is Wyck's. It is breathless, but Raine cannot hear gunfire, not over the vox, or on the wind.

'Sighted?' Hale asks.

Wyck has that jagged grin on his face. Raine can tell just from the tone of his voice over the vox.

'Not Sighted,' he says. *'Round up those highborn bastards we brought with us, and tell them that we found their missing kin.'*

* * *

Wyck moves up slow with his gun drawn and pointed, his Wyldfolk at his side. Above them, the shielding flickers. It feels like knives running over his bones and makes him see shadows when he blinks. The shield doesn't feel like void. It feels like fear, captured and set to work. But before Wyck and his Wyldfolk even get near the shield, there is the more immediate problem.

In front of Wyck, lights are burning. Flares, mostly. They are all scattered around a deep, still pool that's bigger than some of the minor lakes back in the Vales. The water looks like blood in the red burn of the flare-light. Statues of the God-Emperor watch the water too. The changing light transforms His face, making it wrathful.

Around the pool and between the statues, there are figures kneeling. Must be almost one hundred of them. They are as still as the water. Their blue and white uniforms are recoloured in red by that hissing flare light. Not one of them turns as the Wyldfolk approach them.

'Sarge,' Crys whispers. 'What in the hells is going on here?'

Her voice sounds slow to him. Painfully so. He could swear those stimms he took from Kolat are stronger than what Lye used to give him.

Either that, or what she said was true, and maybe the doses really are killing him.

The way he's feeling right now, that thought makes Wyck want to laugh. He has to take a breath. Count it out, just like he told Haro.

'The Kavrone said that their second company were trapped here,' Wyck mutters. 'But they don't look trapped.'

'They look spellbound,' Crys whispers, with fear in her voice. 'Is it the water?'

'The water's for cleansing,' Awd murmurs. 'Those who came here for healing had to pass through it first.'

Wyck has heard of practices like that. They do something similar on Antar's coast's edge. Take the sick and the injured down to the sea and walk them into the water. The salt and the cold is meant to aid them. Not so in the Vales. The black lakes give nothing.

They only take.

He holds up his hand for the others to stop. The left, with the Wyldfolk's mark on it, so they know he means it.

'Sarge,' Crys whispers.

Wyck ignores her and keeps moving. He's close enough now that he should be able to see the closest of the spellbound soldiers breathing through his rifle's sights. *Should* be able to, but can't. Wyck is close enough now to see that their hands are dark with old blood too.

No good, he thinks.

He's about to vox back when he hears bootsteps at his back.

'What is this?'

The spellbound soldier twitches at the sound of the voice. The movement is almost mechanical. Wyck's nerves fire at the sight of it, and his heart starts to thunder in his ears.

No, he thinks. *Definitely no good.*

The words come from the Kavrone's commissar, Vander. The one with the wicked eyes. He strides through the mist past Wyck with Ellervin, that captain of his that barely looks old enough to be tithed. Raine is there too, and Hale. Wyck has never been thankful to see her before, but compared to the Kavrone's commissar, she's a known threat.

'Wait,' Wyck says to them. 'Don't. I think they're spellbound.'

Raine stops. So does Hale. Vander doesn't. He doesn't

acknowledge Wyck's words at all. He draws his pistol and walks right over to the spellbound soldier.

'On your feet,' Vander says, loud and clear.

And as one, the spellbound soldiers around the pool get to their feet.

'Vander,' Raine says, warningly. She raises her pistol.

The spellbound soldiers turn, with sharp, twitching motions, like wooden dolls puppeted by cord.

Vander snarls. Ellervin murmurs something in his own tongue.

'Mists alive,' Wyck says.

Every damned one of the spellbound soldiers is blinded, just like the Sighted dead. From their bloody hands, Wyck can guess how it was done. As one, the spellbound raise their blades. No rifles. Just knives.

'Stand down,' Vander calls out. 'In the name of the God-Emperor.'

There's a moment like a held breath, where nobody moves and all Wyck can hear is the thunder of his heart, then as one, the spellbound speak with a voice that isn't theirs. One that sounds like old, dry leaves turning. A witch's voice.

'Oh, you poor fools,' they say. *'Your God-Emperor is dead.'*

Wyck's finger tightens on the trigger of his lasrifle, but before even he fires with all of his stimm-given speed, there's a boom from Raine's pistol and the spellbound soldier closest to Vander spills over onto his back. His head spills open too, and that's what does it.

It lights the firefight inside the Sanctum of Bones.

The fight quickly becomes a chaotic rush that reminds Raine of how the scholam's lower levels would flood, back on Gloam. A violent, inescapable rush. The spellbound soldiers might not be armed with rifles, but they refuse to fall until they are forced to. Raine has taken cuts from a dozen blades. Blood runs down her sword-arm and soaks through her tunic at the waist. She grits her teeth and pushes the pain aside.

'Heart-strikes,' Raine shouts. 'Head-shots! Quick, clean kills!'

Raine lets her forward momentum carry into her next upward strike. Evenfall's powered blade separates the soldier's head from his body. It doesn't bleed as it falls. The smell of old death rolls up like fog from the ocean. Raine is already turning and firing her pistol again. Another of the spellbound soldiers falls backwards into the cleansing pool. They don't thrash or scream. They just drop. Around her, the Antari light the Sanctum with las-fire. Through the melee, she sees Vander's Kavrone do the same. They have broken into ordered, disciplined pairs, with one soldier covering the other. Despite the fact that they are firing on their own spellbound kin, they do not hesitate. Vander has had to sling that longrifle of his. There's no room for it in a space like this. Instead he uses his own sword. It is not a duellist's sabre, but a lightweight double-edged blade, built for closeness and speed. He uses it deftly. Clean cuts and parries, opening the space around him as she has around her. Despite all she might think of him, Raine cannot deny Vander's skill as a fighter.

One does not last as a regimental commissar on the bleeding edge of the Bale Stars Crusade without knowing how to kill.

Raine's pistol runs dry and before she can eject the magazine, one of the spellbound soldiers lunges for her. His eye sockets are ragged holes in his face, and his lips are blue and split. Raine backhands him with the weight of the bolt pistol. The blow caves in the soldier's face and sends him reeling. It should be more than enough to kill, but the spellbound soldier still arches and twists and tries to bury his knife in her chest.

The blade never lands.

A thunderclap of force turns the spellbound soldier soft and broken and he collapses.

'We must find the one controlling them,' Raine says. 'We kill the psyker, and the spell is broken.'

Lydia Zane steps over the mess she has made and tilts her head. She breaks another of the spellbound soldiers with just a curl of her slender hands.

'We will not find her so easily,' Zane says. 'This is the work of Cretia Ommatid. She Who Watches. Who counts herself the Sixth of Nine.'

Raine grits her teeth at the mention of one of the Nine. 'All the more reason to find her, and kill her,' she says.

Zane nods her head. Her nose is bleeding slowly down her pale face.

'I hear Ommatid's laughter in the way the spellbound move. She thinks this a game. A fleeting amusement.'

And oh, is the amusement fleeting. The rasping voice of Cretia Ommatid echoes from every one of the spellbound soldiers. *As are so many things, when you see as I do.*

The spellbound soldiers stop fighting as one and collapse.

A new game, I think.

This time, Ommatid's voice doesn't come from the spellbound soldiers. It echoes inside Raine's head, a delighted whisper. Shadows crowd her vision and Raine tastes blood.

Yes, Ommatid hisses. *A new game.*

One by one, every loyal soul succumbs to Ommatid's whispers around Lydia Zane. Their thoughts turn dark like ink spilling across cloth, and the Sanctum rings with screams.

+It is false,+ pulses Zane, as loudly as she can. +Ommatid shows you lies!+

If they hear her words, they do not heed them. Las-fire lights the Sanctum as the two regiments fight back against the nightmares given to them by Ommatid and fight each other in their blindness.

'No,' Zane says. 'Not like this.'

She protects them from themselves and from each other. Zane engages gun safeties. Ejects powercells. Twists knives out of hands. She deflects las-fire and solid shot with flickers of telekine shielding. Every action is an effort, because Zane feels the pressure too. Ommatid's whispers pry and pull at the edges of her mind, setting her birds crying and beating their wings, but Lydia Zane is practised in ignoring whispers. She focuses all of her attention on Cretia Ommatid herself.

And on where she is.

+Oh, no,+ comes the voice. +I am not ready to come out yet, my sweet. I am busy with my games.+

Zane is forced to one knee by the immensity of Ommatid's will. Beside her, Calvar Larat would have been no more than a dim, old lumen light. Ommatid is a witch-fire, scorching and bright and hungry.

+I am so glad to see you here,+ Ommatid pulses. +My lovely, broken thing.+

Blood bursts from Zane's nose and runs from her false, silver eyes.

+I am not yours,+ Zane replies. +My soul belongs to no one save the Emperor.+

There is a pause that Zane knows to be softly amused. She can almost see the quirk of Ommatid's smile, though she has never seen the traitor's face.

+Does it now?+ Ommatid teases. +If that is true, then why

is it that your kin tried to betray you? To break you. You cannot trust them, because they do not understand you. They *will not* understand you.+

Zane does not answer. Instead she starts to murmur her centring words in an effort to force Ommatid out. Zane feels her affected sigh as trailing fingers up her spine.

+I would treat you so well,+ Ommatid says. +But you are blind in more ways than one. Wilfully so. It will be your end. The manticore will come for you again, for he cannot afford to call it off.+

Zane shudders. A long string of drool runs from her clenched teeth.

+The manticore,+ she pulses. +You mean the King of Winter. The one who meant to put me in a casket. The one who sent his soldiers.+

Ommatid's laugh is discordant music. +The King of Winter,+ she pulses. +How quaint.+

+Who is he?+ Zane lashes at her, trying to force the answer.

This time Zane truly does see Ommatid's smile. It blooms in her head like a resolving pict. From shapes to sharpness. Blackened teeth and bloody lips. Glittering, green gemstone eyes.

+Oh, my sweet,+ pulses Cretia Ommatid. +Now that would be telling.+

+Ommatid shows you lies!+

Zane's voice makes Tyl stagger and shake, even though the witch is half a kilometre below in the bottom level of the Sanctum. Tyl sees it do the same to Jeth and to Myre. Their heart rates spike momentarily in her helmet's display.

'Teeth of winter,' Jeth snarls.

But Tyl isn't looking at him. She is looking at the shield, and the figure approaching from the other side. The world beyond the shield is smeared and blurry, so all Tyl can see is a shadow, painted in monochrome. The singing she could hear before grows louder and becomes more distinct too.

That voice.

She knows that voice.

'Tyl,' Jeth says. 'What is this?'

Tyl takes a couple of steps backwards as the shield flickers and distorts. She keeps her gun up and braced and her finger resting on the trigger. Jeth and Myre do the same beside her as a hole opens in the shield like eyelids moving apart, and the figure steps through. He stops his singing and stands there in silence with snow hitting his carapace plate. He has a hellgun drawn on them too. Red crystal lenses watch them from the painted face of his mask. The painted face that Tyl knows as well as she does the one who wears it. As well as the singing voice. Her heart rate more than spikes this time and her finger comes away from the trigger of her rifle. Saying the name hurts like a twisted knife in the chest.

'Rol?'

He lowers his rifle, just a fraction. 'Hey, Cass,' he says.

Tyl feels like she's lost her balance as Rol takes a step forwards. There is a deep fissure in his carapace armour that looks as though it was made by a powered blade. Save for that, though, and the strange pendant that looks like a vial on a chain around his neck, Rol looks the same as the last time Tyl saw him, when he had been laughing, like always.

'Stay where you are,' Jeth snarls at Rol. He hasn't lowered his gun a hair. 'Don't move.'

Rol gives a little shake of his head. 'Good to see you too,' he says.

'Thing is,' Jeth says. 'I'm not sure I *am* seeing you, because you're dead.'

'Clearly not,' Rol says.

'What happened?' Tyl says, breathless. 'We thought we had lost you.'

'I was lost, for a while,' Rol says. He puts his hand to that mark on his carapace plate. 'The Sighted got the drop on me in the forges. They took me to a dark place with the intent to kill me.'

He laughs, that familiar, soft laugh.

'Turns out that I'm harder to kill than they think.'

'How did you get away?' Jeth asks. He still hasn't lowered his gun.

'How do you think?' Rol says.

'I'll tell you what I think. I think that Rol is dead, and that you're a Sighted trick.'

'Aye,' Myre says. 'You're a lie.'

Tyl heard what Zane said, but she can't believe it. Fel told her to trust her eyes and ears, but he also said to trust her heart, and it's that last one that's telling her that Rol is as real as she is.

'I'm not a lie,' Rol says.

'Then how did you come through the shield?' Jeth asks.

'This pendant is a key,' Rol says. 'I took it from some scouts.'

'Sure,' Jeth replies.

'I'm telling you, I'm not a lie,' Rol says, again.

'Prove it,' Tyl replies.

Rol lowers his hellgun and slings it. He holds his hand out, palm down, the way they do when they train. When they take oaths.

'Tyl,' Jeth says. 'Wait.'

Tyl ignores him. She slings her own gun and takes a step towards Rol, then reaches out and puts her hand flat on top of his. Her heart was right. He's as real as she is.

'You're alive,' she manages to say. 'But how?'

Rol leans in closer. Save for that new mark, every pit and scuff on his armour is exactly how it should be.

'Because they changed my fate,' he says.

Then he moves, faster than she's ever known him to. Too fast to stop. Rol grabs her by the arm and drives his combat blade between her ribs, then throws her backwards. Tyl lands hard and rolls. All of the air leaves her lungs. The pain makes her half-blind and her heart thunders.

He cut her. Rol who is her kin. As good as a brother to her. He *cut* her.

Tyl sees everything happen through lidded eyes as she struggles back to her feet with blood soaking through her fatigues and dribbling all over the floor. Rol moves fast, hitting Jeth so hard that his mask shatters and he falls against the wall of the corridor and goes still. Myre fires on Rol, but he knocks her shot wild and puts her up against the wall by her throat.

'*Rol!*' Tyl screams his name this time.

His mask turns to her.

'Caiden,' she says, using his given name in the hope he'll snap out of it. 'Stop.'

He keeps looking at her as he twists his hand and breaks Myre's neck. Tyl feels as if the ground has fallen away. She screams and fires at him as he drops Myre and comes for her. Even half-blind and bleeding, she hits him twice before he closes the gap and knocks her onto her back. Rol's armour is smoking from where the las-fire has grazed him and glanced from it. He disarms her and throws her gun clear first, then her knife, then he puts his knee on her chest so she can't get free.

'Looks as though the captain really did turn his back on you,' Rol says.

'You don't know a thing about it,' Tyl manages to say. 'The captain has done no such thing. Not like you.'

Rol laughs, and it sounds like a bad echo of his voice.

'Sure he did,' he says. 'Because he let his heart tell him what to do and not his head. Because he's compromised by it. That's what Cretia told me.'

'Ommatid,' Tyl says the name like a curse. 'What did that witch do to you?'

'She didn't leave me for dead in the forges, for one thing,' Rol says. 'Not like you.'

He reaches up, unhooks his mask and pulls it free to show his face. Pale and freckled, with eyes so light they might as well be silver. Exactly as she remembers it, like his mask.

Save for the fate-mark cut into his skin, struck through. The day of the forge.

'She changed my fate,' Rol says. 'Gave me a new one to keep me from the After. Saved me from death.'

Tyl shakes her head. Her fingers are going numb, and her vision is blurring. She knows it won't be long before she blacks out.

'You haven't seen it,' Rol says. 'You don't know what it's like to hang over the edge like that. To know it's over and to be offered a way out.'

'And all it costs is your soul,' Tyl snarls.

Rol sighs. 'You get nothing without giving something in trade,' he says. 'You know that.'

'Ommatid is using you,' she says. 'You are nothing but a weapon.'

'And you?' Rol says. 'What do you think that winged eagle you wear means? We are all just weapons to be used. At least I know what I am being used for.'

'Well, I'd rather be used in the name of light than of darkness,' Tyl says.

Rol looks wounded then, as if he were hoping for a different answer.

'She said you'd say that too,' he says, with a sigh. He takes his hellgun from his belt and points it at her face. 'Maybe you'll change your mind when you see it. When you're hanging over the edge like I was.'

Tyl hears the pistol whine as it builds charge. That's when she moves with all of the energy she has left and all of the speed she can muster. She pulls his combat blade out from between her ribs and buries it in his neck. Rol fires the pistol reflexively and misses her by a handspan. Then he slumps sideways, choking.

'There's no changing fate. No escaping death.' Tyl drags herself into a sitting position against the cold wall of the corridor. 'A Duskhound should know that.'

He gasps and whines, blood spreading across the floor. It looks black.

'*Cass*,' he says to her.

Then his eyes go glassy and his limbs go still and Tyl sees a new fate-mark take shape in the blood on his face. It matches perfectly to the time-code in her mask's display. Right down to the second. Tyl feels a tear slide from the corner of her eye under her mask. She goes to the pouch on her belt. Her hands shake as she opens it and takes out the auto-cauteriser and burns the knife wound closed. She lets her head rest against the wall and looks down the corridor at the shield.

The shield they have been tasked with dropping.

Then Cassia Tyl takes a long, slow breath, drags herself to her feet and goes to fetch her gun.

* * *

Severina Raine finds herself alone in a corridor hewn from old stone. There is a gentle thrum carrying through the walls and floor. Rhythmic, like a heartbeat. A push and pull.

The ocean.

The wind howls around her, carrying flakes of snow that sting her skin and melt against her greatcoat. Torches snarl in sconces, flickering in the wind. Raine moves up with her pistol raised, her boots echoing on the flagstones of the floor. On the wall to her right, there are letters painted on the wall in red.

Honour. Duty. Faith.

Raine lowers her pistol slowly and holsters it. She reaches out with one of her gloved hands and puts her fingers to the word 'faith'.

'Do you have it?'

The words echo strangely, as if spoken by two voices. Raine looks around to see a man standing there, dressed in white, with a red sash slung across his chest. His medals glitter in the firelight and his eyes glitter too. Behind him stand four Lions of Bale. Their faces are hidden by dark cloth masks.

Executioner's masks.

'Faith, Severina,' says Lord-General Militant Alar Serek. 'Do you have it?'

Raine drops her hand away from the letters. She salutes him without thought, an instinctual reaction.

'Yes, lord,' she says. 'My faith is my shield, and my sword.'

He shakes his head. 'If that is true, then why are you carrying so many doubts?'

Raine blinks. 'Doubts?' she says.

Serek takes a few steps towards her.

'About the crusade,' he says. 'About those who serve alongside you. About Mardan Tula's death.'

He narrows his eyes. They look different to Raine, not as blue as she remembers them to be.

'Doubts about yourself,' Serek says.

Raine curls her fists. 'My doubts about the crusade are founded, lord,' she says. 'The Kavrone. Sylar. They killed Tula to conceal their own actions. They are moving against you.'

'Are they?' he asks her. 'Or are you seeing traitors in every corner because you *want* to see them. Because you want to believe that your sister was incapable of breaking faith.'

Raine shakes her head. 'No,' she says.

'Is it because you want to believe yourself infallible?' Serek asks her. 'Unbreakable?'

His words feel like cuts. Like gunshot wounds. She cannot stand them, nor the idea that she has disappointed this man that she so admires.

'No,' she says, through her teeth.

'You took a soul off the line today, against orders and without seeking permission,' Serek says. 'You are acting against High Command, because of your doubts. You are acting against the crusade. Tell me, Severina Raine, what is the name we give to those who act against the crusade?'

Raine tries to speak, but the words escape her.

'The word is traitor,' Serek says.

His voice distorts and breaks up like a bad vox-signal, and those eyes of his are definitely not blue. They are green, and faceted like gemstones.

On either side of Raine, other figures take their places against the wall. To her right, Mardan Tula, with ligature bruises marking his neck. Andren Fel, bruised and bleeding, his grey eyes flat as if he is broken.

'No,' Raine says.

To her left, Raine sees Lucia. Always Lucia. Looking at her

sister is like looking in a mirror. Her warm brown skin. Dark eyes. Stark white scars.

The blood, blooming on her tunic from the firing squad that shot her.

'Say it,' Serek says. 'Admit what you have done. What you are.'

Raine has her back against the wall. Against the word 'faith'. She puts one hand to the cold stone and feels the thrum of the ocean through it. Raine looks at Serek and at the Lions of Bale with their guns held across their chests and she grits her teeth, tasting blood and cold air and smoke from torches.

'No,' she says. 'Because I know the truth of my heart. I know the strength of my faith. I am no traitor.'

Raine raises her hands in front of her chest and makes the sign of the aquila.

'And I know that this is a lie,' she snarls. 'And I will not be broken by it.'

The world flickers, just like the torch light. Like a corrupted pict-capture. Serek smiles at her, and it looks in no way as it should.

'Yes, you will,' he says, and his voice echoes and doubles. 'Everyone can be broken.'

Serek holds up his hand and the Lions raise their guns as one, but they do not fire on her. The Lions fire on Tula first and he dies all over again, slumping down against the wall, leaving a thick trail of blood down the word 'Honour'.

'I will not break,' Raine shouts again.

Then the Lions point their guns at Fel and fire. Raine cannot help but blink reflexively at the *crack* of las-fire, nor can she help the way her heart aches as Fel dies too with his blood spattered across the word 'Duty' and across her face and throat. Raine blinks again.

'I. Will. Not. Break.'

The words burn on the way out as the Lions turn to point their guns at Lucia.

'I was wrong,' Lucia says.

Her voice doesn't echo or distort. It sounds exactly as Raine remembers it from the last time they spoke.

'I thought that I could not be broken,' she says. 'That I could not fail, and neither could you.'

She looks at Raine with tears in her dark eyes and puts out her hand. Her fingertips brush the sleeve of Raine's greatcoat.

'I was wrong,' she says again.

And the Lions fire, and Lucia falls, and just like the first time it leaves Raine with a vacancy in her soul. A part of her taken. Extinguished. Raine feels her whole body start to tremor, though she knows that this is a lie. She drags her eyes from Lucia and looks back at Serek.

'I will not break,' she says, her voice barely a whisper.

The Lions turn their guns on her now and Serek shakes his head.

'It is over,' he says, and he sounds disappointed.

'Service is my duty,' Raine says, as the Lions take aim. 'Duty is an honour.'

She snarls the words through her teeth and through the blood in her mouth.

'The greatest honour is to know true faith,' she says, as they open fire.

Daven Wyck staggers and falls against something. The bole of a tree, rimed with frost. He blinks hard. Snorts blood back into his nose. Tastes it in the back of his throat.

'What?' he mumbles.

His own voice echoes back at him from between the other

trees. *What, what, what,* until it sounds like a crowd of accusers. Wyck raises his lasrifle and braces it against his shoulder, pointing it into the mist and the forest until the word stops echoing back at him. Everything is pin-sharp from the stimms. Bright with shadow and light. He smells damp earth and stagnant water and hears the rustle of leaves. Wyck's heart hammers and it's not just because of the dose. It's because he knows exactly where he is.

But he can't think how he got here.

'No good,' Wyck says to the forest.

That echoes back at him too. *No good, no good, no good.*

Wyck pushes himself away from the tree, leaving a bloody handprint on the bark.

Just like the last time he was here.

The echo of his voice fades away to be replaced with another sound. Another echo, only this one is mournful and hollow and it makes his heart want to stop in his chest.

Howling.

He hears howling.

Wyck starts running without looking back. He can't look back because he knows what he'll see. Vicious shapes trailing smoke. Coalfire eyes and snarling maws.

Duskhounds, come to take the soul that they are owed.

The howling follows at his heels as Wyck throws himself through the trees, snagging on branches that reach like claws, and roots that try to trip him. He feels the heat of the hounds at his back. The howling is deafeningly close.

Wyck breaks the treeline and sees it. The lake, stretching out like a black mirror. He doesn't stop running until he's in the water to his waist. It is freezing cold.

Only then does he look back.

But the shoreline is empty. He can't hear the howling

anymore. Just the lapping of water and the gentle knocking together of stones pushed by the lake's edges. The wind pulls at his fatigues and ruffles his hair.

They are gone. He outran the hounds.

Wyck starts to laugh so hard that it hurts and makes his eyes run.

'That's right!' he shouts at the shoreline. 'Not this time!'

That feeling fades along with the laughter as something pushes against him in the water. It bobs to the surface with a gasp of old air. A body, floating face down, wearing black carapace armour and stuck through all of the soft joints. Wyck takes a step back, and the lakebed gives under his boot, miring him. He bumps against another body. The blank, this time. Blood blossoms from the knife wound in the soulless man's chest, turning the water even more black. More bodies swell and rise and float to the surface. No Sighted. No cultists or fanatics or curselings.

Just the others.

Wyck backs up until the water is up to his chest. It presses on him and makes it hard to breathe. Another body emerges from the blackness. Pale like a moonstone from a long time spent at the bottom of the lake. Grey eyes, wide with horror. Another knife wound, but no blood from one so old.

Raf.

What have you done, Dav?

His old friend's words are the push of the water and the clatter of stones. They are the thunder of Wyck's heart.

'Shut up,' Wyck shouts, but his voice doesn't echo now. The only echo is Raf.

What have you done? What have you done? What have you done?

The water rises and presses and Wyck starts thrashing to

get clear of the grip of it and the echo of his dead friend's voice, but he can't see the shoreline now. Can't see anything but Raf's grey eyes, wide with horror. He fires his rifle until the cell empties. Then a pair of blue-white hands burst from the lake's surface and wrap themselves around him, pulling him under.

Lydia Zane cannot keep Ommatid out, certainly not of her kinfolk's minds, but there is something that she can do. She bows her head and concentrates all of her strength. By categorisation, her primary abilities are telekinetic. Like her regiment, she is made for breaking. Telepathy is secondary, it is harder for her to use and to control. It costs her even more than her other gifts.

But she has little choice.

+You want to play games?+ she pulses to Ommatid. +Then let us play.+

Zane squeezes her eyes shut and feels the world wash away until she cannot smell the burn of las-fire or the cold stink of the dead. Frost patterns over her skin and the old wounds open up across her body. Her blood soaks sluggish into her robes.

She opens her eyes again to a vast star-scape. The stars are aligned as you would see them from the coast's edge on Antar, in the spring when the sky is clearest. The planet turns slowly below her, dressed in green and grey, just like those who call it home. Zane sets her feet down on nothing at all. Her birds circle her lazily.

A figure stands opposite her in the blackness, haloed by stars. She wears a robe made of hundreds of gossamer-thin layers. Hundreds of colours, too, if such a thing is possible. The woman is thin too. Almost semi-transparent, just like her robes. Her feet are bare and bloodied and her eyes are two green gemstones set into a pale, drawn face. Her hands are curled like claws, with jagged, broken fingernails.

Zane starts to tremble at the sight of her, because looking at Cretia Ommatid is like looking into a broken mirror.

'Oh, well isn't this a delight?' Ommatid says, with a wide, pointed grin. 'You spoil me, my sweet.'

With effort, Zane takes a step towards Ommatid, trailing flakes of frost. She draws her dagger, spun from Antari darkwood.

'Your world is wild,' Ommatid says, looking down at Antar as it turns. 'Quite beautiful, really.' Her crystal eyes snap up to meet Zane's. 'Would you like to guess the number of fates in which I have seen it burn?' she rasps. 'I can give you a hint if you'd like. It is more than the number of times that I have seen you win this fight.'

Zane shakes her head. 'I know fate,' she says. 'As do all from Antar. You are not its master.'

Ommatid laughs, and it echoes from every star.

'No,' she says. 'I am not its master, but I am favoured by it. I see many paths. Many choices. I see the shadows that cling to the heart of your precious crusade.'

Zane tightens her grip on her spun wooden dagger. Ommatid tilts her head.

'You would so love to know, wouldn't you?' she says. 'Which faces are just masks. Whose hearts have turned black. How they were turned.'

Ommatid takes a step forward. They are almost within arm's reach of one another now. Zane's birds cry over and over. Warning calls. The bindings inside Zane's head ache and the cables embedded in her scalp click and hum.

'Your mistake is believing that souls can be turned at all,'

Ommatid says. 'Souls cannot be forced or fooled. They *choose*. Out of ambition, or greed. Fear or fury. The path to truth is written into every mortal soul. It is only in following it that we become free.'

'Free,' Zane says, softly.

The spun blade shakes in her hand. Her mouth is thick with drool.

'Free,' Ommatid says. 'And you could be too, my sweet. You just have to choose.'

Free, free, free, echoes the first of Zane's birds.

'Look within yourself,' Ommatid whispers. For a moment, her voice is that of Zane's mother, from the day beneath the singing tree, long ago. 'See the path. See the truth.'

Zane takes a ragged breath and closes her eyes.

'I see it,' she murmurs. 'The truth.'

'And your choice?' Ommatid asks in her mother's voice.

Zane's eyes snap open and she plunges her wooden knife into Ommatid's chest. No hesitation. A deep cut. Just like Wyck told her. Zane pulls the blade free again and Ommatid's blood scatters, freezing as it leaves her body to make new stars in Antar's night sky.

Fall, says Zane's other bird.

'I agree,' says Zane, to the bird.

And she grabs Ommatid by the shoulders as the nothing beneath their feet falls away and the two of them tumble down, towards the turning face of Antar below.

Severina Raine snaps awake on her knees in the Sanctum of Bones with Ommatid's lie echoing after her. Her chest burns from the Lions' gunshots and from having what really matters twisted against her. It would be so easy to give in, in that moment. To allow the pain to break her.

But Severina Raine is made to endure pain. She is made never to give in. So she grits her teeth and gets back on her feet though her limbs ache and her mind is reeling. She wipes blood from her nose onto the back of her glove.

Raine sees Vander nearby. He has his sword drawn, in guard. She can see the way he shakes as the dream peels away. Raine shouts his name, but he remains still, save for that shaking. When she approaches him, he is murmuring something in his sharp-edged accent.

'I meant to stop it,' he is saying, over and over. 'I can still stop it.'

Raine does not trust Vander. She does not know if he is a part of Sylar's plan, or just oblivious to it, but she knows that here and now, she needs him. Until she is sure, she cannot condemn him, as much as she loathes him.

'Vander!' she shouts.

This time, he turns to look at her, but his green eyes are dull and distant. He raises his sword drunkenly, as if to strike her.

And for the second time in as many days, Raine curls her fist and punches him. The blow knocks Vander reeling and makes him stop his murmuring. He shakes his head, hard, and lowers his sword.

'Ommatid did this,' he snarls. 'I will kill her.'

'For once, something we agree on,' Raine says.

This time, when Vander looks at her, his eyes are clear and furious. 'You will never lay your hands on me again,' he says. 'Is that clear?'

Raine ignores him. She won't make a promise that she knows she cannot keep.

'We must rally those left standing and make Ommatid pay for her games,' Raine says. 'Look around you. We are moments away from broken.'

Vander does as she says. Sees what she does. That the Antari and the Kavrone are bloodied and in disarray. Some are dead.

'You are right,' he says, and it sounds as though it pains him.

The two of them draw their bolt pistols and fire them into the air. The twin booms echo hard and loud into the shadows, reverberating off the Sanctum's distant walls.

'Enough!' Raine yells.

And they turn to look at her. Beside her, Vander raises his sword.

'The Emperor watches,' he shouts. 'Will you be found wanting?'

The answer comes as a rolling 'no', from both regiments. Raine sees the Antari helping one another to their feet. Those who can be helped. She sees Hale and Odi and Koy, all bloodied and limping, but living. The Kavrone do the same. With their uniforms tarnished and blood-spattered, they don't look all that different to the Antari.

'Courage in His sight,' Vander shouts. 'Always!'

Those words. The ones she heard from Lucia, once. More of her sister's words echo for Raine, then. Words from the dream.

I was wrong.

And Raine denies them, because she thinks that she is the one who was wrong about Lucia all this time, and she is determined to prove it.

'We will not be broken,' Raine cries. 'Not today. Not ever!'

The Antari cheer and they rally and Raine's own words ring in her ears. More words from the dream.

I will not break.

Daven Wyck comes to with lungs full of water and hands dragging him clear of the lake onto the shore. He thrashes free, coughing and heaving and gasping for air, then rolls to his feet and goes for the one who was dragging him like that. The one who tried to drown him.

'Dav!'

The voice stops him short before he can bury his knife in the chest of the figure. The figure holding their hands up and trying to get back from him.

Awd's voice. Awd's hands, with the Wyldfolk's mark on his palm.

Wyck lowers the knife. It's an effort to do it.

'What?' he says. 'What happened?'

'You wouldn't stop,' Awd says. 'So I put you under to see if it would wake you.'

The realisation happens slowly, like everything else around him. This isn't the Vales. There's no black lake. No shore. The floor underfoot is blood-slick tile. The water at his back is the cleansing pool. He's in the Sanctum of Bones with his kin.

'It was a damned witch-dream,' he says.

Awd nods. That's when Wyck notices the las burns dappling Awd's flak armour. One or two have gone through. He glances down at his rifle. At the powercell, blinking on red. Empty.

'I shot you,' Wyck says.

Awd nods. 'Not badly,' he says. 'Whatever you saw sent you mad. Too mad to land any kill-shots.'

'Sorry,' Wyck says.

The word surprises him. It clearly surprises Awd too.

'I don't think I've heard that word out of your mouth once,' Awd says. 'Not in all the time I've known you.'

Wyck shrugs like it doesn't matter. Like he doesn't care. 'Don't get used to it,' he says. 'Find the others. We need to regroup and get back in the fight. Find that witch and kill her.'

Awd puts his hand out to stop him before he can pass by. 'You kept saying something,' he says. 'When the dream had you. Something about bodies in the water.'

Wyck goes cold, as if he's back in that black lake.

'It was a witch-dream,' he says. 'That's all.'

'You swear that's all it is?' Awd asks.

Of all the Wyldfolk, Wyck has known Awd the longest. Only Crys comes near in terms of time and blood spent. They both owe each other, though Wyck has always been careful to keep the balance in his favour. Awd is the closest thing he's got left to a friend.

Which is why he won't tell him the truth of it.

Wyck nods and holds up his hand. The one with the Wyldfolk's mark on it.

'I swear,' he says. 'On blood spent.'

There's a flicker in Awd's eyes. One that Wyck can't quite recognise.

'Alright,' he says.

Then he turns away to go and find the others.

Cassia Tyl holds Rol's pendant in an outstretched hand, as far from her body as she can. As far from her heart. She can still feel the chill coming from it, though the hallway is already cold with the snow that's still falling.

'Are you sure we should use it?' Jeth asks.

He has had to take off his Duskhounds mask because Rol shattered the eye lenses and split the plasteel when he hit him. Jeth's dark skin is a patchwork of bruises, and his nose is rebroken, but at least he's still alive.

Unlike Myre.

'We don't have a choice,' she says to Jeth. 'We need to get inside the shield and complete the mission.'

Jeth frowns, but he doesn't argue.

Tyl takes a step forwards. As the vial swings close, the shield starts to shimmer and part and a hole opens in the face of it. The closer Tyl gets the more it peels apart until there's room for her to step through and let Jeth pass after her. The instant he's through, she wants to drop the pendant and shatter it under her boot, but she can't, because they might yet need it. Tyl puts the thing in a pouch at her belt, with Jeth frowning at her all the while.

'Once the shields are down, we destroy it,' he says.

Tyl nods, then she glances back to where Myre is slumped against the wall. Rol is lying not far from her. All of that blood has turned thick in the cold.

'Blow the charges,' Tyl says.

Jeth hits the command key on the bracer at his wrist and the hallway blooms with light. The roar is dampened by the shield. Chunks of tile and glass and armour are deflected by it with smears of colour. Myre and Rol. Both gone now. Truly gone.

'That will bring the Sighted running,' Jeth says. 'We should move.'

Tyl looks for a second longer as the smoke rolls against the psychic shield, questing and pressing. Through it, she sees fire and blackened iron. Broken glass and debris.

But no remains.

'Let's finish this,' she says, turning away.

'Commissar.'

Both Raine and Vander turn at the voice. Yuri Hale approaches them through the dead with his command squad in tow. The captain is badly bruised, and his flak armour has been blackened in places by las-fire. Makar Kayd is bleeding from a deep head wound. He is hefting both his vox-set and the company standard. Behind him, Lye and Rath have their rifles slung so that they can carry a limp, shaking figure between them.

Lydia Zane.

When they get close enough, they lower her to the ground. Both of them unconsciously wipe their hands clean on their fatigues. Zane is murmuring and shaking. Her false eyes remain firmly closed.

'She hasn't stopped,' Hale says. 'Not since the dreams faded.'

Raine takes a couple of steps towards Zane. She draws her pistol on the psyker. Vander steps up too, though Zane isn't his to watch or judge. The Antari look on, wary.

'She is broken,' Vander says. 'Dangerous.'

Raine listens to Zane murmur and picks up her slurred words.

'She is the reason we are no longer dreaming,' Raine says, lowering her pistol. 'She is keeping Ommatid out. Drawing her eyes.'

'I heard her,' Hale says. 'I remember it now. In the dream I heard her.'

'Ommatid shows you lies,' Lye says, with a nod. 'That's what she said.'

Raine remembers it too, though she couldn't recognise it at the time. Zane's voice carrying in the roar of the ocean and the tremor in the cold stone at her back.

'She is still dangerous,' Vander says.

Raine puts herself between Zane and Vander. She can feel the eyes of the Antari on her. Rare are the occasions that she feels firmly on the same side as her regiment. Rare are the occasions she can feel their want to cheer for her, even over the life of a witch.

'She is dangerous, you are right,' Raine says. 'To our enemies. To Ommatid.'

She holds his eyes.

'I am the regimental commissar assigned to the Antari Rifles,' she says. 'Which means that Lydia Zane is mine to judge. And my choice is to spare her life.'

Vander narrows his eyes. 'So be it,' he says. 'Another decision for which you will answer.'

'Gladly,' Raine says.

Tyl knows when they are close to the source of the shield. Not just by the thick, serpent's coils of cabling that run along the walls and ceiling, or the elevated presence of the Sighted. It's the sense of unease. The physical sensation like a blade running down her back, catching the knots of her spine. The way the walls seem to bend and bleed. To narrow and close. The way that she keeps catching shadows out of the corners of her eyes.

And then there's the whispering.

She watches. All is what she watches. She sees. All is what she sees. She knows. All is what she knows.

'This place,' Jeth says. 'We should have burned the lot to the ground.'

He is bloodied and breathing hard, leaning against the wall of the corridor. The two of them have passed through a maze of connecting rooms and corridors to get to the spire's centre. Tyl has seen antechambers still set up for surgeries, and mortuary pits where the bones of the dead are boiled and cleansed, ready to be made into something new. Those that could not be used have been set into the walls of every corridor and every room, to watch and grin until they turn to dust with age.

'I'm still considering it,' Tyl replies.

Jeth smiles. It looks like it hurts.

'There are mounted guns on the door,' Tyl says.

She is using her combat blade as a mirror to see around the corner into the next corridor, where the overhead cables lead. Even in the reflection, the shape of the space keeps changing.

'It is manned and fortified, and there are two scouts moving up too. I don't think they want us around.'

Jeth snorts. 'Could say the same for them,' he says. 'Pattern?'

'Eleventh hour,' she says.

'Sounds about right,' Jeth says.

He pushes away from the wall and stands up straight. That looks like it hurts too. Jeth takes a krak charge from his belt. Tyl holds up her hand, open, and waits for the right moment. Then she closes her hand in a snap movement, and the two of them round the corner. Tyl goes in front and puts two las-bolts in each of the scouts. Jeth lands that krak charge at the far end of the corridor, where the mag-component snaps it to the doors behind the Sighted and their mounted guns. Tyl hears the guns spin up and the Sighted shouting in Laxian, then the grenade goes off with a colossal *boom*. Krak is meant for armour breaking. It'll go through a Chimera's hull if you attach it in the right place. It blows the doors inwards and twists the guns into ruin along with their gunners, but the rest of the Sighted have already cleared the barricades and are running in a headlong charge. Tyl sees six. Or maybe it's eight. The corridor shrinks and wavers around her. Tyl fires on the closest, a woman with blazing green bionic eyes and curved blades in the place of her hands. She disappears when the las-bolt hits her, but not because she's dead.

It's because she was never there. Just a trick, like Zane said.

'Ghosts,' Tyl shouts, backing up.

Tyl goes side by side with Jeth so that the Sighted can't split them up. They choose their targets. Some of them bleed.

Some of them don't. One of the Sighted grabs onto Tyl's arm. He feels real enough, as does his blood when she opens up his throat with her combat blade. Some of it hits the ceiling. As the Sighted sinks to the ground, more take his place. Tyl's vision fills with rolling black eyes and wide-grin mouths. She fights like a cornered animal. It's not training anymore. It's instinct.

Then Tyl thinks of the pendant. It breached the shield.

The *psychic shield*.

She gets her fingers around the pendant and pulls it free from the pouch at her belt. It is burningly, agonisingly cold. Despair washes over her. The Sighted recoil from it as one, then Tyl drops the vial and breaks it under her boot. There's an unholy scream that runs fingers along all of her nerves, and then the ghosts vanish, leaving the true Sighted behind.

Two of them.

Tyl puts a las-bolt in one and Jeth breaks the other's neck with a twist of his hands, then they both stand there a moment, breathing raggedly.

'Guess that thing did come in useful,' Jeth says, then spits a clot of blood onto the floor.

Tyl looks to the door, blown open by the charges. The whispers echo loudly from inside as she moves down the corridor towards it. The walls around her expand and contract like lungs. Tyl picks her way over the barricades and the twisted guns and the Sighted dead, and steps through the jagged remains of the doorway into the chamber beyond.

It is a circular space that might have once been an observation chamber for procedures undertaken by the Sanctum's healers. Cables hang in loops from the ceiling and snake down the stairs to the centre where they trail up and connect to a set of nine metal thrones. Thrones with witches fused into them. Every one of them has been messily blinded. Tyl can't tell if it was done to them, or if they did it with their own hands.

'Emperor's mercy,' Jeth says, from beside her.

Tyl walks down the stairs towards the thrones. Her breath mists the air and shadows coil around her legs. Dread coils around her heart in turn. The whispers are screams now, issuing from the mouths of every one of those witches. She approaches the closest of them with her rifle up and ready. It is a woman, this one. Thin as springtime ice. Her teeth are blunted, broken stubs from where she has clattered them together as the shield draws her power. There are tear trails painted through the blood on her face from her empty eyes. She is murmuring something different now. Something more urgent.

'Protect the engines. Protect the engines. Protect the engines.'

Lightning arcs across the witch's scalp and she raises her empty eyes and looks right at Tyl.

'Grant their fates,' the witch screams. *'Give them death!'*

Pressure squeezes behind Tyl's eyes and bursts light across her vision.

'Execute,' she slurs.

And the two of them open fire. They keep firing until the screaming stops and the mist retreats and everything finally falls silent. The pressure eases and Tyl's vision stops dazzling. She activates her vox-link.

'Duskhounds checking in,' Tyl manages to say. 'Shield is disabled. The way is open.'

TWELVE

Alpha-Grade

The building that houses the Departmento Munitorum records on Laxus Secundus is an imposing hulk of marble and leaded glass. Like the city district around it, it has been remade for war. The windows are shuttered and shielded. The lip of the roof is looped with razor wire. Gun-nests have been built on the stairs that lead up to the doors. The approach is shattered rockcrete and wet mud and a high, barbed fence runs around the perimeter. A security checkpoint built from flakboard and corrugated plasteel stands at the gated entrance. As Fel approaches, one of the guards stationed inside it comes out to meet him. The guard carries a cut-down lasrifle with a wicked bayonet. He is wearing a raincloak with a hood, but the rest of his gear is soaked from standing out in the constant Laxian storm. His hands are painfully red from the cold, and going by the set of his shoulders and the frown on his face, he's more than a little pissed off about it.

'Hold there,' the guard says. 'This is a secure area.'

His accent is familiar from that night at the landing fields. It's a giveaway that the man is Kavrone, though he wears no colours or pins. It's what Fel might have called a coincidence, if he were fool enough to believe in such things.

'Name,' the Kavrone says, flatly.

'Andren Fel. Eleventh Antari Rifles.'

The guard's frown deepens. 'Thought your lot were assaulting the city today,' he says.

Fel could say the same about the Kavrone, but he doesn't. That won't do him any favours.

'Believe me, I wish that I was,' he says. 'But instead I'm standing here, in this damned endless rain.'

The guard laughs and there's a small change in his bearing.

'I hear you,' he says. 'What's your business?'

'There's a requisitions adept named Lori Ghael stationed here,' Fel says. 'I need to speak with her.'

It's only half a lie. There's that outstanding missive from Ghael and the Departmento about troop allocation for the Duskhounds. The one he has been putting off.

'You got a script?' the guard asks.

Fel nods. He takes out the order script and shows it. It's watermarked with the Departmento seal. The guard takes it in one of his weather-raw hands and reads it over.

'Can't be too careful,' he says, without looking up from the script. 'There have been security breaches across the front. Behind the lines, if you can believe it.'

'Is that so?' Fel asks him, without missing a beat.

The guard nods. He rolls up the script and hands it back. 'From what I hear everywhere under this sky is dangerous,' the Kavrone says.

Fel puts the script back in his pocket, and laughs. 'You'd think it was a warzone,' he says.

That makes the Kavrone laugh for a second time.

'I'll vox up,' the guard says. 'She'll have to come down and verify in person. Security, you understand.'

He puts his fingers to the vox-bead in his ear and passes the message up.

'Oh, you'll need to leave that pistol of yours, of course,' he says, when he's done.

Fel unhooks the holster for his pistol and hands it over. He expected to have to do it, but it sits poorly with him nonetheless.

'Security,' Fel says back to the guard. 'I understand.'

Ghael doesn't take long to come down to the gate. Like before, she is wearing fatigues and boots. Today she also has a heavy rain jacket and a patterned scarf wound tight around her neck. Just like before, though, the expression on her face is one of faint amusement.

'Captain Fel,' she says, with a tilt of her head. 'I wasn't expecting you.'

Fel nods. 'Things have escalated,' he says. 'It's a poor time to be undermanned.'

Ghael huffs a breath into the cold air and narrows her eyes, with that half-smile of hers still in place. Fel can see the question – of why he's here, and not on the line – plainly in her face, but she doesn't ask it. It's a risk, that moment. Ghael could easily blow the whole thing, but Fel has a feeling she won't because then she won't get to ask her question.

'He's alright,' Ghael says to the guard. 'Verified.'

The guard shrugs his shoulders and buzzes the gate. It unlocks and swings open and Fel goes inside. It closes and locks again behind him. Ghael turns away and back towards the complex. The guns on the nests track them as they walk up the marble steps.

'Autocannon mounts,' Fel says. 'They aren't messing around.'

Ghael snorts a laugh. 'It's not very welcoming, I'll grant you that. Security has been increased over the last couple of days. More guards. New guards.'

They pass into the complex building proper. The entry hall is a domed structure with a high roof. The floor is marble, and slick with rainwater. Adepts hurry to and fro with sheaves of orders and requisitions. Their voices become an anonymous, echoing muddle of languages. Watching them go are yet more guards, with those same cut-down model lasguns.

'It's strange,' Ghael says, as she leads Fel across the entry hall, 'just how many of those new guards are Kavrone.'

Those last words come from Ghael in Antari. Her accent is coast's edge, like Tyl's. Like Rol's was. The choice to use their homeworld's tongue makes Fel realise that just like the last time they spoke, Lori Ghael knows more than those around her.

'Strange,' Fel says, in Antari too. 'That's one word for it.'

Ghael's office is a room deep inside the labyrinthine structure of the Departmento complex. It isn't a small room, but it is made to feel as though it is by all of the records and paperwork stacked on every surface. There are charts pinned to the walls. Troop listings. Requisition orders. Records of the dead, long enough to reach down and bunch where they hit the floor. Fel finds a space in the middle of it all that's big enough to put his feet in.

Ghael steps over and around her paperwork to her desk. On it is a dust-caked cogitator with a speaker mount. She depresses one of the chunky trigger-keys and the speaker hisses, then music starts. The strum of strings and echoing drums. Fel recognises it immediately as music from home.

It puts him right back on the edge of the Northwilds' black forests.

'They let me play it because it helps me concentrate,' Ghael says. 'Makes me more efficient.'

Ghael cranks a dial and the volume increases, then she rounds her desk and perches on the edge of it with her arms folded. She is tapping her ink-blackened fingers against her arm.

'You should be in the Sanctum with your hounds,' she says. 'But you're not. I know for damned sure that it's naught to do with that order script I sent you, so what is it?'

Fel watches her carefully. There's a tension in her that he's seen before in others.

Like something hunted.

'What do you think it is?' he asks her.

Ghael stops her tapping, but only to pick up a handful of papers from her desk. She riffles through them quickly. More quickly than is natural.

'I couldn't forget it,' she says. 'What you said that night about the guns. Steadfast-made. What Krall and Brannt said too, about the Strixians. He was wrong, I thought, but I wasn't sure. I don't like to be unsure.'

She puts the papers down and leans over to pick up another handful.

'So I went looking,' she says. 'And I found something.'

Fel's hand drifts to where he'd usually wear his pistol, just by instinct.

'What?' he asks her.

'Krall was right about us sending guns to the Strixian Ninety-Ninth, and I was right about them being dead. And now the Strixians are not the only ones.'

She holds out a crumpled piece of paper. It's a transcription, and it must have been one she made herself, because it's in Antari. The script is spiked and cramped.

'Krall and Brannt,' Fel says, scanning the page. 'When did this happen?'

'A promethium container went up at their new work assignment the day after the fight club,' Ghael says. 'After one of the Kavrone landing sites was breached.'

'One of the landing sites?' Fel makes it sound like a question.

'Begging your pardon, captain,' Ghael says. 'But don't give me that shit.'

Fel looks up at her. She is more pale than usual, and back to tapping her fingers. She nods at the paper in his hand.

'Whatever it is you are hunting, it doesn't want to be found,' she says. 'It'll kill to stay hidden.'

Fel doesn't break eye contact with her. The song playing through the speaker is slow and mournful. One for winter.

'All the more reason to keep hunting,' he says.

'Then you'll be killed too,' Ghael says, flatly. 'Or worse, dishonoured.'

He knows that she's right, just as he knows what his answer is.

'It would be a small price to pay for the sake of the crusade,' Fel says. 'For the regiment.'

For Raine, he thinks.

Ghael's human eye narrows and the lenses of her augmetic eye spin to mimic it.

'It wasn't just those records I pulled,' she says. 'I found everything that I could about you, too, Andren Fel.'

That feels like exposure. Like an intrusion. Just like her asking him to tell the Duskhounds' story to those from outside.

'I know that you were born in the Northwilds,' she says.

'Orphaned at seven years old. That you proved an exceptional candidate during training at the Schola Antari.'

She pauses and clears her throat, as if her words are sticking.

'I know what they did to you at that place,' she says. 'That they tested you over and over again, and found you unwilling to break.'

She doesn't say how they tested him. She doesn't have to. Fel remembers it well enough. The submersion tanks and going for days without food or water or sleep. Fighting far beyond first blood. Sometimes with weapons. Sometimes with his bare hands. He remembers the shocks and the lash and the flash of knives. She's looking at him with a sort of sadness now, as if everyone living isn't made by one kind of pain or another. As if there's an alternative.

'I know that your combat record is exemplary,' Ghael says. 'No black marks. No punishment orders. You have never turned your back on a fight or on your squad until today. That tells me that whatever it is you are looking for here is beyond important.'

'So you will give me leave to find it?' Fel asks her.

Ghael takes a deep breath. 'No,' she says. 'As much as I know I am going to regret it, I'm going to help you.'

'What about the risk of being killed or dishonoured?' Fel asks.

Ghael shakes her head. 'I might not be a soldier, but I still serve. My life belongs to the crusade, to the Emperor, same as yours.' She pauses. 'And we are Antari. That means loyalty before the threat of death.'

It's an old adage. One that Fel is surprised to hear from the mouth of a Munitorum adept.

'Aye,' he says. 'Thank you.'

She waves the words away.

'So, what is it that you need to find?' she asks.

'I need to get into the central archive,' Fel says. 'To the alpha-grade records.'

Lori Ghael puffs air out through her cheeks. 'That's all?' she asks, flatly.

'That's all.'

She shakes her head, but she is smiling.

'You know,' she says, 'I really thought it'd take a lot longer before I started regretting this.'

The alpha-grade records are kept in the undercroft of the Munitorum complex. It seems appropriate to Fel, given that he's looking for something deliberately buried.

'You need high level clearance to get inside,' Ghael mutters, in Antari.

The two of them are walking through the marble hallways of the complex together towards the heart of it. Ghael smiles and nods at those who pass her, including all of the guards.

'Clearance I have,' Fel says. 'Or codes, anyway.'

She gives him a sideways glance.

'How in the hells did you get alpha-grade codes?' she asks, before shaking her head. 'You know, actually, don't tell me. It's best I don't know.'

'Surely,' Fel says.

'The codes will get you through the door,' Ghael says. 'But what were you planning on doing about the guards? They wouldn't exactly take you for an adept.'

'Slipping by them if I could,' he says. 'Quieting them if I couldn't.'

Ghael lets out a slow breath. Under the grin, she's nervous.

It's why she brought a bundle of records and slates with her. Something to hide the shaking of her hands.

'Quieting them,' Ghael says. 'Not killing.'

Fel shakes his head. 'Not killing. I am a soldier, not a monster.'

She only looks a little bit relieved by that.

'And why wouldn't they take me for an adept?' he asks.

Ghael looks at him flatly. 'The fatigues, for one thing. Never mind the fact that I have never in my life seen an adept built like you. It would be like painting a wyldwolf's fur and trying to pass it off as cattle.'

Fel laughs at that. It makes Ghael jump.

'Didn't think your kind did that,' she says. 'Laugh, I mean. Don't they take that from you at the scholam?'

'I told you,' Fel says. 'I am a soldier, not a monster.'

Ghael turns into a side corridor, and Fel follows her. It isn't nearly as grand as the main hallways. The marble cladding stops, exposing the bare stonework. Fel remembers it from the schematic and the landmarks he made, like the high-gain vox cabling that runs overhead. It's a part of the complex's nervous system. Security and power. Vox transmissions.

'Your codes had better work,' Ghael says. 'You'll only get one go at this.'

'They'll work,' he says. 'I trust the one who gave them to me.'

Ghael glances back at him. 'Trust,' she says. 'There's more in your tone than just trust.'

Fel knows what she is getting at, as much as he knows he won't speak of it. It's another intrusion. One too far.

'The records,' he says, instead.

Ghael looks at him and her mouth quirks in a smile, despite the shaking of her hands.

'There it is,' she says, and she stops at a heavy door that's marked with block words in four different language scripts.

It reads *AUTHORISED PERSONNEL ONLY*.

Lori Ghael puts in a code and pushes the door open. The room beyond is small and cramped. Set with heavy gauge cables and breaker levers. Manual switches and generatorium. Fel ducks inside the room and pushes the door closed.

'What are you doing with this kind of access?' he asks her.

Ghael shakes her head. 'Not my access,' she says. 'A friend's. Saw him put the code in once, and like I told you, I don't forget.'

'And where is this friend now?' Fel asks.

Ghael checks the chrono at her wrist. 'In the mess,' she says. 'For another fifteen minutes.'

'You're sure about this?' Fel asks her. 'You're not too far gone to turn back.'

Ghael looks back at him. Her augmetic eye glints in the low light.

'People are dead,' she says. 'And if there is a chance that what I've pledged my life to is being poisoned and corrupted, I'm not going to sit by and let it happen.'

She turns back to the breaker levers and cables.

'Now go,' she says. 'And I'll make you some shadows to hide in.'

There are two ways into the undercroft from the main floor. A stairwell that's keenly guarded, and an elevator shaft that is equally so.

At least until the power goes out.

There are no exterior windows in the heart of the complex, so when Ghael cuts the power, it goes dark as the witch's hour. But it's not just darkness that Ghael makes. Alarms begin to blare from elsewhere in the complex that draw the two guards away from the elevator they are guarding and to the source of the noise, because they think nobody will use it in the dark, without power to the mechanisms. They shout to one another over the alarms as they go and the stablights mounted on their rifles skip over the walls and the tiles of the floor.

And they skip over Fel entirely as he slips by them, hidden by the clamour and the dark.

He makes his way down the hall to the elevator doors without using the stablight he carries. Moving in the near-dark is second nature, even without optics. It's the way he was trained at the Schola Antari. The masters would cut the lights during fight training, or make them do it under flickering strobes. They'd sit Fel in the isolation cells and have him stare into the shadows until he learned how to read them.

It's the kind of learning you don't forget.

Without power, the elevator won't raise, but he doesn't need it to. Fel takes the combat blade from his belt and pushes it into the gap of the door to pry it open. Just wide enough to get through. Inside, the chains descend into darkness. Down to the undercroft. He takes hold of one like a rappel line. The doors fall closed again under their own weight, and Fel descends the elevator chains. He goes slow so that he lands quiet on top of the cage, then drops into it, landing softly. The doors at the bottom are closed too. It's the greatest risk of contact, this moment, but it's still easier than the stairway would have been.

Fel pries open the lower set of doors the same way as up at the top. The corridor beyond is low-ceilinged and angled further down. It is dark.

And it is completely empty.

As Fel leaves the elevator behind, the emergency lighting flickers on, bathing everything in dim red light. He waits a moment, but the pict-feed lenses mounted into the ceiling stay dark, like dead eyes.

The heavy door at the end of the corridor is keypad locked. Fel inputs the code that Raine gave him, and the door locks release with a hiss. He pushes the door just enough to hear what's inside. The air that comes from within is just about warm, and has none of the damp of the corridor outside. There's not a sound carried on it, save for the hum and click of cogitators, so he opens the door the rest of the way.

The room beyond is well-lit, clearly on a separate circuit to the rest of the complex. It is huge and circular, like a strategium hall. Tall stacks run floor to ceiling, as thick as trees can get if they are left well alone. Each stack holds rows upon rows of physical records, as well as datacrystals and pict-feed logs. The whole thing looks as though someone tried to build a forest who had never seen a real one. As Fel moves between the datastacks with light casting through the spaces between them, it feels a bit like a forest too. It's all the knowledge, he thinks. That's what he was always told. That the forest remembers things. Soaks them up like it does rainwater. This is the same. All of those deeds and lives, all the blood spent, all captured in ink and crystal. Overhead, servo-skulls hum absently and scan the shelves, paying him no mind. They clack their jaws and spool data, then move to the next record.

From up ahead, Fel hears murmuring. He slows and puts his back to one of the stacks, then looks around it for the source of the noise.

An old woman moves away from him down one of the

aisles. She is hunched and thin, dressed in heavy robes and supported by an array of multi-jointed augmetic legs. They hiss as she stops.

'Five years,' she says, to herself. Her voice is dry and coarse, like turning pages. 'Five thousand, five hundred souls. Numerical symmetry.'

She makes a gasping, rattling noise. It takes Fel a moment to realise that she is laughing. Then her spider's legs start moving again. They take her straight up the side of one of the stacks. He crosses the aisle quickly and keeps going towards the centre, towards the alpha-grade records.

The alpha-grade records are all held in one combined cogitator system. A behemoth, set with blinking lights. Cables coil from it like wasted limbs. At the base of the stack is a viewscreen and an input console with heavy plastek keys that are worn and dirtied from use. The word 'query' blinks in block capitals on the screen. Fel checks the aisles around him and the stacks above, then types his query.

ACCESS ALL RECORDS, STRIXIAN 99TH REGIMENT.

The cogitator built into the stack spools and clicks. It sounds bad-tempered. The screen flickers and then autofills with a response, one letter at a time.

AUTHORISATION REQUIRED. ALPHA-GRADE.

Fel inputs the code that Raine gave him again and prays inwardly, because he doesn't dare speak aloud.

The cogitator ticks and burrs for what seems a long time, while the cursor blinks green against grainy blackness, then the screen autofills again with lists and lists of records. There are hundreds of documents pertaining to the Strixian 99th. Fel cross-references them with another phrase.

CORIS BELT, THE.

Fel is rewarded with a record of the Strixians' destruction at the Coris Belt, just as Raine said. To a soul. He changes his phrase.

HYXX.

The same. Destroyed again, to a soul.

GHOLL.

The same.

CAWTER.

Again.

And again, and again. A dozen battlefields. A dozen deaths. *Hells*, Fel thinks.

He goes back to the beginning. To the record of their founding. The document is dense with Munitorum jargon, but Fel can get the shape of it. Ten thousand souls taken from a dozen different worlds. The regiment is cited as fleet-based, but they have no homeworld. No operational headquarters. They are made from nothing and nowhere.

Like ghosts.

At the bottom of the record, underneath the crusade seal, there are the names of those associated with the founding. Lord-Marshals. Commissariat. Departmento officials. Fel doesn't recognise a single one of the names, and then there's the matter of the regiment's founding date. It sticks in Fel's head, because it's a date that all who serve in the Bale Stars Crusade know.

The reconsecration of Steadfast, one month to the day after the recapture. The greatest celebration in the history of the Bale Stars Crusade. A day they made songs for. Fel gets a very bad feeling, seeing that date in connection with the Strixians. Like losing the ground underfoot.

He enters another query into the cogitator, requesting the records for every one of those associated with the founding.

The cogitator spools, whirs, then spits out a list of records, each one of them marked with the same red lettering.

KIA.

Fel has seen death records before. They usually specify the way of it, post-humous commendation or dishonour. Not so with these. They are all unusually spare on detail, but that is not the only thing which unites them. Like all death records, they are countersigned by a chief medicae. In this case, by the *same* chief medicae.

Surgeon-Major Isabella Luz.

Fel checks his chrono. He has no more than eight of Ghael's minutes left. It'll have to be long enough. He sets a new query.

ACCESS ALL RECORDS, SURGEON-MAJOR ISABELLA LUZ.

The cogitator churns and clicks, then skips a beat. Fel flexes his fingers absently.

The screen autofills with a list of records. At the top is Luz's own service record. It is marked the same way as the ones before it. In red, with the letters 'KIA'.

Another ghost, though this one had a life before she died.

Along with Luz's service record, Fel has access to all of her case notes and studies. To every cut that Isabella Luz ever made. Most of them are pict-feed captures or vox-thief recordings. There's one in particular that snags his attention, because of that damned date again. The reconsecration of Steadfast. He tries to play the record, but the cogitator clucks angrily. The screen flickers, and text autofills.

INPUT PASSCODE, it says.

Fel's bad feeling gets a whole lot worse. Every record here is protected by alpha-grade measures. For the recording to require an extra passcode means it's more than important.

More than alpha-grade.

He frowns and backs out of the records, then plugs in the datakey that Raine gave to him and copies everything to it. The Strixians. The dead. Every cut that Isabella Luz ever made. He knows that doing so has likely triggered an alert somewhere and that whoever buried the files will soon know that they have been accessed. It's a choice that can't be unmade. One that might make him just as dead as all of those others, if they catch him.

But that's the trick to it, he thinks, as he pulls the datakey, just like with any other operation.

You don't get yourself caught.

Fel has not long made it back through the elevator doors on the main floor when the lights come back on and the guards reappear around the corner to return to their post. They both stop in the corridor at the sight of him. They are holding their rifles at ease, but he can see the moment before movement in the way that they stand. He won't have time to take them both out before they can shoot him, or raise the alarm.

'What are you doing down here?' asks the first.

Fel holds up his hands and softens his voice when he speaks.

'I don't quite know where here is,' he says. 'I was looking to get out when the lights went and I lost my bearings.'

The second one frowns at that. It pulls at the scars on his face. Scars that say he knows how to fight.

'You lost your bearings,' he says, slowly, as if he's turning the words over.

Fel thinks about how quick he'd have to be. How much he'd have to hurt them, and how poorly that sits. He's careful not to let it show. Not to let them see the moment before movement.

'Like I said, I was just looking to get out,' he says, with a shrug. 'Before someone misspoke their rites of maintenance.'

The second one stays frowning, but the first one snorts a laugh.

'It wouldn't be the first time,' he says, and he steps aside to let Fel walk by. The second one does too, after a moment.

'You'd better find your way out,' the guard with the fighter's scars says. 'And go careful not to lose your bearings.'

Fel laughs at that, because it's what they want to hear.

'Understood,' he says.

THIRTEEN

Blades at your back

Severina Raine cannot dismiss the dream and the anger she felt at the sound of the word *traitor*. She lets that anger push her as they advance upwards through the Sanctum of Bones. With Cretia Ommatid occupied by Zane, the Sighted have returned in force, flooding from the spire's darkness to protect their master. Like always, they count oath-breakers and fanatics amongst their ranks. Biologis adepts, and surgeons with augmented hands for cutting. Even the sick fight for them, just as Vander said, still clad in their gowns and bandages, with their wounds turning to rot.

Raine ducks behind the cover of a tipped gurney as glass jars burst from solid shot just above her head. Fragments scatter around her, like snow with sharp edges. This place was an augmetics implantation suite before the war. It is lined with cots. Multi-limbed surgical rigs hang from the ceiling, armed with cutting blades and wicked drills. Channels are cut into the floor to help the blood flow away. It is doing so now, though it is black and thick and slow from the Sighted dead.

'Ommatid must be close,' Hale says. 'They refuse to fall back.'

Grey Company's captain is crouched beside Raine, taking cover too. He is bruised badly, with one eye as good as closed by it. Hale ejects the cell from his laspistol and pushes a fresh one home. He fires around the cover. More solid shot hits the tiles in answer, sending splinters into the air. Across the room, on the other side of the blood channel, the Kavrone fire from behind cover with their marksman rifles. Where the Antari are made for breaking, the Dragoons are made for precision. Excision.

'She is getting worse, too,' he says, nodding to Zane.

The psyker has been dragged into a sitting position, kept behind cover. Zane bleeds steadily and slowly from her nose and ears. It mats the furs she wears around her shoulders, making her look all the more like a wounded animal. Zane murmurs in slurred Antari, her breathing misting the air. Carrying her with them has slowed them and put them in danger, but Raine will not have her left behind. Not when she is giving so much to keep Ommatid's claws from their minds.

'Keep her safe,' Raine says. 'No matter what. No matter who threatens her.'

There is understanding in Hale's grey eyes. He nods.

'Now,' Raine says, over the vox this time, to the rest of them. 'Push through!'

As Raine gets to her feet, there's an explosion from the far side of the implantation suite, followed by a series of screams. The gunfire from the Sighted fanatics stammers and stalls. Raine breaks cover to see that the door at the far end of the suite has been breached, blown inwards by a demo charge. The suite strobes with hellgun fire from the two figures in matt-black carapace who set the breach.

'*Apologies,*' Cassia Tyl's voice is hoarse and edged with pain. '*We were waylaid.*'

Daven Wyck goes headlong into the smoke and the fray. Everything is made sharp by the stimms. Crystal clear as the Sighted fanatics move slow around him. They are all skin and bones and bandages. Some have the bloodsoaked cloth wound around their eyes, though they still fight like they can see and still try to cut him with jagged blades and shards of black glass.

But they are so very slow.

Wyck ducks the strike of the first fanatic and answers it with one of his own, burying his knife blade straight between the Sighted's collarbones. It goes in deep and grinds against something. Spine, maybe. He pulls the knife clear and kicks the fanatic onto his back. There's not much blood, and what's there is black and smells old. Beside him, Wyck sees Jey lock up his lasrifle trying to fire. The fanatic he was shooting at smiles wide and goes for him with an augmetic arm that ends with silver-tipped claws. Jey's pale grey eyes widen in slow motion.

Wyck throws himself at the fanatic, knocking him to the floor. Those silver-tipped claws rake across Wyck's flak armour and snag deep in his knife arm, sending it numb. Wyck grabs the Sighted's head with his other hand and slams it against the tiles. The first time the fanatic just goes dizzy and blank-eyed. The second time there's a breaking sound and a splatter of blood. Wyck's heart thunders and he finds he can't quite catch his breath. Over the ringing in his ears he hears Jey say something. It takes a second to filter through.

'Close,' he is saying. 'That was close.'

Around them, the firefight has stopped. Wyck gets up off the dead fanatic and wipes black blood from where it has spattered on his face. Jey is looking at him funny. His grey eyes are still wide. It's a look Wyck has seen before, from more folk than he can count. From Raf, all that time ago. From others before that too, because he's never been the kind to pull his punches. It's shock, that look. That, and a little disgust. He should be used to it, but with the witch dream still hanging over him it puts hooks in his soul and makes him feel discomforted, like a bright light shone in his eyes.

It makes that silver aquila weigh heavy around his neck.

'Give me your rifle,' he says to Jey, as if there's nothing wrong.

The void-born hesitates a second.

'Don't make me ask twice,' Wyck says.

Jey blinks a couple of times and hands over the gun. Wyck ejects the cell and resets the firing control, muttering a soft word to the rifle as he does so, before pushing the cell into place and handing it back.

'They lock like that when you don't treat them right,' Wyck says.

Jey nods a little too quickly. 'Right,' he says.

'I don't know who is the more vicious, the Sighted or your kind.'

The voice belongs to Justar, one of the Kavrone Dragoons. He is a sergeant too, marked by his gold epaulettes and the trim of his gloves. Hale told Wyck that Justar's squad runs the edge too. It made Wyck laugh when he said it. From what he's seen, the Kavrone know nothing at all about the edge. Justar looks down at the fanatic's body with disgust. At the mess of it, and the wide arc of black blood.

'You call yourselves wild, but feral would be better. Savage.'

Wyck looks down at the body too. Then at Justar, with the las-burns on his blue and white armour. The scores and scorch marks on that Steadfast pattern rifle he carries.

'It's all killing,' Wyck says. 'Whether it's pretty or not.'

Justar scowls and mutters in his own tongue. Wyck has served in the field alongside the Kavrone plenty of times, often enough to pick up a few things.

'Words like those, I think it's you who is being savage,' he says. 'Isn't that right, highborn?'

The look the Kavrone is giving him, he's liable to start a fight. A part of Wyck wants him to, so that he'll have an excuse to hit back. To break Justar's unbroken nose. His heart stammers and his fists curl of their own accord. The room runs like paint. Bright. Aching. Everything is so damned loud.

'Careful, Antari,' Justar says, warningly.

Wyck can't say anything back. Can't see right. He has to shut his eyes.

'Sarge.'

Justar is gone. It's Crys he's looking at now. She frowns slow. Micro-expressions that crease her eyes and pull at the scars on her face. Wyck remembers her getting those scars. Remembers the way she screamed. All that shrapnel. Such a mess.

'What?' he says to her.

'We're moving,' she says.

She is. Everything is. Slowly like he's underwater. Under the surface of the lake with the wraiths giggling in his ears. With their cold hands around his throat so he can't get air. Can't get out.

'Moving,' Wyck says, trying just to breathe. 'Right.'

* * *

Antar's sky is thunderhead grey, like the roaring sea below it. The wind howls as if it is trying to outdo the ocean's bad temper, rattling the leaves on the singing tree. Birds cry. Both Zane's crows, and the seabirds who call the cliffs their home.

'It has been a long time since I have seen such a place,' Cretia Ommatid says.

She is slumped against the bole of the singing tree, still bleeding from the knife wound in her chest. It is not a physical wound, of course. It is a different kind of hurt. A deeper kind. But despite it, Ommatid is still grinning. Not beaten.

But Zane does not have to beat Ommatid. She just has to keep her busy.

Ommatid tilts her head back to look up at the crown of the tree.

'Do you see the way that the branches grow from a single point and spread, sometimes even turning back on one another?'

Cretia Ommatid lowers her chin again and locks her crystal eyes on Zane.

'It is like fate, and just like those branches, some fates are sure. They could take the weight of a body.' She grins wider. 'Of a hangman's noose. But not all of them. Some are fragile. Fleeting. They will be broken by the storm.'

Zane snorts a laugh. 'Such wisdom,' she says. 'There is little wonder that you are elevated amongst fools.'

Ommatid's grin turns serrated.

'Fools,' Ommatid says, tasting the word. She spits bloody on the long grass. 'No. We are *enlightened*. Freed from our bonds and our limits.' She tilts her head. 'Don't you ever wonder what that would be like?' Ommatid asks. 'To be free?'

For an instant, the scene tears away. Everything but the singing tree. The sea and the wind are replaced with the sound of screams, and Zane sees how it would be to be truly free. How she would break and injure and kill and revel in it. How her false eyes would blaze with unlight as a great, winged shadow unfolded itself from her back.

'No,' Zane says.

The vision disappears, and the cliff returns. The song of birds. Ommatid, with her razor grin. Zane wipes her bloody nose on her sleeve and coughs. It rattles her lungs. She limps over to Ommatid, drops to her knees and pushes her spun wooden knife against the traitor's throat. A bead of blood runs down the darkwood blade.

'What you offer,' Zane says. 'It is poison. It is wicked.'

Ommatid lets the knife press in. 'They all think so, to begin with,' she says. 'But pain lends perspective. It is as I said, they all choose, just as your lost hound did.'

Zane frowns. 'A lost hound,' she says. 'You mean Caiden Rol.'

Ommatid nods and it makes more blood run down the blade.

'He resisted at first,' she says. 'So desperate to die for his crusade. For his *Emperor*. But when your Duskhound saw what truly waits beyond, he changed his mind. He begged me to spare him.'

'No,' Zane says. 'You are lying. Duskhounds cannot be broken.'

Ommatid shakes her head. 'He was not broken,' she says. 'He was *saved*. I offered Caiden Rol a new fate, and he chose it gladly.'

'More lies,' Zane hisses. 'Fates cannot be changed.'

'Oh, my sweet,' Ommatid says, with a smile. 'Of course they can.'

The scene changes again then, returning Zane to the

Sanctum of Bones. To a cold and darkened chamber lined with heavy, rune-marked caskets, just like those that Zane saw in her dream. Shards of mirrored crystal have been placed on the floor to form the Sighted's spiral mark, only this time a throne sits in place of the eye at the centre and in the throne, connected to it by needles and cables and bound by restraints, is Caiden Rol.

The Duskhound is without his mask and his armour, and his face is so bloody that all Zane can really see are his eyes, glassy and unfocused. He is as still as the dead. He *should* be dead, but his soul hasn't twisted free all the way. It is tethered, somehow. Kept from the After. Zane feels a tear trace its way down her cheek as Cretia Ommatid approaches Rol, walking the spiral barefoot and leaving bloody prints on the mirrored shards. The caskets around Zane begin to hum and the spiral of bloody mirrors starts to glow and glitter and light until it is afire with Ommatid and Rol at its centre. Zane can hear screams. Terrible, echoing screams, coming from within the caskets.

Coming from those like Zane, who are gifted.

'No,' Zane whispers. '*No.*'

Then Ommatid puts her hands on either side of his head and Rol starts to scream too. The fire reaches so high and burns so brightly that for a moment it is all that Zane can see, writhing and contorting in shapes that look like faces. The screaming is deafening, from the gifted and Ommatid and Rol alike, and Zane finds she cannot help but scream with them.

But then as suddenly as it began, the screaming stops. Zane knows that every one of the psykers in the nine caskets are dead. She feels their souls twist away as the fire burns down to reveal Ommatid still standing, and Rol, still sitting in the throne.

But now he is changed.

He is awake, his grey eyes focused and clear. He is not bruised, or injured. All of that blood on his face has gone.

Save for the fate-mark that has opened in his skin.

'No,' Zane says, again.

And the Sanctum of Bones blows away like smoke, returning her to Antar's coast's edge.

'See,' Ommatid says. 'Fates can be changed, for a price.'

Zane is still shaking from the sight of the caskets and the fire and the fate-mark. They are indelible, marks like that. They seep all the way through to the soul. Zane presses harder on her darkwood knife.

'Why did you do it?' she asks. 'Why Rol?'

'Because fate is the sum of countless instances,' Ommatid says. 'In order for something grand to unfold, many small things must happen first. Particular paths must be chosen at the correct time. Lives must be ended, or spared. And of course, blood must be spilt.'

'That is why you are telling me all of this,' Zane says, softly. 'Because you believe it will allow something grand to unfold.'

'Clever little thing,' Ommatid says, with a proud smile that turns Zane's stomach.

'The fate-engines,' Zane says. 'What will you do with them?'

Ommatid laughs. It is a vicious noise.

'Oh, my sweet,' she says. 'It is not what *we* will do with them that should concern you. It is what the manticore will do with them.'

'The manticore,' Zane rasps. 'Who is the manticore?'

But Cretia Ommatid does not answer her. Instead, she laughs again.

* * *

The two Duskhounds left standing are both scored and scorched. Bruised and bloodied. When Tyl breathes, she sounds winded. There is a wide, dark bloodstain on her fatigues from a bad wound in her side. Jeth is dragging a limp and he has had to cut his face to ease the bruising trying to close his right eye. Raine knows that it isn't really the wounds that hurt them. They are built to take punishment. Used to physical pain. What will hurt them is the fact that only two of them are left standing.

And Raine knows just how badly that will hurt Andren Fel, too, when he finds out.

'What happened up there?' she asks.

They are moving up through the Sanctum of Bones, through a chamber lined with boiling vats, sluices and catch-trays. Clusters of candles stand around them, half as tall as the Antari are. Polished skulls watch them from recessed niches on the walls. Tyl is still wearing her Duskhounds mask, so Raine cannot see her face, but there is a hesitation in her before she answers. A visible tensing.

'They tried to break us. Ommatid tried.' Tyl puts her hand to that wound at her waist. 'She underestimated what it would take.'

'The shielding was fueled by witches,' Jeth says. He has that same sour tone to his voice that the other Antari do when saying the word *witches*. 'Nine of them.'

'They kept saying something, over and over,' Tyl says. 'Protect the engines.'

'*Engines.*'

Raine stops and turns to look at Lydia Zane. Lye and Rath drop her bodily to the ground as lightning arcs from her scalp. The psyker lands on her hands and knees.

'Throne,' says Lye. 'Oh, *Throne.*'

Rath and Lye both take a step back from the psyker. Raine

doesn't. She moves closer and drops into a crouch so she can hear exactly what Zane is saying.

'Engines,' Zane slurs again. *'Fate-engines.'*

Then she raises her hand and points, trembling, past Raine, before slumping forwards once more.

'What in the hells are fate-engines?' Hale asks.

'Something definitely worth burning,' Tyl says, coldly.

Raine nods. She does not know any better than they do what the fate-engines are, but Sylar's order from the briefing is ringing in her ears.

Capture. Excise. Preserve.

The fate-engines are what the Kavrone general wants. She would stake her honour on it. Cold runs through Raine like a winter's gale as she looks to Vander and his Dragoons. They are still moving up through the chamber in the direction that Zane pointed.

Towards the fate-engines.

'We move,' Raine says, as the Kavrone engage with the Sighted once more. 'Now.'

Hale and his command squad are slow, because of Zane. Too slow to keep up with Severina Raine as she enters the fray alongside the Kavrone Dragoons. She cannot let Vander and his regiment get away from her. Cannot let him reach the fate-engines first. She runs the edge, alongside Wyck and his Wyldfolk. Gereth Awd's flamer fills the air with smoke and ashes. Yulia Crys fights like a brawler. The two new recruits stick together, protecting one another. Wyck is out alone, in the centre of the storm, like always.

Raine grabs hold of the wrist of a Sighted fanatic who tries to cut her with a jagged glass knife, and twists it. She feels the bones break. He drops the knife, but he doesn't give up on trying to cut her, reaching for her throat with his other hand. His hand is a silver claw of curved blades that Raine catches on the blade of her sword.

'For those who truly see,' the fanatic rasps. 'For the lords of fate and change!'

'No,' Raine says. 'For the Emperor.'

And she fires Penance at point-blank range. The fanatic spills backwards. His black blood hits the ceiling and hits Raine too. She spits onto the tiles before turning to face the next threat with her limbs burning. She refuses to tire. Refuses to slow. Raine strikes and parries and takes cuts in return until she is alongside Vander. The Kavrone's commissar is cut and bleeding too. Between every swing of Raine's sword she sees Vander cleave fanatics in two with his own. He kicks and punches and fights for his life. Around him, the Kavrone make clean shots with their modified rifles. Centre-mass, like a combat drill.

Like a firing squad.

'Push through!' Vander shouts. 'Courage in His sight!'

The words ring in Raine's ears. She remembers hearing them from Lucia, all of those years ago. Remembers the wildness of her sister's eyes, and the words that followed shortly after.

Faith has been broken.

Severina Raine has spent a decade hating her sister. Dismantling every memory that she held dear in the belief that Lucia betrayed the crusade. She has built walls around herself and her heart, and put all of that anger and hate into every battle she has fought, only to find out that it is all built on lies.

Raine falters then, slowing just for an instant. It is how she sees so clearly the moment in which Vander sends a

Sighted fanatic staggering backwards with a strike from his sword. The fanatic falls flat on his back and his layered, padded coat opens, revealing the cluster of grenades strapped to the Sighted's chest.

'Your Emperor cannot see you here,' the Sighted says, and he laughs.

And before Raine or Vander can do a thing about it, he triggers the bomb vest.

The explosion takes Wyck off his feet and puts him against the wall, hard. The impact drives the air out of his lungs and fractures something in his chest. He sits there for a second, struggling to breathe. He shakes his head, but it just makes his ears ring worse. White blossoms of light print on his eyelids when he blinks. There's a fire roaring in the chamber. Everything is getting thick with smoke. He can taste it. Ash and death.

Just like Cawter all over again.

Around him, his Wyldfolk are down. He hears moans and screams under the ringing in his ears and sees Crys lying there. She's not moving.

'Get up,' Wyck says to himself.

He puts his hand out and tries to get to his feet, but his legs go and he falls again. He thinks maybe there's something fractured there too. The fall jolts the air back out of his chest. He can't do it. Can't get on his feet. Can't get to them.

Not on his own.

Wyck takes one of the vials from a pouch at his belt. The liquid inside it is dark red, like old blood. His heart accelerates just from holding it. He knows the risk. Knows that he should have listened to Lye when she told him to stop. But he can't, because without it he can't get up.

Wyck uncaps the auto-injector with his thumb and punches it into his leg. He takes a deep breath and counts it out and waits for the stimms to hit him. For his vision to tunnel and sharpen. For his heart to fight like it's trying to get free. Then he gets to his feet. It hurts so bad that it makes him shout, but he doesn't fall. He staggers through the ash and the smoke over to where Crys is lying. There is blood matting her hair and running down her face.

'Yulia,' Wyck says.

He drops to one knee and puts his hand on her shoulder. Crys snaps awake and swings for him. It's only the stimms that make him quick enough to grab her hand and block it.

'Whoa,' he says. 'That's enough of that.'

Her eyes go wide and she rolls to sit up. Wyck helps her onto her feet.

'Sarge,' she says, her voice raw. 'What happened?'

Wyck remembers what he saw in the seconds before the explosion blinded him and took him off his feet. The Kavrone Dragoons firing their lasguns, and in amongst them, the two commissars. Raine and Vander. Wyck looks over to where the fire is burning itself out. The blast put a hole straight through the floor, cutting the Wyldfolk off from the rest of the regiment, who are stirring on the other side. It turned several of the Kavrone into nothing more than a mess. He can't see any amongst the dead that wear the black. No sign of Raine.

'I think they might have killed our commissar,' Wyck says to Crys.

'*Wyck.*' Hale's voice is hoarse over the vox. '*Are you still alive over there?*'

'For the most part,' Wyck says. 'What now?'

'*Keep moving,*' Hale says. '*Run the edge. We have the witch slowing us, but we will make our way around to find you.*'

'Run the edge,' Wyck says, as if there's ever another way to live. 'Understood.'

Severina Raine comes to with a start and raises her pistol instinctively, pointing it into the empty darkness. It takes her a moment to lower it again, and to calm her heart. Raine sits herself up. The action makes her cough, bringing up masonry dust and blood. She spits on the stone floor. Her head rings from the explosion.

The *explosion*.

Raine looks up to see the collapse. It must be twenty feet above her. Everything up there is on fire and thick with smoke. Raine can still hear las-fire echoing down from above, but on this level, all is quiet save for the settling of rubble. She has to get back up to her regiment and back into the fight. Raine gets to her feet slowly, leaning on the rubble to do it. She tastes blood again. Everything aches as the world turns around her. Very still bodies lie everywhere. Most are Sighted, and yet more are clad in Kavrone blue, but there is one in Antari splinter. All of them are surrounded by dark puddles of their own blood. Raine checks the Antari first. It is Tian, of the Wyldfolk. He is burned so badly that she can only tell by what's left of his tattoos. The Kavrone are just as bad. Just as dead.

Raine stops and tries to catch her breath. It is coming short and shallow. She puts her fingers to the vox-bead in her ear.

'Hale,' she says. 'Acknowledge.'

There's a roar of static that tells Raine her vox-link is shot. She winces and takes the bead out. With the static gone, and the ringing in her ears fading slowly, Raine can hear another sound.

Someone else, struggling to breathe.

She raises her pistol and snaps the stablight live. The beam illuminates the space. The collapsed stonework and shattered chunks of flagstone. Shards of glass.

And Lukas Vander, slumped against the rubble, pinned in place by the length of rebar that has punched through him at the shoulder. His right arm hangs at his side, useless.

'Raine,' he says.

She moves over to him, her boots sticking in his blood as she does so. Vander's face is drained white, but he is still scowling at her. His breathing is shallow too. It sounds wet.

'I hate to say it,' he says, between breaths. 'But I need your help.'

Raine doesn't move. She is still thinking about the fate-engines and about broken faith. About that moment at the commissariat hub when his composure broke, just for an instant.

She knows that she will not get another chance like this one to know the truth about Lukas Vander.

'Raine,' Vander says, again. 'Are you addled? Stop staring at me and help me.'

'I will help you,' Raine says. 'But first I want you to tell me what really happened to Mardan Tula.'

'What?' he asks, blinking into the light.

'You heard what I said,' Raine says.

Vander's scowl deepens. He struggles against the rebar but gives up as the bloodstain on his tunic spreads and his breathing starts to whine in his chest.

'You saw what happened to Tula,' he snarls.

Raine drops into a crouch so that she can look him in the eyes and read him more easily.

'I saw,' she says. 'But I don't believe it, and if you were any kind of commissar then neither would you.'

'You have no right to question my purpose,' Vander says, through his teeth. 'You are a damned half-breed with cowardice written in your blood.'

Raine knows that he means every word. Vander has never been anything but honest about how he feels about her. It's that honesty that makes her question whether he could really be complicit in the actions of his regiment.

'Answer my question,' she says. 'Tell me what you think really happened to Mardan Tula.'

Vander exhales a long breath.

'Fine,' he says, through his teeth. 'I believe that it was suicide, just like the reports say.' He spits blood onto the tiles. 'I believe that Mardan Tula invited the rope around his neck, even if he did not set it himself. He thought himself above consequences. Above reproach. None of us are that, save for the Emperor.'

'So who do you believe would want Tula dead?' Raine asks.

To her surprise, Vander laughs. It is short-lived, and sounds agonising.

'Everyone,' he says. 'We are commissars. Every soul in the regiments wants us dead.'

He gestures weakly past her to where the ceiling collapsed. 'If you think for a moment that any one of those ferals you serve with are weeping over you right now, then you are more of a fool than I thought.'

'I would not expect them to,' Raine says. 'I expect them to serve, and to fight. To do so with courage in the Emperor's name. And I trust them to know that I will have a bullet or a blade waiting if they don't.'

Vander snorts. 'Trust,' he says. 'There is no place in this world for trust.'

'So you trust no one,' Raine says.

'Not a soul,' Vander says. 'Not the Kavrone. Not you, or any of the others we serve with. Certainly not Tula.'

He shifts slightly, trying to ease the pressure on his shoulder. The rebar grinds against his bones.

'Not like you,' Vander says. 'You trust your Antari, despite all that they are. Despite what you are.'

'No,' Raine says. 'I do not trust the Antari. I understand them and I know their limits. What will drive them, and what will break them. There is a difference.'

Even as Raine says them, she knows that the words aren't entirely true. There is one soul amongst the Antari that she trusts, but she'll be damned if she'll say so to Lukas Vander.

'And Tula?' Vander says.

'Tula was commissariat,' Raine says, by way of answer. 'He was a good man.'

'A *good man*,' Vander says. 'Do you know that it was him who told me what your sister did? How she betrayed the crusade by leaking information to our enemies. How she tried to get the Lord-General Militant and half of High Command killed.'

'That's a lie,' Raine snarls.

Vander shakes his head. His breathing rattles in his chest. 'Why would I lie about it?' he asks. 'I gain nothing from speaking ill of the dead. Despite what you may think of me, I have no interest in being cruel for the sake of it.'

'What cause could he possibly have to tell you that?' Raine asks.

'His own,' Vander says. 'Mardan Tula was a political animal, Raine. He told people what they needed to hear if it would get him what he wanted. That's what I meant when I said that he set his own noose. That kind of act makes enemies.'

'So you *do* believe that Tula was murdered,' she says. 'But you are willing to let the act go unpunished because you feel that he deserved it?'

'I never said that,' Vander says. 'All crimes must be punished.'

The words are half of an old adage that Raine heard a hundred times or more during her training.

'Every slight answered for,' she says, completing it.

Vander's green eyes are distant. Unfocused.

'Do you know what it is about you that I so hate, aside from your blood?' Vander's voice is weak now. It has lost all of its edges. 'I hate your honour, and your loyalty. The fact that you sound so much like a commissar.'

He takes a ragged breath.

'I hate the fact that you are going to help me now,' he says. 'And that I am going to owe you for it.'

Raine hates it too. She doesn't want to help him, nor does she want his debt, but she cannot leave him to die without cause or confession. It is not how she does things.

'This is going to hurt,' she says.

Vander nods his head. Raine holsters her pistol and puts her arms around his chest. She takes his weight, and then lifts him, slowly and surely off the spar of metal. It snags against bone and muscle, making Vander cry out as she pulls him free. She sits him down again on the floor, then takes off the sash she wears and winds it as best she can around his wounded shoulder. When she pulls it tight, he curses. Then Vander gets to his feet unsteadily, without her help, and the two of them go to find a way back to their regiments.

'The manticore,' Lydia Zane hurls the words at Ommatid. 'Who is the manticore?'

Ommatid laughs. She is bleeding from her nose and around her crystal eyes.

'The one who holds your leash will learn his name,' she says. 'The outsider clad in shadow-black. Ask her, if you truly want to know.'

Zane snarls. The grass stirs and brushes against her and her robes snap around her like wings. The singing tree shakes. She pushes harder on the blade at Ommatid's throat.

'You will tell me *now*,' Zane says.

Ommatid does not flinch at the knife's pressure, she merely smiles all the wider.

'Oh, my sweet,' she says. 'Do you think that you can intimidate me? Do you believe that you have me trapped here, on this ghost of your beautiful world?'

Zane feels a deep cold run along her bones, then, that locks her in place. Frost begins to pattern the trunk of the singing tree around Ommatid.

'I am here because I want to be,' Ommatid says. 'I am here because of you, and your little birds.'

Zane does not mean to say the words. They just boil up from inside her.

'You can see them,' she whispers.

'Of course I can. Pretty little things they are too. One black. One white. Mirrors, and opposites.'

'They are just echoes,' Zane says. 'Made by the things I have done, and nothing more.'

'They are so much more than echoes, just as you are so much more than *Epsilon*.' Ommatid reaches out and puts her cold hands on either side of Zane's face. 'I have watched you for a long time, in the years gone by and the ones yet to come. Your fate lies not with the Antari, or the blind. You are destined for enlightenment, but you must choose. Place your feet on the path to truth and follow it.'

Zane sees herself clearly in Ommatid's crystal eyes, then.

'*No,*' she slurs, through her teeth.

Because in the reflection, she too has crystal eyes in place of her silver ones.

'Your kin would have you break others until you yourself are broken,' Ommatid says. 'The manticore would spend your strength like coin to change his own fate. They only seek to use you until there is nothing left to use.'

Zane moans through her locked jaws, because those words, at least, are true and Zane knows it. She has known it since the day she came into her powers.

'The path awaits. The *Nine* await,' Ommatid says, sing-song. 'You need not be lonely, or hated. You need not be bound, or caged. You can be strong, and free, as I am.'

'*Free,*' echoes Zane's crow. '*Free!*'

'Choose,' Ommatid says, again. 'Think of all that you could be.'

And Zane does think of it, and it scares her more than the manticore or the fate-engines, or even death itself.

Because there is a tiny part of her that sees the beauty in it.

'*No!*'

Zane screams the word, and the ice in her limbs shatters. She cuts Ommatid's throat with the darkwood knife, but Ommatid does not choke, or spasm or tremble. She does not die. Instead, Ommatid sighs with blood running freely onto her many-coloured robes. Her fingers trace Zane's face gently as she lets go.

'Until next time, then,' Ommatid says.

And then she vanishes, and Zane finally allows the dreamscape to collapse. A peal of thunder splits the sky as the sea boils away and the singing tree burns and splinters and turns to dust.

And then Zane's eyes truly open to the Sanctum of Bones.

To Nuria Lye and Ari Rath and Yuri Hale. Zane draws a breath that burns and makes her cough. Her kinfolk let go of her arms and she falls to the floor, hard. She retches up blood and bile onto the tiles.

'Hag's *teeth*.' Rath's voice is an underwater murmur.

'Zane,' Hale drops to one knee. 'Where is she? Where is the traitor witch?'

Lydia Zane looks up, with blood running down her face and the taste of acid and ocean in her mouth.

'Gone,' she manages to say. 'Ommatid is gone.'

Awd's flamer roars, lighting the corridor. Wyck feels the heat of it at his back like the balefire breath of the hounds from the witch-dream. The reflected light glimmers in the gemstone eye of the Sighted fanatic who is trying to kill him, turning the crystal red. The fanatic is built big. As big as Crys. Wyck cuts him deep. Arms and chest. Those kinds of cuts should slow the fanatic, but they don't. He grabs Wyck by his throat and slams him up against the wall of the Sanctum. It knocks the air clean out of Wyck's lungs and shifts his cracked ribs. Makes him drop his knife from numb fingers. Wyck struggles for air with his vision dazzling.

'What do you see, Antari?' the Sighted hisses, through pointed teeth. 'The edge of death?'

Wyck's vision is crowding with shadows. Howling echoes in his ears, louder even than his heart can beat.

'Not mine,' he manages to say.

Then he curls his off-hand and punches as hard as he can into the Sighted's gemstone eye. Something in his hand breaks, but so does the Sighted's eye socket. Wyck feels the stone push in, and the fanatic screams and drops him. Wyck falls hard, air rushing back into his lungs. It burns like several hells, but Wyck gets to his feet, picks up his knife and cuts the Sighted's throat. Cuts his screaming short. Blood paints a line through the air, glittering like stars.

Like stars.

Wyck takes a ragged breath and looks around himself. The corridor he is standing in is deep into the Sanctum, far from the rest of the regiment. Right on the edge. The walls are arched and wrought from dark iron. Flickering, erratic lumens illuminate the corridor in stuttering bursts, showing up the ironwork jutting from the walls like teeth and the puddles of black water rippling at Wyck's feet as the Sighted's twitching body shakes itself still. At the end of the corridor is a massive set of engraved doors. The carvings on them are of bodies laid open to the air. Of cables and bones.

Wyck goes cold from the inside outwards.

He's seen this place before, in the dream that Zane shared with him. Her voice bounces around in his head, unwanted and unpleasant.

Blades, at your back.

Wyck turns on the spot with his knife raised in guard and finds himself looking at his Wyldfolk, and at Justar and the five that are left of his damned Dragoons. There are no Sighted. No blades.

Just those who run the edge.

Wyck lowers his own knife and tries not to laugh. He's not sure which of the two things is more of an effort.

'Yulia,' he calls out to Crys. 'Get those doors open.'

'Got it, sarge,' she says, with a grin.

She heads over to the doors and starts to set her charges. Despite her new scars, and everything the Sanctum has done to her, she still whistles as she does it. It's always the same song with her. Something from home. It echoes strangely around Wyck, making his ears ache. He moves away from the door and puts his back against the wall.

'You might want to do the same,' he says, to Justar.

The Kavrone sergeant looks at him with that same disdain as before, but he doesn't argue.

'Your kind really do revel in it, don't you?' he says. 'Fighting. Burning. Breaking.'

Wyck's smile goes no deeper than his teeth. 'There's precious little else to revel in with lives like ours,' he says. 'Might as well take what you can while you're standing.'

Justar shakes his head.

Crys sets the detonator line and rolls it out as she takes her place opposite Wyck, beside the Kavrone. She whistles out the last bar of that song and then thumbs the trigger. The explosion happens slow to Wyck. Light first. White to yellow, like a captured sun. Then the dust and plaster in clouds. Then solid chunks of wood land all around him, clattering off the ironwork. The noise of it rings out and Wyck hears Crys laughing, loud.

'Spectacular,' Justar says, flatly, dusting debris from his fatigues.

'Your words, highborn,' Crys says, with that grin she gets from breaking.

'Let's go and see exactly what it is they are hiding,' Wyck says.

He runs through the mess that's left of the doors. Over debris and through the smoke. Motes of fire spiral past his eyes as he tracks his rifle side to side, looking for Sighted to kill, but Wyck finds no Sighted. No contacts.

What he finds makes him stop and lower his rifle, slowly. He goes cold again from the inside out. Nine great, grey caskets sit in the chamber, linked by cables and patterned with frost. The sigils etched into them burn like phosphor flares. The caskets connect by oil-slick pipes and tubes to a throne that bristles with needles. There is broken glass and blood on the floor around the base of it. The blood is old, and painted into a shape that Wyck can't keep looking at. One that seems to move. One that feels as though it looks back.

'No good,' Wyck says.

He hears something else that Zane said, then, clear as a springtime sky.

Worse than death.

'What is this?' Awd has fear in his voice, honest and open. He is standing shy of that bloody spiral. They all are. Not one of them will cross it.

'A witch circle.' Crys isn't laughing now. 'That's a witch circle.'

She is right. Wyck knows it. Even if he hadn't seen Zane's dream, he'd be able to feel it in the air. Around him, the Kavrone move.

'Secure the chamber,' Justar is saying. 'And the machines.'

Wyck turns and stares at him. 'What in the hells are you doing?' he asks.

'Our orders are to capture and preserve,' Justar says. 'So I am capturing. Preserving.'

His speech is slow and deliberate. It's not just the stimms making it sound that way. Justar is doing it on purpose, as if Wyck is stupid.

'No,' Wyck says. 'Our orders don't extend to heretic machines. To witch circles. This isn't the kind of thing you preserve, it's the kind of thing you burn.'

Justar steps up to him. The Kavrone is of a height with Wyck, but much broader. Built like a boxer. From the look on his face, he is used to using that to get his way.

But then going by his unbroken nose, he hasn't had to back that look up very often.

'You don't get to decide what the orders extend to, Antari,' he says. 'You shut up and enact them.'

Wyck thinks about those toy soldiers that High Command sent after Zane and about the caskets and the terror she felt in the dream that she shared with him.

'No,' Wyck says. 'I don't think so.'

Justar goes for his sidearm. Wyck sees the movement in half-time, just like the explosion, and he snaps the butt of his rifle into the Kavrone's face before Justar can raise his gun. It knocks the Kavrone reeling, making him drop his pistol. A welter of blood hits the floor. Wyck kicks the pistol away and lets his rifle swing by the strap. He gets Justar in a hold and puts his combat knife up against the Kavrone's throat. The rest of Justar's squad draw on him, but they can't get a shot without going through their sergeant. Wyck doesn't have to look to know that his Wyldfolk have drawn their own rifles on the Kavrone in turn. Tension fills the air like the charge before a storm.

'Drop your damned guns,' Wyck shouts at the Kavrone. 'Or I cut to kill.'

'He's bluffing,' Justar says, through his teeth.

'I'm really not.' Wyck presses on the blade enough to draw blood. 'But please, test me.'

Justar is breathing quickly under that blade. He has the heartbeat of something afraid.

'Do what he says,' Justar orders his squad. 'Lower your guns.'

The Kavrone do as they are told and allow the Wyldfolk to disarm them and put them against the wall. Haro and Jey keep their rifles drawn on them. Wyck feels curiously proud of the void-born in that instant.

They are truly Wyldfolk now.

'You will hang for this,' Justar says to Wyck as he eases the blade from his throat. 'You're a damned traitor.'

'Traitor,' Wyck says. 'Funny, I could say the same about you.'

Then he hits Justar hard enough to put the Kavrone on the tile floor, unconscious. Wyck orders Haro and Jey to take the rest of them into the corridor where they can't interfere.

'You take Justar,' he says to Awd. 'I'm going to help Crys set the charges.'

'Dav,' Awd says. 'Would you have done it?'

'Done what?'

'Cut to kill,' Awd says.

Wyck glances down at the blade in his hand. There is blood dried into the serrations. He blinks and looks back at Awd.

'I didn't have to,' he says.

Awd has got that same expression on his face as before, only this time Wyck thinks he understands what it is.

Disappointment.

Wyck watches from a safe distance as the machines go up. The explosion isn't white to yellow this time. It burns blue and it sounds like screams. In the aftermath of it, he hears Justar laugh. The Kavrone is sitting against the wall with his hands bound. That broken nose of his has swollen up badly.

'Here we are,' he says. 'Now you really will hang.'

Wyck follows where Justar is looking to see Yuri Hale and the others approaching them. Zane is on her feet now. The witch comes close, stopping just short of arm's length away. Her face is painted with blood that is only broken by the tear trails from her false eyes. She is still crying now, somehow.

'You burned the fate-engines,' she rasps.

Her words make him flinch. 'You mean the caskets,' he says. 'What were they, really?'

'The Sighted use them to cheat the After,' Zane says. 'To trick death.'

She looks at him sidelong.

'All for the price of your soul.'

Wyck can't quite believe her words, because he knows for a fact you can't trick death. Not indefinitely.

No matter what price you pay to do it.

'Wyck.'

Hale's voice pulls Wyck's attention from Zane. The captain has his laspistol drawn, and his eyes look cold as lakewater. Awd is stood behind him. Lye too.

'Drop your rifle,' Hale says. 'The sidearm and the knife too.'

Wyck doesn't drop a thing. He just puts his hands up to show he won't use them.

'Yuri,' Wyck says. 'The machines had to burn. They were witch-work.'

'I know what the machines were,' Hale says. 'Zane told me. This isn't about that.'

Wyck feels sweat run between his shoulder blades. He wonders how obvious the double-dose he took is right now. Hale raises his pistol and points it for a kill shot.

'Now drop your damned weapons like I ordered you to,' he says.

+Do as he says.+ Zane's voice in his head is like a heated needle. +If you fight or you run, he will kill you.+

Wyck is dizzied by the words, because he can see the truth of them written in Hale's face. He slowly unslings his rifle and puts it down. Then the sidearm, then the knife. Wyck is acutely aware of all the eyes on him. Of being unarmed and vulnerable.

'Bind his hands,' Hale says.

It's Lye who comes forwards to do it. Wyck tries to catch her eyes, but she won't look at him. She just snaps the bindings shut around his wrists and steps away as if he's something dangerous.

'Captain, wait,' Crys says.

The combat engineer steps up beside Wyck. All that blood and time spent has made her fiercely loyal.

'Come on, now,' she says. 'Whatever is meant to have happened, there's surely no need for this.'

'There's a need, Yulia.'

The words come from Awd. He stands there with dread in his eyes as if he's the one with a gun pointed at his face.

'Because he is a murderer,' Awd says. 'He killed four souls, sworn to the Throne.'

Wyck realises then what this is about and why Awd asked him about the bodies in the water and cutting to kill.

He realises what Zane actually meant when she told him to watch for blades at his back.

Crys laughs loud. 'Shut up, Ger,' she says. 'That's not true.'

She looks at Wyck, all of that loyalty written in her grey eyes. All of that faith.

'Tell them, sarge,' she says.

Wyck has been lying since he learned to talk. Keeping secrets and carrying them with him. Especially after Cawter. It should be easy for him to lie to Crys now, too, but he finds he can't.

It's that damned silver aquila around his neck. It is so heavy.

'Sarge,' she says, again, and her voice breaks a little.

And Wyck watches as the loyalty and the faith drains out of her eyes and is replaced with that same look he gets from everyone else.

Disappointment, and disgust.

FOURTEEN

Failure means death

It has been hours.

Or at least to Daven Wyck it *feels* like hours.

Hours of sitting with his back against cold, bare stone, waiting. He spent the first fw minutes staring at the rough-coat walls and counting the tiles on the floor. Fifty-six. Then counting the loops in the chain connecting the binders on his wrists. Ten. Then the comedown hit him, and counting became too much. The headache first, pressing in like a stormfront and pushing on the back of his eyes. The ringing in his ears. The shaking. Though some of that could just as well be down to the waiting.

Waiting for death.

Wyck rests his head against the cold stone. It does nothing for his headache. He wonders if it'll happen in here. If after all his running, it'll happen in the Sanctum of Bones, in a holding cell where the walls are marked with bloody scratches from whatever was held here before he was. If after everything else he's done, he'll die for helping to save the life of a Throne-damned witch.

'Stupid,' he says. The room catches his voice. There's no echo in here. 'So stupid.'

Wyck doesn't mean to start laughing. It just happens. He laughs so much it hurts. So much that his eyes run and he can't tell whether it's even laughter anymore.

And then he hears the door bolt slide across. Loud, like a gunshot. It makes him flinch. Before the door can open, Wyck runs his hand across his face and uses the wall to stand up because if this is really it, and this is where he dies, then he'll do it on his damned feet.

'Daven Wyck.'

Severina Raine's outsider accent twists his name. Wyck had thought her dead, just for a while. That he'd escaped her judgement. Wyck looks at Raine standing there. Her shadow-black coat is blood-spattered and torn by fire and cutting edges. She holds her bolt pistol at her side, her dark eyes unreadable. He realises he should have known better. That she wouldn't die so easily.

That you don't escape the judgement of a commissar like Severina Raine.

'Commissar,' he says, and his voice is a rasp that sounds weak, which makes him angry at himself.

Raine walks into the room, but she is not alone. Zane is with her. The witch is bound too, her thin wrists manacled, though Wyck knows she could break them easily if she tried. It's a show of faith. Of obedience. Wyck's eyes catch with her silver ones, and a word pushes into his head.

+*Kin*.+

It's almost enough for Wyck to start laughing again.

Raine drags two chairs into the middle of the space.

'Sit,' she says.

Wyck does as he's told and Zane does the same beside him. Raine doesn't sit. She stands and watches them both, so still that she could be carved from darkwood.

'You know why you are here,' Raine says. 'The charges set against you.'

Wyck nods.

'Four counts of murder,' Raine says. 'Against men sworn in service to High Command.'

Wyck thinks about the lake in the witch-dream and all of those that rose to the surface. The real count is closer to the number of links in the chain at his wrists than it is to four.

'It was me,' he says. 'The lot of it. Zane did nothing.'

It's all of those dead that makes him say it. All of the things he has done. His ugly secrets and his sins make him try to save Zane, even though she's a witch, and she's already as good as damned. Because she is Antari, and so is he, and if he is to be judged today then he'll take one decent act with him into the After. Zane flinches beside him, as surprised at his words as he is.

'What are you doing?' she hisses. 'Commissar, his words are false.'

Raine shakes her head. She still has her pistol drawn. The steel of the casing glints in the lumen light and her eyes glint too, as she stares at Wyck.

'I know they are,' she says. 'And those are the only lies that I will hear from you, sergeant. Is that clear?'

Wyck realises then that Raine has never fallen for any of his lies. That she has always seen through to the sharp edges of his soul. It should horrify him, knowing that, but it doesn't.

Somehow, it's a relief.

'Clear,' he says. 'Yes, commissar.'

Raine nods.

'Now,' Raine says. 'The truth.'

Severina Raine stays standing as Wyck and Zane recount what happened. The more they tell her, the more tempting it is to pace, to act, as they describe how four men sworn to High Command came to take Zane under the pretence of reassignment. A reassignment that had no Antari backing or Munitorum approval. It is just like what Raine found in Tula's records. Zane would have been registered MIA, just like the other psykers. Sent to join all of the other ghosts.

'And when you intervened,' Raine says, to Wyck, 'what did they do?'

He is flexing his fingers in an effort to stop his hands shaking. Raine has seen him do it before. If you didn't know him, you could take it for nerves.

'They told me it was above my clearance,' he says. 'Then they tried to shoot me.'

Raine knows that he is telling the truth. There is a way to Wyck's voice when he lies.

'So you killed them before they could kill you,' Raine says. 'Before they could take Zane.'

He breaks eye contact with her for a moment and looks to the pistol she holds at her side, then he rolls his shaking hands into fists.

'Yes,' he says.

'He was not the only one to do the killing,' Zane says.

The psyker looks physically diminished after facing Cretia Ommatid, almost as if she has been starved. There are dark hollows around her false eyes, and her veins are stark under her skin.

'I broke one of the soldiers,' she says, absently. 'He shattered easily. Like eggshells.'

'Mists *alive*,' Wyck says.

He is already sitting as far as he can from Zane, but he recoils from her anyway. To Raine, that hatred has always seemed rather a double standard for someone as damaged as he is.

'Before he broke, I caught the edges of the soldier's memories,' Zane says. 'They were shattered too. In pieces. But there were images.'

Raine is practised at hiding her emotions. It is a necessity as a commissar to keep your balance at all times, just like running those icy gantries over the ocean. To be sure and swift in your choices. But the more that Raine hears, the more difficult it is to remain balanced. It is the fact that the traitors managed to slip by her and get to one of her own regiment. It makes her heart burn. Makes her want to do much more than just pace the room.

But she cannot. Not yet. Raine takes a steady breath.

'What images,' she asks, evenly. 'What did you see?'

'Machines,' Zane says. 'Needles, being pushed under skin. I saw them in the soldier's memories, then again in my dreams.'

She takes a ragged breath.

'I did not know it then, but it was the fate-engines I saw,' Zane says. 'They are fuelled by the gifted. By taking power from those like me and using it to change the fate of another soul.'

Wyck shakes his head. His manacled hands move to make that superstitious Antari gesture of steepled fingers.

'Justar and his lot wanted the engines preserving,' he says. 'You are telling me that they meant to use them?'

Zane shakes her head. 'Not for themselves,' she says. 'It is the King of Winter who seeks the fate-engines.'

Raine blinks at Zane's words. At having the story Fel told her be twisted.

'The King of Winter,' Wyck says. 'You're talking about the old stories.'

'I am talking about a monster who seeks the hearts of the strong,' Zane snarls. 'I saw it in my dreams.' Zane shakes her head. She has paled, even more so than usual. 'Ommatid spoke of him too,' she says. 'Though she called him by another name.'

'What name?' Raine asks.

'Manticore,' Zane whispers. 'She called him manticore, and said that we would know him soon enough. He is one of us, not one of them. Hidden amongst loyal souls.'

Wyck shakes his head again. 'And you're going to trust the words of a traitor witch?'

Zane turns her silver eyes on him, furious, and Wyck flinches away from her.

'I do not *trust* Cretia Ommatid,' Zane snarls. 'She is wicked, and false. She *lies*.'

The cables at the psyker's scalp hum, and Raine catches the scent of ozone. The chair Zane is sitting on rattles.

'Control,' Raine says, firmly.

Zane exhales a long breath before nodding.

'I do not trust Cretia Ommatid,' she says again, as if it bears repeating. 'I trust what I saw in my dreams and what I felt.'

'What did you feel?' Raine asks.

'The manticore is afraid of death,' Zane says. 'It has known the touch of the After. It has been bloodied by the jaws of the hounds, and it seeks a way to undo it for good.'

'To change fate,' Wyck says. 'In exchange for its soul. That's what you said.'

Zane looks at him sidelong. 'That is what I said.'

Wyck curses again, in Antari.

'Enough,' Raine says.

Just as she told Vander, Raine does not trust either Wyck or Zane, but she does understand them. They are two of a kind. Broken edges that can be used effectively, if handled carefully. They can be relied upon to act and react in ways she can anticipate. It is the reason that they are both still living, despite the risks they pose.

'Listen to me carefully,' Raine says. 'Because I will say this only once, and have no doubt that I mean every word.'

She looks at each of them in turn. At Wyck's flint-grey eyes, and Zane's false silver ones.

'Not a word spoken in this chamber leaves it,' Raine says. 'Not about the Kavrone. Not about the one called the manticore. Is that clear?'

'Yes,' Wyck says.

'Aye,' says Zane.

'You are both Antari,' Raine says. 'You know the importance of loyalty. Know that we fight for the Bale Stars, and for the Emperor, no matter what that means, or who we have to face to do it. We will not back down, or become complicit in corruption.'

Raine ejects the magazine from her pistol and takes out two of the shells. One for each of them.

'Both of you have killed in cold blood,' she says. 'The punishment for such an act is death.'

Neither Wyck nor Zane speak. They just look at the shells in the palm of Raine's gloved hand. Their death sentences, wrought in steel.

'I will stay those punishments,' she says. 'On the understanding that you were acting out of loyalty, and you will do so without question in future. That if you see or hear anything else, you bring it straight to me. Do we understand one another?'

'Yes, commissar.'

This time the answer comes from both of them, without hesitation or a trace of deceit. That's another thing Raine understands about the two of them, and the Antari in general. They place a great value on debts owed, and on what is given being repaid. By staying their sentences, she has placed them firmly in her debt. Raine finds manipulation distasteful, but it is another skill that she is practised in. Another necessity, for a commissar.

'Good,' Raine says. 'Because failure will mean death.'

Zane nods. 'As it always does,' she says.

Raine finds herself nodding too.

'Yes,' she says. 'As it always does.'

Steadfast, before

Severina Raine sits in the hallway with her fists locked together tightly. So tightly that her nails dig into her skin. So tightly that her hands can't shake in the way that they so want to.

'Cadet.'

The word makes her look up. It comes from the guard. The big one, with the cruel scar that has turned one of his eyes porcelain-white and useless. He has a heavy pistol at his belt and a lasrifle slung across his chest. His uniform is black, like Severina's own.

Executioner's black.

'It is time,' he says.

Severina gets to her feet. Her legs try to shake now, just like her hands. She follows the guard down the hallway, keeping her eyes on his back, and not on the bare rockcrete walls, or the heavy, windowless cell doors set into them. Her boots ring on the stone floor, and she is reminded for a moment of that day long ago. The day an officer came to explain that her mother was dead.

'In here,' the guard says, and he indicates the last of the heavy doors. 'Five minutes. No longer.'

Severina reaches out and releases the bolt on the door. It echoes in the silence of the corridor. She pushes the heavy door open, steps into the cell and takes her seat in the empty chair, bolted to the floor. Then she finally looks at the cell's occupant, whose hands are knitted together, too, and bound by silver chains that lock to the table in front of her.

'Sister,' Lucia says, softly.

Her eyes are flat, like dulled metal. Bruising presses in on them, and coils itself around Lucia's throat. Old blood is dried around her nose.

Coward's blood.

'Do not call me that,' Severina says. 'You have no right.'

Lucia nods. 'No,' she says. 'I suppose not.'

Lucia falls silent and still. The penitent's shift she wears hangs from her, as if she has not eaten in weeks.

'Will you say nothing?' Severina asks.

'What would you have me say?' Lucia says. 'What could I possibly tell you that could ease that agony you feel? Do you want me to tell you that I regret my actions? That I was fooled, or framed?' She shakes her head. 'They would be lies, Severina, and no matter what else I have become, I will not lie. Not to you.'

Severina is no longer able to control the way she trembles. All of the pretty words she imagined saying melt away like snow and the only ones left are the ones that hurt as badly as she does.

'How could you?' Severina asks. 'How could you give in to it, after everything we promised one another?'

Lucia reaches across the table, as far as the chains will allow. Her fingertips barely brush against Severina's wrist, making her recoil. That is when her sister's eyes go from flat to glittering with tears.

'I did not give in,' Lucia says. *'But I did fail. I failed the crusade. The commissariat. I failed mother, and I failed you.'*

She leans back again and pulls her hand away.

'The price for failure, Severina,' Lucia says. *'What is it?'*

For an instant they are just girls again, reading by candlelight when they should both be asleep. But that memory, like all of the others, is damaged now. Tarnished.

'Death,' Severina says. *'That is the price for failure.'*

The words fall heavy between them.

'I followed what was in my heart,' Lucia says. *'And in turn I have broken yours. For that, please know that I am truly sorry.'*

Severina shakes her head. She has to do it to keep herself from crying.

'My heart is not broken,' she says. *'Attachment is a weakness and I am better rid of it. Better rid of you.'*

Lucia blinks, then she nods. A tear traces its way down to her chin.

'Yes,' she says. *'I think that you are.'*

There is still time left but Severina cannot bear the cell any longer, nor the sight of her sister. She gets to her feet, aching now as well as trembling. Burning with rage and hate, and most of all, with grief. She turns her back on Lucia and puts her hand on the cell door.

'Goodbye, Severina.'

Severina does not answer. She just opens the cell door and walks out without looking back.

FIFTEEN

The truth is contained within

Lydia Zane listens to the psy-reader tick and scratch in time with the commissar's pen against the page, and tries not to think of Cretia Ommatid, or what she was shown in the Sanctum of Bones. What she felt, upon being offered freedom and companionship.

It is just another test, she thinks. *Do not break.*

The psy-reader ticks more quickly, and Zane squeezes her false eyes closed.

Please, do not break.

'Tell me about the tree,' Raine says.

Zane has told the commissar many times about where the singing tree grew, and how she heard the Emperor's voice in the rustling of its leaves, but she has never spoken of what happened afterwards.

'The singing tree,' Zane says, softly. 'Not long after I came into my gifts, it caught afire.'

She stops and breathes and smells it again. The burning

of the singing tree. The acrid taste of smoke plays over her tongue.

'Everyone in the village ran to the tree,' Zane says. 'They tried to douse the flames, but they were fierce and strong and they would not die until the white bark was blackened and the leaves were ashes.'

She digs her fingernails into the arms of the chair. The binders on her wrists dig into her skin. The commissar keeps writing and Zane's birds sit on either side of her, watching.

'They said that it was witch's work,' Zane says. 'That I had done it.'

Her voice catches, and the psy-reader's needle does the same. The commissar stops writing, and glances at the psy-reader as it draws jagged lines like tongues of flame. Like those Zane saw in the vision, burning around Ommatid and Rol.

Such screaming.

'I pleaded with the villagers,' Zane says. 'With the priests and the traders. With the elders. With my mother, and my father.'

She remembers all of those grey Antari eyes, so full of fear and hate. That same look that she has earned every day since, from every one of her kin.

'They did not believe me,' Zane says. 'So they bound my hands and covered my eyes. They cut off all of my hair. Then they took me deep into the forest where the night was coldest and left me there. Scattered ocean salt around me in a witch's circle.'

Raine frowns. 'You did not argue?' she asks. 'Or fight?'

Zane remembers how she had felt as her hair was cut roughly with a blade. As they dragged her with her feet snagging over roots and wet earth until they dropped her bodily to the ground and said those words. The ones that she told

Kayd could not hurt her, but they always do, because she hears them in the voices of her mother and father.

Spare me the ways of the witch.

She had been afraid too. But her fear had been of what would happen if she tried to fight them. Of what a mess her gifts would make. Of proving she was what they thought her to be.

A monster, in a daughter's skin.

'I did not argue,' she whispers, tasting blood. 'I did not fight. I waited in the heart of the forest for the witch-finders to come and take me away. To go up to the stars where I would no longer be alone. Where I would belong.'

Raine's expression this time is harder to read.

'And did you?' she asks. 'Belong?'

Zane shakes her head. 'No,' she says, softly. 'I did not.'

'And the tree,' Raine asks. 'Did you light it afire?'

Zane's hands tremble as she remembers that night. Falling asleep to her mother's song.

Dreaming of flames.

Her jaw aches, and her eyes do too. Deep within the sockets, as they did when she lost them.

'I never meant for it,' she whispers. 'I did not know then the power of dreams.'

Raine nods. 'Like when you dreamt of the King of Winter?' she asks. 'Of the manticore?'

Zane nods. It is an effort to raise her head again.

'He wants everything,' she says. 'The stars. All the spaces in between. He will consume all of the good hearts until no more remain.'

She takes a ragged breath.

'Ommatid said that you would be the one to know him,' she says, before she can stop herself. 'Ask the outsider, she said.'

Raine shakes her head, and for a moment Zane wonders if this is still a testing.

'I have my suspicions,' the commissar says. 'But I cannot be certain.'

'Perhaps certainty is close,' Zane says. 'Or perhaps the answer is already at hand, but hidden.'

Raine puts her hand into her pocket and takes out that timepiece that she so treasures. She tilts the face of it as if to check the time.

'Will that be all, commissar?' Zane asks.

Raine looks at the readout and at her notes.

'Yes,' she says. 'Unless there is anything you would like to tell me.'

Zane looks at the two birds, sitting silently beside Raine. Their eyes are like beads of jet.

'No,' Zane says. 'Not a thing.'

Daven Wyck stands with his back against the wall in the hallway of the old scholam, listening to the wind howl. To his kinfolk moving around. Talking and singing. He picks up the smell of smoke on the wind. Of petrochem, from the yard outside.

Of blood, from where it has soaked into his fatigues.

Wyck puts his hand in the pouch at his belt and takes out the bolt shell that Raine gave him. He lets it sit in the palm of his hand. The shell is heavy and cold and marked with a graven aquila, like the one on the chain around his neck. That is heavy too. Growing heavier by the day.

Wyck has been running from death since Cawter. Since he left his name painted in ashes under the jungle canopy. By rights, holding the shell should feel no different. It's just the fate he is owed, made real. Just the duskhounds' due.

But it does feel different, this time. It makes the After feel closer, yawning wide like jaws. Waiting. Wyck can feel judgement looming too. The counting of his many sins. Wyck realises that it is not just death he has been running from, all this time, but from everything he has done. From every instinct and every decision.

From every cut, quick and deep.

Wyck rests his head against the cold stone for a moment longer and listens to the howl of the wind as he puts that bolt shell back in the pouch at his belt, next to the one that holds the vials. He runs his hands over his face and stands his aching body up straight, then follows the hall the rest of the way to his squad's assigned quarters.

The door is wedged open, so they don't notice him when he steps through it. His Wyldfolk are all sitting together in a ragged circle, talking. Or all that's left of them, anyway. Tian's cot is undisturbed, his spare kit still sitting on top of it. His prayer papers and his darkwood idol from home.

'Room for one more?' Wyck asks.

They stop talking then and turn to stare at him. Crys and Kane. Jey and Haro. But especially Awd. The look on his face, you'd think he'd seen the dead walk.

'Sarge,' Crys says. 'What happened?'

'I spoke with the commissar,' Wyck says. 'And then she let me walk.'

Awd's face is drained pale. Wyck can see the tremor on him.

'Then those souls, sworn to the Throne,' Awd says. 'You didn't kill them?'

His Wyldfolk stare in silence and wait for the answer. For the lie that Raine gave him to tell. Running water echoes from elsewhere in the building.

Drip. Drip. Drip.

'No,' he says. 'I killed them.'

'Sarge,' Crys says. 'What are you saying?'

She's desperate to have him redeemed, Wyck can see it in her face. He feels much worse about that than he does the killing. All the things he's done, and still she looks at him that way, as if he could be a saint, or anywhere close.

'They weren't sworn to the Throne,' Wyck says. 'They were Sighted, wearing High Command's colours. That's why I killed them.'

'Then they were enemies,' Crys says. 'Infiltrating. They meant to hurt us and you stopped them.'

Wyck nods, and that part, at least, isn't a lie.

'I knew it,' Crys says. 'Knew it couldn't be right.'

'Do you swear it?' Awd asks.

Crys scowls at him. 'He said it, Ger, and the commissar let him go. Isn't that enough?'

'You know that it isn't,' Awd says.

Crys moves like she's about to hit him.

'It's alright, Yulia,' Wyck says.

He holds out his hand, palm up. The one with the Wyldfolk's mark on it. He takes the knife from his belt and draws it across the old scar to open it again.

'I swear it,' he says, careful in the way he chooses his words. That he chooses only truths. 'I swear that I killed those who meant to hurt us, and that I did it to protect my kin.'

The blood wells up slow. He rolls his hand and squeezes it tight and blood drips onto the floor. Wyck thinks about his words, chosen so carefully. That he just said kin, meaning Zane, and that he said it in the moment of an oath. He thinks about that bolt shell he carries, the twin to hers, and he knows that it is a truth now. The two of them really are kin, whether he likes it or not. They are bound together by death, made and owed.

'You believe me now?' Wyck asks.

Awd nods. He has more than paled now. 'I believe you,' he says, softly.

Severina Raine sits on the floor of her quarters with the datareader she took from her desk. It sings and spools as the projection snaps live and Lucia's words resolve once again.

For my sister. The truth is contained within.

Raine has the timepiece in her hand. The brass has warmed to her skin. She thinks about the King of Winter, and what he wants. She thinks about what Lucia said to her in the penitent's cell, all of those years ago.

I followed what was in my heart.

Raine's fingers hover over the keys a while before she inputs the passcode carefully and slowly.

H.E.A.R.T.

She hits the input key and the hololith snaps to black. When it resets, Raine finds herself looking into her sister's dark eyes for the first time in more than a decade. Raine hits the key to stop the recording before Lucia can speak and her sister freezes with a spare half-smile on her face.

It is too much to bear, that smile. That look in her sister's eyes. One hundred memories come flooding back that Raine thought she had buried or dismantled. Running the gantries with Lucia in Gloam's chill wind. Training as children with wooden blades while their mother applauded. Poring over maps and learning speeches and playing word games together until it was so dark they could not see one another. Lucia's last word in the game was always *goodnight*, but Raine would guess poorly on purpose so she could speak with her sister for longer. Lucia humoured her, every time.

Raine wants to leave, then, but she cannot stand. She wants

to speak, but she knows that she will cry. So she does the only thing she can do. What she came here to do.

She presses the key, and listens to her sister speak.

'My sister,' Lucia says, and her voice is just as Raine remembers it. Clear, and strong. So much like their mother's. 'If you are watching this, then it means that you too have followed your heart.'

She pauses, and that smile slips away. The recording was captured before Lucia was incarcerated. She isn't starved or bruised, and she still wears her commissariat black.

'If you are watching this, it means that you too have seen the darkness at the heart of the Bale Stars, and our crusade. I am sorry that it had to be you, just as I knew that it could be nobody else. You have always been the kind to seek the truth.'

Lucia laughs, and it is a sad sound.

'To ask questions,' she says. 'You always were asking questions.'

Raine laughs too. It happens without intent, just like the tear that follows it and paints a cold trail down her face. She wipes it away quickly, as if it will leave a mark.

'I promised you the truth,' Lucia says. 'And it will not be easy to take. For that, I am sorry too.'

Lucia pauses and takes a breath. In the background of the recording, Raine hears a fierce storm.

'The darkness,' Lucia says. 'It is not colouring the crusade. It *is* the crusade. The corruption touches every part of it, and the roots of it are in High Command.'

She shakes her head.

'They sent us to fight on foot on Virtue instead of collapsing the ice caverns from orbit because they were looking for something. For the same thing the Sighted had wanted from Virtue. Psychically-active crystal, hidden in the ice. The Sighted use it for rituals. For rites. I saw things on Virtue that should not have been possible. One of the Nine, killed in action, then active again not a day later. Not healed. The death was *undone*. After we took back Virtue, huge quantities of that crystal were shipped back to Steadfast under the cover of a ghost regiment.'

'The Strixian Ninety-Ninth,' Raine murmurs, in the same moment that her sister does, their two voices becoming indistinguishable.

'It is not just the crystal that they are moving,' Lucia says. 'But weapons too. Armour. Sometimes even souls. They allow the transport fleets to be intercepted by the Sighted, who use our own weapons against us. They leak information and tactical data to keep the Bale Stars in conflict, ensuring that the war machine endures. Ensuring that they endure.'

Listening to Lucia's words is like standing before a cold sunrise. One so bright that it picks out everything in hard, uncompromising detail and shows up all of the flaws.

'That is the reason that they want the crystal, too,' Lucia says. 'To endure beyond the threat of death. They are powerful enough to create a regiment of ghosts in order to do it. To manipulate a whole fighting arm of the crusade to their own will in order to capture heretic artefacts and then fool the Munitorum into moving them. They mean to wrest power, and they do not need to gather allies to do it, because from High Command, every soldier sworn to the crusade is already an ally.'

Lucia sighs and she rubs at her face with the back of her hand. The capture is so unstable and aged that it is the first indicator that Lucia is crying.

'What should you do,' Lucia asks, 'when you cannot tell how far the rot has spread?'

Raine is shaking now, just as she did when she saw Lucia last. 'Burn it all down,' she whispers. 'To ensure you catch it.'

'I meant to burn it, but in this I have failed,' Lucia says. 'My enemies have discovered me, and soon I will be just another ghost. Another soul spent to keep the war machine alive. I wish that I could have told you in person, but they would have killed you just as they will surely kill me. I could not allow that to happen, so I hid the truth away knowing that you would seek it, because you always do.'

That smile appears on Lucia's face again, just for a moment.

'You will not fail as I did, Severina,' she says. 'You will not break as father did. You will not be like me, or like him, or even mother. You will be your own legend, and for that, I am so very proud.'

And that is where the pict-feed capture stalls and ends, on Lucia's face and that sparest hint of a smile. Raine aches from the day. From the fight in the Sanctum. From the dreams given to her by Ommatid. From the blast that should have killed her and from every duty she had to fulfil before she could find her way to this room in peace and finally unlock the truth her sister left her. Every one of those aches pales now compared to the one in her chest. She was wrong. She let her sister die, and then killed her over and over in her memories too, every day, for a decade.

Raine puts her hand out as if to touch the hololith, and it dazzles around her fingertips.

'Sister,' she says, softly. 'I am sorry.'

Wyck turns his hand and looks at it in the dim light. At the blood from the mark he reopened and the ashes on his fingertips from painting Tian's name. The smell of the smoke clings to his fatigues and to his skin. They burned Tian's darkwood idol too. It didn't seem right for anyone else to have it.

'Dav.'

Wyck's name is the first word Awd has spoken to him in hours. He says it quietly because Haro and Jey are asleep in their cots. Wyck doesn't know where Crys is, or Kane. He wonders for a moment if they are together somewhere.

Wyck sits back on his cot. 'What do you want?' he asks.

Awd is sat on the floor. He won't look Wyck in the eyes.

'I thought it was true,' he says. 'I let my heart get twisted, when I should have known better.' Awd shakes his head. 'It's because of the forges,' he says, and then he sighs. 'No, not just that. Because of Gholl too. Drast. Because of Hyxx and those priests. You remember?'

Wyck nods. 'You know I do.'

Awd does look him in the eye now. 'Fighting like that, where every face is an enemy. It's an ugly way to do it. It splinters away the soul, piece by piece. A little more, every time. You know what I mean?'

Wyck thinks about those fights and the ones before it too. He thinks about running from death and all the things he has done.

'You know I do,' he says, again.

'When I heard about the bodies, I got to thinking that maybe you were an enemy too,' Awd says. 'That maybe you'd gotten splintered so badly you'd broken. Snapped.'

Wyck thinks about holding that shard of glass to Nuria Lye's throat. Splintered. Broken.

Snapped.

'So you went to Yuri,' Wyck says.

Awd nods, still looking at the floor. 'I couldn't let it lie. I tried, believe me, but I couldn't work those hooks out of my soul.'

He finally looks up then.

'If you wanted me out,' Awd says. 'If you wanted me dead,

I would understand it. I betrayed the mark. Betrayed the blood we have spent.'

Wyck looks down at his hands. At the ash and the blood and the mark made twice now. He thinks about his death sentence. About the Kavrone and the fate-engines and the fact that the fighting will only get more ugly from here.

'No,' Wyck says. 'I don't want you out. Don't want you dead, either.'

'You don't?' Awd asks.

'I want you to watch over the others,' Wyck says. 'Mind them. Make sure they aren't getting splintered too badly. Especially the void-born. Yulia will help. She's always had too much of a heart.'

The words are clearly not what Awd expects, because he doesn't answer in any way but to frown.

'Do you understand me?' Wyck asks. 'I need you to say you'll do it.'

'I understand what you're asking, Dav, but I don't understand what you're asking it for.'

Wyck shakes his head. 'Just give me an answer,' he says.

'Alright,' Awd says. 'I'll mind them.'

'There's another thing,' Wyck says. 'I want to know who it was who told you about the bodies.'

Awd is quiet for a moment. He glances over at Jey and Haro to make sure they are still sleeping.

'And if I tell you,' he says. 'What will you do?'

'Set them straight,' Wyck says. 'That's all.'

'You swear?' Awd says.

'I swear,' Wyck replies. 'One time before the commissar's pistol is enough.'

Awd sighs, long and heavy. 'Kolat,' he says. 'It was Ely Kolat.'

* * *

Andren Fel waits by those same words painted on the wall, just as Raine did for him before. He turns the datakey in his hands. It is such a small thing, the datakey, but it means so much. It might change everything.

Might be as much a death sentence as a bullet.

He rolls his hand around the datakey at the sound of footsteps approaching. It is Raine, but she is not wearing her commissariat uniform. No coat. No cap. She has on plain training fatigues and boots. A black vest and a short thermal layer jacket. The clothing she wears for sparring and combat drills. Her dark hair is wound in a crown braid like always, but much of it is escaping as if she has been woken from sleep. Judging by how exhausted she looks, though, she certainly wasn't sleeping.

'Captain,' she says.

There is something different in her voice too. Fel thinks it might be the sound of hurt and he wonders just how bad the Sanctum was.

'Commissar,' he says, because that is how this works. 'Not dead yet, then.'

The smile on Raine's face is so slight that most wouldn't catch it.

'Not yet,' she says.

Fel opens his hand and shows Raine the datakey, and she nods. They walk in silence through the building that was once a scholam, to that same room as before. Raine is masking a limp from the fight and her knuckles are split and bruised. Fel feels guilt over it. Not that she is hurt, but that he should have been there to get hurt with her. He pushes open the door to the scholam's old library and the smell of damp and decay hits him all over again. Like old trees, turned sickly. It's that map, being eaten away.

The Bale Stars, turning black and rotten.

Fel shuts the heavy door behind them and the papers scudding on the floor settle. Raine stands in amongst them with her arms folded tight across her chest. He crosses over to her. In the years he has known her, and in all of their time spent fighting together and otherwise, Fel has never seen Raine look so thoroughly dismantled.

'What is troubling you?' he asks her.

Raine unfolds her arms and runs one hand over her hair. That is why it has come so loose.

'Just an old injury,' she says. 'Tell me what you found.'

Fel knows she means more than she says, and not to press her on it. Her will is her own, as it always has been.

'I found the Strixians,' he says. 'And those who made them.'

He connects the datakey to the portable slate he is carrying and passes it to her. Raine pages through the records, taking them in quickly with her keen eyes.

'Do you recognise any of the names?' he asks her.

Raine frowns. 'No,' she says. 'Not one. Not from records or reports or even stories. Ghosts, in all the ways it can be true, looking at these records. Every one of them listed as killed in action.'

'But they are ghosts accounted for by the same medicae,' Fel says.

Raine nods. 'Who is herself a ghost.'

Fel asks her for the tablet back and pulls up the medical records attributed to Isabella Luz. He hands it back to Raine.

'This record is locked with a passcode on top of the alpha-grade authorisation,' he says. 'Look at the date.'

She does, and her frown deepens. Raine moves her fingers over the keys, and types a word into the slate. It whirs for a moment, and then a word blinks green on the projected screen.

AUTHORISED.

Fel stares at it.

'What code did you use?' he asks. 'What is higher than alpha-grade?'

Raine takes a breath.

'Manticore,' she says.

The pict-feed opens to a wide shot of a medicae facility like any number of others that Raine has seen across the crusade front. A flakboard room, bare and clinical. Isabella Luz sits on a stool to speak into the capture device. She must have been in her late thirties when the capture was taken. Her skin is mid-brown, her hair shaved down to the bare scalp. Her eyes are keen and hazel coloured, but they sit in an exhausted face. There is a minor spatter of blood on the collar of her uniform that continues onto her throat.

'Begin recording,' Luz says. 'Surgeon-Major Isabella Luz. After-action report for the battle of Steadfast.'

Luz goes on to list casualty numbers. Those who went missing. Those who were killed. The numbers are astronomical, even to Raine, who knows well the cost of war. Steadfast is to this day the largest undertaking in the crusade's history. Their greatest triumph.

Or at least it has always appeared to be so.

'This doesn't bode well,' Fel says, quietly.

Raine shakes her head. She knows they are standing at the edge of the shadow. She can feel it.

Luz finishes her lists and her recordings of numbers, and then she stops and rubs absently at that blood marking her throat.

'The Lord-General Militant was wounded badly today facing down the traitor calling himself Dektar the Ascended.

Such cuts would have killed a lesser man. The walk back even more so.'

Luz pauses and shakes her head.

'Five miles,' she says. 'With one lung collapsed and lacerations to three major organs. He still tried to fight his Lions when they wanted to put him under and bring him in.'

Luz leans her elbows on the desk the capture device is mounted on. She wrings her hands as she speaks.

'I was able to stabilise him,' she says. 'And to repair a good deal of the damage that Dektar did, though Serek will have scars and pain for the rest of his days.'

Her voice skips over those last few words, and she squeezes her eyes shut and hides her face in her hands for a moment.

'I cannot do it,' she says. 'I swore to him that I would say nothing, but I cannot uphold that oath. Not even to one such as him.'

She checks over her shoulder, as if someone may be watching, then looks down at the desk as she continues, and not into the lens of the capture device.

'The rest of the Lord-General Militant's days will be few.' Luz takes a breath. 'In the course of saving him, I found the death sentence already written into his blood. His bones. Marrowblight, the worst I have ever seen.'

Raine realises her hand is shaking as she holds the slate. She hears Fel take a breath through his teeth. Neither of them have moved since the record started. Raine feels frozen, locked in place right down to her heart.

'This cannot be a part of it,' Raine says.

'No,' Fel says. 'It can't be.'

But she doesn't feel sure, and she can tell from Fel's voice that he doesn't either.

'The marrowblight is advanced,' Luz continues. 'Too advanced to do anything much about but offer comfort and care. If he were to cede command, he could perhaps hope for three months.'

She takes a ragged breath and a rueful smile flickers for an instant on her face.

'He told me to get him four months without ceding a thing. That he will not back down because the odds are poor. I will do as he asks because that is my duty, but I cannot go without recording this matter. That, too, is my duty, no matter how much it pains me.'

Luz shakes her head as if to clear it and wipes at her eyes with the back of her hand. She reaches out to end the recording, and the capture skips for a moment before restarting again. The room is the same, but Luz is different. She looks even more exhausted than before. Her eyes are wide and wary.

'Begin recording,' she says, and her voice is hoarse. 'As I feared, the Lord-General Militant's condition is deteriorating. He is shedding weight and muscle. Cannot keep food down. His body is poisoning him.'

Luz doesn't try not to cry this time. Raine feels a tear slide down her own cheek too.

'He forgets,' she says. 'That is the worst thing. Forgets to take his medication, or things he has done. He forgets where his scars come from, and I have to tell him his own legend. Tell him the hero that he is. He fights the sickness as he fights everything, with conviction and with a powerful will, but this sickness cannot be beaten by either of those things.'

Luz pauses and her hand goes to the aquila on the chain around her neck.

'Only faith can aid him now,' she says. 'He prays. I pray. That is all either of us can do. As of this recording, I am still the only one to know his true condition, but I will not be for long. We will not be able to hide it anymore, or he will die, and then everyone will know.'

Luz shakes her head.

'And then we truly will be lost,' she says.

Then she reaches out and cuts the recording again. When it restarts, Isabella Luz is completely still and staring. Her eyes are not keen.

'Begin recording,' she says, and her voice is cold and flat. 'On this day, I commit to record the death of Lord-General Militant Alar Serek. Our greatest hero. Our brightest light, gone out. Gone to the Emperor's side.'

Luz is so still it looks as though the recording has stopped, but then gets to her feet and lashes out, knocking the pict-feed capture device to the floor of the medicae facility, where it lies with the lens cracked. The vox pick-up still catches the sound of a pained, wordless yell from Luz before the record ends.

'This isn't...' Fel says, and then he pauses. 'It's a lie.'

His voice is just a raw whisper, and he is shaking as he stands there. He looks hollow. Broken. Raine knows this, because she feels just the same.

'There is one more recording,' Raine says.

The final record of Surgeon-Major Isabella Luz spins up and flickers to a start. She sits in a different medicae facility now, between a different set of flakboard walls. The recording starts with Luz looking back over her shoulder. When she turns to face the lens, Raine sees that same hollow look in Luz's eyes too.

'On this day, I retract from the record the death of Lord-General Militant Alar Serek,' she says. 'Because he has returned to us. He lives.'

Raine knew Luz's words were coming, but they are still hard to hear, because she can guess what is coming next.

'Not just lives,' Luz says. 'He *thrives*. The marrowblight still endures in his blood and his body, but he is stronger now than he was before he fought Dektar the Ascended. He remembers everything.'

Luz pauses. She closes her eyes in that same way she did on the first recording and takes a deep breath.

'I should be rejoicing,' she says. 'I should be celebrating the miracle that restored our greatest hero, but I cannot, because this is not a miracle.'

Luz leans right into the lens.

'He is different,' she murmurs. 'Changed. It is his eyes. They are *so* blue now. And then there is the matter of the mark.'

She puts the flat of her hand to her chest, above her heart.

'Here,' she says. 'There is a scar that is not a scar.'

'No,' Raine says, despite herself.

'It is a fate-mark,' says Isabella Luz.

The recording ends abruptly. Raine's knuckles are pale as she grips the data-slate.

'Serek.' She has to say it aloud to make it real. 'The Lord-General Militant. He is the manticore. The shadow at the heart of the crusade.'

Raine's hands are scarred, like the rest of her body. Scars earned fighting for the Bale Stars. For Serek.

'He has betrayed us all,' she says.

Raine can't find the strength to keep standing, so she goes to her knees and puts the slate down amongst the scattered histories of the Bale Stars. Years of blood spent and war made and souls lost.

'All for a lie,' Raine says. 'He was a *lie*.'

She thinks of a dozen moments in her own history. Amongst

them, the conversation she had with Serek on Hyxx, at the Temple of Unlight. Lucia's graduation day on Gloam. The forges, when he spoke of her mother. Gholl, in Caulder's Reach. The day she saw Lucia, at the holding cell. A visit that the Lord-General Militant allowed to happen.

Serek. It was all Serek.

Raine doesn't intend the agonised sound she makes. It just happens.

Fel drops to his knees beside her and puts his arms around her. Raine lets him. She leans into the embrace and returns it in kind, just for a moment. It feels as though if she lets go, she might become untethered altogether.

Lost.

'What will we do now?' he asks, and he sounds lost too.

Raine has spent her entire life knowing the answer to that question, no matter who asks it, and why. She knows the answer just as clearly now too. It's just the saying it. She lets go and pulls away from Fel, then gets to her feet and gives him a hand up to his.

'We drag it out into the light,' she says. 'All of it. The Strixians. The Kavrone. Serek himself and any who have fallen with him. Every one of them must face judgement.'

Raine looks Fel in his storm-grey eyes.

'This is your last chance,' she says. 'To walk away from this. This path will be bloody, and there is no turning back.'

'Not a chance,' he says. 'I swore it, remember? Until the end.'

Raine nods. The words feel final.

'Until the end,' she says.

Steadfast, before

The guard with the porcelain-white eye closes the door behind Severina and bolts it. The sound echoes again. It reminds Severina of a gunshot and makes her think of the handful that will end Lucia's life. She puts her own hand to her chest. It is hurting so badly that she is surprised the hand doesn't come away bloodied.

'Severina.'

She looks up at the sound of her name. The man who spoke it stands in the corridor, flanked by two guards in black carapace and furs. He is tall and strong, dressed in ceremonial white, with that red sash she remembers slung across his chest.

'Lord-General Militant,' she says, dropping into a bow.

'Enough,' he says. 'At ease.'

Severina stands up straight, but she is not at ease. She cannot be. Not in this place, with him present. With him knowing full well why she is here. Serek waves his guards away. The one with the porcelain-white eye goes too, leaving them alone in the corridor.

'Did you speak with your sister?' Serek asks.

'Yes, lord,' Severina says.

'And what did she say?'

Severina thinks for a moment about that tear tracing its way down Lucia's face.

'It does not matter, lord,' she says. 'Because my sister is a traitor, and a traitor's words are worth less than nothing.'

Serek nods. His ice-blue eyes are thoughtful.

'I am glad to hear you say so,' he says. 'Your mother was an Imperial hero. A fierce and honourable soul. If you are to survive, then you must be the same.'

Severina feels the weight of that expectation then. Of her mother's legacy. Every medal. Every moment, down to the grand ceremony of her state remembrance service.

A hero, even in death.

'I will give everything,' Severina says. 'Heart and soul, as she did.'

'As we all must,' Serek says. 'When you join the crusade, both your enemies and your allies will test you. Every choice will matter. Every choice will change you, so you must never forget the lessons you learned at the scholam and before it.'

Severina nods.

'Duty, honour and faith, lord,' she says.

It is Serek's turn to nod. 'In time, you will come to consider your sister's failure another lesson,' he says. 'One about loyalty. You know what awaits Lucia Raine at dawn tomorrow.'

'Death,' Severina says, making an effort to sound strong as she does so. 'The fate of all traitors.'

'Never forget that. Never turn your back on the Bale Stars, or the crusade. On your allies, or on me, or the same fate will await you.' Serek tilts his head. 'And I think the memory of Thema Raine deserves better, don't you?'

Severina thinks of her mother and how she would feel if she knew of Lucia's fate. It makes her heart ache all over again.

'Yes, lord,' she says.

'Good,' Serek says. 'Then we understand one another.'

'Of course,' Severina says.

'Then I bid you goodbye, Severina Raine,' Serek says.

He makes the sign of the aquila.

'For the Bale Stars,' he says.

Raine makes her own aquila in turn.

'For the Emperor,' she replies.

And then Serek turns and walks away, his polished boots echoing on the flagstones.

And that sound, too, could as well be gunshots.

SIXTEEN

Lighting fires

Andren Fel walks back towards the Duskhounds' assigned quarters without really seeing. Without hearing, either. His mind is noisy with the truth.

Serek. It was always Serek.

Fel has spent his life serving the crusade. Before he served it, he trained to serve it. Save for his faith, it's the only constant he has ever known.

He stops walking and just stands there for a moment. It feels like the floor is tilting beneath his feet. His ears ring like a charge has gone off. It takes Fel a moment to recognise the sensation, because he feels it so rarely.

Panic. He is panicking.

It takes all of Fel's concentration just to find his balance again, which is why he doesn't notice Cassia Tyl until she is right beside him.

'Captain,' she says.

She is out of breath, and every one that she does take sounds like agony. Fel frowns.

'Cass,' he says.

It is the first time he has seen her since getting back. Since the Sanctum. Tyl is without her carapace or her mask. Her fatigues are bloodstained, and her face is bruised and cut. It's her eyes that are the worst part, though. Fel sees agony there too and gets another bad feeling to go alongside all of the others.

'What happened?' he asks her.

Tyl glances down at her hands as if she is hesitant to speak, and that is when Fel notices the blackening of her fingertips from ashes. His balance goes again.

'Who?' Fel asks.

'Myre,' she says, softly.

Fel has lost many over his years of service. He has learned how to deal with death. To take the hurt and stay standing. In that moment, though, he finds he can't. Myre is gone, and he wasn't there.

They lit the fire, and he *wasn't there*.

'You said the words without me!' He doesn't intend to shout at her. It just happens.

'I didn't know where you were!' Tyl raises her own voice in return. 'When you would return, or if you would at all. I couldn't leave Myre waiting for her name.'

Fel shakes his head. It's not a good enough reason. 'We are kin, Cassia. We do it together, always.'

'We are *kin*?' Tyl snaps. It's a tone she has never used with him. 'You left us. Followed your heart and not your head.'

'That's enough,' Fel says, warningly. 'You don't know what you are talking about.'

'I saw you,' Tyl says. 'Just now, with the commissar, leaving that place you go to. She asked it of you, didn't she? Gave you another duty to do, and you picked her over us.'

'Shut up, Cass,' he says.

'That's where you go, on those nights we don't fight.' Tyl's face twists in an ugly way. 'What is it, captain, a midnight dance?'

'Shut your damned mouth,' he shouts at her.

She punches him, then, square in the face. Fel's vision dazzles for a second and he tastes blood. His temper breaks like kindling, and he grabs hold of Tyl by the front of her fatigues and puts her up against the wall.

'*Enough*,' he says.

Tyl stops fighting him and looks at him, stunned.

'Throne of Earth,' Tyl murmurs, in Antari now. 'You love her, don't you? I can see it in your face.'

Fel lets Tyl go and takes a step back from her. 'Leave it alone,' he says, though he knows that it's too late for that.

'You do.' Tyl sounds dumbfounded. 'You damned fool. She is a *commissar*, Dren.'

Tyl only calls him by the shorthand of his name when she really wants to talk to him and not her captain. When they are being kin, and not just soldiers.

'I know that,' Fel says. 'Believe me.'

'It'll be the death of you, one way or another,' Tyl says.

Those words settle heavy on Fel, because he can't deny them.

'I know that too,' he says. 'But I trust her. Severina might be a commissar, and an outsider, but she is much more than the sum of those things. She's a fierce heart, Cass.'

Tyl shakes her head at his use of Raine's given name, but all of the fight has gone out of her.

'I don't doubt it,' she says. 'But it doesn't make you any less of a fool.'

Fel shakes his head. 'You might be right about that,' he says.

Tyl puts her hand out, and the two of them clasp wrists. It's a gesture of forgiveness.

'Nobody else learns of this,' Fel says. 'I want your word.'

'You have it,' Tyl says.

'And just to be clear,' Fel says. 'You never take a swing at me like that again. Is that understood?'

Tyl's face colours, and she holds up her hands. 'Understood, captain,' she says.

'Now, tell me about Myre,' Fel says. 'I want to know how it happened.'

Tyl looks down the corridor as if she is worried that she will be heard. Fel is reminded of the pict-feed capture of Isabella Luz.

'It was Rol,' she says, softly. 'I know it sounds like dream-talk, but I swear to you, it isn't.'

Fel is already hurting from everything he has seen and heard today and from everything he now knows, but there is still plenty of room for another hurt as Tyl tells him about finding Rol again in the Sanctum of Bones. About everything he said to her. Everything he did. She gets so far through the retelling and just stops. Her hand goes to her side, where there is a good deal of blood staining her fatigues.

'You had to kill him,' Fel says.

'Yes,' Tyl says quietly.

Fel can't help thinking of when he recruited the two of them. Rol and Tyl had come up from the scholam as a pair, and stayed that way in every fight after, like shadows for one another. As good as blood.

'I'm sorry, Cass,' he says, softly.

Tyl shakes her head. 'Me too,' she says.

She takes a deep breath and shakes her head as if to clear it.

'I just can't understand it, captain. It truly was him. Not a ghost, nor an illusion. It wasn't glamour or a mask. It was Rol, but he had given up everything. How can that be?'

Fel shakes his head. 'I can't explain it,' he says, and it is the truth. He wouldn't know where to begin. 'But he is not the first, and he won't be the last.'

Tyl frowns. 'What are you saying?'

'I'm saying that things are going to get worse and that our enemies won't always be easy to see, or to face. I know that you think I am a fool, but I mean it when I say I trust the commissar, and you should too. I swear to you that I will explain everything, but I can't yet. Not until I know it is safe to do it.'

'Captain,' Tyl begins. 'What–'

'I can't,' Fel says, but he makes a quick motion with his hands, in the battle-sign that only the Duskhounds use.

Enemies, it means. *Surrounded.*

Tyl's eyes turn wary. She nods her head slowly.

'Understood,' she says.

Fel realises there is something amiss the moment he enters his quarters and the automated lumens flicker on. He draws his pistol on instinct and scans the room. His carapace armour and his weapons are still secured by genetic lock. His kitbag is stowed and the handbound book of litanies is sitting where he left it on the thin mattress. The blanket is folded neatly and undisturbed. There are no boot prints, save his own.

It's the table that's different, or more precisely the two tin cups he left on it. They are the ones he uses for making windfall tea and reading the leaves. The ones he takes with him when he goes to see Raine. One of them has fallen onto the floor.

Fel treads lightly as he crosses the room to where the tin cup is rolling on its curved edge, catching in the draught that blows through the gaps in the mortar of the walls. He nudges at the cup with the toe of his boot, and it rolls a little more, but nothing else happens. Fel exhales a long breath, then shakes his head.

It's the day, he thinks, making him paranoid.

He holsters his pistol, then stoops down and picks up the cup. It is the one that he gives to Raine. He scored a pattern of thorns into the rim of it, because you should always read from the same one so that the fates don't get tangled. Raine laughed when he first explained it to her, but now she understands and she listens. Sometimes she even lets him tell her what he sees in her fate.

Fel has never tried to hide from Raine what he feels. There would be no point, even if he wanted to, because she would see right through it, as she does with everything. But they have never acted on it, no matter what Tyl might think. Fel has no doubt that he means something to Raine, but she is a commissar, and he is a soldier, and that means something too.

Fel goes to put the cup back down on the table, and realises there is something else amiss. Something that doesn't belong, and makes him flinch to see it. It is a twist of metal, with a red glass lens set into it and silver cables coiled up like insect's legs. It's only when he puts his hand out and takes hold of it that he realises what it is. An augmetic lens.

Lori Ghael's augmetic lens.

'Cass,' Fel shouts, and it's all he gets to do, because as soon as the lens breaks contact with the metal of the table he hears a familiar sound.

A charge triggering.

There's a deafening roar and a flash of light and a huge pressure wave. The room turns around him and he ends up on the floor on the other side of it, by the door, struggling to breathe. Struggling to see. Fel tries to get to his feet, but only makes it halfway before falling again. He puts his right hand out to catch himself, only to find that it is gone, and most of his arm with it. It is just blood and bone. Jagged shards of shrapnel have buried themselves in his chest and his stomach. He is bleeding badly. Really badly. All over the floor.

'Hells,' Fel manages to say, and it uses up the last of the air in his lungs.

He hears Tyl shouting something over the ringing in his ears and sees her move into his narrowing vision as it washes in shades of grey. He wants to tell her to get clear in case there's another charge, but he can't get the words together. Can't see her clearly. Tyl's words become a rush and a mumble until he can't hear them at all. The world disappears and leaves him in darkness, just like those isolation chambers. Shapes in the shadows. On the edge, with his heart going arrhythmic, and the rest of him going numb. Fel hears a different voice. Raine's voice.

Until the end, she says.

SEVENTEEN

Consequences

The medicae facility used to be the scholam's own hospital ward. It is all tiles and steel, and it catches the echoes of machine noise and of the wounded. Catches the echo of Raine's boots on the tiles as she pushes her way through to where they have taken Andren Fel. All of that noise is a rush and a roar, like the ocean.

Like the explosion.

She had heard it, even from the other wing. Felt the tremor through the stone.

Raine's hands are already fists, but now she curls them so tightly that her knuckles ache with it.

Nuria Lye sees her coming. The medic is standing beside the curtained-off bays. Her scrubs are bloodsoaked, and there is some in her hairline too. She opens her mouth to speak, but Raine doesn't give her chance.

'Does he live?' she asks.

Lye nods. 'Just,' she says. 'It is bad, commissar.'

Raine knew it would be, but that doesn't make it easy to hear.

'Let me see him,' she says. 'See how bad it is.'

Lye runs a hand through her hair and sighs. 'Yes, sir,' she says.

Lye takes her over to one of the bays.

'He is in and out,' she says. 'On a good deal of meds. He won't be able to tell you much, if anything, and I'd beg you not to press him.'

Raine nods. On the face of it, she is there in her capacity as commissar, to find out what happened and punish those responsible. That's what Lye sees, because that's what Raine lets her see. But Raine knows where she can lay the blame for this, and so much else. The visit is because she cares, and Raine realises exactly how much when Lye pulls that curtain back.

Andren Fel is cut as if by a dozen blades. Shallow wounds mark his face and throat, and there are dark circles of blood on the bandages around his chest from much deeper ones. He is stuck with intravenous needles for pain medication, blood and fluids.

'He was full of shrapnel,' Lye says, in a low voice. 'He's lucky he made it here, the amount he bled.'

Raine is only half-listening. She is looking at where they have had to cut away Fel's right arm, almost to the shoulder. Raine takes a breath and smells counterseptic.

'Leave,' she says to Lye.

The medic does as she is told immediately. Raine's voice allows for nothing else. The curtain behind her falls closed again. Raine waits for Lye's boots to recede before she approaches him. Before she speaks.

'Andren,' she says.

He stirs, just barely, but he doesn't wake or answer her. Raine wants to say his name again. She wants to shake him just so that he'll wake and speak to her because she can't stand how still he is.

'I warned you,' she says. 'But you wouldn't walk away. You had to be so honourable.'

She shakes her head. 'I wish you had walked away,' she says.

'Not dead yet.'

Fel's words stun Raine. His voice doesn't sound like his own and when he opens his eyes, they are glassy. His pupils are like pinpricks in the grey.

'No,' Raine says, softly. 'Not yet.'

She moves closer. Close enough to reach out and touch him.

'What happened?' she asks him.

He frowns and she sees the fingers on his good hand curl.

'I can't remember,' he says. 'Not a thing but fire.'

His words are halting. Raine can see how it hurts him to talk.

'It's alright,' she says, and her words are halting too. A different kind of hurt. 'I will hunt down the ones who did this. This, and everything else. I will break every last one of them.'

Fel nods. 'I know,' he says. 'I know you will.'

Raine looks at the mess that is left of his arm and listens to the rattle of his chest as he breathes.

'Andren,' she says. 'I am sorry.'

He shakes his head.

'Until the end,' he says. 'I swore it.'

'I know,' Raine says. 'But it is too much to give.'

'No,' Fel says. 'It isn't. Not for you.'

Raine shakes her head, because he's wrong. It is too much to give and it is too much for her to take, too, because despite how hard she has tried to keep her heart her own, she has failed. She has allowed herself to care. To trust.

To love him.

Raine takes hold of his good hand and laces her fingers in his. She means to say it, then. To tell him exactly what he means to her. But his grey eyes have closed, and he is still and silent again, save for his breathing.

'Rest easy, Andren Fel,' Raine says, though she knows he cannot hear her. 'I still have stories I owe you.'

Tyl has washed her hands with boiled water, scrubbed them until the skin is red, but still she can't get rid of the blood under her fingernails.

Her captain's blood.

Tyl looks up from her hands at the sound of footsteps as Raine emerges from the curtained medical bay. The commissar's face is set in the same way it always is, giving away nothing. Her eyes, though, are an altogether different story.

They are full of pain, and rage.

Tyl feels guilt then at her earlier words, and the way she scorned Fel for giving up his heart.

'Commissar,' Tyl says, before she can change her mind. 'A word.'

'Of course,' Raine says.

The rage is there in her voice too. Running underneath it like water under ice, and just as cold. The two of them walk together out of the medicae facility and into the scholam proper. To the outside, where the wind carries their words away.

'The rumour mill says that the Sighted infiltrated this place,' Tyl says, looking at the posted guards, and the gun-nests. The Valkyrie gunships, crouched on the yard like hawks over prey. 'That they were the ones to plant that device.'

'And what do you think?' Raine asks.

Those furious eyes of hers bore into Tyl. It feels as though she can see right through to her soul. Tyl makes an effort to hold Raine's gaze.

'I think that if the Sighted were to infiltrate this place then they would have burned the lot to the ground and cut us to ribbons. I think that this was something else. Something personal.'

She pauses and considers her next words carefully.

'I think that it was done to get to you,' Tyl says.

Raine's face doesn't change.

'The captain wouldn't tell me what is going on,' Tyl says. 'He said it wasn't safe to.' She huffs a humourless laugh. 'But he did tell me that enemies surround us, and he told me that I should trust you.'

Tyl holds out her hand, palm down to the ground, the way she does when the Duskhounds make their oaths.

'So this is me trusting you,' she says. 'This is me swearing what's left of the Duskhounds to you anew, on the understanding that we will bleed whoever did this to my captain.'

Finally, there is a change in Raine's face, and Tyl sees a glimpse of that heart of hers. Fierce, like the captain said. Raine puts her hand on top of Tyl's.

'We will bleed them,' Raine says. 'I swear it.'

It is falling dark again when Wyck makes his way down to the tankers' lot. Like last time, it is noisy with the songs of repair and reconsecration. This time, the damage is much worse, though. Every one of the Fyregiants he walks past is blackened and broken, and there's a space in the line where *Mountainsong* would rest, if she weren't dead.

He finds Kolat with *Stoneking* at the end of the line like

always. He's not on his own this time. There's another of the crew with him, that idiot who is bigger even than Crys. The two of them are stood up on the Demolisher, talking. *Stoneking* is torn open all across her chassis and her turret.

'Hey, Ely,' the idiot says, when he sees Wyck. 'I think we've a lost one here. Are you lost, infantry?'

Kolat turns and looks. His goggles are pushed up on his head, so Wyck can see the way his eyes go wide, even with the half-dark and the distance. There's not a hint of that steel smile of his.

The whole thing is almost worth it then, just for that look.

'Get out of here, Curi,' Kolat says.

The big idiot shrugs and drops down off the tank. He passes by Wyck with the intent of shouldering him as he goes. Wyck sidesteps it, and Curi nearly loses his footing in the mud.

'Careful there, armour,' Wyck says. 'You spend enough time sitting on your arse as it is.'

Curi scowls and squares up to him.

'I told you to go,' Kolat says, as he drops into the mud. 'Don't make me say it again.'

Curi clearly knows Kolat well enough to know not to argue. He shrugs again with that scowl still on his face, then he walks away up the line. Wyck looks at Kolat standing there. He's got a thick-headed hammer in one hand.

'What are you doing here, Wyck?' Kolat snarls.

'What am I doing here,' Wyck says. 'That's not really what you're asking, is it? What you're really asking is why I'm still living, despite your best efforts. Despite you ratting me out to my own.'

Kolat raises that hammer of his a little in answer and Wyck shakes his head.

'You aren't going to brain me with that,' he says. 'Not here, where everyone can see. Not unless you're as stupid as your crewmate. I didn't come here for a fight.'

'You?' Kolat says. 'Not here for a fight? Why does that sound like a lie?'

Wyck laughs, because Kolat has never been able to tell when he lies. 'Either you put the hammer down, and we talk, or I'll rat you out like you did me. I'll tell the commissar all about what you did to Edra, and you can see if you walk away from her.'

Kolat blinks and glances up the line where the others are all working, then he curses in his southlander dialect and drops the hammer into the dirt. The head of it buries itself in the mud.

'Talk,' he says.

'Good call,' Wyck says. 'Here's the thing. You tried to get me killed, Ely, and that sits very poorly with me.'

Kolat shakes his head. 'You're the one who did the killing and hid the dead in the water. I just reported what I saw.'

It comes back to Wyck in flashes then. The rain. The cold. The smell of the dark, still water. The euphoria at surviving a fight that blackens and rots and turns to guilt and anger. There was a time he'd just push all that away. Let it sink, like the bodies. It's not been so easy, lately. Not since the forges, and the pendant he took. Not since the look Jey gave him in the Sanctum. The same look Crys gave him when they took him away in chains. He was in the right when he made those kills, but he didn't do it because it was right. Not really. He did it out of instinct. Out of the need to hurt, and be hurt.

He did it because he is splintered, like Awd said. Snapped.

'That's true,' Wyck says. 'But you still sold me out. Not only that, you tried to turn my own against me. That knocks the scales out. It means you owe me.'

Kolat's shoulders slump a little. Whatever else he is, he is Antari, and he knows the value of an owing.

'So report me,' he says, bitterly. 'Like you said before. Make it even.'

Wyck shakes his head. That bolt shell he carries is heavy, like walking into water with a pocketful of stones.

'No,' he says. 'Even would be me telling your crew. The big idiot Curi. Vurn, and Lieutenant Frayn, with her holy soul. There are many things I'll do, but not that.'

'What, then?' Kolat asks.

Wyck thinks about the next ugly fight. About enemies all around them, and the jaws of death opening wide and dark.

'I want more stimms,' he says. 'As strong as you can come by. I want them every time I ask for them, with no thought of payment or owing, until I'm not here to ask anymore.'

Kolat scowls. 'Fine,' he says. 'No payment or owing, for as long as you're here. You have my word.'

'Good,' Wyck says.

He turns to go, then, but he stops and looks back before he does.

'Oh, there's something else,' he says.

'What?' Kolat asks, glaring at him.

'If you try to come after me ever again, I'll tell Zane that you were the one to rat us out.'

Kolat's eyes go wide again. 'You wouldn't give me up to a cursling like her,' he says. 'To a witch.'

'I would,' Wyck says. 'In a heartbeat.'

Kolat spits on the ground. 'You are a bastard, do you know that?'

Wyck nods. 'So everyone keeps telling me.'

EIGHTEEN

Bale's Heart

Raine watches through the armourglass as the surface of Laxus Secundus falls away beneath the bulk lander. The city of Defiance and the war-broken land around it become distant enough to look like a spreading stain, and then the lander breaks the cloud layer, and she loses sight of it altogether.

'The rest of the regiment are under way, commissar.'

The voice belongs to Yuri Hale. Like her, the captain is also wearing a dress uniform. His is solid grey, save for a sash and beret in forest green. The icon of the Rifles pinned to Hale's beret is made from painted enamel, and not from gold or brass.

'You look ill at ease,' Raine says.

Hale's smile is wry. 'It's the ceremony of it,' he says.

Raine turns and looks out to the clouds. They are thinning and breaking as the lander leaves the poisoned sky of Laxus Secundus behind.

'It is the accepted protocol,' she says. 'When attending a strategium called by the Lord-General Militant.'

The summons had come shortly after Raine's visit to see Fel in the infirmary, and it had been unequivocal. The entire regiment were to pull out of Defiance immediately, and report to fleet command for their next deployment. Raine remembers the closing line, stamped in red ink.

By order of Lord-General Militant Alar Serek. For the Bale Stars. For the Emperor.

It is an effort for Raine not to drive her fist into the armourglass of the viewport.

'Perhaps it is protocol, but it still seems needless to me,' Hale says.

Formality always does to the Antari, because their own ceremonies are an equaliser, not a show of power, and Raine knows that is exactly what the call to the strategium is.

It is Serek, showing them just how powerful he is.

The strategium hall on board the Retribution-class warship *Bale's Heart* is a monstrosity built from steel and gold. Banners hang from the vaulted ceiling, rippling in the recycled air. The gold thread catches in the starlight from the arched viewports. Baroque, detailed murals span the walls, wrought in paint and plaster and gilding. Raine sees Steadfast, and Paxar. Hyxx and Virtue and dozens of other battlefields. She might have been proud to see it once, to stand in this hall and look upon the crusade's many victories, but now no matter where Raine looks, she sees only lies.

'I have never seen a gathering like it,' Hale says.

If he was ill at ease before, Hale now looks entirely discomforted. Raine sees the same look on the faces of every one of the four Antari captains sent to represent the regiment.

'Not since Steadfast,' Juna Keene says.

Like her captains, the Antari general is in dress greys, her rank marked by the white cuffs and lapels. She waits with her arms folded across her chest. Keene has been general since the day Raine joined the regiment. She is tough, and clever. A good commander.

'You were there, at the reconsecration?' Raine asks.

Keene nods. 'I was not tithed long then, of course,' she says. 'But I saw it. Saw the Lord-General Militant confer the first of his Lion's Honours. Saw them collapse the last bastion.'

She pauses, and a smile flickers on her scarred face.

'When the dust rolled out from it we all put our hands into it and marked ourselves.' She unfolds her arms, then draws one hand across her chest, shoulder to hip. 'Here, to here,' she says. 'That was our own honour, to be marked as he was.'

Raine looks at the awe written in Juna Keene's eyes. The awe that must have been written in her own, not so long ago.

Another lie, just like all of the others.

'There are the Kavrone,' Hale says, nodding to where they are taking their places.

Lukas Vander is among them, his wounded arm bandaged inside his greatcoat. He is in conversation with Kaspar Sylar. The Kavrone general puts a hand on Vander's shoulder, just for a moment.

The gesture makes Raine wish she had left him to bleed in the Sanctum of Bones.

'The Eighth Paxar,' Hale continues. 'Draxian Air and the Ghollite militia. The Scions of Steadfast.'

'House Stormfall's nobles,' Devri says. 'The court of the High King.'

Raine sees the nobles in their finery, accompanied by cherubim that scatter earth from their homeworld wherever they tread. She sees officers and commanders. Generals, marshals. Castellans and commissars. A hunched and robed cohort of Adeptus Mechanicus magi that vent steam and move on insectile legs. There are representatives present from every fighting force sworn to the Bale Stars Crusade. The enormity of it hits Raine, then. The vastness of Serek's deceit. Because every soul in this room either serves him knowing exactly what he is, or they serve him in ignorance, as Juna Keene does.

Either way, they still serve him.

She is not just surrounded by victories and lies, but by enemies too.

Horns blare from the far end of the hall. Raine is reminded of the battle for the forges. It was only days ago, but it feels like weeks. Like years. Every soul in the strategium hall draws to attention, and Raine does so along with them.

Not a single person in the strategium hall speaks as the Lord-General Militant walks out onto the dais, flanked by two Lions of Bale in their carapace and furs and that kastelan automaton of his. The heavy refrain of the robot's tread sounds like a dolorous heart. Serek is wearing his white dress uniform. White, like the pelt of Zane's King of Winter, with the crimson sash slung across his chest. A mark of honour, and of faith.

Another lie.

'Loyal souls of the Bale Stars.' Serek's voice carries clearly over the crowd. 'Today sees us take the next step on our path towards victory. Towards the restoration and sanctification of this great sector.'

He looks out over the crowd. There are hundreds of people present, but still Raine feels Serek's eyes fall upon her. It feels like being caught in the cold.

'The shipyards of Laxus Prime are that next step,' he says. 'They have been held by the Sighted for over a year.'

There are murmured words at the mention of the Sighted. Curses and prayers.

'They have corrupted the shipyard cluster,' Serek says. 'Given it over to heretic machines and their masters. One of the Nine crouches at the heart of it. It names itself as Ahxon-Pho. Fifth of Nine. It names itself *That Which Creates*.'

There is a machine wail from the representatives sworn to the Adeptus Mechanicus at the name. At the word *creates*. Their cry is static laced with sorrow and rage. Serek waits for it to pass before he continues.

'The shipyards have turned aside fleet actions, and naval strike wings. They have held fast in the face of every assault. They are a jagged peak to conquer.'

Every member of a regiment in the hall is looking to Serek and awaiting the order that will send them to conquer that peak. They yearn for it. Raine can see it in their unblinking eyes.

'To take the shipyards will require a determination like no other,' he says. 'A ferocity, and a capacity to achieve the unachievable. It will require great sacrifice, and it will require blood.'

Serek glances to the plastered, gilded walls.

'Just as it did on Drast,' he says. 'To break the unbreakable fortress of Morne. Just as it did to collapse the Sighted's stronghold on Gholl. To survive the Laxian forges, and the fires of Hyxx.'

Raine keeps her eyes forwards, but she knows that around her the Antari officers have become completely still. Reverent. Serek's eyes fall upon them again, and this time Raine knows that he is looking at her. It is more than cold, that stare.

It is monstrous.

'The Laxian shipyards are a legend waiting to be written,' Serek says. 'And the honour of writing it will fall to the Eleventh Antari Rifles.'

Serek draws his sword and raises it over his head. He roars a cheer that is picked up by every soul in the strategium hall as they turn to face Raine and her regiment. The sound of it is deafening. Baleful. Like being surrounded by a storm. As one, the Antari drop to one knee and bow their heads. Raine is a heartbeat behind them, but she doesn't bow her head at all.

'For the Bale Stars,' Serek shouts.

Raine knows the response as everyone in the hall does, but she has never felt the kind of rage she feels now in saying it.

'For the Emperor,' Severina Raine roars in return, her voice joining the storm.

The five Antari officers are swept up and celebrated, congratulated by pilots and adepts and soldiers alike. Every soul in the room wanted that honour and the chance to spend their blood in the crusade's name.

In Serek's name.

Raine watches it happen, one step removed as she always is. The movement of people around her, the noise, it feels like shell shock. Like being the only one to see that the water has been poisoned, but unable to say a word as every person at the table drinks from their cups.

'Severina Raine.'

Raine looks away from her Antari at the sound of her name, to the man who speaks it. To the man dressed in white, wearing a crimson sash and carrying a gold-hilted sabre at his hip. To the man whose ice-blue eyes glitter like cut gems. No, not the man.

The monster.

'Lord-General Militant,' Raine says, and she makes the sign of the aquila.

Serek's face doesn't change. He takes a step forward so that he is close.

'At ease,' he says, and the words seem deliberate.

Five paces back stand Serek's armed guard, his ever-present Lions of Bale, and his kastelan automaton. Behind them stand the other attending representatives of High Command, sworn to serve him. Araxis, the High-King of House Stormfall. Lord-Castellan Caradris. General-Primary Hu-Sul, of Gholl. Last of all, Raine catches the mismatched eyes of Veris Drake. The Lord-Marshal acknowledges her with the sparest of nods. She wears a single pin on the lapel of her crimson uniform, wrought in gold and jet.

The Lion's Honour.

Raine has never felt less at ease, or more alone.

'Strange,' Serek says. 'That it feels such a long time since last we spoke.'

Like before, it is an effort to hold Serek's stare. An effort not to take that gold-hilted sabre from him and cut him down where he stands. Raine knows that she would never land the blow. That she would be shot dead by his Lions and crushed by his kastelan, or be torn apart by the hundreds of souls in the strategium hall that are sworn to him. She cannot fight him. Not here, not now.

But that doesn't mean that she will back down.

'Much has happened, lord,' Raine says. 'Much has changed.'

Serek smiles then, that same arctic smile that she once wished to earn.

'It is inevitable,' he says. 'For things to endure, they must change.'

'As have your words,' Raine says. 'You told me once that in order to endure you must be a creature of faith. Unbreakable.'

She takes a breath.

'Words I have lived by,' she says. 'Words I have bled for, and killed for.'

'Words are powerful,' Serek says. 'That is what you said to me in the forges. People will die in the name of them.'

He looks to where the Antari officers celebrate with the others. The hall rings with cheers and cries of devotion. Raine's heart is cold and still.

'I meant what I said,' Serek says. 'The shipyards are a legend waiting to be written. A glory that will be remembered and celebrated. The names of the dead will adorn the Hero's Mount on Steadfast. It is a deed worthy of your mother's memory, wouldn't you say?'

Raine's hand actually twitches this time with the need to kill him. With the want to go for that sabre. Serek smiles again. Behind him the kastelan's power fists twitch too, in response. It must be slaved in more ways than just by commands.

She has no threat left to offer, but that of words.

'When I was first assigned to the Rifles, I thought them desperate to burn,' Raine says. 'They believe so strongly in the fates given to them that they seemed fatalistic, almost foolish.'

She looks at the Antari officers now in their plain greys, with honest reverence on their faces. With their scars and their beliefs worn plainly in their skin.

'I underestimated them,' she says. 'I have broken the unbreakable with them. Toppled bastions and tyrants. Burned cities, and bled traitors. I thought at first that they were entirely *other*, but they are not. Not in the ways that matter. Not in the way of our hearts.'

She closes her hand into a fist over her heart.

'Because we are fierce and loyal.' She looks back to Serek. 'And never to be underestimated.'

The Lord-General Militant laughs then. The sound sends cold fury through Raine's core.

'Good words, Severina Raine,' he says. 'Very good words.'

And then he turns and walks away from her, disappearing back into the baying crowd.

Gloam, before

When Severina arrives back at her dormitory, there is something amiss. A box, sitting on her low, flat cot. It is unmarked, save for the scuffing of transit and the prints of dirty fingers.

'Where did this come from?' Severina asks.

'It was here before me,' Illariya says.

She is sitting cross-legged on her own cot, reading from a sheaf of prayer papers. She doesn't look up from them.

'Has anyone touched it?' Severina asks.

Now Illariya looks up. She has a scowl on her face like always. It accentuates her scars.

'Why would they?' she asks. 'It is addressed to you. More special treatment, I expect, for the last of Thema Raine's precious daughters.'

Severina has fought Illariya many times, in training and outside of it, but on this day, after visiting the punishment cell and seeing the traitor that she once called her sister, she does not fight. She does not raise her voice or lose her temper. She just stares at Illariya instead, with her heart aching.

'Get out,' she says, coldly. 'Now.'

There is an instant of unease in Illariya's face. She rolls up the prayer papers and slides off her cot.

'I will get more peace in the chapel anyway,' she says.

She leaves quickly, without looking back. The wooden door shuts heavily behind her. Severina barely hears it, because all of her attention is devoted to the box. She crosses to the cot and sits down beside the box. Takes a breath. Then she picks it up and puts it on her lap. It is not very heavy. Not enough to contain weapons. Something slides around inside it when she tilts it, gently.

She should take it to the abbots. Progena are supposed to give up their personal effects. They are given everything they need by the scholam. Uniform. Training. Weapons.

A home, when nothing else is left to them.

She should take it to the abbots, but she doesn't. Instead Severina breaks the seals on the box, and lifts the lid.

And then her heart truly does ache.

Inside the box is a book titled 'The Many and Gloried Astra Militarum Regiments of the Bale Stars'. It is worn and foxed, with cracks in its leather face. The foiled letters have worn smooth. Severina takes the book out with care and moves the box aside. The smell of the book is the smell of old parchment and candle-smoke. Of nights spent reading, long past when she should have been sleeping.

Of playing word games with Lucia.

Something drops onto the leather cover of the book and runs into the cracks. Severina puts her hand to her face and brushes away a tear. She is so angry. So sad. So worn and damaged, just like the book. She takes hold of the leather cover of the book and runs her hand down the face of it, then she hooks her fingers beneath it and pulls until the cover buckles. Until the spine breaks and the binding comes unbound. Then she tears the pages *out in handfuls and lets them fall to the floor around her like snow. Like spent shells. She tears and tears until there is nothing left to break and then she sits there breathing and aching and trying not to cry again.*

And that is when she hears it. The ticking, soft and regular like a heartbeat, coming from the box beside her.

She turns and looks into the box. The timepiece is settled into a corner like a frightened thing, the brass casing catching the lumen light. Severina puts her hand into the box and takes hold of the timepiece. She looks at the bone and glass of its face, the beautiful brass casing and chain. She thinks of all the times she woke before Lucia to see her gripping the timepiece tightly, even in her sleep, the chain looped between her fingers like a noose.

Severina turns it over. The back of the case is plain and unmarked. She takes her training knife from her belt, and holds the timepiece steady as she pushes the point of it into the brass. She does it slowly, and jaggedly, slipping once and nicking her hand. One letter at a time, she carves Lucia's name into the brass. When it is done, her hands are bloody, and so is the timepiece. It stings. All of it.

Severina gets to her feet and goes over to the window. It is a narrow opening in the wall, like an arrow-slit. The wind howls through unimpeded, carrying tiny flakes of snow with it. Severina holds the timepiece out of the window. It spins by the chain. Below, the hungry ocean roars, waiting for her to drop it. To let go. Under the sound of the wind and the ocean, Severina hears that ticking. Regular. Like a heartbeat. She wills her arm to move and her hand to open. She wills herself to hurl the timepiece into the ocean and her memories with it. To be unbreakable.

But she can't.

A pained noise escapes her, and Severina draws her arm back inside. She sinks to her knees and drives her closed fists into the floor until they are bloody too. Until there's a breaking in her fingers and in the face of the timepiece she is still holding. That is when she stops. When the glass goes. A tiny crack, in the top of the face.

Broken, like she is.

Severina stays like that a while. Long enough for the cuts to slow their bleeding and for snow to gather on her clothes and in her tangled hair. Then she slowly lifts her hand and puts the timepiece into the pocket in the chest of her tunic.

The one close to her heart.

NINETEEN

A jagged peak to conquer

Raine stands in the strategium aboard the battle-cruiser *Wrath Unending* and looks upon the Laxian shipyards. The jagged peak that they have been tasked with conquering. The legend, waiting to be written.

The battle that is intended to be her last.

The schematic is rendered in ink on parchment in excruciating detail, and is so large that it lays over the massive strategium table like a shroud. Recent pict captures lie scattered on top of the parchment, taken by the fleets sent to the shipyards before this one. Those who failed.

'Your objective is the command core,' Juna Keene says.

The Antari general is standing on the opposite side of the table from Raine, with three of her captains. Hale and Devri and Sun. It feels strange to Raine to attend a briefing with only three, and not four.

Without Andren Fel.

Keene leans forward and points to the command core. It

is a spherical chamber connected by two bulkheads to the outer core – a ring of adamantium and void-safe armour-glass that is linked to the shipyard's multi-layered docks and berths and build basilica by void-sealed gantries. Looked at in abstract, the shipyards are insectile. A central body, surrounded by many jagged, jointed legs. On the schematic, the command core looks small, but going by the scale indicator on the schematic, that chamber alone is the size of the strategium hall on the *Bale's Heart*. Taken as a whole, the shipyards are bigger than the forges on Laxus Secundus were.

'Where are we to land, sir?' Hale asks.

Hale is out of his dress greys now, and back in his fatigues where he is comfortable. He leans on the edge of the table, taking in the schematic's details.

'Not at the core, I bet,' Devri says, with a grin. 'Or this would hardly be worthy of a legend.'

Keene smiles thinly. 'Not at the core,' she says. 'Each company will land at a different location on the shipyards' voidward side.'

She has to move a short way down the table and the schematic to point them out.

'Blue will hit the upper docks,' she says. 'Gold, the repair berths beneath.'

Keene leans a little further to indicate a massive chamber on one of the shipyard's docks.

'Grey, into Build Basilica Delphi.'

Keene picks up a handful of the scattered picts from the table.

'The last fleet to hit the shipyards was combined Navy and Astra Militarum,' Keene says. 'Two full companies of Paxar soldiery, and Tempestus support.'

'And what happened to them?' Devri asks.

She hands the picts around. The one that she passes to Raine is blurred and monochromatic, but it still sets her on edge. She hears Karin Sun mutter an Antari curse under his breath.

'The Sighted turned the shipyards against them,' Raine says, looking at the hundreds of frozen, floating dead in the pict. 'Sent them into the void.'

Keene nods. 'The magos, Axhon-Pho, is in control of the shipyards' systems. Connected to them. That is only possible from the command core, even for one of the Nine.'

'So, it will see where we are, and what we are trying to do?' Hale asks.

'Yes,' Keene says. 'But there is an advantage in the magos' connection to the shipyards.'

She traces one of the finely inked lines on the schematic with her finger. It leads from the command core to a location in the shipyard's upper reaches, not far from Blue Company's landing zone.

'Axhon-Pho is connected to all of the systems. For all intents and purposes, it and the shipyards are one and the same.'

Devri rubs at his unshaven jaw, thinking. 'So, we hurt the shipyards, and we hurt the magos,' he says.

'Precisely,' Keene says. 'That's your aim, and Sun's. Blue will go for the spinal auguries and blind it. Gold will destroy the auxiliary power nodes and starve it.'

'And Grey?' Hale asks.

'Yours is the kill, captain,' Keene says.

Yuri Hale smiles, then. It pulls at the scars on his face. 'Aye, sir,' he says.

Karin Sun puts down his pict and looks at Keene. 'I have a question, general,' he says.

Keene glances at him and folds her arms across her broad chest. 'If it is about destroying the shipyards, then don't ask it. This is capture and control. We preserve as much of the facility as we can.'

Sun shakes his head and goes back to frowning at the schematic. 'Fine,' he says. 'Then I do not have a question.'

Devri claps Sun gently on the shoulder. 'One day,' he says.

A smile breaks the thunder of Sun's face, then, just for a moment.

'So how do we get close enough to kill the magos?' Hale asks.

'The flotilla will exit the warp as close to the shipyards as they can, at the outer limits of the system's Mandeville point. They will push through the long-range defences, drop you at your landing zones and then proceed to target non-critical areas on the opposite side of the shipyards from you in an effort to draw the magos' eye.'

'Nothing like running under fire, sir,' Devri says, and he grins.

'You will need to run, too,' Keene says. 'The flotilla will only be able to maintain position for so long before they have to retreat. Command can ill afford to lose the ships.'

But they can afford to lose the Antari, Raine thinks. *For the sake of Serek's lie.* She has to put down the pict before she creases it in her hands.

'How long do we have?' she asks.

'Six hours,' Keene says. 'At most.'

Devri gives a low whistle. He's not quite grinning now.

'It will be enough,' Raine says, firmly.

She needs them to believe it, because belief is what will get them through this fight, and the one to follow. To lose this battle would not just be to lose the shipyards.

It would be to lose the Bale Stars altogether.

'This legend is ours to write,' Raine says. 'We will not fail in that. We will fight fiercely, and we will endure. In the Emperor's name.'

All four of the officers echo those last four words together, with their closed fists held over their hearts.

'Warp exit is in two hours,' Keene says. 'See to your companies and make good your oaths. The Laxian shipyards are the gateway to the western arm of the sector. Victory here changes everything.'

Raine looks down at the vast shape of the Laxian shipyards again. A reckoning, written in black ink.

'Yes, general,' she says. 'It will.'

TWENTY

A legend, waiting to be written

The void unfolds on the viewscreen in front of Taran Vadri like a painted backdrop. Like a flag, being shaken out and made to fly. The pressure that comes with warp travel fades, the nausea recedes like the tide going out and Vadri sees the Laxian shipyards, a massive, jagged star of iron and steel set against the real stars. They dropped from the warp as close as they could. As close as they dared to. Beyond the shipyards Laxus Primary is a dull, grey orb. Orbital defences hang in the planet's orbit, glittering like bright stones.

'Status, augur-master.'

The voice belongs to the shipmaster. Kasumi Sho never seems to need a moment to recover from translation. Vadri has heard her say that she relishes the jolt of it, and he can believe it. Sho relishes everything. Gambling. Debate. Drinking.

But especially battle.

'Translation successful,' Vadri says, as data tracks down one side of his vision, fed straight into the lens that replaces his left eye. 'Just waiting for the others to catch up, sir.'

Sho laughs loudly, like she always does. She is standing, because no Navy officers born of Paxar have command thrones, just a pulpit to shout from. Sho's regalia of green and gold is bright under the bridge lumens.

'And we once again prove the value of our name,' she says. *'Far Runner!'*

Everyone on the bridge knows how to answer, Vadri included. It is a reaction, like blinking.

'Far Runner!' he shouts with the others, as the other ships in the flotilla tear their way from the warp and join them in real space. Their sister-ship, the Sword-class *Equinox*. The Gothic-class *Blade of Coris*, and lastly, the *Wrath Unending*. The grand cruiser is a bullish slab of old wounds and armour plating, scored and scarred from hundreds of years of being at the heart of a fight.

Vadri has never in all his years of service seen a more beautiful ship.

'Flotilla translation complete. Positioning within tolerances.' Data flares red in the false lens of Vadri's eye. Long-range augur chimes ring. 'And we appear to have drawn the station's ire.'

At first it is just the station's long-range automated defences. Lance fire that splashes across the shields as the escorts move into position to protect the larger ships.

'That's quite enough of that,' Sho says. 'Put out their eyes, please, Daxx.'

'Aye,' the gunnery officer replies. 'Forward lances, firing.'

'Forward lances,' slur the gunnery servitors in unison.

They fire a split second before the *Equinox* does, collapsing the long-range defence systems as they push towards the iron tangle of the shipyards in formation. It feels close, to Vadri, as if he could reach out and touch the *Wrath*, or the *Blade*, but in reality they are hundreds of kilometres apart. As the flotilla breaches the outer defence lines, Vadri's augurs start to sing again.

'Enemy movement,' he says. 'They are launching escorts. Two Cobras on an intercept heading.'

Sho laughs again. 'Two Cobras,' she says. 'I thought this was a shipyard. I thought this was a legend, waiting to be written. Give me an intercept course and shunt power to the forward lances. We will soften them for the *Wrath*.'

The bridge is noisy with acknowledgements and relayed orders. With vox-chatter from the attack squadrons preparing to launch. Vadri feels the *Far Runner* thrum in his bones as they enter the outer range of the Cobra-class destroyers. The shields flicker. Lance fire lights the void. Vadri sees it and he acknowledges it, but he does not focus on it, because he is trying to understand the augur readings and the data that is tracking across his vision. He frowns.

'More movement, shipmaster,' he says.

The bridge shakes and the lumens gutter. Sho curses emphatically in her own tongue. Just like the *Wrath Unending*, it's a beautiful thing.

'If you can't tell me what it is, Taran, then I don't know what you're sitting there for,' she says. 'Daxx, get me a firing solution on those Cobras before they slip by us.'

There's an *aye* from the gunnery officer. The attack squadrons have launched now, too, and are engaging with the enemy's own. They are tiny specks in the starlight. Vadri half-sees one of the enemy Cobras light and list as Daxx's lances punch through her shields. She vents air and debris into the void like blood into water. Their sister is baring her teeth at the other Cobra, but Vadri sees what is beyond them too, now, and he wants to curse like Sho.

'Shipmaster,' he says, feeling warp-tense all over again. 'The movement is a battleship.'

Vadri takes a breath. He can see it now, massive even at distance. A gloried skeleton, with some of her bones still open to the void. Old and angry and made for the kill.

'Apocalypse-class,' he shouts. 'It's the *Starforged Sword*.'

Vadri knows the *Sword*. Every Navy soul does. She was one of the most honoured battleships of the Bale Stars fleet before her near destruction at the Coris Belt. Before her relocation to Laxus for refit and repair.

And now the damned Sighted have her.

Vadri feels a tear trace from his remaining unaugmented eye as the augurs ring louder in his head. Deafening.

'She is preparing to fire,' Vadri yells. 'Nova cannon!'

Sho cries an order from her pulpit that Vadri only hears half of over the impact alarms. Something about forward shields. It's not enough. Nothing they can do is. Not against a nova cannon. Vadri makes sure not to blink as the fire comes for them.

Because that infernal fire, like the *Wrath Unending* and Sho's violent cursing, is beautiful.

Toka sees the *Far Runner* and the *Equinox* go in an instant through the armourglass of his cockpit. The explosion shakes his Fury Interceptor around him and puts her into a roll. Shakes through his body and makes him bite his tongue. Even with the glare visor in his helmet dipping, it still momentarily blinds him. A good number of the other fighters are caught in it and vaporised in an instant. Dark shadows against the white.

'Emperor's mercy,' he says, between breaths.

Toka has time for nothing else, because the battle won't wait for grief. He puts the Fury into a steep, spiral climb to get clear of the spreading debris, and to try to shake the traitor interceptor still hanging on his tail. Ahead of them, the *Starforged Sword* churns forward in the blackness like a creature of myth, pushing past her ailing Cobra escorts.

'Evris,' he shouts. 'Clip that hawk or we'll be as dead as the *Far Runner*!'

'On it!'

The gunner's voice is thick, as if he's injured. Toka feels a flare of concern, but he doesn't have time for that either. He'll just have to check on Evris when the battle is done.

Or find him by the Emperor's side if they don't survive it.

Toka pulls the Fury over and around, spiralling into a steep fall that puts them past the enemy interceptor at speed. Not too fast for Evris, though. Lascannon fire splits the dark and splits the enemy interceptor too, right along her hull. She crumples and detonates and breaks into pieces and Evris whoops, like he always does. It makes Toka do the same. He can't help it. It's all instants, a fight like this. An instant of grief. Of worry. Of fear. Of joy.

Then Toka sees the two remaining ships of the flotilla engage the part-repaired Apocalypse-class. The *Blade of Coris* and the *Wrath Unending* are massive ships, but they are dwarfed by the *Sword*. That difference means danger, but it also means they can outmanouvre her. As Toka watches, they pass alongside the *Starforged Sword*, and open up with their broadsides. The *Sword* replies in kind, and his visor dips all over again.

It's another instant to count with the others.

One of pride.

'Missile count,' he says to Evris.

'One rack,' Evris replies. 'It's the last of them.'

'Then let's not waste them,' Toka says, and he pushes for the *Starforged Sword*.

They take fire from enemy interceptors that Evris answers in kind. He catches most of them and clips the rest. They take hits from debris and from pieces of the *Far Runner* and the *Equinox*. Even at speed, with the starlight and the lance fire and the roar of the Fury, Toka catches split-second glimpses of bodies in the void.

And then they are on top of the *Starforged Sword*. Beneath them, the battleship bleeds. The *Blade of Coris* and the *Wrath Unending* do the same. They are made for punishment, but they cannot endure indefinitely.

Nothing can.

'Fire when I say,' Toka says. 'We will only get one shot.'

He rolls the Fury, and even with his pressure suit compensating, it dizzies him. He tastes blood. The Fury shakes as lance fire from the *Sword*'s dorsal arrays track them. Toka sees it then, the gap in the *Sword*'s skin where her bones show through.

'One shot,' Evris says. 'Now I see what you mean, Lam.'

The Fury screams through the *Sword*'s voids, and into the space between her exposed bones. Automated turrets punch into her hull and clip her wings and knock out the telemetry. Toka tastes blood again as he cracks his head on the airframe, but they are inside. Going too fast to stop. Ironwork zips past.

'Do it,' he says to Evris.

'Aye.'

The last of their missiles streak from the Fury into the innards of the *Starforged Sword*. They fly through the fire of it.

Toka's instruments scream. Explosions trigger and catch and carry through the battleship's bones. He hears Evris whoop like he always does and he can't help but do it too. There's a moment when they break through the fire and the destruction where it is silent save for the Fury's engines and the hiss of air escaping from Toka's suit.

'Lam,' Evris says, over the vox. 'I'll see you, alright?'

Toka nods.

'I'll see you,' he says, in his last instant.

Daven Wyck can't help closing his eyes in the instant that the assault craft drops from its mag-clamps in the *Wrath*'s hangar bay and starts to move for the shipyards. It knocks the air right out of his lungs, though not by the force of it. It's because he feels the same way about the assault craft as he does about troop transports. About all ships. That they are just another kind of tin can, waiting to be torn open by fire. Wyck tries not to think about what's outside. About lance fire, and venting air. The void-lost dead, and behind them, nothing. So much nothing.

Wyck's eyes snap open again as a colossal tremor shakes the assault craft. It creaks and howls around him, and he waits for it to happen, for the craft to tear open and spill the lot of them out into the void to die in the cold and the silence.

But it doesn't. Instead, the assault craft rights itself and the lumens flicker back up. Red, like the inside of something living.

'Emperor's bloody *wounds*,' Crys says. 'Thought that was it, there, sarge.'

She is seated and harnessed like the rest of them. The rest of his Wyldfolk. Rom Odi's Hartkin. Lara Koy's Mistvypers. Hale's lot. The commissar and Zane. The compartment is all body heat and the smell of cold metal and smoke and sweat. Hale had tried to make Wyck strap himself into a seat too for the launch and the breach. Said it was safer. Wyck wouldn't do it because he never has. Not since Cawter.

Not since he watched Keller and the others burn.

'One minute!' Hale shouts over the racket of the engines and the impacts and everyone praying and muttering. Over Zane, humming her damned atonal songs. Wyck hears everything loud and clear because of the dose he took before they boarded. He took double, because he knew it would be bad, and because of that bolt shell he carries.

Wyck looks to his Wyldfolk, sitting there with their hands rolled into fists around their harnesses. Their spirits are lit. Their eyes too. Not like his, with violence waiting to be made and the push of stimms. His kin are fighting for the value of duty. For virtue and honour and all those things Wyck has never felt.

But he's not going to stop them feeling it. Not when it might be the last time.

'Thirty seconds!' Hale shouts, and the proximity alarms start to go.

'You go fast, and you don't look back,' Wyck shouts to his squad, over the noise of the alarm. 'Fight the Sighted until they are dead, or you are, but make sure you cut them before you go.'

There's a jolt that unsteadies him on his feet. He hears the magclamps fire. They all unclip their harnesses, get to their feet and draw their guns and knives.

'Because we are Wyldfolk,' Wyck continues. 'And what does that mean?'

'Cuts from us always kill!' they answer him, as one.

And then there's another *boom* as the breach charges go,

blowing them a way into the shipyards. Air rushes into the compartment through the toothed hole it makes, cold and smelling of iron. Wyck sees the dark, strobing innards of the shipyards beyond and hears the chatter of gunfire and the scream of alarms.

'Let's go!' Wyck shouts.

They follow him, first up. First out. Running the edge, like always.

'I knew it,' Crys says, as they run.

'What?' Wyck asks.

'That you had a good speech in you somewhere,' she says, and she laughs. 'Inspirational words.'

Wyck doesn't laugh with her. He can't find the want to, because they don't feel like inspirational words to him.

They feel very much like last words.

TWENTY-ONE

On the edge of the After

Build Basilica Delphi is a colossal chamber built from black iron and pitted steel. Part-built pieces of starships hang overhead, casting long, dark shadows that fall across Severina Raine and the Antari of Grey Company as they make the push across the basilica towards the void-gantries that will lead them to the shipyards' core. Raine's boots ring off the grated decking as she runs to meet the enemy past the immobile shapes of lifters and heavy-duty machinery. Beside her, Tyl and Jeth run too. The Duskhounds are like two extra shadows, sticking close by. Raine looks left to see Hale and his command squad. On her right, Koy and her Mistvypers. Ahead, Wyck and his Wyldfolk. The rest of Grey Company are lost to smoke and distance and darkness, but Raine can hear them running and fighting. Las-fire strobes in the half-dark. Every breath Raine takes smells like stagnant water and blood. Like corruption. A constant, thrumming chant echoes through the shipyards' vox-emitters.

<Seek thee avoidance of atrophy,> it says, in an atonal, machine blare. *<Only by Nine.>*

The Sighted are everywhere, pushing and pulling like the tide. Most are soldiers clad in blue and grey, with cloaks of mirrors, or feathers pushed under the skin and crystals set into the sockets where their eyes should be. But not all. Through the melee, Raine sees dockworkers and shipwrights too. Adepts and tech-priests. All with their loyalties torn away, and with red-raw fate-marks carved into their skin.

For things to endure, they must change.

Serek's voice echoes in Raine's ears as she plunges her sword into the chest of one of the Sighted. The traitor is wearing a red uniform that should be patterned with cogwheels and angular, runic text, but every one of those icons has been defaced and oversewn to create new, hateful shapes.

'Only by Nine,' slurs the Sighted, with blood bubbling over his blue, cracked lips.

Raine pulls her sword free and he falls, dead.

'Onwards!' she cries into the vox. 'In the Emperor's name!'

Along the line, Hale's Grey Company roar a cheer as they break through the Sighted's lines. The sound echoes around the basilica, right up to the part-built ships overhead. Over four hundred souls, spread out across the vastness of the basilica. Everyone fit enough to fight.

Everything that Raine has left to her.

<Seek thee knowledge unsought. Only by Nine,> echoes that machine voice.

Ahead, dozens more of the Sighted flood through the massive door at the far end of the chamber that leads to the void-gantries. The heretics drop mobile cover as their weapons crews set up gun emplacements. Gunfire clatters against the decking and cuts the air by Raine's head as she ducks behind one of the huge, immobile lifter machines on the deck with the Duskhounds at her side. Jeth keeps firing around the cover as solid rounds ring against the machine like a winter storm. Along the line, Raine can just about see Daven Wyck and his Wyldfolk through the smoke, holed up in the same way. She hears the distinctive, echoing *boom* of Yulia Crys' modified grenade launcher firing.

'More are coming, commissar,' Tyl says. Her voice is calm and steady as she checks her vambrace's display, despite all of the running and fighting. 'I'm picking up a lot of movement.'

Yuri Hale drops into cover beside them with blood welling and soaking through the arm of his fatigues from where one of the enemy rounds caught him. His command squad are with him. He waves Lye away when the medic tries to take a look at the gunshot wound in his arm.

'We have to break through now,' Hale says. 'If we let them slow us, we fail. We die. All of us.'

He looks to Lydia Zane. The psyker is sitting with her back against the machine and her legs drawn up like a sorrowful child. Raine realises that, even now, Zane is barefoot. Her feet are black with blood that only mostly belongs to the enemy. Her face is bloody too. Almost animalistic. Zane hasn't been the same since the Sanctum, and her time spent facing Cretia Ommatid in a space that only the two psykers could see.

'Make us a path, Zane,' Hale says.

Zane blinks, and then looks at him.

'A path,' she says, absently. 'A path to truth.'

Jeth curses loudly and ducks back behind the cover. His carapace armour is chipped and smoking from impacts.

'They are advancing,' Jeth growls. 'Whatever you're going to do, do it now.'

'I did not know then the power of dreams,' Zane murmurs, as if she has not heard him.

Raine moves to stand in front of her. 'Lydia,' she says.

Zane's head snaps up at the mention of her given name. Her lips are parted like an animal breathing under stress, exposing blood-pinked teeth. Bolts start to turn in the machine frame at Zane's back. Raine keeps her pistol pointed at the deck, ready to raise and fire in an instant if she has to.

But only if she *has* to.

'Control,' Raine says. 'You are Lydia Zane. Primaris psyker. Graded Epsilon.'

A thin line of blood runs from Zane's nose. The psyker touches her hand to her face and then looks down at her bloodied fingertips. She nods, as if in understanding.

'Eleventh Antari Rifles,' the psyker says.

Detonated rounds paint the air gold around Lydia Zane as she makes a path to the vaulted doorway, and through the Sighted defending it. The deck creaks under Zane's feet in the wake of her telekine shield, and her power. Her two birds sit on her shoulders and cry joy as she claps her hands together, and the closest of the Sighted snap and break and turn to meat and bone and nothing more. The enemy start to scream, and then to run, but there is little point in running from gifts like Zane's. She raises her hand and turns it and tears a hole in the plating of the deck for those who run to fall into. Some she pins with twisted spars of metal. Some she throws against the armourglass viewports. Some she tears limb from limb, and that is easiest of all, because there is little resistance to be found in flesh and bone. Emotions soak into the air, and into her skin. Fear and anger and hatred that crash against her as if she is walking into an ocean tide.

They only seek to use you until there is nothing left to use.

Cretia Ommatid's words echo in Zane's mind, as they have been doing since they spoke in the Sanctum. Since Ommatid tried to tempt her.

Think of what you could be.

'No,' Zane snarls, through her teeth.

Her concentration falters and a stray round breaches Zane's kine-shield and clips her thigh, spraying blood. Zane falls to her knees and she does not think, then. She just acts, with her birds crying loudly in her ears and her mind.

FREE.

FALL.

Zane cries out and slams one closed fist onto the floor. A spear of telekinetic force lances out from her, tearing a furrow through the deck, and through the Sighted. There are screams and pops and flashes as guns detonate in hands, and bones break, and dozens of souls are unmade in an instant. Blood-mist hits Lydia Zane's skin like ocean spray, and all falls finally, blessedly quiet, save for that machine voice coming from the vox-emitters over her head.

<*Seek thee life everlasting. Only by Nine,*> it says.

As if in answer, Cretia Ommatid's voice rises up inside Zane's head again.

Think of what you could be.

And Zane kneels there and looks at what she has wrought. At the blood and the mess and the ruin and at her birds, flitting from corpse to corpse.

The Nine await.

Ommatid's voice is a test, just like the night Zane spent alone in a circle of salt under Antar's dark sky. Just like the commissar's questions, and the two birds that follow like shadows. She must never stray from the path towards the light. Never place one foot on the spiral.

'I am Lydia Zane,' she murmurs to herself, over and over. 'I am Epsilon. I am Antari.'

And with great effort, she gets back onto her feet.

On the shipyards' void-gantries, with the stars hanging all around her, Raine learns exactly why it is that the Sighted call Axhon-Pho *That Which Creates*.

The creations the magos sends to kill Raine and Grey Company are part-mechanical horrors. There are dozens of them, some crawling on multi-jointed arms and legs and some running upright, with awkward, juddering spasms of their limbs. Each of Axhon-Pho's creations are built of dead flesh that clings stubbornly to iron and adamantium and bone. Multi-coloured crystal shards jut from their bodies, and their hands and feet are bladed. Where they should have faces, they just have silvered mirrors set with vox-grilles that broadcast the magos' ceaseless preaching.

<Creation is necessary violence,> they blare. *<Only by Nine.>*

Raine plants her feet as another of the creations comes for her, its bladed feet clattering against the bloody, oil-fouled decking. There is no cover to speak of on the gantries. No option other than to fight their way through. Around her, Hale's command squad engage with the creations. The Duskhounds' hellguns light the gantries with fully-automatic las-fire. Shouts and curses come from Wyck's Wyldfolk. Everywhere, the clash of blades and the smell of blood.

'No backwards steps,' Raine cries, as she meets the creation's blades with her own sabre. 'Do not falter!'

Her powered blade severs one of the creation's four arms at

the elbow. It does not recoil, and the blaring of Axhon-Pho's words continues uninterrupted.

<By violence is purity found. Only by Nine.>

Raine catches a glimpse of herself in the creation's mirrored face as it lunges for her. Of bruises and cuts and hollow eyes.

She looks so much like Lucia did, that day in the cell.

Raine shouts, wordlessly, as she turns aside one of the creation's grasping, bladed hands with her sabre and fires her bolt pistol point-blank into the creature's mirrored face. The silvered mask shatters, covering Raine in shards that cut her face, bloodying her further. One of the creation's remaining bladed arms snags her as it falls twitching onto the deck, cutting Raine deeply across her sword arm. With her arm burning and her fingers trying to go numb, she severs what is left of the creation's head with her sabre, and it finally shakes itself still.

But there is no respite.

Raine gets moving again, firing the last round in her pistol's magazine at another of the magos' creations. The bolt-shell's detonation shatters what passes for its ribcage, but the creation does not stop until Lydia Zane forces it to. The psyker disassembles it violently, shearing joints and pulverising flesh with a clap of her thin, pale hands. Zane's breathing is rapid and shallow and blood is soaking through her slate-grey robes where she was shot, despite Nuria Lye's field treatment. Ahead, Cassia Tyl kills another of the creations with precision fire from her hellgun, putting a smoking hole straight through its mirrored mask, even as Jeth is slammed against the armourglass of the gantry wall by a third. The Duskhound yells and punches his combat blade over and over into the back of its neck, as it tries to claw through his carapace plate and his mask. The company vox is loud with chatter.

'They'll have us for dead! Push through!'

'I need a medicae here!'

'Hartkin, acknowledge. Mistvypers requesting aid!'

'I can't get to you, Lara.'

Then there is an agonised shout that Raine catches even over all of that noise.

'Ari!'

The cry comes from Makar Kayd. Grey's vox-operator charges with his lasgun raised at the monster that has Ari Rath pinned on the decking, but he is not quick enough to prevent Axhon-Pho's puppeted creature from opening the banner bearer's throat with its claws. Raine sees blood mist the air. Hears Hale shout too. Kayd gets knocked onto his back, and the creation rears. Raine runs to intervene.

And then a massive tremor runs through the void-gantry that nearly knocks Raine from her feet. The overhead lumens cut out, replaced with red emergency lighting. Axhon-Pho's preaching falters, becoming an enraged, atonal scream. His remaining creations crash to the ground, as if their minds have abandoned them. Tyl and Jeth make sure that they will not wake again with bursts of hellgun fire, while Wyck orders his Wyldfolk to secure this section of the gantry. Raine ejects her pistol's spent magazine and reloads, ready for the next fight.

'Getting comms, sir,' Makar Kayd says, to Hale.

The vox-operator sits himself up, winded and bloody, and Hale takes the handset from him. Raine drops to one knee beside them so she can hear it. Kayd's eyes stray to Ari Rath's dead body as he adjusts the vox-set's dials. He shakes his head even as the connection stops hissing and becomes clear.

'This is Gold, checking in. Auxiliary power is down,' Karin Sun says.

There is a pause and another hiss of connection.

'*Good work, Kar.*' Devri's voice over the long-range link is undercut by las-fire and screams, but he still sounds as though he is smiling. '*You got to blow something up, after all.*'

'We'll see you at the core, Karin,' Hale says.

'*Understood, Yuri,*' Sun says. '*Though the bloody magos has us locked out of the gantries. We are–*'

Sun never gets to say what they are doing, because his next words are stolen by Axhon-Pho's mechanical voice blaring all around them. Over the emitters, and the vox.

<Deliver the faithless unto darkness,> it says. **<Only by Nine.>**

A second distant tremor rattles the gantry and Raine catches one last shouted word over the vox-link through a roar of static and screams that sends her cold to her core.

Decompression.

'*No,*' says Kayd.

'Gold, do you read me?' Hale says. 'Gold, acknowledge!'

Hale slams his fist on the deck.

'*Gold!*' he says, again.

But there is no answer from Karin Sun. Instead, the voice that breaks the static belongs to Sale Devri.

'*Kar is gone,*' Devri says. The hurt in his voice is plain to hear.

Hale blinks. Raine sees hurt in him too, just for an instant, before he buries it.

'You have to blind it,' Hale says. 'And quickly.'

'*I'll cut out the bastard's eyes,*' Devri says. '*Just get yourself to the core and send the magos screaming to the hells.*'

'By fire and thunder,' Hale says.

'*Aye,*' Devri replies, with a darkness in his voice. '*By fire and thunder.*'

* * *

Daven Wyck's hands are slick with blood.

His heart hammers in his ears as he throws himself into another fight and into another squad of Sighted soldiers that are holding the bulkhead door leading to the next section of the void-gantry. Wyck drops the first with a flurry of las-fire, and the second with the butt of the gun, breaking the Sighted's fate-marked face open to the air. More blood. Around him, his Wyldfolk are fighting too. To Wyck, it all looks to be happening slowly. In between heartbeats. Deafening, painful heartbeats. Crys has one of the Sighted on the ground, her big hands around the soldier's neck. Jey and Haro are back to back, rifles up. Awd fires his flamer, making what's left of the enemy fall back. Second-hand heat rolls over Wyck, bringing with it the smell of burning.

Like Cawter.

Like Keller and others.

The memory makes him falter for what feels like forever, but can only really be a second or two.

It's still long enough to get shot.

The shotgun blast impacts against Wyck's flak armour and knocks the air clean out of his lungs. The Sighted who shot him is grinning. His eyes are crystals, and his own chest-plate is a silver mirror. The Sighted pumps the combat shotgun and goes to fire again, but Wyck isn't faltering anymore. He is furious. He snaps his own rifle up and fires as he moves. The first shot knocks the Sighted's aim out, so the shotgun blast puts dents in the deck to Wyck's left instead of taking his head off. Wyck's second las-bolt sends the Sighted's black blood up the armourglass behind him, and then Wyck is too close for the rifle at all. He lets it swing by the strap and slams the Sighted into the armourglass and buries his knife up and under that mirrored chest-plate. Twists it.

'The darkness waits for you,' the Sighted hisses, as he dies. 'It hungers.'

Wyck recoils from the Sighted, letting him fall to the deck. He is dimly aware that the fighting around him has stopped, but the Sighted's words have him frozen.

The darkness waits for you.

Wyck is suddenly even more aware of the void pressing in on the gantries. Of the endless, shapeless, frozen nothing waiting on the other side of the armourglass.

The darkness waits for you.

He thinks of the howling of the hounds, and the After, even more infinite than the void.

His heartbeat becomes faster. More painful.

He can't breathe.

'Dav, we've got company!'

Awd's words filter through the rushing in Wyck's ears and the thunder of his heart, and he turns away from the armourglass to see the bulkhead door the Sighted were guarding grinding upwards. A clade of ten skitarii stride through, painted in the enemy's colours. They move with a killer's grace on slender, backwards-jointed metal legs. Red lenses glow balefully in their domed face-plates, and their powered blades sing a dirge as they raise them.

'Emperor's *wounds*!' Crys shouts. 'They are infiltrators!'

Wyck is about to ask what in the hells that means when he is all but knocked from his feet by a blaring, agonising wall of noise. Everyone around Wyck collapses to their knees. The only reason Wyck doesn't fall too is because the stimms won't let him. That double dose he took keeps him upright. Instinct makes him put himself between the infiltrators and his Wyldfolk. Wyck's eyes are streaming and his limbs want to lock, but he still manages to raise his rifle and fire. The burst of las-rounds hits one of the infiltrators right at the heart of the spiral painted on its face-plate, sending sparks and black fluid into the air. There's a momentary gap in that damned awful wailing.

'Get up!' Wyck shouts to his squad.

His Wyldfolk start moving, but they are so *slow*. Wyck's vision swims from that noise the infiltrators are making. He tastes blood. Tastes ozone from the crackling edges of the powered blades as one of the infiltrators lunges for him. Wyck has to roll badly to duck the skitarii's powered blade. It hits the deck instead and cuts a furrow straight through it. Wyck gets to his feet and empties half of his lasgun cell into the infiltrator's torso before burying his knife right between its eye-lenses. The blade goes in up to the hilt and sticks, but the infiltrator doesn't fall. Instead the skitarii's arm snaps out like a misfire, knocking Wyck off his feet. He loses his grip on his rifle and crashes against the wall and slides down it, struggling to breathe. Then the infiltrator turns and points its stubcarbine at Haro. The void-born is still trying and failing to get up.

'Haro!' Wyck shouts, dragging himself to his feet. 'Move!'

She doesn't, but Awd does, with a yell. He turns his flamer on the infiltrator and washes it with promethium. The clinging fire burns away the robes and what little is left of the man it was made from, then the infiltrator's stubcarbine detonates like a set charge, making a twisted wreck of its arm. But the damned thing still doesn't die. It turns fast, cutting Awd across the chest with its powered blade. He cries out and goes over.

And something inside Wyck snaps.

He throws himself at the smouldering, spasming machine creature and manages to knock it flat. Manages to pull his knife from where he left it, though it makes his arm scream to do it. Makes him scream too. He buries the blade in it three more times. On the third strike the knife snaps off inside, so he sets to pulling the cables free with his bare hands until all the thing can do is twitch.

Until he realises how quiet it is, save for the ringing in his ears and the beating of his heart.

None of the infiltrators are blaring noise at them anymore, because they are all crumpled and collapsed around him, patterned with frost.

Wyck looks up to see Zane standing there with blood running in a thick stripe from her nose. It drips in half-time onto the front of her robes. The commissar is with her. Everyone is with her. All looking at him.

No. Not everyone.

Wyck gets to his feet and goes straight to where Awd is lying. The powered blade opened him up across his chest. The flak didn't come close to stopping it. Awd is breathing like a panicked animal and pumping blood all over the floor.

'Dav,' he says, between shallow breaths. 'It's bad. It's really bad.'

Wyck doesn't need telling. He shouts for Lye, but she's already dropping to her knees opposite him and pulling her kit and her needles.

'Hey,' Wyck says, and he clicks his fingers to get Awd's attention. 'Look at me. Keep your eyes open.'

Awd does as he's told, but his eyes are foggy. Lye is trying to stop the bleeding. She's red to her elbows, and she has that look on her face that Wyck's seen before.

The look that tells him it's worse than bad.

'I promised I'd do it,' Awd says. 'That I'd mind them.'

'There's minding, and then there's being stupid,' Wyck says. 'Throne, that was stupid.'

Awd laughs, though it's not a joke. Some blood comes with it. 'Never promised anything about that,' he says.

Awd takes a breath and Wyck sees the way air bubbles in the wound.

'I'm sorry, Dav,' Awd says.

'What for?' Wyck asks.

But Awd doesn't answer. Instead, he just seizes and rasps a breath and then goes still. Wyck curls his hands into fists. It hurts to do it, because he's cut across the palms and the knuckles from killing the infiltrator. Skinned. Ragged.

It doesn't stop him from slamming his fist onto the deck and cutting it all over again.

'Dav,' Lye says.

'Not a word,' he snarls.

He gets to his feet and goes to fetch his rifle. Wyck sees Haro and Jey looking at him. Crys too. The great big fool has tears running down her face. She opens her mouth to say something, but he turns away because he doesn't want to hear it from her either.

Not a damned word.

It takes almost four hours for Raine and the Antari to reach the end of the void-gantries.

Almost four hours, and a great deal of blood.

Raine's body aches from cuts and bruises and from every fight before this one. Every blow she parries with her sword makes her ache all the worse, but still she does not stop. She cannot stop. So Raine refuses the pain and the exhaustion as she fights her way through the Sighted defending the last section of the void-gantries. Raine opens one of the Sighted from hip to throat with her sabre, letting her momentum lend strength to the blow, before using that same momentum to slip past another as he tries to cut her in turn. This one is clad in blue carapace armour and a mirrored helm and wields a wave-bladed sword made from dark metal. Raine hears the hum of the sword as it parts the air by her head.

'Change is creation,' the Sighted says, as he swings for her again. 'Change is death.'

Raine catches his sword on her own, and pushes the Sighted back a step. He hisses behind his mirrored mask.

'And so is death creation,' he says. 'Only by–'

The Sighted's last word is lost to the *boom* of Raine's bolt pistol. The explosive round shatters the man's helm and his head beneath it and his body falls heavily onto the decking, gouting black blood. Around Raine, the fight is in full flow. Another of the Sighted cuts Yuri Hale and nearly takes that same eye he was so lucky not to lose. Hale answers with las-fire from his pistol that paints the deck with blood like a starfield. Lydia Zane slams one of the heretics against the armourglass and breaks him. Tyl and Jeth make quick, efficient kills, dropping many of their enemies before they can even close range. Raine sees Wyck snap the neck of another Sighted with a twist of his hands, shouting as he does it. Raine draws her sword through another of them. Through the last of them. The heretic falls hard and rasps a noisy breath, and then dies.

'And now for the door,' Hale says from beside her, breathless.

The bulkhead door blocking the way ahead is massive, as wide as the gantry and made from one solid piece of reinforced plasteel that's easily as thick as the hull of a tank. The Sighted's spiral mark has been daubed on the face of it, at least six feet high. As Raine approaches it with Hale and his squad she can see that the spiral is made up of words.

Only by Nine, it says, over and over again.

Raine scowls and spits onto the deck. This close to the core, the floor is crowded with jagged clusters of crystal and puddles of oil that mingle with all of the spilt blood.

'Wyck, set Yulia to work on the door,' Hale says. 'I want it broken.'

'Aye, sir,' Wyck says.

The splinter pattern on Wyck's fatigues is almost lost to filth and blood. His face is cut and bruised, and his fair hair is dark with ashes. Only the aquila on the chain around his neck remains bright and clear to see.

'Be precise,' Hale says. 'The void has taken quite enough from us today.'

Wyck glances momentarily at the armourglass viewport, and Raine sees him take a breath.

'Got it,' he says, and he shouts for Crys and moves off to the bulkhead.

'How are we doing, Nuria?' Hale asks.

The medic is almost as bloody as Wyck. She shakes her head and sighs. 'I won't lie, Yuri, it could be better.' She glances back to where the rest of the squads are mustering and keeping watch. 'The Fenwalkers are as good as dead. Only the new recruits left standing. Koy's watching over them as well as her own, now. The Hartkin have fared little better. We're looking at one in eight dead, or worse.'

Raine feels the weight of their losses heavily then, and not just Grey Company, but Blue and Gold too. All of them. Hundreds of Antari souls, damned to die by High Command because of what she knows.

'Their sacrifice will not be wasted,' she says, as much to herself as to Hale and Lye. 'We will make the enemy pay in blood for those we have lost.'

Hale nods. 'Aye, commissar,' he says. 'For every death.'

'Breach is set, captain,' Crys shouts.

The combat engineer jogs back towards them, trailing a line of det cord. Everyone else gets at least as far back as Crys does. Five charges are affixed around the edges of the bulkhead door, with det cord running between them along the seals. Raine knows that the charges are custom-made, like all of Crys' demolitions kit. Built for the job at hand, and the environment they face.

'When the bulkhead goes, we push straight through,' Hale says, over the company channel. 'No hesitation. Go for the kill.'

'Aye, for the kill!'

The answer comes from every squad sergeant left standing.

'On my word, Yulia,' Hale says.

'Yessir,' Crys says, with a grin.

'Break it,' Hale snarls.

Crys flips the switch on the detonator, and the det cord lights in a bright white instant, like the heart of a star. The charges follow, triggered by the cord. They detonate so quickly that Raine can't separate the noise. It all just becomes one long *boom* and an exhaled plume of smoke that stings her throat and her eyes, and then it is over, and there is nothing left of the bulkhead but a twisted, splintered mess, and through the doorway, the outer core.

'Go!' Hale shouts. 'Straight through, for the kill!'

Raine breaks cover alongside the Antari and runs for the outer core, through smoke and freezing cold water from the fire suppressors. A storm, inside the shipyards. Everything is painted crimson by the emergency lighting. Alarums wail, but louder still is the machine voice of Axhon-Pho.

<*The unenlightened will perish,*> it says. **<*Only by Nine.*>**

Raine sees the outer core in glimpses as she runs through

the smoke. It is a massive circular chamber, lined with thick knots of piping and cables. The Sighted have built several rows of fortifications and barricades from scrap and sandbags between the gantries and the bulkheads that lead to the command core. Targeting lasers pierce the smoke all around Raine as she reaches the first row of barricades and vaults them, landing amongst the Sighted on the other side. They are still reeling from the explosion that destroyed the door. Some are bleeding. Some aflame. Las-fire strobes in the smoke, and the fight becomes a series of instants painted in red and gold.

Firing Penance and sending black blood scattering across the deck.

Lydia Zane splintering bone and metal alike with a clap of her hands.

Daven Wyck slamming one of the Sighted against the barricades.

Cassia Tyl killing with whispers of hellgun fire.

Yuri Hale's chainsword snarling and sending more black blood into the air.

And then over the shouting and the gunfire and Axhon-Pho's droning, Raine hears something else.

The high-pitched whine of automated turrets.

'Take cover!' she shouts into the vox.

Raine ducks back onto the other side of the barricades as the automated turrets fire, cutting through the smoke and clattering against the barricades and the deck. The order echoes down the line from the squad sergeants and from Hale. Shouts echo too. Screams. Sparks fly everywhere. All along the line, the Antari of Grey Company seek safety in the shadow of the barricades as the heavy gunfire tracks along it, splintering metal and plasteel. Raine sees one of Koy's Mist-vypers hit by it, splintered just as easily. Dead in an instant.

'Zane!' Hale shouts, from beside Raine. 'Shields!'

The psyker is on her knees, shaking and bleeding badly from that gunshot wound in her leg. She looks down the line and holds up her hands, making barricades for the barricades where she can, but her shielding is flickering and faltering.

'I cannot protect them all, captain,' she says, through blood and drool. 'It is too far. It is too much.'

'Do what you can,' Hale says, as he unhooks the vox handset from Kayd's kit.

'This is Grey,' Hale says. 'Devri, do you read?'

'I hear you, Grey,' he says. Devri sounds like he's in pain. *'I'm almost at the auguries. We've got resistance.'*

Zane is moaning through her teeth now and weeping from her false eyes. Frost spreads out from her across the deck. Raine ducks again as a high calibre round slips through and takes a chunk out of the barricade by her head.

'Resistance or not, if you don't blind the magos, we're dead,' Hale says.

Zane cries out then and her limited shielding fails. Screams echo. Silhouetted figures spill away from the barricades, torn apart by gunfire.

'*Now*, Devri!' Hale shouts, into the handset.

And there is a huge tremor that rattles the deck underfoot. For an instant the gunfire and the magos fall quiet. In that moment, Raine can hear nothing but the cries and the moans of the dying.

'Auguries destroyed,' Devri says, over the vox. *'Go for the kill, Yuri.'*

'Aye,' Hale says. 'For the kill.'

Daven Wyck sinks down with his back against the barricades. Him and his Wyldfolk are right out in it, leaving the rest of Grey behind. So slow. Hard rounds clatter off the deck around him, throwing sparks into the air. Wyck puts his hand to his side. It comes away so red it's almost black, and he realises he's been shot. Realises that's why it hurts and why he's so dizzy. He can't remember it happening. Can't remember much of anything, save for splinters. Thrown punches. Hip-fire. Snapped bones. Strangling. Screams that could be his or could be theirs. That could just be echoes for all he knows because he can't tell the edges from the centre anymore.

He rests his head against the barricades for a second and takes another vial out of the pouch at his belt. His vision is already pin-sharp. Everything is already so loud. But the gunshot wound will make him slow.

And he can't afford to be slow.

Wyck uncaps the vial with his thumb and punches the auto-injector into his arm. It hits him hard, because he's already running the edge. Already on the edge. It makes him knock his head against the barricades and grit his teeth. Makes him almost choke on his own spit.

Then it makes him get up on his feet. Take a breath. Wait for the chatter of guns to skip and then run from cover and into the teeth of it. Over the barricades and the sandbags they've slung up. There are five of the Sighted. Six. Maybe ten. It's a blur of colours and shapes and sound. Yelling. The *crack* of las-fire. The thunderclaps of solid shot. Everything smells of iron and dirt and old flowers. More thrown punches that jolt his arm. Make his knuckles creak and ache. More bones that break under his hands and his boots.

More screams. Could be theirs, or his.

Then it's over. Wyck doesn't know exactly how he ends up on his knees, but he does. Throwing up onto the treadplate, so it goes into all of the grooves. There's blood in that too. Blood everywhere.

So much of it, everywhere, always.

He gets to his feet again as the others catch up to him. Their faces run like water as the room turns. It should just be Crys and Haro and Jey, because that's all he has left, but it's not. Wyck sees Awd too, cut through. He sees Tian, all broken. Efri and Dal and Vyne. Yevi and Nial and all of the others that have gone on without him. Last of all there's Keller, burned black save for his grey eyes.

What have you done, Dav? the dead ask.

'Too much to forgive,' he answers them, his voice barely a whisper.

And then Crys takes hold of him by the shoulders and shakes him and the dead vanish. Wyck shrugs her free before his nerves can fire enough to make him hit her.

'You don't look right,' she says, her voice made low and slow. 'Don't sound right.'

He almost tells her it's because he's not. Because he's wrong. Made badly. Broken and snapped, but he doesn't. Instead he tells her what he always tells her, because soon it won't matter anyway. Because of all his sins, lies are surely the least.

'It's nothing,' Wyck says.

Raine feels the tide turning as she cuts and shoots and kills her way towards the command core alongside Yuri Hale and the rest of Grey Company. Raine's hands are slick with blood and sweat, and her bones ache. Smoke stings her eyes and leaves her lungs raw, but they are so close.

Victory is so close.

And then the emitters overhead click live with a whine

and Axhon-Pho's voice echoes again, but this time it is more than just monotone.

It is *enraged*.

<Kill the faithless,> it says, over and over. *<Kill the faithless.>*

And a twinned bellow echoes in answer.

Raine looks to the source of the roar to see a hulking creature approaching through the smoke. No, not a creature. A *creation*, made from bone and flesh and metal to look like an apex predator. The thing is nearly as big as a Taurox, and it moves spasmodically on four limbs that end in clawed feet. Jagged crystal scales cover its body and forelimbs, and exhaust pipes jut from its shoulders. The creation's face is no more than a silvered, asymmetric skull with slack, fanged jaws, that looks neither animal or human. Two more faceted crystals sit in the creation's hollow eye sockets. It twitches and bellows again without moving those slack jaws, dribbling oil and fluid onto the deck.

'Five *hells*,' Jeth says, from beside Raine.

And the creation lowers its head and charges forwards.

'Fall back to the barricades!' Hale shouts. 'Do not stop firing!'

Raine fires on it, the bolt shells detonating against the creature's crystal hide, scattering shards and spraying the deck with oil. Las-fire from the Antari glances from the creation's scales and clatter from its silvered bones. Hellgun fire chips splinters from its jaws and skull.

But the creation doesn't stop.

It lands amidst the Antari, reeking of death and scattering oil. It guts Makar Kayd with a swipe of its claws. Knocks one of the Hartkin into the barricades and crushes another underfoot. Zane manages to save herself and Nuria Lye with a kine-shield but the psyker is on her knees and screaming. Tyl and Jeth stand their ground, still firing. Aiming for the eyes and the dead flesh between its scales. Raine hears Yuri Hale shout in Antari. The meaning of the words filters through to her as the creation turns towards him.

Go back to the hells.

Hale cuts the creation deeply across its forelimbs and face with his chainsword. The toothed blade skips and grinds over bone and metal, sending splinters and oil into the air. The creation falters and staggers and its limbs misfire and for a moment it seems it might fall and go still.

But then the creation rears and bellows and slices him with its massive, hooked claws.

Hale's chainsword goes skittering away and he falls to his knees with blood spilling from the deep wounds in his face and throat and chest. Somehow, Hale still manages to raise his laspistol in a shaking hand and fire it up into the creature's face, shattering its jaw.

'*Back to the hells,*' he manages to say again, over the vox.

And then the creation slams him onto the deck, and he goes still. Raine hears Lye scream. Hears Jeth curse. She yells too, wordlessly, firing her bolt pistol on the creation until it clicks empty. It comes for her then, bellowing all the while. Las-fire halos it. Tyl shatters one of the creation's crystal eyes. Raine stands her ground with Evenfall in guard. She has to kill it. She has to survive. She cannot allow the shipyards to be the death sentence that Serek intended it to be.

She will not die here.

Raine allows the creation to get so close that she can smell the terrible death-stink rolling from beneath its ruined jaws. It swings a massive claw to cut her, snagging her along her hip and ribs as she ducks inside its reach. The pain is dizzying, but she is close enough now to see herself reflected in the faceted crystal of its remaining eye.

Close enough to plunge Evenfall to the hilt up into the creation's skull.

The creation spasms and bellows and knocks Raine backwards, sending her crashing onto the deck. That is dizzying too. And painful. As Axhon-Pho's creation thrashes and collapses to the deck, spilling oil and shedding sparks, Raine tries to sit herself up, but realises she can't. Her armour is a ruin, torn open by the creation's claws. She is bleeding a lot. It bubbles up and over her hands as she tries to stop it, turning her black uniform even more so. Raine's vision smears and blurs as the Sighted start firing again and someone puts their armoured hands on her and drags her into cover behind the barricades. She sees a Duskhound's mask through lidded eyes, and nearly says Andren Fel's name.

'Eyes on me, commissar,' Cassia Tyl says. 'You can't die here.'

Raine shakes her head. She can't die here. Not with the fight unfinished and with Serek still standing and the crusade fighting on blindly in the name of a lie.

She will *not die here*.

Raine tries to stand but she only makes it as far as her knees. Her sabre falls from her hand. Her pistol too. Tyl shouts for Lye as Raine manages to put her hand into her greatcoat pocket and take out the timepiece, printing blood into the name carved into the back of the case.

She hears her sister's voice then, from the datacrystal recording.

You will not fail as I did, Severina.

You will be your own legend, and for that, I am so very proud.

Raine's vision tunnels until the only point of light is the timepiece's case, and her sister's name.

'Lucia,' Raine whispers, as the darkness overcomes her.

'Hale is down!'

Lara Koy's voice over the vox is distorted by distance. Muted by the screaming and shouting and the hammering of Wyck's heart in his ears. He takes cover behind the barricades with Sighted las-fire cutting holes in the smoke around him. He is breathing hard. Bleeding badly, from the wound in his side. So dosed up that colours are dazzling and his skin feels as though it's afire.

'Lara, I'm going to need you to repeat that,' he says, his voice hoarse.

'Yuri's dead, Dav.'

Wyck blinks, and his hand falls away from the vox-bead in his ear. Yuri too. Gone to the After with Awd and Efri and Dal and Vyne and so many others. So many dead who don't deserve it. Who aren't owed it.

'What about Devri and Blue?' Wyck asks.

'I cannot raise him without long-range vox. We're on our own. The magos' damned creatures are everywhere, and we've not long before we lose void support.'

Wyck chances a look around the barricade. There is only one more Sighted barricade between him and the bulkhead doors that lead to the command core. To the magos.

To the end.

'We need a plan, Dav,' Koy says, in his ear.

Wyck ducks back behind the cover as las-fire splits the air. He thinks about Karin Sun and Gold Company blown out into the void. Killed in an instant.

Wyck takes a deep breath, and it hurts to do it.

'Leave it to me,' he says, into the vox. 'Just keep drawing their eyes.'

'What are you going to do?' she asks.

'Enact Yuri's last order,' he says. 'I'm going for the kill.'

He cuts the connection before she can argue with him.

'What's the plan, sarge?' Crys says, from beside him.

The combat engineer is covered in ashes and dirt, and her flak armour is split across the chest-plate. A bloody wound carves its way along her scalp through her short, dark hair. Jey and Haro are still with her too, firing around the cover at the Sighted's lines. The void-born don't look like new blood anymore. They are just Wyldfolk, now.

'We're going to send the magos into the void,' Wyck says. 'How many charges do you have left?'

Crys pulls the last of her kit from her belt. A tight-wound bundle of demo charges, and a remote trigger.

'Just the one, but there's no real range on the trigger,' she says. 'I'll have to be with it when it goes.'

What the Sighted on the gantries said comes back to Wyck then.

The darkness waits for you.

'No, you won't,' Wyck says. 'Give me the charges.'

Crys' face falls in what seems like slow motion.

'Sarge,' she says.

'No,' Wyck snarls at her. 'I won't have your death to bear too. Not with all of the others. Now do as I say and give me the damned charges.'

Crys shakes her head. A tear paints a clean line through the blood on her face.

'Damn it, Dav,' she says.

But she passes him the charges. They are heavy and cold in Wyck's hands.

'You get me to the door, and then you fall back to the others,' he says. 'Clear?'

'Yes, sir,' Crys says.

She claps him on the shoulder then with her left hand. The one with the Wyldfolk's mark on it.

'Go fast,' she says.

Wyck nods. 'And don't look back,' he tells her, and he means it.

His Wyldfolk get into position beside him.

'Ready?' Crys asks.

Wyck feels the weight of the demo charges and the bolt shell he carries and the aquila around his neck and he nods.

'Ready,' he says.

And then he breaks cover and runs for the bulkhead door. Las-fire cuts the air around him. Punches holes in the deck. Nicks his legs as he runs. Wyck staggers but he doesn't fall. Doesn't slow. He hits the barricades and vaults them. Shoots one of the Sighted in the face and breaks another with the butt of his rifle. Crys knocks another to the deck. Jey guts one with a knife. Haro sends one spilling over backwards. The last two of the Sighted fall back towards the bulkhead. Wyck shoots one of them down and Crys gets the other, but they have already triggered the bulkhead door. A siren blares and the door begins to grind closed and Wyck runs for it, dropping into a slide under the door before it slams shut and seals with a hiss of pressure. Wyck gets to his feet with his ears ringing and his bones aching. He is alone in the vast command core, separated from his Wyldfolk. The circular chamber is lined with cogitator banks and lit only by the starlight coming through the armourglass viewports and the glowing crystals jutting from the deck like standing stones. Wyck takes a breath and gags. The command core stinks of death. Bared skulls and bits of bone lie everywhere. Torn sinews and slicks of blood. Some of it is animal, but most is not. Tangled loops of pipes and cables snake over and through the mess, sweating oil and coiling up to the raised central dais where they connect to the shadowed, jagged shape that sits on it.

The magos. Axhon-Pho.

<Flesh given purpose,> it burrs. *<Only by Nine.>*

There are even more bodies on the dais, scattered around the magos like kills in an ursa's den. The loops of pipes and cables stir and slither over one another as the magos turns to face him, clicking like an auspex return. It rears up on nine mechanical legs. Black robes stitched with crimson spirals hang from what remains of its torso, thin and tattered. Multiple arms protrude from beneath those robes, bladed and augmented and set with weapons. The face inside the magos' hood is a spiral of red crystals and lenses set around a central vox-emitter.

<Kill the faithless,> the magos blares.

Wyck runs for the viewport as the magos claws its way down from the dais towards him. Jagged bolts of lightning spear from the magos' weapon arms, arcing to the deck and the cogitators and scorching the air around Wyck's head. One of the cogitators detonates, sending Wyck from his feet. He lands badly amongst the blood and the ruin, shattering his wrist. His rifle skitters away and is lost amongst the cables. The magos stalks closer on its spider limbs, with that auspex-click, hunting him. Wyck goes in the pouch at his belt and takes out another of his vials. The dose hits him even harder than the last one did. Blood runs from his nose and his heart aches in his chest as he gets back on his feet. More lightning hits the deck. He can smell the metal and blood stink of the magos as it lunges closer. Through the armour-glass, the void looms wide and dark and strung with stars. It's like looking at death itself. Right down the throat of the hounds. Wyck should be afraid, but he isn't because of the weight of the bolt shell he carries. Because of the weight of the aquila around his neck. Because he is tired of the blood on his hands and the ghosts in his head.

He is tired of running from death.

Wyck drops into a slide as the magos tries to take his head clean off with one of those bladed arms. He slams Crys' improvised charge against the armourglass where it sticks, and then rolls to his feet, ready to thumb the trigger.

And then one of the magos' bladed arms punches into his chest, straight through the flak. Wyck coughs blood.

'No good,' he says.

Wyck's feet leave the deck as the magos lifts him. The movement makes the blade shift in his chest and he cries out, going blind for a second. His body is going numb fast. He can't make his fingers work. Can't thumb the trigger. The magos tilts its head and blurts noise at him and Wyck sees himself reflected a dozen times in the shattered red crystals of its eyes. No rifle, no knife. Only the silver aquila on the chain around his neck left.

<And so destiny is written,> the magos blares, so loud his ears ring. *<Only by Nine.>*

'We'll see about that,' Wyck says.

Half-blind from pain and damn near dead, he thumbs the detonator trigger.

The world turns sideways as the magos is sent reeling by the explosion. Wyck ends up on his back on the treadplate as the viewport cracks along its length. Tectonic, like old ice underfoot. The magos screams again.

And the viewport blows out.

There's a rush and a spin and the world turns again. The magos disappears into the void. Bits of glass rush past. Droplets of blood. Wyck's ears ring, and it sounds like howling. He hangs in the emptiness waiting for the blackness to take him with agony running knives over his body inside and out. A memory presses in from the edges of his misfiring mind.

That day back home. He'd walked into the black lake to try to get the blood off his hands. To get rid of the knife he'd used. It wasn't supposed to go that way. The fight was only meant to go to first blood. Just a way to get some extra coin for him and Raf and the others, but once he'd started fighting, he'd not been able to stop. Then Raf had to come and find him. He had to ask him that damned question.

What have you done, Dav?

It wasn't supposed to go that way, but then Raf had pushed him. Punched him. Fought him. So, Wyck had fought back but the knife was still in his hand, and then it was buried in Raf's chest.

It wasn't supposed to go that way.

Awd said that it's war that splinters a soul. Makes it snap. Wyck knows that's not the truth of it. That some things are made badly in the first place. They start off broken. Weak. He waits for the void to take him. For the hounds to come and drag him to the After to be judged for all of his sins and the blood on his hands. He is ready for it. Ready to answer for everything.

But there is no howling. There are no balefire eyes, or yawning jaws. Instead, Wyck hears a voice ringing in his head, dim and distant.

Kin, it rasps.

Something Wyck can't see tethers him, keeping him from that break in the armourglass. Away from the void.

Away from death.

Emergency measures kick in. Shutters slam down, sealing the void out and allowing the core to repressurise. Wyck falls hard onto the deck and air forces its way back into his lungs. It burns badly. His whole body burns. He can't move or speak or even blink. The bulkhead door grinds up slowly, and his kinfolk move in. Lydia Zane limps into view and falls to her knees beside him. She is bloodied and burned and looks for all the world like a devil sent to haunt him.

'I owed you a debt,' Zane says, as unconsciousness comes to claim him. 'Consider it paid.'

TWENTY-TWO

What was lost

Andren Fel wakes to the sound of screaming. The noise pulls him up and out of dreams that cling to him, refusing to fade. Dreams of fire, and smoke. Dreams of Severina Raine's voice, echoing, though he cannot see her for the fire.

I still have stories I owe you.

Fel finds himself in a small, stark room, with whitewashed walls. There is no door, just a plastek curtain that shifts and creases in the recycled air. The room smells of counterseptic, and of blood. Fel hears screaming again, coming from beyond the curtain. He hears shouts in answer too. The snarl of tools and a repeating *ping* that sounds like auspex returns, or a monitron tracker. Fel gets himself sat up, though it hurts to do it. Every breath burns. His eyes are heavy, and his mind is slow. It takes a moment to understand what he is seeing and hearing. For him to recognise that he is in a medicae ward and to remember why.

Fel looks down then at his right arm.

'Hells,' he says, and his voice is hoarse.

The augmetic replacement is made of silvered steel, and it goes almost all the way to his shoulder. His arm aches, though it shouldn't be able to, and the augmetic fingers twitch of their own accord, like a misfire. It takes Fel three tries to make it stop. The servos inside the augmetic whine and burr. What happened starts to filter back in, then. The explosion. Bleeding a lot. Seeing Raine in the aftermath. She had asked him what happened, and he hadn't been able to tell her, but Fel remembers now. The cause of the explosion was a contact charge. One that he failed to notice until it was too late. Whoever set the bomb had made a trigger of Lori Ghael's augmetic lens as a message, and a punishment.

Ghael is dead, because she helped him.

Fel feels all the heavier now. His augmetic hand twitches again, trying to close. He has to find Raine and tell her about Ghael's death.

Fel pulls the needles feeding him medication from under his skin. That takes three tries, too, because his augmetic hand is clumsy and slow. Blood spatters on the tiled floor and the machines by the side of his cot start to ring urgently. Fel manages to get to his feet, but then the room starts turning around him and the walls run like wet paint, and he finds he can't see so well. When the orderlies come running and shouting, it sounds as though they are underwater. He can't fight them when they make him sit back down on the edge of the cot. Fel has to keep looking at his hands until everything stops spinning. That augmetic catches the light a lot. He'll have to do something about that.

'What in the hells do you think you're doing?'

Nuria Lye sounds as though she is underwater too. It does nothing to make her sound less angry, or tired. When Fel is able to look up, he sees that she looks it too. The chief medicae's grey eyes are bloodshot and hollow. Her lip is split and her scalp is grazed.

She looks as though she's been fighting.

Unease claws at Fel, then.

'I missed a fight,' he says. 'What was it?'

'You need to rest,' Lye says, with a shake of her head. 'Or you'll miss a good deal more.'

Fel shakes his head and the room turns again. He has to put his good hand down on the cot-frame. 'Tell me what I missed,' he says.

Lye puffs air through her cheeks. 'High Command sent us after the Laxian shipyards,' she says. 'And we took them back, but it cost us.'

It's not just unease that Fel feels then. It's dread.

'How much?' he asks.

'Your Duskhounds are still standing, but not everyone was so lucky.' Lye shakes her head. She blinks a couple of times as if her eyes are stinging. 'We lost almost forty per cent across the regiment. Karin Sun and damn near all of Gold. Dol and his Fenwalkers. Half the Wyldfolk. Ari too. And Yuri Hale.'

Fel takes a breath, but it doesn't seem to help. All of those losses still feel like being drowned.

'Gone to His light,' he says, softly.

Lye nods. 'Aye,' she replies. 'Evermore.'

Then Lye takes a deep breath and her no-nonsense frown returns. 'Now, rest, like I said. That arm won't settle until you do.'

Fel shakes his head. 'I can't,' he says. 'I need to speak with the commissar about what happened on Laxus Secundus. You have to call for her.'

Lye's face colours, and she shakes her head.

'I can't, captain,' she says. 'Raine was killed in the ship-yards too.'

Everything goes distant in an instant. Muffled, like the shock after a flash-charge. Fel's augmetic hand twitches again and this time he doesn't try to stop it. He just lets it misfire while he tries his best to breathe, remembering Raine's voice in his dreams.

I still have stories I owe you.

Fel slams his augmetic hand against the rail of the cot and puts a dent in the metal. He wants it to hurt like it did before, but now he can't feel a damned thing.

'It will get easier,' Lye says. 'Once the injury isn't so new.'

Fel knows that she means his arm, which is why he doesn't tell her that she's wrong and that it won't get easier, because he should have been there to fight with them, and he wasn't.

Because he owes Raine more than just stories, and now she is gone.

TWENTY-THREE

For the Bale Stars

Lord-General Militant Alar Serek is in agony. Every step he takes down the marble and gilt hallway that leads to the main audience chamber on board *Bale's Heart* sends pain rolling outwards from the old scar that runs from his shoulder to his hip. From the mark he was given. Serek does not allow the pain to show on his face. He does not limp, or falter, and his breathing remains steady, because in this he is practised. He has been hiding the pain for over a decade.

But not for much longer.

Soon, he will have the machines.

Soon, everything will change.

Serek passes by the hanging portraits of those who came before him. The brightest and fiercest sons and daughters of the Bale Stars rendered in cracked and flaking oils. The paintings are cared for, and tended, but even still the name plates have tarnished and their eyes have faded, because no legacies left by the dead can outlast time. Serek stops at the end of the hallway and the last of the portraits. His kastelan stops in the same instant, keeping silent watch as Serek looks at the portrait of the last Lord-General Militant to hold rank before him.

The artist captured Thema Raine well. Her severity, her scars and her keen eyes. Even down to the way she held herself so straight, as if she could never be bowed. Never broken. Long ago, Serek used to think that was what it took to hold dominion over the Bale Stars. Just standing straight, and never breaking. But it is so much more than that.

You must give *everything*.

The roar of triumphal horns carries from the audience chamber ahead of Serek, and he turns away from Thema Raine, and her keen eyes. He walks up the marble steps towards the audience chamber with that ever-present pain coursing through him. His kastelan follows close, and slow. A pair of attendants open the heavy curtains, and Serek steps out onto the dais to another kind of roar, coming from those arrayed before him.

The audience chamber's gallery hall is arranged like a cathedral, lined with rows and rows of marble pews on either side of a central aisle. None of the pews are in use, because all present are standing. At the sides of the hall stand those who have come to bear witness. Sylar, and a select few of his Kavrone officer cadre. The Paxari Naval delegation, and House Stormfall's lesser nobles. A number of Serek's own Lions of Bale. In the gallery rows stand those who are to be honoured.

The remaining members of the Eleventh Antari Rifles are clad in their dress greys with hardly a thought for medals or glories. Instead, they are decorated with cuts and bruises and bandages. They all wear colour bands to mark their companies. Serek sees blue, and grey, but very little in the way of gold. Serek has read the reports, and the lists of the lost. Over half of the regiment's infantry were killed to claim the Laxian shipyards. It is a good deal of blood to spend, but like so many things it is necessary, for the crusade.

For the Bale Stars.

The other five members of his High Command are already present, and already seated in their own finely made thrones on the curved dais. High-King Araxis and Veris Drake bow their heads as Serek walks past them to where his throne waits. He does not sit; instead Serek draws his sword from the scabbard at his hip, because blades and words go hand in hand. Because both can cut and kill in equal measure. Because that blade always reminds him of who he is, and why he has been chosen to stand above all others, to shape the fate of the Bale Stars, and those who serve them. Serek's kastelan waits at his back, and two more of his Lions take guard positions on either side of him, their fur-trimmed cloaks stirring in the recycled air. On Serek's left, Io Karandi. On his right, Mateu Vostal. The pariah's presence is discomforting, but necessary.

'On this day, a new legend has been written,' Serek says. 'Like all legends, it has been written in blood, by the faithful and the loyal. By those willing to sacrifice everything in the name of something greater.'

He looks out at the Antari. They are scarred and augmented and built strong from fighting. Despite all of that, they still seem transient. Impermanent. Their lives will be short and bloody and then they will be gone. Their names and their deeds will pass into memory, but even that will not last. Those who remember die, and their memories go with them.

Death is an equaliser, which is why Serek has given so much to deny it, because he is not equal. He is *chosen*.

But he will allow them their moment of glory, impermanent as it may be.

'The Bale Stars see your sacrifice,' he says. 'As do I. We see your bravery and your loyalty, and we recognise it.'

He raises his hand and draws it across his chest, following the shape of the old wound given to him by Dektar the Ascended. The wound that put him on the path to change and to the truth. It aches even more fiercely then. A reminder of what he is, and what he needs to be, just like the sword he carries.

'I confer the Lion's Honour on every soul that spent their blood at Laxus,' he says. 'Both the living, and the dead. On your captains. Your sergeants. Your infantry and on your commissar.'

There is a murmur then in the audience chamber as the doors at the far end open. The victory banners hanging above the central aisle stir and four figures resolve with a scattering of psy-frost. Two are storm troopers, dressed in black carapace and armed with hellpistols. The third is the Antari psyker, frail and wretched. Serek barely pays them heed, because his attention is on the fourth figure. The one dressed in commissariat black, with a peaked cap on her head and her bolt pistol drawn.

'Lord-General Militant.'

The voice rings out clear. That pitch and inflection. Just like her damned sister. Just like Thema, who Serek once knew and respected. Who he emulated, until he realised that standing straight and remaining unbroken were not enough.

'I refuse the Lion's Honour,' Severina Raine says, as she walks down the central aisle. 'As do my regiment.'

The chamber erupts with noise as the other members of

High Command react to Raine's words with indignant rage. Serek holds up his hand and they all fall silent.

'Severina Raine,' he says, with deliberate calm. 'I was told that you were dead.'

She stares up at him from the gallery floor, unflinching. If it weren't for her intent, he could almost be proud of her.

'A lie, lord-general,' Raine says. 'But a necessary one, because I know the truth.'

Serek could order her shot in that moment, but he doesn't, because he wants to see if she will have the strength to say it.

He wants to see if she truly is Thema Raine's daughter.

'And what truth is that?' he asks.

Raine levels her pistol at him.

'That you have embraced darkness, and betrayed the Bale Stars Crusade.'

As soon as Raine says the words, the chamber erupts into clamour. Serek's Lions raise their guns and point them at her. Not just the two on the dais. The guards around the edge of the chamber too. On either side of her, Tyl and Jeth raise their own hellpistols in answer. Shouts and orders echo off the walls of the audience chamber and Raine watches Serek through the iron sights of her pistol as the Lord-General Militant shakes his head.

'I am so very disappointed in you, Severina Raine,' Serek says, and the room falls silent again. He sheathes his sword and sits down in that throne of his as if nobody in the chamber has a gun levelled. 'I gave you every chance, despite the failings of your blood, and now you stand here on a day meant to glory our victories and you dare to level your weapon at me. You dare to accuse me of betraying the Bale Stars Crusade.'

He looks down at her from his throne, his blue eyes glittering like cut crystal.

'I have given everything in the name of this crusade,' he says, coldly. 'Lower your weapons, while you still can.'

Raine knows that, at least, to be the truth. She does not look away from those unnatural eyes of his as she speaks again.

'Including your soul,' Raine says, just as coldly.

Serek shakes his head. 'You share your sister's failings,' he says. 'And you will share her fate.'

He gestures to his Lions. 'Get her out of my sight.'

As the Lions step down off the dais and onto the gallery floor Raine hears the powercells of Tyl and Jeth's guns whine. Her finger tightens on the trigger of her pistol.

'No.'

The Lions freeze at the sound of the voice. A voice Raine knows so very well, one that she wishes she had never doubted.

'I want to hear it,' says Lord-Marshal Veris Drake. 'All of it.'

Serek turns to look at her. 'Veris,' he says, warningly. 'Do not be a fool.'

Drake's eyes narrow in that approximation of a smile. 'Alar,' she says, giving his forename as much deliberate weight as he did hers. 'If you have committed no sins, then where is the harm? Surely Raine's words will only damn her further.'

'Unacceptable,' says Gulieta Vallah. The fleet commander's face is a snarl as she draws her sabre. 'This is dissent. Treason!'

The drawing of Vallah's sabre shatters decorum like a dropped glass and within seconds High Command is divided between Serek and Drake. Not just High Command, either. Every soul in the chamber. Kaspar Sylar breaks the line and points his gilded, ornate laspistol at Veris Drake.

'You are a damned disgrace,' the Kavrone general snarls. 'This is not about Serek. This is about your ambition.'

Drake laughs. 'Ambition?' she says. 'Kaspar, please. We both know who of the two of us has killed for the sake of ambition.'

The sound Sylar makes in response is practically animal. Raine hears his pistol arm and charge.

'You *dare*,' he roars. 'You dare to question me. To question the Lord-General Militant.'

'Nobody is above questioning,' says Lukas Vander.

He draws his own pistol with his uninjured hand and puts it to Sylar's head.

'Not for a commissar,' Vander says. 'I would hear Raine's charges.'

The chamber is held at stalemate. Held like a breath. So Raine takes a step forwards into the teeth of the Lions, and towards the throne and the king who made it for himself.

'Lord-General Militant Alar Serek,' she says. 'The charges against you are that of treason and corruption. Of the use of psykers and heretical machines taken from the enemy to prolong your own life and your control over the crusade. Of the abuse of military assets to acquire those machines.'

Raine takes a breath.

'You are accused of murder. Of complicity in the deaths of hundreds, not least of Surgeon-Major Isabella Luz, who you killed to conceal the greatest of your sins. The willing embrace of corruption.'

She clicks the hololith projector she carries live and holds it up in her hand for all to see. The audio blares from the vox-emitters Tyl and Jeth rigged to their kit.

'He is different.' Isabella Luz's voice echoes in the silence of the chamber. *'Changed. It is his eyes. They are so blue now. And then there is the matter of the mark.'*

Raine sees those blue eyes go wide. Serek begins to move. He opens his mouth to speak.

'There is a scar that is not a scar,' Luz says. *'It is a fate-mark.'*

There is a long, aching moment of silence. Of shock and dismay, that rolls through the chamber like an ocean wave.

'I will not stand for this,' Serek says. He gets to his feet. 'Not from you, or any other.'

'Is it true?' Drake asks. Her voice is hollow, and full of rage.

Serek snaps around to look at her. 'Of course not,' he says.

'Prove it,' Drake says.

Serek flinches. He takes a breath, and his hand goes to his chest as if it hurts him.

'Throne, it *is* true,' Drake says, softly.

'You do not understand,' Serek snarls. 'You cannot. I have given *everything* for this crusade. I have torn down cities. Laid waste to armies. I have taken every wound and stayed standing, but it was still not enough. I would have lost everything I have given, and everything that I have done. My crusade and my sector, all because of a weakness in my blood.'

When he looks back at Raine there is so much hatred in his crystal-blue eyes.

'I denied it,' he says. 'I changed my fate for the sake of *my* Bale Stars. For the sake of *my* crusade.'

'No,' Raine says. 'You denied it for the sake of no one but yourself.'

And she fires her pistol. The *boom* of it echoes in the vaulted chamber, and Serek falls backwards into his gilded throne. Blood mists the air.

And the chamber erupts with agonised noise and gunfire.

Lydia Zane cannot help feeling the pull of sorrow, watching Alar Serek fall and die. Not because he had not earned such a death. His sins more than fated it. Zane feels sorrow because a part of her believes that Serek's sins grew from noble intent. From momentary weakness, when remaining strong mattered most.

Zane blinks away the sorrow as she throws herself through the melee that the audience chamber has become. Her bare feet slip on the bloodied floor. Her limbs ache, and her lungs burn with every breath. Without her gifts, Zane is weak. Limited. But she knows exactly who it is who has taken them, and she will have them back.

She will use them for what is right. She will remain strong.

The soulblind Lion is heavily-built and tall with a blunted, war-scarred face. He is well-armoured and well-armed, too, with a pistol and rifle and a brutal combat blade, but the Lion is distracted by Raine and Tyl and Jeth and the execution of his master. He does not know that Zane is close until she has punched her darkwood dagger into his back, into the space between his carapace plates. Into the space just beside his spine.

The soulblind Lion cries out then, and drops his pistol. Blood wells over Zane's hands as she pulls the blade free again. The Lion twists around and drives his fist into her face. Zane falls onto her back and the Lion comes with her, leaning all of his weight on her chest. He puts his big, blunt hands around her throat and squeezes. The absence of his soul worries at Zane even as he chokes the life from her. Zane's false eyes stutter and dazzle. Her lungs burn and over the ringing in her ears she hears him speak.

'You're nothing without your magicks, witch,' he snarls.

Those words make Zane's heart stir, even as it aches and struggles and thunders in her ears and she screams through her teeth and punches the darkwood blade into his left eye.

The Lion lets her go, moaning shapelessly with the blade buried so deep. He rolls clear of Zane and seizes and shakes and dies slowly. Slowly enough for Zane's voice to return to her.

'Even without my magicks, I am still Antari,' she rasps. 'And that is enough.'

The audience chamber is a warzone.

All around Raine, the Lions of Bale advance, firing into the crowd. The Antari surge forwards and fight back even though they are unarmed. Juna Keene knocks one of Serek's Lions to the ground with a heavy punch from her augmetic arm while Sale Devri fires a stolen pistol, defending her. On the dais, the remaining five members of High Command are intent on killing one another. Veris Drake is taking cover behind her ornate, gilded throne, trading fire with Lord-Castellan Caradris. General-Primary Hu Sul is locked in a duel of sabres with Gulieta Vallah. High-King Araxis is crawling along the marble to escape danger, his fine robes tattered and spattered with blood.

'Traitor!'

Raine turns at the sound of Kaspar Sylar's voice as he fires on her with his ornate pistol. The high-yield las-round impacts against Raine's chest-plate, winding her, and knocking out her aim. Before Sylar can fire again, a loud *boom* splits the air and Sylar falls messily onto the marble floor, executed by Lukas Vander.

'Raine!' he shouts, over the noise. 'The kastelan!'

Serek's slaved automaton steps down off the dais with a heavy thud. Crimson lights glow from within its face-plate as it turns its domed head towards Raine. She raises her pistol and fires three times as it moves inexorably towards her. The bolt-rounds put craters in its metallic hide, but the kastelan keeps coming with smoke trailing from its armour and lightning crackling around its heavy fists. Raine takes a step backwards, and fires again. That shot shatters the kastelan's face-plate. Tyl and Jeth chase her gunfire with their own high-powered las-fire. The kastelan blares machine noise and staggers, blinded. Raine ducks away as it swings for her, crashing its powered fist against the floor and powdering the marble. She draws her sabre. Evenfall is made for endings, and it sings as Raine splits the kastelan's armour with it, cutting a deep groove up the front of the automaton's chest and its domed head, sending sparks and smoke into the air. The power fields on the automaton's fists flicker and die, but it still rears up again, blaring static and shedding sparks and shaking the marble with its ponderous, inexorable tread. It raises its massive fist again.

And then the kastelan automaton crumples and folds and bends and ruptures, catching fire as it dies. The automaton falls forwards and hits the marble with a thunderous *crack*, still burning. Felled, like a tree.

Lydia Zane falls to her knees beside Raine. The Antari psyker is bloodied and bruised, panting like a hunted animal.

'It is not over,' she rasps, and points to the dais.

A spear of light lances up from Serek's gilded throne, stealing Raine's vision for a split second. When her sight returns, Alar Serek is on his feet once again. His white tunic is painted red with blood and his arctic eyes no longer remain.

Blue fire burns in their place.

There is a mournful roar around Raine from every soul in the chamber. She hears cries of *Chaos*, of *traitor* and of the Antari word that means *sent-from-the-hells* as they all recognise Serek for what he has become.

'Heretic,' Raine says, and she points her pistol at Serek, and pulls the trigger.

The others all fire on him too. Everyone who can. Light blooms on the dais a second time from las-fire and detonating pistol rounds, but when it clears, Serek still stands. The blue fire in his eyes burns all the brighter.

'*Enough,*' he says.

And everyone in the chamber around Raine freezes. Silence falls like a shroud as Serek descends to the gallery floor with his sabre drawn. It trails splinters of darkness that look for all the world like feathers. He moves for Raine, almost too quickly to see, and she barely turns aside his sword with her own.

'*You look at me with such hate,*' he says, his voice a twinned echo of the one she knew.

'Because you are a monster,' Raine snarls.

She turns his sword aside again and brings Evenfall around in a glittering arc. It is as fast as she has ever moved.

Fast enough to cut him.

Evenfall's powered blade draws a thin red line across Serek's sword arm. Black blood sprays into the air. Raine catches the scent of death as Serek bellows and attacks again. Raine parries, but it rattles her arm so numb that she cannot catch his next strike. The one that plunges straight through her armour and into her chest. She loses her grip on her sabre and her pistol. They clatter to the floor beside her as Serek kicks her onto her back. He puts his boot on her chest, and Raine's vision dazzles.

'*I am not a monster,*' Serek says. '*I am what is* **necessary**. *In the decade since Steadfast we have reclaimed more worlds than in the first thirty years of the crusade combined. We have felled tyrants, and toppled citadels, but our enemies are changing and so too must we. Only through change can we endure.*'

'No,' Raine manages to say, 'we endure through faith. We

endure through will, and great sacrifice in the God-Emperor's name.'

Serek shakes his head. **'The God-Emperor,'** he says, coldly. *'I dedicated my life to service in His name. I fought and bled and killed for Him, but when my body failed me, and I looked to Him for salvation, He turned His golden eyes elsewhere. After all I had done.'*

'Because He does not deal in mercy,' Raine says. 'To seek it is weakness.'

'Weakness is limiting yourself,' Serek says. *'Weakness is knowing that great power lies within your reach and failing to use it. With those machines I could change* everything, *Severina. I could reverse the massacre at Coris. I could undo the Shattered Years. I could twist the ropes of fate around the Nine and unmake them. I could restore the Bale Stars, edge to edge. Every injustice, undone. It is not too late.'*

The balefire in Serek's eyes flickers and he extends his hand to her.

'I can spare you. I can spare everyone.'

For an instant, Raine thinks of it. Of the unwriting of all those wars, and the blood it would spare. She thinks too of Lucia. Of what it would mean to be able to bring back her sister, and to undo that particular injustice. To unsay all of those terrible things that she said, and to be made whole again.

But then Raine thinks too of what Lucia said those years ago on the platform over Gloam's angry ocean.

They wanted to build a new world, and poison seemed a small price to pay.

And she knows that no matter the reward, poison is always too much to pay.

With incredible, blinding effort, Raine reaches out and

grabs her bolt pistol. Raises and fires it. Bloody mist scatters across her as Serek staggers backwards, bleeding anew from that old wound of his. Bleeding black. His hold on the others breaks, and they right themselves and rally and fire upon him. The hail of las-fire pushes him backwards as Antari hands pull Raine back to her feet. Keene and Devri. Raine's blood drips onto the marble as she advances on Serek and raises her pistol again. The Antari follow her. The Kavrone too. Vander and the Lions that are left standing. Serek is pushed back against the edge of the dais by the weight of las-fire and by Lydia Zane. The psyker bleeds anew through her bandages as she forces the monster that was once Alar Serek to his knees, burned and bleeding and trailing smoke.

'Lord-General Militant Alar Serek,' Raine says, between ragged breaths. 'I find you in dereliction of your duty to the Bale Stars Crusade, and to our Holy Lord on Terra. The punishment for this is death.'

Serek looks up at her then, and for a moment, his eyes are not lit by balefire. They do not look like cut crystal. They are a deeper shade of blue, like a twilight sky. They are his own.

'I just wanted to live,' Serek says, softly. 'I was afraid. Angry.'

Raine shakes her head. 'There is fear in everyone,' she says. 'And anger. It is what we choose to do in the face of it that damns or defines us.'

Serek nods, slowly. 'Those are good words, Severina Raine,' he says, in his odd, echoing voice. 'Words to die by.'

And then Raine pulls the trigger, and her pistol barks and Alar Serek does die.

Truly, this time.

The Wrath Unending, *before*

Raine calls only for a chosen few. Those that she has the best measure of, whose responses she can best predict and direct. The first is Juna Keene. The Antari general is a necessity. Without her, the plan will not work. Raine calls for the three captains, too, to help her enact it. Yuri Hale, Sale Devri and Karin Sun. The last of Fel's Duskhounds and Nuria Lye. Last of all, Raine sends for Lydia Zane, because the plan will not work without her, either.

And because there is little point in trying to keep secrets from a psyker.

The meeting takes place in a disused storage chamber in the lower decks of the Wrath Unending *during their warp-transit towards the Laxian shipyards. Old wounds from the* Wrath's *many fleet engagements mar the walls and deck. The damage has been repaired, but not concealed. Like the Antari, it wears its scars openly.*

'This feels like trouble, commissar,' Hale says.

He sits on one of the old crates beside Devri. Karin Sun stays on his feet, with his arms folded.

'I am inclined to agree, captain,' Juna Keene says. 'What are we doing down here, Raine?'

The Antari general is seated too, on another of the crates. Keene makes a show of looking at ease, but Raine can see suspicion in her grey eyes.

'You found the manticore,' Zane says, absently. 'That is why we are here.'

The psyker is sitting with her legs crossed beneath her on the treadplate of the floor. Like always, when they are aboard ship, she is barefoot.

Keene frowns. 'Manticore,' she says. 'What are you talking about?'

'This is what the captain spoke of, isn't it?' Tyl asks. 'What he couldn't tell me.'

'It is what he bled for,' Raine says. 'What so many have died for.'

She takes out the datakey from the pocket of her greatcoat and loads it into a portable hololith projector which she places on the floor.

'It is the truth,' she says.

And then she spools up Isabella Luz's records and lets them play. It is no easier to watch it a second time, even after speaking with Serek and seeing the truth of it in his face. Raine wants to cry out all over again. The Antari are silent throughout, and for what seems a long time afterwards too. All Raine can hear is the burn of the *Wrath*'s engines.

'He is the manticore,' Zane says, softly. 'He who was afraid to die, so he twisted free of the noose.'

'Serek,' Keene says. 'This cannot be true.'

The general gets to her feet as if she wants to leave but goes nowhere. She just stands, tensed like a threatened animal. Nuria Lye thumps her fist against the crate she is sitting on and curses softly, in Antari. Raine catches the phrase oath-breaker.

'Serek killed Dektar the Ascended,' Hale says, with his head in his hands. 'He liberated Steadfast and Paxar and saved us from death in the forges. He is the crusade.'

Karin Sun says nothing, but Raine sees a tear roll down his blunted, scarred face. He doesn't try to brush it away.

'It can't be,' Devri says. 'It just can't.'

Cassia Tyl shakes her head. She looks resigned. 'Of course it can,' she says, in a hollow voice. 'Fate-marks don't lie. Serek was broken by the threat of death.'

'And he made a choice that changed him,' Jeth says.

'The man that Serek once was is dead,' Raine says. 'He died on Steadfast, all of those years ago. He died the moment he made that choice.'

She pulls the datakey and Isabella Luz's frozen face disappears.

'Serek means for me to die at the shipyards,' she says. 'He is willing to sentence the entire regiment to death if needs be, to keep his secret.'

She looks at the Antari.

'But we will not die. We will emerge from the Laxian shipyards victorious, and then we will expose him for what he truly is.'

'He will come for you,' Zane says. The psyker speaks with cold certainty. 'The moment he learns that you live, he will hunt you. He cannot afford to stop.'

Raine nods. She hasn't stopped thinking about it since leaving the Bale's Heart.

'I know,' she says. 'That is why he must believe me dead.'

'And once you're dead?' Karin Sun asks. 'What then?'

'Serek is bound by the expectations of the rest of High Command,' Raine says. 'He could not call an order like that and let victory pass without a ceremony to mark it. He will look upon it as a display of power. A chance to show anybody left who might challenge him what happens to those who do. Serek thinks himself above reproach, and that in itself is another advantage.'

'Nobody is above reproach,' Keene says. 'Nor beyond the reach of death and judgement.'

'Just killing Serek is not enough,' Raine says. 'He has to be exposed. Torn down in front of everyone else. It is not enough to cut out the source of the rot, everything touched by it must be removed too.'

Raine takes a breath.

'But I cannot do this alone,' she says. 'So, I am asking you to stand with me.'

There is a moment of silence amongst the Antari. Raine knows that they are waiting for their general to speak. Juna Keene raises her augmetic arm and turns her hand to look at it.

'I earned this arm fighting on Cawter in Serek's name, hoping that I could prove myself as strong as he was on Steadfast.'

Keene exhales a slow breath and extends her hand. Raine grips Juna Keene's hand, and the general claps her on the shoulder.

'We will stand with you, Severina Raine,' she says. 'Loyalty, before the threat of death.'

'For the Bale Stars,' Raine says. 'For the Emperor.'

The Antari all speak those last three words with her. Keene lets go of Raine's hand. She nods her head and gestures to her captains.

'We have much to do,' she says. 'So, let's get to it.'

Everyone leaves the room then, save for Cassia Tyl. Raine knows what Tyl is going to say before she speaks.

'You'll want this keeping from the captain,' she says.

Raine hasn't stopped thinking about that since leaving the Bale's Heart either, and she knows her answer. It's just the saying of it.

'He cannot know,' she says. 'Not any of it.'

Tyl's face clouds, but she nods her head. 'Operational risk, commissar. I understand.'

Raine nods, though it's not just about operational risk. She trusts Andren Fel with her life. She will not tell him her plan because *she knows that he will try to aid her, when he can't. That he'll likely get himself killed into the bargain. Raine knows what it will do to him, to think her dead, but it cannot change her answer.*

All that Raine can do is hope that she is still standing at the end of all of this to ask his forgiveness.

TWENTY-FOUR

An empty throne

Severina Raine stands in the audience chamber aboard the *Bale's Heart*. The blood has been cleaned from the marble, but the damage from gunfire remains. From the killing shot she fired on Serek. The damage is deep. Cracks spread through the stone from it, long and dark. The damage done to Raine runs deep too. Every movement pulls at the stitching and cautery in her chest. Her broken ribs ache, as does the gunshot wound she took from Sylar. But she is still standing. She endures, just like the marble, and the *Bale's Heart*.

Just like the crusade.

'It will stay like this.'

Raine turns at the sound of Veris Drake's voice. The Lord-Marshal has one of her arms bound in a sling, and she leans on a finely made cane as she approaches Raine. With her are General-Primary Hu-Sul of Gholl, and High-King Araxis. They too are injured. Exhausted.

They are all that remains of Bale Stars High Command.

Drake puts out her uninjured arm and brushes her fingertips across the damaged marble.

'To repair the damage would be to forget,' Drake says. 'And we must never forget.'

Raine nods.

'But we must rebuild,' Drake says. 'The crusade must endure. In order for that to happen, the truth about Serek cannot be allowed to spread. It would destroy morale. Destroy everything we have given so much to save.'

Raine feels hollow. 'So, he is to be given a hero's death,' she says.

Drake nods.

'And those who know the truth?' Raine says, coldly. 'Will they be offered the same?'

High-King Araxis chuckles at that. 'You were right about her, Veris,' he says. 'She is much like Thema.'

Raine glares at him. Drake waves her hand before she can speak.

'We have given much thought to it,' Drake says. 'Any complicit in Serek's actions will be sentenced, but there will be no more deaths for the loyal. You and your Antari have already paid dearly enough.'

Drake puts her hand on Raine's shoulder and for a moment Raine feels as though she could be a child again, standing in the grand hall decorated in her mother's name. But this day is different. This hall is decorated with damage, and the Bale Stars have lost more than just one hero.

'You dragged Serek into the light through sheer will and devotion,' Drake says. 'And those things should never be wasted. You will continue to serve, as your regiment will.'

Her hand falls away again.

'After all,' she says, 'we still have a crusade to fight. In the Emperor's name.'

Raine nods. She feels tears threaten at the corner of her eyes, from exhaustion, and agony.

But most of all, from pride.

'In the Emperor's name,' she says.

Steadfast, after

Severina Raine stands alone in the vast, dark shadow of the Hero's Mount and watches the engraving servitor slowly cut her sister's name into the marble. She is dressed in plain training clothes, and not her uniform. She does not carry her weapons. In this, she is here as a sister. As a good heart, and nothing more. Devotional candles flicker in the cold wind as the blade cuts the shapes of Lucia's name. It reminds Raine of doing the same to the timepiece, all those years ago. Of trying to let go.

Only this time, it feels as though she actually can.

She knows that Fel is there before she catches sight of him out of the corner of her eye. He doesn't say a thing, just stands beside her as the servitor cuts the name and as dust from the marble falls like snow and those candles continue to flicker. Then it is done and the servitor folds back its arms and moves along the mount. It will never be short of names to carve.

Raine takes the timepiece from her pocket and looks at it. At the crack in the face and the way the case has buckled and tarnished. At the name, carved into the brass. She feels the steady ticking against her palm, soft and even, like a heartbeat. Then Raine closes her hand around it and walks over to the wall. She puts the timepiece down amongst the candles and picts and letters for the lost then runs her thumb over the case one last time, before stepping back again.

'That's it done,' she says, and the words apply to so many things. 'It will be strange to go and leave it here. To leave her here.'

'Think of it not as leaving her, but as letting her rest,' Fel says.

Raine nods. Her eyes sting, as if from the wind.

'It's good to have you back,' she says. 'To have you here, for this.'

'I wouldn't have been anywhere else,' he says. 'I will stand with you always. Until the end.'

Raine turns to look at him. Fel is without his carapace armour, just dressed in plain fatigues with the sleeves rolled back. The metal of his augmetic arm reflects the candlelight.

'Let me see,' she says.

He offers her his hand, and she takes hold of it in her own. The augmetic is a good one, well made and strong, but Raine feels grief over it nonetheless. Guilt.

'It's a lot to lose,' she says, and she lets go.

Fel shrugs his shoulders. There's a softening in his grey eyes. 'I can think of much worse things,' he says.

'I am sorry for keeping the truth from you,' Raine says.

'You don't need to apologise for doing what's right,' he says. 'Or for being strong enough to do it.'

Raine can't think of how to answer that. Instead, she

reaches out and touches his face, tracing the shape of that old scar that runs down his cheek to his jawline.

'I have never told you exactly what you mean to me,' she says.

He smiles, just a little, then puts out his hand and brushes her hair back, away from her face.

'Yes, you have,' he says, softly, and in that moment, they aren't soldiers. They aren't serving. She is not an officer, and neither is he.

They are just souls.

A crusade to fight

On board the *Pyre's Light*, the Antari induct their new blood. Swear them into squads and give them their marks and their myths. Raine hears it and sees it as she makes her way back to her posted quarters. Later, the Antari will fight for the joy of it, as they always do on the nights before a deployment, because it is the way of things. Even though Raine can never partake in that, or any of their other rites, she finds it a comfort. There is value in things that endure despite hardship.

Raine lets herself into her quarters and the overhead lumens activate to reveal two figures waiting for her. Before she can process who it is, she pulls her pistol and points it.

'Come now, Severina,' says Lord-Marshal Veris Drake. 'We are all friends here.'

Raine lowers her pistol and holsters it, but she doesn't lower her guard, because Drake's words aren't entirely true.

Because the other person in the room is Lukas Vander.

'Raine,' he says, in that same cold way he always does,

though there is less disdain in it than there was once. Than there was before Serek.

Raine pulls the bulkhead door closed behind her and spins the lock.

'To what do I owe this visit?' she asks.

Drake gets up from the folding chair she is sitting on. She has to lean on her cane to do it, because the damage done during the fight on the *Bale's Heart* could not be entirely undone.

'I will be blunt,' Drake says, as if Raine would ever expect differently from her. 'High Command is weak. The command echelons are a mess. We have never been more vulnerable.'

Raine narrows her eyes. 'But that is not why you are here,' she says. 'And it is certainly not why *he* is here.'

'In that, you are correct,' Vander says. 'And believe me, I am not here by choice, either.'

Drake gives him a withering look. 'Enough, Lukas,' she says. 'I am here because I do not believe that corruption within the crusade died with Alar Serek. Because I need watchful eyes, and faithful hearts. I need those that I can trust to seek it out.'

Raine frowns. 'We are already tasked with guarding the souls of our regiments,' she says. 'We will not fail in that.'

'Of course,' Drake says. 'But I need you to guard more than just the souls of your regiments. I need you to do so for the crusade, and I want you to begin with this.'

She takes something out of the pocket of her robe and places it in Raine's hand. Something that Raine has not seen since she gave it to Mardan Tula, what seems like a lifetime ago. An auditory damper disc that Tula could not tell her the origin of. Not because he didn't know, but because it was beyond classified.

'And if I refuse?' Raine asks.

'We both know that you won't.'

'How can you be sure?' Raine asks.

'Because I know you, Severina Raine. Because you are not the kind to refuse a duty, or back down from a trial.'

Drake smiles then. Not that narrowing of her eyes, but a real smile.

'Because you are a commissar,' she says.

ABOUT THE AUTHOR

Rachel Harrison is the author of the Warhammer 40,000 novel *Honourbound*, and the short stories 'Fire and Thunder', 'The Darkling Hours', 'Execution' and 'A Company of Shadows', featuring the character Commissar Severina Raine. She has also written the short story 'Dirty Dealings' for Necromunda, as well as a number of other Warhammer 40,000 short stories including 'The Third War' and 'Dishonoured'.

YOUR NEXT READ

WARHAMMER 40,000
CADIAN HONOUR
A MINKA LESK NOVEL
JUSTIN D HILL

CADIAN HONOUR
by Justin D Hill

Sent to the capital world of Potence, Sergeant Minka Lesk and the Cadian 101st discover that though Cadia may have fallen, their duty continues.

For these stories and more go to **blacklibrary.com, games-workshop.com**, Games Workshop and Warhammer stores, all good book stores or visit one of the thousands of independent retailers worldwide, which can be found at **games-workshop.com/storefinder**

YOUR NEXT READ

DOUBLE EAGLE
by Dan Abnett

The war on Enothis is almost lost. Chaos forces harry the defenders on land and in the skies. Can the ace pilots of the Phantine XX turn the tide and bring the Imperium victory?

For these stories and more go to **blacklibrary.com**, **games-workshop.com**, Games Workshop and Warhammer stores, all good book stores or visit one of the thousands of independent retailers worldwide, which can be found at **games-workshop.com/storefinder**